DATE DUE

MAY 1 6 2000

MAY 24 2000	JUL 2 7 2000	
JUL 0 5 2000	SEP 1 6 2000	
AUG 1 7 2000		
AUG 2 9 2000		
OCT 1 0 2000		
MAY 3 0 2001		
MAY 3 0 2001		

Demco, Inc. 38-293

THE BOOK BORROWER

THE
BOOK
BORROWER

A NOVEL

ALICE MATTISON

WILLIAM MORROW AND COMPANY, INC. / NEW YORK

It is the policy of William Morrow and Company, Inc., and its imprints and affiliates,
recognizing the importance of preserving what has been written, to print the books
we publish on acid-free paper, and we exert our best efforts to that end.

Library of Congress Cataloging-in-Publication Data
Mattison, Alice.
The book borrower : a novel / Alice Mattison.—1st ed.
p.   cm.
ISBN 0-688-16824-8 (alk. paper)
1. Title.
PS3563.A8598B66   1999
813'.54—dc21   99-21961
CIP

Printed in the United States of America

First Edition

1   2   3   4   5   6   7   8   9   10

www.williammorrow.com

For Susan Bingham and Sandi Kahn Shelton
and in memory of Jane Kenyon

THE BOOK BORROWER

Тноисн she was pushing a baby carriage, Toby Ruben began to read a book

———

On a gray evening in late November 1920

———

and the wheel of the carriage—a big, skeletal but once elegant Perego she'd found in somebody's trash—rolled into a broken place in the sidewalk. The baby, tightly wrapped in a white receiving blanket, glided compactly from carriage to sidewalk. He didn't cry. Like his mother, the baby would be troubled more by missed human connections than by practical problems; also the three-second rule held: as if he were a fallen slice of bread, Ruben snatched him up and ate him. Kissed him passionately and all over, dropping the wicked book into the carriage. She put the baby back where he belonged and picked up the book, but she didn't read for at least a block. Then she did read.

———

On a gray evening in late November 1920, an observer who happened to be making his way up the hill from Dressler's Mills to the streetcar line that ran to the principal square of Boynton, Massachusetts, might have noticed a sturdy young woman hurrying through the mill's gates. The air was full of cinders, which must have been why she reached up to tie a veil over her face, though she did so with a gesture so casual, so obviously

———

Ruben had to cross a street. She closed the book. It was thin, with black covers, not new.

—Want a book? a woman in the park had said.

The woman wore a blue-and-white-checked dress like a pioneer's, but sleeveless. A wide neckline bared her freckled chest; with good posture she chased serious, muddy daughters in pink pinafores. Ruben's baby, Squirrel, was three months old.

—Go, Squirrel, go, Ruben shouted, just so the woman, sweeping by, would speak.

—What? Sunny hair rose and settled.

—He's trying to put his thumb in his mouth.

The woman leaned over to look, her hair over her face, and Squirrel found his thumb for the first time. Excellent, said the woman, Deborah Laidlaw, straightening, then giving a push to the small of her back. She left her hand there. When their conversation, skipping some subjects, arrived at sex and husbands, Deborah said, Jeremiah has intercourse only to music.

—Any music?

—Folk songs.

It was 1975.

—Fuck songs! Ruben was surprised to have said that. Her hair was dark red but thin, and she was shorter than this impressive Deborah. In the songs, Ruben supposed, people built dams, harpooned whales, or cut down trees, while Jeremiah penetrated his wife.

—History. He'll read any book about history, said Deborah, but mostly trolleys.

—Trolleys?

—Streetcars. He's obsessed with the interurbans. But there aren't any songs about trolleys.

—Clang, clang, clang went the trolley! sang Ruben, flat—who never sang for anyone but the baby.

—Doesn't count. Want a book?

Jeremiah had found it in a used bookstore. He had begged Deborah to read it, but she only carried it back and forth to the park in a striped yellow-and-white cotton tote bag.

—I am not interested in trolleys, said Deborah. Jeremiah has a theory about the person in the book. I don't care.

—It's history?

—A woman writing about her early life. About her sister.

—It sounds interesting, said Ruben politely.

—Good. You read it.

Ruben took the book: *Trolley Girl,* by Miriam James.

—You can't *keep* it, said Deborah; Ruben was embarrassed—but they'd meet again. The daughters were Jill, who talked, and Rose, a big baby. Jill collected sticks and demanded to throw them into the river, a narrow glinty stream visible through trees. So Deborah carried Rose on her hip, striding away from Ruben, down a wooded slope where the carriage couldn't follow. Ruben watched: the back of a muscular woman walking in sandals, her dress disheveled by a child on her hip, and an earnest child running carefully, turning every few feet—this way!—as if only she knew where to find the river. Ruben had never been in this park, though she'd lived in

4   the city for most of a year, busy being pregnant. Forever she
would have to remind herself that Deborah hadn't made the
river.

She pushed her glasses up her nose and started for home.
How snug and well-outfitted she would be when the Squirrel
could ride on her hip, leaning confidently against her arm—
one short leg in front and one behind her—pointing like Rose,
who used her mother as a friendly conveyance. Now he was
only a package. At the sidewalk she opened the book. Then
came—terrible to think about—the broken place, and then,
when she'd just begun the book again, the street to cross, and
a dog she looked at. But now.

———

reached up to tie a veil over her face, although she did so
with a gesture so casual, so obviously ineffectual, that the observer—if he had any reason to watch her at all—might have
wondered what occupied her mind enough to distract her
from the imminent risk of a cinder in the eye. Perhaps she
was afraid of missing her trolley. She walked steadily and energetically uphill, though her skirt—modestly long for a
woman in that experimental year—was twisted around her
legs by the wind at each step. The girl yanked it free and
hurried toward the main street.

When she reached it she turned the corner, and if our onlooker has kept up he would now notice another girl leave
the shelter of a shop entrance—a milliner's, closed for the
night—and hurry toward her. "Goosie, your hat's crooked,"
said the newcomer, looking irritated. Under the light of a gas
lamp she reached up to untie and retie the other's errant veil.

"*Goosie,*" said the other girl, a little contemptuously.

"I've called you that since I was a baby."

"I know. But we're not babies now, Miriam Lipkin."

———

Jewish? thought Ruben.

———

"I wish we were babies." They weren't beautiful. They
looked like a pair of nicely brought up Jewish sisters. Our
onlooker, even in Boynton, even in 1920, could discover
business more rewarding than the scrutiny of these two—and
since their streetcar is approaching anyway—let's forget the
observer. I'm going to follow them onto the trolley myself.
I'm Miriam, who forty-four years ago was the girl in the
doorway of the milliner's, and the one climbing the hill is my
sister Jessie, or Gussie, or Goosie—names were fluid in those
immigrant days—a clerk at the mill. She's now facing me
with her back to the hill she's just climbed, like a cutout figure in front of a complex diagram: triangles upon triangles,
trapezoids here and there. The sloping mill roofs, in shades of
gray and black, are grouped behind her as if she's an icon of
American labor. And she's climbing onto the trolley. Trolley
girl, someone called her, not many months after this moment.
The name makes her sound like an ingenue in a gay straw
hat taking the streetcar to the fair, but Jessie was frivolous
only as a joke. On the cindery day in November I'm recal-
ling, Jessie had been a member of an anarchist cell for several
years. She'd once had urine thrown at her while she made a
speech on the Boynton common.

"Isn't it supposed to be good for the hair, Miriam?" she'd
asked me that night as I walked her home, loyally trying
not to mind the smell. Jessie's hair was stringy. She wondered if the urine might give it body. At home, our father
screamed at her for an hour. Our mother cried. Mother always cried. She wasn't good for much besides crying. I
sound angry and I am. After all this—all that I am about to

describe—was over, I escaped from the millinery shop and eventually I went to college. I studied Latin. "Miriam" is almost an anagram of "I am *ira*." I am anger. My widowed mother lived with me in my rent-controlled Manhattan apartment for twenty years. She died two months ago, and now that her nagging voice is no longer in my ears, maybe I can pay attention to what I remember, what I am still so angry about.

———

—Squirrel's mommy!

—'quirl mommy!

Ruben stuck the book between the mattress and the side of the carriage, as though Deborah and her girls didn't know about it. It was a foolish, old-fashioned book. The little yellow-haired girls caught up, Jill running, Rose tumble-running.

—Do you want a *job*? called Deborah. I forgot. I told someone I'd—

Irritating. Did she look so poor?

—Doing what?

—Teaching. You said you were a teacher.

Had she? Presumably. She said, Maybe I'm no good. Ruben thought of her old, faraway teaching job, of standing in comfortable sun saying Paragraphs! to young people: then for some reason all laughed together, teacher and students.

—You don't have to be good. The pay is terrible.

But Ruben was good. Now they took telephone numbers. Deborah taught child-care workers preparing for the high school equivalency exam.

—Is it math? I can't teach math.

—Sure you can. Mostly it's English. Teach what you want. They'll never take the exam no matter what we do.

Ruben was lonely and slightly miserable, home alone all day with Squirrel. In her pregnancy she'd done nothing but read, here in a new city where she had no friends and had come only

because her husband had been hired as assistant budget director
in the public works department. All week Ruben pictured him
talking on the phone or, seen from behind, pacing a corridor
with windows, sun at his left, though she wasn't aware of any
such corridor in his office.

Sweat was on Deborah's face and chest above the blue-and-
white dress. Her skin was freckled and flushed. She wore eye
makeup. Her shoulders were broad. She looked as if she could
drive a stick shift or put on a party. Ruben, who hated to drive,
couldn't even push the carriage properly.

—I pushed the carriage into a hole because I was reading.
The baby fell out.

—Is he all right?

—Because I was reading that book.

—Jeremiah's book? Well, nobody forced you.

—I'm not blaming you!

Deborah Laidlaw picked up Squirrel and held him before
her, hands around his chest. Squirrel—without a neck at the
moment—blinked. The receiving blanket dropped to the
ground. Deborah ignored it. He and she stared, Squirrel's eyes
finding something to look at—the gold cross at Deborah's
throat?—and Deborah put him back into the carriage, now
picked up the blanket. She said, You must never read while
pushing the carriage. Said it as if Ruben were so young or so
stupid she might not know.

Never mind what Ruben lacked. Her mother hadn't said the
right things; or was dead; or had never existed, so that Ruben
had to be made by committee from glossy scraps of magazine
ads. She blinked like her son because her eyes stung, took the
rebuke, liked it.

—I do want a job. But when Deborah turned away again,
Ruben thought of her mother, who had existed, but was dead.
Not her favorite inner story, the story of her mother's death: a
story of temper and its consequences. Ruben did not tell it to
herself just then, but she opened the book.

———

My parents were Jewish immigrants from the Ukraine.

———

So were Ruben's grandparents. Maybe they knew one another.

———

I have a feeling that nobody in our family had followed the kosher laws for generations. I once saw a photograph of a shtetl in Russia, including a pig. The caption pointed out that the pig proved that Jews and non-Jews lived in close proximity, but I think it may have proved that my great-grandparents were somewhere around. On the High Holy Days my parents dressed up and went to the movies, where my father translated the subtitles into Yiddish for my mother. They wanted the neighbors to think they were in the synagogue. Not that they didn't consider themselves Jewish; not that they didn't do half a dozen Jewish things—well, religiously. We dressed up on Purim. My mother cooked matzoh ball soup. We ate no bread on Pesach. My mother fasted on Yom Kippur until shortly before lunchtime, while my father screamed about hypocrisy and superstition. Then she had a cup of tea and a dry roll, complaining that it was too dry. An hour later she had another roll, with butter.

I had two sisters. Jessie was two years older than I, and I was three years older than Sarah. My first memory is of my sister Jessie telling me a story to distract me from my mother's screams during Sarah's birth in the other room. It was the middle of the night and we were sitting on the cold kitchen floor. I couldn't believe we could get away with such an infraction, but nobody objected. The story Jessie told was about cockroaches who grew to be the size of people and became teachers in school. Until I went to school and even after, I was afraid my teacher might be a cockroach. Much later I read the famous Kafka story.

Our apartment was full of Yiddish shouting. I remember wishing they'd all speak English, but I'm imposing a memory from much later; when I was little, I myself didn't speak English. In this account, I'm going to write what I remember, even if it could not be true, and I'm going to write about what happened to Jessie when I wasn't present, as if I were Jessie at times. When we were teenagers, we argued about memories and couldn't agree whether some of them were mine or hers. Who was it my father kicked in the head, the one time he lost his temper that badly? We each remembered that he did it to the other. We were both sure it wasn't Sarah. Maybe it never happened. Maybe it happened to Sarah.

———————

—Where is God? said Deborah.

—I don't know anything about God.

—Nobody knows anything about God. Don't you think about that all the time?

—Never, said Ruben. They were pushing Deborah's daughters on the baby swings while Squirrel slept in his carriage. It was raining lightly.

—Then what?

Ruben tried to think what she thought about. Death.

—I too, I too, said Deborah. It was the third time they'd met. Maybe the fourth. You have children, you think about death. I'm pregnant.

—I didn't know!

—I'll show soon. I'd show now in tight clothes.

—When you have more than one child, said Ruben, do you worry less about death?

—Each one is your whole life. Which is not good. There are

already too many people I can't do without. My friends . . . now another one.

Ruben didn't know if she meant another child or another friend. To pull their talk back to its odd already customary place, she said, What do you mean, where is God? Isn't God supposed to be everywhere? Do you mean where physically?

Deborah pushed the swing and Jill said, Higher, higher! Deborah ran under it, faced Jill and kissed her, and pushed the swing back, all the way back, running under it again. Then she turned and began pushing in the usual way. She said, I believe in one God, father almighty, maker of heaven and earth. . . . Then she said, It's not just that bad things happen. Where is God then? Out to lunch? But it's more than that. I want to know—well, I want to know about bad things, but I can't know that. What I want to know for everyday occasions is, Where is God when I push Jill on the swing?

—Aren't you still nursing Rose? said Ruben.

—I'm trying to wean her. Besides, she pinches me. She nurses from one breast and pinches the other. Mine, mine. How's she going to like having a liddly?

—A liddly, said Ruben.

—No moozum, not even once this time, Deborah said.

—What's moozum?

—Oh, it's my word for menstrual blood.

At night Ruben said to her husband, Harry, also called Ruben, Oh, this Deborah!

—What does she look like?

—Medium-sized breasts. Well, medium large, but she's nursing. And pregnant.

—Breasts aren't all I—

—She wears sandals. She looks like an adult. She has fluffy light hair and big arms full of daughters.

—Breasts make me think about your breasts, said Harry.

—They're too tender and sore.

—I don't want to touch them, just to see them.

—You see them constantly. I nurse this kid all day.

—Could you take off your shirt and your bra and walk around a little?

—I'm not wearing a bra. Can't you tell? She shrugged off her shirt and cooked supper, scared she'd spatter something hot on her breasts. But she liked his look, his quiet.

Deborah in maternity clothes, two weeks later, made Ruben want another baby. Ruben had worn peasant smocks with embroidered trim, but Deborah went in for classy gray tunics she wore to the park with straight skirts and panty hose. Pregnancy makes me want to dress up, said Deborah. I don't know why. It's a nine-month festival.

—Shall we have another one? Ruben asked Harry.

—I love Peter, said Harry, a small man with wrinkles in his forehead, more wrinkles when he was happy. Now he wrinkled up like an old man, watching her cook, in her shirt this time. Sure, another Peter.

—Probably we should think of a different name.

—Peter II.

—Vole. Squirrel and Vole.

—Vole is good, said Harry. More than half the time, when she said something, Harry understood. Possibly seventy percent for jokes, and he generally knew the size of a joke, didn't look around for more. But the baby is hard, he said. You said you didn't want another one.

—He's hard.

Squirrel often cried. Her nipples were leather. She nursed him on the toilet seat, once in the bathtub but she was afraid she'd drop him—no, afraid she'd stick him under on purpose. He's hard, she said, but I want another one.

Deborah was at ease with babies on all sides of her.

The phone rang and it was Deborah. Again it was Deborah, even on Saturday morning while they had breakfast. Ruben felt that swirl in the throat, as when the teacher said hers was the best; and she was also troubled.

—What does she want with you? said Harry.

—Want with me! In moments she was in tears.

Then a fight. You can be friends with whoever you want, said Harry. I do *not* claim every bit of your attention, I do *not* claim all your time, you want to be friends with this Deborah, be friends, I don't care. If anybody is having second thoughts it's you, not me.

Apologies.

Sex. Nipples so sore she didn't want him to lie on her, so they did it dog style, but she felt ugly, her breasts hanging low.

—Maybe I *am* jealous, he said.

On Monday, Deborah called for Ruben on the way to the park, but Ruben wasn't ready.

—What do you have to do?

—Vacuum the rug. They stood at the door, Deborah in mustard color, a new maternity dress, her little girls beside her. Ruben didn't ask Deborah in.

—You'd give up time with me to vacuum the rug?

The dismal rug, in midafternoon, when Squirrel wouldn't stop crying . . . If she didn't do it first thing, later it looked like something put into a movie to show that the characters have spoiled their lives.

—I didn't think you were like that, said Deborah.

Ruben said, I'll meet you in the park in ten minutes. She wanted to pee, too. She wanted to change Squirrel. She didn't want to be hurried. But she didn't vacuum the rug. She changed the baby, but when she saw his cap on the shelf she took it because the day was sunny. Under the cap was the book Deborah had lent her. She had forgotten. She didn't ease the carriage down the porch steps, bumping it, hand on the baby's back, as she usually did. She sat down on the top step and began to read. When Squirrel cried, she nursed him while reading, his smooth, light brown efficient head at her breast, her shirt bunched around his head. Deborah always wore a heavy bra whose straps slipped down her bare shoulders, but Ruben, again, had no bra on; not a political gesture exactly (small breasts, easier to nurse), but almost a political gesture.

As usual there was crud on her glasses. She cleaned them with a wet finger and read through streaks.

––––––

My father worked in a ladies' clothing factory, basting in place the collars and cuffs of expensive dresses; then they were sewn by women on machines. He peered as if light hurt and it was painful to take a good look at things. His eyes were red, rheumy, and ugly, with red veins in the whites. When he was young he had read anarchist theory, but as an old man he couldn't read easily and he stared all day at the newspaper.

My mother was brave, but expressed her courage as contempt. Nothing impressed her, everyone was out to cheat her, everyone was her enemy. Stupid irony was her chief means of communication—not clever irony. Only Sarah, the youngest, broke through Mama's disdain. I think after Sarah was born my mother refused sex with my father. Maybe, having given my father a great big no, my mother felt better about children, and enjoyed Sarah.

Several nights a week when we were little, my father entertained men Jessie and I called the Screamers. They screamed mostly in Yiddish, staying until late at night, drinking tea or schnapps. I was convinced that they were bandits. It seemed impossible that they could be invited guests, they made everybody so unhappy. I must have been eight or ten when I first asked Jessie whether she thought the police might be helpful in getting rid of them.

"The police!" she said. "We don't have anything to do with the police!"

"Why not?" My teacher had said we should consult a policeman if we got lost. Like everyone who wasn't an immigrant, policemen had the wrong smell, as I put it to myself, but I wasn't afraid of them. Jessie began an explanation that was far beyond me. I have no idea how she'd learned all she told me: police were bad, the men who visited Papa were good, Papa wanted their visits, she would have liked to be allowed to stay up and listen. The men were planning a better time, she said, when there wouldn't be suffering and poverty, when everybody would have enough money because people would share equally. It was spring, and we were walking home from the market, where Mama had sent us to buy potatoes. The potatoes were in a bag Mama usually carried, and now Jessie carried it. She spoke in a low voice and looked around her, bending her head seriously. For years I connected radical political ideas with potatoes. I thought I had made the connection from seeing a print, somewhere, of van Gogh's potato eaters—people presumably in need of such ideas. But one day, crying on the naked shoulder of a bored lover, I told the story of the walk in the spring, the warmth and the light wind and the new leaves and the potatoes, and I realized where the connection in my mind had come from.

I don't remember Jessie reading the kind of heavy tome I associate with political theory, but certainly there were anarchist newsletters and papers in the house. Once Jessie persuaded Mama to give her some food for a beggar. Mama finally filled a bag with bread and an apple, then—I think I remember—she spat into it. Could she have done that? I certainly remember Jessie carrying the bag to the door and handing it to a ragged man who waited there. The man turned and in profile I saw him take an enormous bite out of the apple. I never asked my mother if she'd really spat. Spitting was different then, an expressive activity, a major health problem. Signs read "No Spitting." What happened to those signs? Did more people spit in the old days than now? Where did the old ones get so much saliva?

Sometimes Jessie was my best friend and sometimes she ignored me and left me to play with Sarah. Sarah was prettier

than we were, but not bright. She adored me, which was flat-
tering, but I quickly grew bored with her. I knew my proper
companion was Jessie.

Jessie and my father shared political ideas but disagreed
constantly. As she grew he took to screaming at her, accusing
her—oddly for an anarchist—of sexual crimes: whoredom,
promiscuity. He blamed her for having big breasts, as if she'd
grown them on purpose to attract the attention of men. In a
household full of women, a man must dream about breasts
and wake in agonized sweat if the women are mostly his
daughters. And what if his wife has rejected him? Sarah, in
time, had big breasts as well, and mine were not tiny.

By telling Jessie over and over again that he believed she
had a sexual life, my father must have given her a kind of
permission to consider having one. Or maybe the talk of free
love in the anarchist meetings affected Jessie. You talk about
it long enough, you need to do it. From the age of twelve,
my sister sat in on the meetings, which were sometimes held
in restaurants and union halls, sometimes at our house. From
the time she was fourteen or fifteen, men—not boys—were
asking her to run errands or deliver messages for them.

I came to understand that sometimes Jessie went with one
or another of these men and "did things," in bed or elsewhere. Probably rarely in an actual bed. I think that at first I
imagined these scenes; later Jessie told me. She had nobody
else to tell, of course, not darling stupid Sarah, and certainly
not our parents. What amazed me was that Jessie loved sex. I
knew about sex, somehow, although certainly my mother
hadn't told me, but of course I thought it must be horrid.
Jessie told me sex was delectable. She told me how to mas-
turbate.

So I will describe something I do know about, though of
course I wasn't there: the night Jessie lost her virginity. She
was in love. She was in love with a printer in his thirties
named William Platz. He had stolen the key to the print shop

where he worked, and at night sometimes he returned there and printed leaflets and pamphlets for the anarchists. Sometimes Jessie helped him. One cold night they were walking from the shop to the union hall, their arms laden with pamphlets on which the ink was not quite dry and had a pungent smell. After a silence, William Platz asked Jessie solemnly if she were a virgin.

"Naturally," said Jessie.

"And do you, like me, believe that men and women should be free to follow their impulses in these matters?"

Jessie had never put such an idea into words, but, having grown up in our household, was somewhat lawless in many ways. She didn't blush.

I said, when she told me about it, "You didn't feel modest or frightened?"

"No, I was happy. I'd loved him for a while, and I didn't know what we'd do if he loved me back, because he was married."

"Will you come with me now?" William Platz had said. She was going with him anyway, to stow the pamphlets in the empty hall, but she understood. On the way, he went into a bakery that baked bread late into the night. Jessie waited outside in the cold and William Platz came out with a big round loaf. He tore off pieces and fed them to her.

"Big pieces or small pieces?" I asked. Big would mean fierce passion and small would mean tender love.

"Small pieces," she said. They made love on William's coat, which he spread on the floor in an upstairs room of the union hall. It was cold; a stove was nearby but it was unlit. Jessie was afraid of rolling over in passion and hitting her head on the cold stove.

William Platz left her not long after, though, and that's how she came to tell me the story.

"Why didn't you tell me right away?" I said. "Were you ashamed?"

"I almost told you, because I was sore," she said. "But I didn't think you'd know a remedy." William Platz dropped Jessie as a lover, but they remained political associates. I didn't see how that was possible but my sister shrugged.

By November 1920 Jessie was eighteen and had moved out of our apartment long since, which infuriated my father because she was working as a clerk at the mill and as long as she lived in the house he confiscated her wages. Jessie didn't graduate from high school; she'd gotten this job when she turned sixteen. When I graduated and got my own job I minded handing my money over to my father, but not as much as Jessie had. All day I'd sew decorations on hats and be polite to ladies, wanting to crush the hats and be rude to the customers, and on the way home at the end of the week, with my money, I tried to convince myself that it would buy a loaf of bread for Sarah, a dress for Sarah, whom I loved.

I don't know why we two sisters were as angry as we were. Many people in our circumstances were at peace. Before Jessie moved out, she systematically stole silverware and sheets from my parents, one piece at a time so it wouldn't be missed. Of course she believed that property was meaningless, but nonetheless. . . .

Often in life there's an obvious next step, but most adults would be shocked at the thought of taking it. We have scruples, habits, and deeply held notions: religion, morality, ideology, or custom, and when someone proposes going to bed or when a cup sits on a table at just the time we lack a cup, we consult an inner rule book. Jessie really was an anarchist. Her mind knew no government.

The anarchist cell in Boynton, Massachusetts, in 1919 and 1920 was sufficiently small and obscure—or Boynton itself was sufficiently small and obscure—that it was not a target in the infamous Palmer Raids during the "Red Scare," when thousands of radicals and others thought to be radicals were rounded up and threatened with deportation. Anarchists in

Boynton mostly contented themselves with writing manifestos and arguing. They read documents aloud to one another in our parlor or in dirty rooms around the city, rooms in which my sister acquired itches of various sorts from men as noble in mind as she. After William Platz there were others, but he was the one she loved. He had broken her heart.

We'd whisper about men on the trolley, now that Jessie had moved out. The millinery shop was near the mill where she worked, as I've said, and we'd meet and ride back and forth together. Ordinarily, on the trip home she'd alight first and I'd watch her stride thumping down the hill, her legs apart—she had a bit of a waddle—toward her rather sordid room. But on the night I'm now describing—I do remember that I began this lopsided account with Jessie and me getting on the trolley after work—she rode all the way with me, for she was coming home for dinner. I was nervous, eager to get her into a good mood so dinner at home wouldn't be spoiled by fights.

"Three hippopotamuses today, one giraffe, two lionesses," I said while Jessie looked out the window as we rode. She was brooding and I was trying to get her attention.

"Did you sell them all hats?"

"Some of them. A lioness roared at me. Did you have adventures today, Goosie?"

"What does that mean? Mr. Franklin praised my alphabetizing. Does that count?"

"I'm glad he's kind."

"Miriam, he's kind because I wear clean clothes and speak properly," said Jessie, "but I don't care for his sort of kindness."

"Why on earth not?" I said. "You do wear clean clothes."

"I'm poor. I'm no different from the men in the mill. I don't want kindnesses they don't receive. We're all just pieces of machinery to the bosses."

I held my tongue.

"Look at him," Jessie said then.

"At who?"

"The motorman." He looked perfectly ordinary.

"The company wants to cut his pay by twenty-five per-cent," Jessie said. "Does he look as if he deserves that?"

"What did he do? How did you know?" I said.

"Not just this man—all the motormen and conductors. There's going to be a trolley strike."

I couldn't imagine it—the fatherly motorman braking the trolley, seizing his conductor by the arm, and departing, re-fusing to take us home. The trolley, it seemed to me, had al-ways been there and would always be, although in fact trolleys were a relatively recent addition to the American scene, and by the time Jessie and I were young women, the trolley period was almost over. The lines had been stretched across the vast acreage of the United States at the turn of the century, and they were all over the place. I know I can't con-vey what it was like. All the routes intersected everywhere. The streetcar was something safe and rattly anyone could walk to the corner and jump on. We could also ride out into the country, simply, without going downtown to a big station and getting a fancy schedule and buying a ticket in advance. The interurbans hurtled through the fields; my favorite line ran along a river and within a few minutes, instead of staring at tenements and brick factory buildings, I was spotting tur-tles sunning themselves on rocks. The trolleys were every-where—but cars and buses were becoming prevalent. There were fewer riders all the time. The trolleys were owned by private companies, as I was soon to understand, and when the company in Boynton calmly announced that the workers were going to have to accept a twenty-five-percent pay cut, they were doing something that seems impossible now but was not uncommon at that time.

We left the motorman, that night, to his troubles, and went home to dinner. I remember, next, Jessie bending her head to laugh at something I said—something irreverent, I suppose. I try to bring back the image of my mother, at her end of the table. What was she thinking—besides, that is, worrying that there wasn't enough meat? She looks at Jessie in the gaslight, in my imagination or my memory, and what happens then? She notices that Jessie's collar looks dirty (it's interesting that I remember Jessie talking about clean clothes, because often they weren't), that Jessie's big hands are in danger of knocking over Papa's tea, that her laugh is loud. Mama doesn't understand the conversation; that would be hard on anybody. We made no effort, by this time, to speak in Yiddish or to translate. Still, I'll bestow upon my mother some fondness for Jessie, and I don't think I'm lying. Fanny Lipkin, then, saw how the light made an arc shine on her oldest daughter's head, and she had the impulse to touch the bright part, as if she thought it might feel different from the rest of Jessie's hair. There was no way to say such a thing, not in Yiddish, which Fanny was forgetting, and certainly not in English, so Fanny would have felt the wish in images, not words. Her hand tingled with the pleasure she'd feel, stroking her daughter's head—do I go too far?—and instead she reached toward the child nearer her, Sarah, and brusquely set her collar and hair to rights. She wet a finger and cleaned Sarah's cheek, and Sarah arched her back and leaned away.

"The Lake Avenue line?" Jessie was saying. For we were, in fact, talking about trolleys. I was. As transportation, not as symbols of the struggles of laborers or the injustices of the powerful. "You're not being clear."

"The country," I said. "She lives on a farm, with chickens." Fanny tried to listen.

I'd made a friend. I brought my lunch and ate it on a bench on the Common, and there I'd met a girl who worked in a bookstore, and who had invited me to take the Lake Avenue trolley to visit her on Sunday, and to bring my sister

Sarah. I didn't actually know whether she lived on a farm, but her family certainly kept a few chickens.

"Who is this friend?" said Papa.

Friend Fanny understood. "A Jewish girl?"

"Not Jewish," I said.

Jessie was restless. Her nervous face, which had exaggerated, slightly bulging eyes, moved in and out of the gaslight. She began clearing plates, her skirt slapping furniture. Her big arms came down between my father and me, between me and my mother, like black lines, coming down, rising, again and again. At last, tea spilled.

"How far?" Papa asked, turning to look at Jessie though he was talking to me. I could see him tense as he watched her. Between us, Jessie and I broke his heart, but I did it more delicately.

"What difference does it make how far?" I said. "It's on the trolley line. We've passed it on the way to Lake Park."

"The Ferris wheel?" said Sarah.

"Next thing you'll want to go to Europe," said my father. "Sarah will ask me for carfare to Russia."

"I'd like that," said Sarah seriously.

"Better to stay in America," said my father, equally seriously. "Even with this President Harding they've just elected, who is not an intelligent man, even with him, better to stay here." He patted Sarah's arm and my mother reached out to pat her other arm.

"President Wilson, President Harding," said my mother, leaning across the table, trying to get it. Her gray hair was untidy and she still had her apron on. I'd been attempting to teach her to read. I wanted her to become a citizen, but she didn't for many years, not until reading was no longer required. Women were about to get the vote and I'd been telling her about voting, but she had no interest.

"Ah, President Wilson," said Papa. We'd all heard this before. "If only people had listened to President Wilson." Woodrow Wilson was the only American politician who had been enough of an idealist to appeal to my father. Wilson understood that Europe was a real place and that people there were human. If President Wilson had prevailed, Papa was always telling us, and the League of Nations had been set up to match his envisioning, we'd have had true peace, not this skittish peace that Americans celebrated with foolishness and noise, this flimsy peace full of suspicion and hate.

"And poverty. And injustice," interrupted Jessie, also not for the first time, not that she had much faith, ever, in President Wilson. "Your President Wilson deported Emma Goldman."

"He's a sick man. Others did this. Wilson did not do this." Papa had gradually stopped attending the anarchist meetings as the complexities of life in America had become more interesting to him, and now he had become afraid of radical activity, worrying that he'd be deported even though he was an American citizen. The Screamers no longer came to our house, but wherever they had gone, Jessie had followed.

Papa ignored Jessie and kept talking. I was the only one listening, not that I couldn't already recite what he was saying. My mother couldn't understand English, Sarah couldn't understand politics, and Jessie couldn't understand President Wilson, that mild compromiser who allowed people to be rounded up and imprisoned out of fear of radicalism. But I see myself looking daughterly as Papa explained that President Wilson respected all countries, not just this one. Daily my father had exhorted Congress, from our dining room table, to ratify Wilson's treaty and support the League of Nations, but he had failed.

"If Wilson had won—"

"Oh, Papa, enough," Jessie said, stopping on her way to the kitchen with a platter. "There are troubles in this country

that President Wilson didn't know how to fix. You know
there are. You yourself are a worker."

"I see no Cossacks. I hear of no pogroms in this country."

"But there's hatred of Jews. I feel it at the mill. And how
do they treat Socialists? And what about Emma Goldman?
But worst is the poverty." Jessie carried the platter into the
kitchen and I stood up to help. I could hear Jessie clattering
plates. Then she came back. She could never keep from making a speech. "When they send me on an errand through the
cutting rooms," she said, a little hoarsely, her dark eyes bulging, "or the floor where the machinery is, I'm shocked at
what I see—creatures so pale and wrinkled with hard work,
they're scarcely human."

"I know about hard work, my daughter."

"And wages are being cut everywhere—"

"Your wages?" said Papa. "At the mill?"

"No, not so far, but the trolley men—"

Suddenly Father was in a rage, standing up, pounding the
table. "I do not want to hear about the trolley men! I do not
want to hear about my daughter screaming in the streets,
throwing stones at police! They will rape you and kill you!
This will be my shame for letting you hear those foolish men,
when you were a baby!"

He sank to his chair and buried his face in his hands, but
Jessie was shouting louder than he. "In a country where business tells the government what to do, what can workingmen
do except strike? And how can decent people not support
them? A strike is honorable. Helping strikers is honorable.
You expect them to take a twenty-five-percent cut in wages?"

"Not my daughter!" he screamed. Sarah ran crying from
the room, and I followed her, but I continued to hear their
voices.

Jessie didn't stay to help finish washing up. The announce-
ment that Sarah and I would be taking the Lake Avenue trol-

ley out into the country on Sunday had been lost in the debate, which had given Sarah and me half a headache each, we said as we worked in the kitchen. I felt close to Sarah, for once. She was able and smart at the sink if not in school, and got the joke about half a headache, somewhat to my surprise. I felt distant from Jessie, who had gone out into the night with her crazy notions, and it made my throat tight and my stomach queasy to feel distant from Jessie.

———

—You never came.

—I started reading. Deborah and the little girls stood in front of her. Squirrel had fallen asleep in Ruben's arms. She yanked her shirt down.

—What are you reading?

Ruben laughed. That book.

—Jeremiah's favorite book? Is it any good?

—I don't know. She should have gone to the park. Now she wanted to be with Deborah.

—They want you to teach at the Center. I was saving it to tell you in the park. She called me last night. She's calling you tonight.

—Who?

—Carlotta. The director. Can you start next week?

Ruben was afraid to drive a car and so she contrived not to have one; cars shriveled in her care. The next week, she took the bus. She found the building: an old school, remodeled and turned into a day-care center. She walked in through a crowd of children, some black, some white, who chased one another like puppies. She had to ask two grown-ups before someone led her to the basement, where five women sat at a round pressed-wood table in the middle of a huge, shadowy room. The school table had an aluminum base but the edges tilted when Ruben or the students put their elbows on it. All but one student were black. They didn't smile. Ruben talked too much. The women were ashamed at what they didn't know. They made the table rock, then backed away from it, discovering reasons to hurry back to the babies they cared for. What efforts someone had gone to, winning them time off, winning them Ruben. The director, it turned out: Carlotta, a big, loud, black woman who hurried through after half an hour, shouting encouragement. Her voice resounded in the bare room, which had been the school's gym. Far across the room were two high windows, with squares of sun below them, but otherwise the classroom was dark. Dusty bulbs hung in cages.

—No, we don't all work *here*, the friendliest one corrected Ruben. Me and Lily work here. The rest of these girls come from Barrett Street. The other city day care.

—Oh, of course. But which one was Lily? One was Dorothy, but which? The friendly one, who turned nodding toward Ruben, was Emma.

Deborah, who taught different students at different times, wasn't there. Ruben had imagined classrooms, with Deborah down the hall.

—Let's see what you know, Ruben said. They knew nouns but not verbs. All but Emma could read, some haltingly. Ruben had no idea how to teach Emma to read.

—What we really don't know is math, said Cecile, the white woman. Emma, smiling, didn't know what *a third* meant. Ruben tore paper in thirds, broke imaginary cookies in thirds. Emma, they all said with fondness, don't you even know *that*?

The day of the second class, the sleepy-looking sitter canceled because of a cold. Ruben brought Squirrel along. Ooh, said the students, as if they'd never seen a baby up close, as if there can never be enough babies. Emma took him from Ruben's arms. Handed a baby, the class sat back and the table didn't wobble. Each took her turn patting his back, smoothing his damp blue shirt. Ruben, distracted, had them read. A newspaper lay on the table and they passed it around. Patty Hearst had been captured! Friendly Emma could not read *captured*. She could not read *radicals*.

The page in the math book was on graphs. It was hard to explain, and Ruben, too, would rather have played with Squirrel. She tried to remember not knowing what a graph was. She liked watching other women hold her baby, though it made her feel young and ignorant. He settled unshyly against each bosom.

In the park, next day, it was cool, and brown leaves blew into Ruben and Deborah's faces. Rose cried with something in her eye, and Deborah stood her on a bench and got it out with the wet corner of a tissue. Crouching, Deborah was big, in a denim tent dress and a gray poncho. She grasped Ruben's arm when she straightened herself. Well, did you see? Deborah said. They caught Patty Hearst.

—When the baby comes, said Ruben, Squirrel will have someone to play with.

—He'll have plenty of people to play with, as soon as he can play, said Deborah. Squirrel sat up in an umbrella stroller. He didn't have enough muscle tone yet not to look squashed. Deborah laughed at him, mushed in his bright blue sweater and hood, not much face, and Ruben looked and laughed, too.

Jill was at nursery school. Now Deborah swung her arms, bending in the fallen leaves under gray clouds as if to chase Rose, though she didn't; but Rose ran anyway, fell and ran, fell and ran, laughing.

—I was so happy when she turned into a revolutionary, said Deborah. Now I want to sneak her out of jail.

—Who?

—Patty Hearst.

—But that was totally unreal. How could she turn into a revolutionary? I was ashamed of her, said Ruben.

—Why couldn't she?

—Because they were just a bunch of criminals. They kid-

napped her. And I don't think you can *turn into* a revolutionary.

Deborah shrugged. They made her father give money to the
poor. It was like a ransom.

—But they were violent and destructive, said Ruben. Is violence ever all right?

—Patty Hearst is an idealist, said Deborah.

Ruben was irritated, but she didn't want to talk about Patty
Hearst. Patty Hearst made her feel guilty and uncomfortable.

—Teaching is good, she said. But hard.

—Don't worry about it, said Deborah. They pay so little.
Whatever you do is fine.

Ruben looked to see if she meant it. But they want to learn!

—Oh, they'll learn.

—How long have you been doing it?

—A year.

—Do they ever take the test?

—One did. But she was different.

In Ruben's presence, two students had talked about Deborah's class. We did laugh, they said, shaking their heads. We
did *laugh*.

The next day Ruben's sitter was over her cold, and the class
elbowed and rocked the table, backed away. Emma had not
come.

—Where's Emma?

—She's no good at this. She can't do it.

But without Emma, Ruben was lonely. Nine chairs were at
the table, the empty ones nearest the teacher.

Nobody understood graphs.

Ruben struggled, explaining what she read in the students'
book, her head tilted toward the door as she listened for Emma.
Out of her anxious head came an idea, and she drew a bar
graph showing how many children each woman had. She was
on it. Hers was the shortest line. The five of them, she and the
four who'd come, leaned over the table together, hands

splayed. Big Cecile had four children, little Lily had five, while lively Dorothy had three and scared Mary two, but Mary also cared for her niece. Ruben didn't know how to show that on the graph. The graph was in ink; finally she lengthened Mary's line in pencil.

—A niece is different? said Mary.

Various voices: Not so different. Not different at all.

Ruben heard Squirrel's cry as she walked into her house. Her milk let down. She had not thought of him for three hours. She'd fretted her way home, thinking how to lure Emma.

Too cold to stand in the playground and watch Rose run in the leaves, Ruben and Deborah walked, Rose in Squirrel's stroller, Squirrel in a sling on Ruben's chest.

—All the way home, said Ruben, I fuss about the class. Good fussing. Yesterday I forgot Squirrel. I forgot I had him.

—When I teach, said Deborah, I walk in thinking of God.

—What does that mean?

—You couldn't teach if there were no God, said Deborah.

—You couldn't?

—But that's not what I'm talking about, said Deborah. I started in the wrong place. I walk in thinking about God, but then I forget God. I forget to worry about the babies.

—The babies aren't God.

—No, said Deborah, the babies aren't God. They walked some more and Deborah said, God wants the babies. God could kill the babies.

—I don't think I like your God, Ruben said.

Deborah said, I think God doesn't care much about whether they live or die. He has other plans for them. And maybe He wants them because we want them. They could die because we love them.

—I think maybe you're crazy, said Ruben.

—Just because we love them, said Deborah, stopping and looking at her, they could die.

—Not *because.*

—Because. I think because.

They stopped for a light. Ruben swiveled her head to watch for traffic turning when they crossed. Baby Rose in the stroller led the way into steel and combustible gasoline.

—You think God kills babies because mothers love them?

—I don't know why anyone dies. Not many babies do, not many. Deborah patted her big belly. She had to stretch to push the stroller.

—Do you want me to push that?

—I'd rather push than wear Squirrel. My back would hurt more.

Deborah was quiet for a while. Then she said, still pushing, It has something to do with love, the danger they're in. I know it does. We put up with the students, but we don't love them.

—Oh, said Ruben, interested. This I have thought about. This is my only contribution to philosophy. This is the Three Levels of Stuff.

Deborah laughed. I like the way you say *stuff.* You have a Brooklyn accent.

—I do not, said Ruben, though she was from Brooklyn. She had worked out the Three Levels of Stuff when Squirrel was first born, during those frenzied, lonely weeks. There are three levels of stuff, she said. First level: food, shit, and sleep.

—Sex?

—I don't know about sex. She hadn't thought about sex when Squirrel was first born.

—Go on. Second level?

They walked. Let me explain third level first. Third level: art, maybe God, death.

—The spirit.

—The spirit, said Ruben. First level things make you think of third level things. When you take care of a baby you know he could die.

—I think sex is both, said Deborah. It's both first level and third level.

—Maybe.

—But what's second level? said Deborah.

—Second level, said Ruben. Second level is offices.

—Offices?

Where Harry had rushed when she was frantic because the baby had vomited in the wrong way, the dangerous, possibly fatal way she'd read about. Where she pictured Harry stopping as he walked down a corridor in which the sun made squares on the floor, holding a file folder open in his right hand, reading something slightly unsatisfying that had just been typed.

Ruben said, Offices exist so the people in them can forget about death. Like the place where you get a dog license.

—Oh, I want a dog! said Deborah.

—Oh, me, too.

Ruben couldn't remember why she started to talk about the Three Levels of Stuff, but Deborah said, So you think teaching is second level, and that was why. Deborah continued, But teaching can be third level. Teaching proves the existence of God.

—Now how is that? But Squirrel cried. And when he stopped, after Ruben shook him back to sleep, bouncing as she walked, Deborah turned, bigly and warmly, to Ruben, her mouth open in a loose oblong, her light hair on her face. Are all mothers afraid? she said.

—I don't know. But I'm glad I found you. Since I am and you are.

—Oh, yes, said Deborah. But sometimes I think we talk each other into it.

Ruben felt a stricture in her throat. You want to take this walk? It's not too tiring?

—Maybe we should turn back now, said Deborah, and Ruben said little on the way back.

·   ·   ·

When the sleepy sitter had a toothache, Ruben brought Squirrel to class again. He cried and she nursed him. The group argued about breast-feeding. Lily said, Nobody's eating from my breast but my boyfriend.

—That is so foolish, girl, said Mary. Forget you said that, before you *think* how foolish it is.

After class, Ruben didn't need to hurry. Let me see where you work, she said to Lily.

Lily led her, with Squirrel in her arms, upstairs where small children ran, mothers talked, teachers shouted—some affectionately, some coldly. A woman reached to touch Squirrel. Then Emma came out of a classroom, carrying two babies.

—Emma, Emma, why don't you come to school? said Ruben. But Squirrel was crying. She bounced him on her arm, but he cried.

—It didn't work out, said Emma. She smiled indulgently. It just didn't work out.

—But I *want* you.

—That's nice of you to say. Emma had a big body. The babies she held were both black, and Ruben felt outnumbered. Emma waited to find out whether Ruben wanted to say something else, as they listened to Squirrel cry, and then she said, Naps for my honeys, here, hoisting the babies higher and letting them settle. One laughed. And she crossed the hall and went into another room.

—Oh, drag her by the hair, Deborah said that night on the phone.

—I'm going to go up and drag Emma down by the hair, Ruben said to the rest of her group, before the next class.

—Don't you touch her *hair*, girl, she spends hours straightening that hair! But they grinned.

—And when I bring her, for God's sake don't insult her!

Ruben tried three rooms where everyone pointed where she should go, agreeing—Yes, Emma should go—and finally walked into the room where Emma worked. Emma came, impressed. They walked down the stairs together. Ruben had pretended to be a certain kind of person and everyone had believed she was. As they walked down, Ruben asked, Why don't you let your hair go natural? But now she'd gone too far.

Emma still couldn't read. Ruben was exhausted that night. Maybe it was a mistake. Emma couldn't do it.

The next time, Ruben was afraid to look, but when she did there were five women at the table. She threw her bag onto the table to celebrate and the table shook and everyone laughed. Emma kept coming. She hugged Ruben often. She couldn't learn.

Deborah was huge. She hugged Ruben, too. In the cold, Deborah and her girls came to Ruben's house and they ate grilled cheese sandwiches. Deborah took over the stove because only she knew how to make the sandwiches so her girls would eat them. She made sandwiches for herself and Ruben, too. She buttered the bread inside and outside and Ruben could feel them both grow fatter. Deborah said, Toby, you aren't fat, you're gorgeous.

—Nonsense.

—It's true.

Ruben considered herself. Red hair, center parted. Slightly fat. Glasses. Not beautiful, not that it mattered, not the sort of thing she thought much about.

—Did you ever sleep with a woman? Ruben said.

—No, did you?

—Never. Did you ever think about it?

—Of course. Let's, some day, said Deborah.

Deborah stood behind her as she ate at her kitchen table, and Squirrel lay back in his white slanting plastic chair and roundly looked at them from the middle of the table. Rose and Jill played with pieces of sandwich and talked to slimy babies that were apple slices, dancing them up and down. Deborah kissed Ruben's scalp and ate a bite of Ruben's remaining half sandwich. Ruben did not turn around. She could feel Deborah's pregnant belly against her head, warm and firm. The window faced south and the winter sun came in behind her and around them both, through a stained-glass yin-yang sign in green and blue, coloring a white macramé hanging she'd tacked above the table. She felt sun on her arms. Rose climbed into Ruben's lap and jumped apple slices over Ruben's arm. Were Ruben and Deborah becoming each other? Toby Ruben hugged Rose and noticed the grain of her own oak table, which lay in such a delicate curve that she had to trace it with her forefinger. Something else beautiful: Rose's ear in the sunlight.

A brace of ladies, they walked, that fall and into winter. It grew dark and Rose wept. Once, miles from home, Squirrel cried unceasingly in his stroller. Ruben stuck her hand down his pants to check his diaper pins.

—Use Pampers, said Deborah. You tape them with masking tape.

—Yuck. Ruben hated the feel of Rose's plastic diapers.

—You want pins sticking in him?

—They're not. Squirrel kept screaming. Deborah shrugged as she stretched past her belly to propel a long stroller made for two, in which Jill was asleep and Rose sang mournfully to herself.

—When we walk, said Ruben, where will you put the baby? They laughed, not that anything was funny: it was cold, twilight, they were far from home with their backs toward home. Partly their laughter was guilty. Squirrel still cried. The houses leaned at them, wooden simple houses with three stacked porches. Skimpy wreaths hung on doors, early, or could they be from last Christmas?

—We ought to turn around, Deborah said.

—Are you tired?

—No.

—Nobody else would do this with me, said Ruben.

—Everybody else would call the Child Abuse Hotline. At last they turned. When they reached Ruben's house, they turned again and walked to Deborah's house. Squirrel was asleep. Outside Deborah's house he cried again. Ruben picked him up and rocked him in her arms. The little girls climbed out of their stroller and ran up on the porch in the dark. Ruben's knees hurt with cold and tiredness. Her breasts hurt. Can I nurse him in the street, standing up?

—Doctor, doctor, I have frostbitten nipples! Come inside.

—I'd never get going again. She nursed him, standing, in the street.

—When is the test? Emma asked, at every class. When will I get my equivalency?

The others were afraid of the test and shushed Emma.

—I keep coming, said Emma. I've come every time. Now I want to take the test.

Ruben kept changing the subject. When she talked on the phone to Deborah, she told her about Emma.

—So?

—So what?

—So schedule her for the test.

—How can she? None of the others are taking it yet. She couldn't possibly pass it.

—So?

—What do you mean, so? It would be irresponsible.

—Do what she wants, said Deborah.

It was a way of looking at things, it had nothing to do with Emma. It made Ruben angry. She'll fail, said Ruben. Everybody will think I'm a bad teacher.

—Oh, is that it?

—No, said Ruben. She'll be unhappy when she fails it. She'll blame me.

—Toby, I can't think about that. I'm four centimeters dilated. I haven't slept in a week.

—Maybe you should stop teaching.

—Oh, I bring magazines and read to them.

—Not really, said Ruben, who spent hours late at night planning lessons.

—Somewhat really, said Deborah.

—What do you think Deborah meant? she said to Harry, but Harry didn't care. They were in bed. He'd learned not to touch her breasts, which were just kitchen appliances these days, so he ran his fingers through her pubic hair and began to touch her inside. What did Deborah mean? she said again, but for the first time since she'd had Squirrel, she liked the feeling, she wasn't just giving herself lectures about it.

When Deborah had to go have her baby, Jeremiah showed up on Ruben's porch with the little girls. She had seen him only once before.

—Do we have one of those friendships with husbands? she and Deborah had said to each other. But Jeremiah was nice, and Harry was nice, and once they had all stood on a corner in the wind—strollers, husbands—and talked. Now Jeremiah, a short man, glittery-eyed from fucking to work songs or for some other reason, stood and laughed on the porch because his wife was having a baby quite soon, two weeks early, and Ruben gathered the little girls into her house and talked to him shyly through the partly opened door. It was windy.

—Quick or slow? Ruben asked, through the doorway. What do you think?

—Quick or slow what? said Jeremiah, and she felt herself blush as if he'd caught her in a double entendre, when all she meant was labor. The birth.

—Oh, quick, surely.

—Better hurry then, which was also embarrassing, as if she was throwing him out.

This strange husband smiled and stood. Jill had breakfast, he said, but Rose wouldn't. It was early in the morning. Harry was still asleep.

—I'll feed her.

—She likes—

—I know what she likes. Grilled cheese sandwich. Butter on the outside. Cut into strips. Handled till it's gray. She wanted him to know that she knew.

Harry met her, carrying Squirrel. Didn't Deborah have friends before you?

—I don't mind! Ruben was proud to be the one.

—I didn't mean it that way. I was curious.

—Her other friends are boring.

She baby-sat perfectly. Harry left, Squirrel napped, and she made cookies with the little girls, letting the rug stay dirty. She lifted the heavy daughters onto her kitchen chairs, saying in a perfectly casual, adult voice—just as she planned to speak later to Squirrel—Oh, Jill. Maybe you could dump in this baking soda? She guided Rose's hand. The phone rang.

—Toby, we've got another kid!

—Healthy?

—Oh, healthy, yes, of course!

—Girl or boy?

—Oh, girl. They're always girls.

—What's her name?

—Mary Grace.

Ruben's eyes teared. She would have to kidnap the whole family, maybe even glittery Jeremiah. She would keep them in her bed, all five of them, and take them out to look at them, now that they were perfect, now that they had given that old-fashioned, believing, innocent name to their third little daughter. But if she kept them in the bed, Harry would discover them. Where would she keep them? They would be her secret pleasure. She hung up the phone and turned, blushing and grinning, to the untidy yellow-haired girls standing on her chairs. Then she cried and hugged them.

—Doesn't it need more baking soda? said Jill.

They baked the cookies. Ruben ran out of creative activities long before Jeremiah came. That night she climbed into bed as soon as Squirrel slept. Harry watched television. She'd been reading a library book, but she had finished it. Before that book, she'd read books her students might like, and books about teaching such students. Now, at last, she could read the book Deborah had lent her. Seeing Jeremiah had made her remember it. She was a little afraid he'd ask for it, but of course he didn't. Tired as she was, she got out of bed and found the book in a pile on the dresser.

————

The wintry fog wrapped itself around the union hall, as if to hold tight within its grip the men and women gathered there. I'm inventing this. I wasn't there. I'm looking around that room in my imagination, and I have to admit: it's a crowd of decent people. Some look naive, some look foolish—of course their clothes are old-fashioned to me as I write this in 1964—but there's plenty of intelligence and goodness. The leader, whose attention everyone is trying to get, is my sister Jessie's old flame, William Platz. He's got curls on his forehead and a skinny nose that looks elegant profiled in the lamplight. He's obviously noble, smart, fearless—maybe too fearless? He's suddenly distracted and when I look around I see that my sister has stepped decisively into the room, looking squat and determined: not sexy, but maybe sexy after all, because of her directness. He hasn't gotten over her, though he's gone back to his wife. He's pointing to a chair. Jessie sits. At first she has a hard time paying attention because she, too, has felt something, once again, between herself and William. Also she's thinking of—what on earth?—me. We'd had a quarrel. We'd met before work in the morning. I'd told her the strike would be just as successful or unsuccessful without her as with her. Now I see how angry and nasty a remark that was. I was suggesting she wasn't a leader.

Jessie shook off any thoughts about her uncomprehending sister Miriam and anything else besides the business at hand, and listened attentively, raising her eyebrows as if ideas could be made clearer that way. The discussion was about the trolley strike that had taken place just a few months earlier in Denver. After death, injury, and terrible property damage, the workers returned to their jobs, merely requesting that the scabs be run out of town. The union leader said, "You do not know what this shooting, this loss of life, has done to me. I am a different man. I would do anything to end this bloodshed." The gathering in Boynton considered these words seriously, with strong disagreements. Some thought the Denver union leader was a hero, others that he had betrayed those he was supposed to lead.

Jessie rose to her feet. "If we decide *now*," she shouted, "in exactly which circumstances we'll surrender—" She paused. "If we say *now* that we *could* surrender—well, we might as well give up. We might as well go home." She was hoarse, as she often was when she made a speech: her voice wasn't naturally loud. Her eyes bulged, I imagine, and hairs escaped from her small brown bun. "*I'm* not going home. I'll do what's needed. If someone dies, I will mourn. But I will mourn then, not beforehand. If the rest of you want to go home now—well, then, it will be quiet enough in here that I can think of a plan and know what to do. I hope you reach shelter, all of you, before the snow."

The speech became well known around town. Nobody left, of course.

This group, a combination of anarchists, Communists, Socialists, and the leaders of the trolley men's union, first planned to persuade people to boycott the trolleys during the strike. "Once the public understands what is at stake," said William Platz, "it will demand justice in order to keep the lines running!" There was applause and shouting and happiness, but of course they were kidding themselves, and, in fact, plans were also being made to intimidate potential passengers and keep them off trolleys run by scabs.

It hadn't been my sister's first speech. She literally stood on soapboxes. Mostly people ignored her or laughed at her; sometimes they got angry. Jessie knew that speeches weren't going to keep anybody off the trolleys. The Denver strike, which they'd avidly read about, had been bitterly violent. A newspaper account I've found says that at least five people were killed and thirty injured. Mobs stoned the *Denver Post* building, destroyed the business offices, and tried to demolish the presses because the paper was against the strike. A passenger was struck by a brick. Strikers and sympathizers marched on City Hall screaming "Wreck the Hall." The response was even worse: armed volunteers joined the police, and federal troops arrived to put down the disturbances. The *New York Times* reported on August 7, 1920, that "armored tank cars mounted with Browning machine guns capable of firing five hundred shots a minute are patrolling the streets." The *Times* continued, "Fearless men, aroused by the menace to life and property created by the riots, are armed with sawed-off shotguns and have orders to shoot to kill if necessary." It was in this situation that the strikers gave up and the leader declared himself a changed man.

I'm as staunch an old lefty as anybody, mind you. I'm not siding with the police and the army and the reactionary press against the strikers. I just think the strikers in Denver were stupid: What did they think was going to happen? And given the example of Denver, just three months earlier, what, may I ask, did the trolley men of Boynton, Massachusetts—aided and abetted by my sister—think was going to happen to them?

"Jessie." William Platz caught up to her as she was stepping outside into the night. "May I walk you to your trolley stop?" Heavy irony, here. He'd seduced her three years earlier—taken her virginity. The two of them are about to try to close down the very trolley system to which he is demurely escorting her. Nonetheless comes this invitation that I'm imagining or remembering. Jessie told me about something like this. She liked his solicitude. Already, though she was so young, she had lost any claim to protection from men, and ordinarily she didn't want it. But William Platz jammed his cap on his head and pulled it off again to run his hand through his curls, which the sooty wind blew into tangles. The heavy brown cap was thrust onto his head again. Jessie hadn't tied her veil in place and the ashy breeze nicked her skin. They walked silently together. He knew where she was going—to the Crampton line. It ran into the slum where Jessie had rented a room when she and my father quarreled so badly she had to leave.

Walking up the long hill, they didn't talk. They waited together at the trolley stop and Jessie began to wonder why he didn't make his own way home. Then the trolley came and they got on. As usual, they were surrounded by tired workingmen in gray or brown coats, all of them shaking in their seats with the car's movement. William sat next to her and Jessie took in the slightly damp smell of his woolen coat. She felt a renewed awareness of his body next to her own, as if the inch of air closest to him had its own texture, mixed rough and smooth, and its own dark, pleasant smell.

He touched her, inadvertently or not, and she got the idea that he was going home with her. She thought he'd changed his mind. He'd seduced her and had been her lover for months, and then he'd told her he'd made a mistake, that despite the ideas of anarchism he wished to be faithful to his wife. Now Jessie's feelings were engaged—and hurt a second time. Maybe William Platz had still another lover, who happened to live on this trolley line. Whatever the reason, he jumped up, shook hands with Jessie, and disembarked three blocks before her stop. Jessie went home alone and I think—I indulge myself with thinking—that our lives were changed that night as her heart beat faster, but then more slowly and angrily, defiantly. She studied the motorman's back during those last three blocks. He was a man our father's age, with, she decided, a simple, vulnerable look to his head and shoulders. The motorman needed her. He and she were in the same army.

———

Ruben stopped reading and slept. But the baby woke in the night, and after she nursed him, she couldn't fall asleep again.

———

Lest the reader think it was always night in Boynton in 1920, with a gritty wind blowing, let me say that the Sunday after Jessie's dinner at home was sunny and clear, with cold white clouds moving swiftly across a cold sky. A light snow—the first of the season—had fallen the night before, and a scattering covered fields and roofs. Where dry reeds from the previous summer still stood in the open places, they rustled with ice. Sarah and I looked out the trolley window at the open countryside, on our way to have Sunday dinner with Edith Livingston and her family. I stared at the crisp brown grasses near the right of way until I was lulled by the rhythmic progress of the trolley and no longer saw them.

Sarah chattered about how she imagined Edith might look. "Does she have dimples? I picture her with dimples." I felt shy, and wished I hadn't agreed to go, and to bring along my unpredictable little sister. Once, the trolley stopped because of ice on the overhead line, and the conductor climbed up on the roof and knocked it off with a pole. Sarah was excited about that, too, though she'd seen it done before. It was she who recognized Edith's house from the description I'd been given, and, sure enough, the next stop was Hale Road, where we were supposed to get off, and where Edith, who had no dimples, met us.

All I remember of the walk to the house with Edith, so many years later, is that we saw a dead sparrow on the frozen ground, and Edith, who had a volatile disposition, squatted and stroked and cooed along with Sarah, while I stood by: I was irritated at their sentimentality, and also cold. I was envious, too. My dumb but darling little sister, I thought, would soon be a closer friend of Edith's than I was. Edith was sharp and funny when she wasn't crying over something, but I watched her admire Sarah's broad pink face and easy smile. And Sarah was admirable. I see her smiling up at Edith and me, all but smiling through tears, when Edith had stopped looking at the bird and Sarah was still crouched on the ground. Sarah was smiling at her own foolishness and naturally nobody could resist that. She had on a pretty blue coat that my mother had made. She looked particularly charming in the country. We took a shortcut across a field.

As we were welcomed into Edith's family's house, I was almost sure I heard somebody in the background saying "Jewish?" Sarah didn't notice. I was sure I was right when I saw the expression on Edith's mother's face, which Edith's imitated: they were wordlessly reassuring each other, with big smiles, that *nothing* was wrong. It didn't take me long to figure out that the person who'd spoken was Edith's elderly uncle. I rather liked him anyway, maybe because of his bluntness. But I was upset, too, mostly for Sarah, who was looking with trust and pleasure at the slightly swoopy overdone dark red drapery and upholstery.

We were looked at, meanwhile; we'd do. The uncle greeted us as nicely as anybody. Edith had brothers of all sizes. We sat down. Somebody said grace, which was new to me. The food was like food in library books. There was a vegetable I couldn't name.

My father was a gruff, awkward man, so I found it unsettling when Edith's father turned out to be well spoken, with elaborate manners. "Let me help you to some more roast, Miss Lipkin. Wouldn't you like this crisp piece?" He and the old uncle monopolized the conversation until, now and then, it would be seized by an old woman who was apparently the uncle's wife. Gradually I realized that they were Edith's great-aunt and great-uncle: the aunt and uncle of everyone in the room except Sarah and me. I was unfamiliar with elderly relatives, and relatives who were the heads of large families. My grandparents and great-aunts and great-uncles had been left behind in Europe and were spoken of with such foreboding and regret and guilt that I'd come to think of that generation as a crowd of helpless ghosts, nothing like this vigorous old pair, who were comfortably in charge. Everyone else liked them, too, I soon saw—except Mr. Livingston, Edith's father. Then I began to understand that the old couple were his relatives, not his wife's, and that he worked in a company the old man had begun. It sounded like a factory, but I couldn't figure out what it made. The old man was called Uncle Warren and at least one of Edith's brothers was also Warren. As the conversation became more rapid it seemed that Edith had *two* brothers called Warren, but even the goyim probably didn't carry their odd customs that far. Then I realized that Mr. Livingston—Edith's father—was Warren, and that he now ran the plant, and that his uncle didn't think he was smart enough.

"Of *course* there are Reds in the factory," Edith's father said. "There are Reds everywhere." He sounded more like our own father now, angry. But on the other side.

The old uncle shook his head dolefully. Edith's brothers were becoming restless. The youngest was the one called Warren—Warrie—and he had climbed out of his chair and made friends with Sarah. She played peekaboo with him, and then took him on her lap. "And naturally they've infiltrated the union," Mr. Livingston was saying. "Doesn't surprise me. Damned Bolsheviks."

"Warren," came Edith's mother's voice.

"I mean it literally," said Mr. Livingston. "If the Bolsheviks aren't on their way to hell, I don't know who is. Excuse me. The Underworld, boys, the Underworld."

"Father said 'hell,' " I heard the second oldest brother whisper to the oldest one, who was shushing him. "But he did, he did."

"Hear they're planning a little riot for us," said the old uncle. "Right in Boynton. If the trolley men go out. I suppose that doesn't bother you either?"

"Of course not," said the father, his voice now shaky with anger. "Let them try it. We've got a pretty fine police force in Boynton. And there's the National Guard, if necessary."

I wasn't positive Sarah wouldn't blurt out something about Jessie's politics. Or maybe these men had even heard of Jessie and the anarchists. Sarah, however, was playing elaborate games with Warrie, and now they'd both left the table and tall Sarah was dodging around the furniture as if she were in her own home while the little boy shrieked with laughter. I was afraid Edith's mother would mind, but she looked on almost tearfully, as did, of course, Edith.

"Would you call out soldiers for something like this?" the old uncle asked his nephew, refusing to drop the subject. "I'm just trying to ascertain what you'd do." He sounded as if he hardly cared, and yet the father got angrier yet, and shifted abruptly in his chair, knocking his elbow into Sarah, who had come up behind him with little Warrie Livingston in her arms. He jumped up and apologized, a little impatiently I thought, but Sarah beamed at him and assured him it wasn't his fault. "We aren't hurt, Warrie, are we?" she said. Suddenly there was a new issue. Warrie insisted that Sarah be invited to dinner on his birthday, several weeks hence.

"Oh, you don't have to invite me," said Sarah. But they did invite her—and me, too, as an afterthought. Mrs. Livingston whispered to me that they'd nearly lost the little boy to influenza. Sarah promised to return, and so did I, but Sarah

was the draw for good reason. I'd sat through dinner sniffing
and judging and emitting curlicues of cynicism from my place
next to Edith. Sarah had joined the family and made them
feel better about themselves. The old uncle kissed her when
we left.

A few days later, I locked up the millinery shop in the evening, alone. The owner's mother was sick, and with some
fanfare Miss Fredericks had explained to me what needed to
be done, and, for the last few days, had trusted me to do it
while she hurried home early. I swept the floor and replaced
the hats we'd sold with others I took from boxes and arranged on the expressionless heads, to all of which I'd se-
cretly given names. Miss Fredericks took most of the money
with her, but I liked knowing that some was left—hidden in
a box only she and I knew about—and knowing that Miss
Fredericks believed I wouldn't take it. Dressing the heads was
like playing with dolls, but I'd never had dolls with such elegant clothes as these hats, and when I was sure I wouldn't be
interrupted, I couldn't keep from talking to them. It was a relief to stop sneering at everything for once.

The hats looked stylish to me, but Boynton was a dreary
place and they were probably old-fashioned before we sold
them. Nonetheless, tilted over the painted faces, the hats gave
the forms the calm look—I thought of it as an "American"
look—that Edith's well-dressed mother had worn as she
pulled Sarah and me into her house. Of course, she wasn't
wearing a hat in her own parlor.

The look was nothing like one my mother might affect, nor
did she wear these hats. My passionate mother yanked her
children closer while screaming at us to change. Neither love
nor hats was dainty in our house. My mother wore hats she
seemed to have brought from Europe. Jessie and I told each
other that they had been handed down from remote ances-
tresses who had worn them to kill chickens.

I wasn't above enjoying the escapes into fantasy that my

job offered me, though I was often bored and annoyed in the millinery shop. Now I was engaged in the silliest of those escapes, accepting a party invitation in a false voice while arranging a black hat with a decorated veil over a head sculpted with light brown curls, which I called Louisa, when a knock at the door startled me. I hoped I hadn't been heard. I told myself it was only a late customer. I didn't answer, but the knock was repeated. Then I opened the door, and my sister Jessie pushed past me into the store as roughly as if she thought I might have closed the door in her face. I hadn't seen her for a week. I screamed a little because she'd had her hair cut short since we'd last met, and it seemed for a moment as if she had indeed come to buy a hat, in order to conceal the way she looked. She acted as if she didn't know what I was staring at, and then ran her hand through her bobbed brown hair. "What's wrong with it?"

"Nothing."

"You don't like it."

"You look like a radical."

"I am a radical." Jessie was buxom, as I've said, and not too tall. Her figure made her look motherly until she cut her hair. Now she looked like someone I'd be shy with. I *was* shy.

Jessie walked around the store, unable to keep her hands off the merchandise. "Look at the little rosettes on this veil. How could anybody stand them in front of her eyes?"

"You know. You've worn veils. You look past the little rosettes."

"I don't look past things."

I didn't want to ask if her hands were clean. I tried to finish my work.

"Miriam, do you have any money?"

"What?"

Jessie was upset. She kept swinging her arms as she stood there, like someone on a swift hike. Then she told me about

the trolley ride with William Platz. It pleased me. It made me
know that my sister still lived somewhere inside this woman.
"I want to make him think about me if he wakes in the
night," she said. "If you give me the money you keep here,
we can help support the strikers. William knows I have no
money. He'll think I robbed a stranger in the street."

"She takes the money with her." I had the box of petty
cash, and after Miss Fredericks had left I'd sold one hat and
collected that money, but of course the hat was gone. She'd
know right away that there ought to be $3.98 in the drawer
or one more hat on display. But I didn't tell Jessie there was
money in the store. Now I think my loyalty was misplaced. If
I'd given it to her, maybe she'd have calmed down, sobered
by some sense of responsibility toward me. Maybe she sus-
pected that I was lying.

Jessie left the store, shrugging. Later I learned that she
went to William Platz's house, where she found his wife
alone and confessed to her that William had taken her virginity a couple of years earlier, that he had been her lover, and
that now he had another lover, on Prescott Street. Jessie was
guessing about the second lover, but she turned out to be
right. Mrs. Platz, of course, was the wife of an anarchist, but
he'd come to it late and they were legally married. She herself
was not interested in political theory. Still, she told Jessie that
she was unconcerned with the artificial rules of bourgeois so-
ciety and William could do as he liked. Of course she was
bluffing, but Jessie was silenced.

As she was getting ready to leave, though, William came
home. His wife began screaming at him, and in the end he
left with Jessie. She got him back for a few days. I think he
stayed at her room, where, no doubt, they made love every
hour. Jessie wasn't a bad person. She was brilliant, and we
lived in such a particularly dismal town. When I read Dick-
ens, later, the descriptions of gray, dreary mill towns reminded me of home. Nothing we saw was beautiful or noble.

If Jessie had grown up as she should have—even if my father had stayed with his idealism and thought things through—she'd have been high-minded but quieter. She'd have written forceful letters to the editor of the newspaper. Frustration turned her idealism sexual and violent.

The strike was planned for the following week. The trolley company refused to negotiate and I don't think the workers wanted to negotiate, either. By now it was late December. Jessie appeared at our apartment one evening. She said she'd come to collect any warm clothes she might have left behind when she moved out. Probably she also came to make my parents and me feel bad. She'd just been left, once again, by William Platz, and she needed to share her misery. My parents were predictably panic-stricken over her sheared head, which Jessie had probably forgotten entirely by then. No doubt she came to scare them with plans to shoot the president of the trolley company, and instead she had to defend her haircut. Sarah cried, and demanded to know just how it had been done and where. At an Italian barber's, it turned out.

"Weren't they rude?"

"No, they were perfectly nice." Glancing at Jessie's face, I knew they had been rude.

Sarah ran her hands over her twisted braids as if to make sure she still had them. We'd been interrupted cleaning up after dinner. Jessie insisted she had already eaten, but when Sarah fixed a plate for her she didn't refuse it. After we washed the dishes, Sarah and I followed Jessie into the bedroom. I made Jessie take a jacket of mine I insisted was too short for me. Sarah watched from the bed.

"Goosie," she said abruptly, watching Jessie try on the jacket and smooth her hands over her hips, "you don't believe in free love, do you?"

"What makes you ask that?" Of course Sarah thought Jessie was a virgin.

"Don't women who cut their hair believe in free love?"

"What's wrong with free love?" said Jessie wickedly.

"Don't you want to be married and have babies?" said Sarah. "Miriam's friend Edith says free love will destroy the American family."

"Oh, Sarah, don't listen to idiots," Jessie said. She swept her hand across my dresser, as if sweeping idiots off it, and all my little bottles of scent and toilet water fell down. One broke. Jessie bent to pick up the whole bottles, putting her hand among the broken pieces of glass, while I ran for a rag.

"You'll cut yourself."

"My hide is tough," said Jessie, "but I'm going to stink of this stuff."

She shook her big hands. Sarah reached to smell first one hand and then the other, laughing, and in her gesture I caught a glimpse of womanhood. She seemed indulgent, but she wouldn't stop arguing. "Goosie, if you could meet these new friends, you'd see that you don't have to be so angry. You don't have to change everything American. We're Europeans. We don't know how they do things here."

"You were born here, Sarah," Jessie said. "You can figure these things out as well as I can."

"I think Edith's father knows better than you, Jessie."

"Edith's father! Isn't he the owner of Livingston Brass? Where workers lose their jobs if they relieve themselves more than once a day?"

"Jessie!"

"Look, Sarah, the trolley men are losing a quarter of their wages. What would happen to you if Papa's wages were cut that much?"

"I'd leave school and get a job," said Sarah stalwartly.

"That's no answer."

"Well, I don't know what I'd do," Sarah said. She'd unpinned her braids and was twisting them around her fingers. "But you don't know either, Goosie. Mr. Livingston is a kind man, in a kind family. They invited us to come back for Edith's little brother's birthday."

"Let them start thinking about some other little brothers, over near the river."

"Goosie, Goosie."

"Oh, stop calling me that!" Jessie walked out of the bedroom, clutching the jacket, and Sarah, in tears, threw herself on our big sister.

"Oh, it's all right, Sare," said Jessie, but she left a few minutes later, and Sarah was still crying.

———

Deborah called from the hospital in the morning. They're not letting me out until tomorrow. I'm a prisoner.

—How come?

—Some number. It's minor.

—I want to see Mary Grace! Ruben wondered if something was wrong; no.

—So come here. I want to see you.

—I'll come. She had to take Squirrel along, and she was pretty sure he wouldn't be allowed into the hospital, so she wore him in the sling and put a shirt of Harry's on top and her coat on top of that. She'd worn that shirt when she was pregnant. I'm putting you back in, she said to Squirrel. Surprising: short, red-headed Toby Ruben deceiving the big hospital, of which she was afraid. It had given her the Squirrel and maybe it could snatch him back, an idea no less powerful because it was nonsense. You better not cry, kiddo. She walked to the bus stop, patting his rear.

It wasn't Ruben who broke rules. Apparently she had become Deborah, and she fluffed her hair and stretched, unhunching her shoulders, which were already tight: this baby was too big to be carried on her chest. He slept and slurped his tongue a little too noisily, and slept again—a good friend. Deborah broke rules. She thought of Deborah saying she

merely read aloud to her students. If Lawful Toby tried that,
Director Carlotta would whoosh in like weather to catch her
and hold her up to shame. What have we here, what what
WHAT have we here! White Lady thinks our Black Ladies (and
white ladies) are of no account, not worth trouble, not worth
squints and frowns and headaches?

But there was no question about smuggling Squirrel into the
hospital. Ruben wanted badly to visit Deborah, and see Mary
Grace Laidlaw, that new citizen. Peter the Squirrel had to see
her too; probably he'd marry her eventually.

At the bus stop an old woman disapproved of carrying babies
on chests, and Ruben said, Oh, leave us alone! Probably the
old woman, who drew herself into a seat and inserted herself
in her own tote bag, grimacing, growing smaller and smaller
while the tote bag grew larger and larger—quite probably the
old woman cursed her. For while Ruben crossed the street in
a hurry, buttoning the shirt over Squirrel and holding her coat
as closed as it would get, first she remembered her dead mother,
whom she didn't like thinking about, and then Squirrel made
a sound in his sleep, an *ah*. In the lobby of the hospital he
awoke and she heard him slurp his thumb, so she left and
walked around an endless block with more than four sides,
onto a bridge over the highway, where she walked against the
wind and her baby was socked by wind and was soon crying.
Ruben started to circle the block again. This time she saw a
bench. She took off her coat and Harry's shirt and took off
Squirrel, who was shrieking by now. She pulled up her own
shirt and nursed him, trying to yank the coat around her. She
had never been so cold. People passed and looked at her, but
nobody criticized her. When the baby fell asleep, she put him
back into the sling and got dressed around him. Then she returned to the hospital and asked for the pass to see Deborah
Laidlaw. And was handed it by someone who barely looked at
her.

In the elevator, a nurse winked.

Pass in hand, Ruben hurried down the corridor where Squirrel had been born. They'd think she was tired of him—and sometimes she was. But not bringing him back.

In the room was her friend Deborah, bare-breasted, nursing someone not as large as her breast. Jill was leaning over her mother and Rose was lying on the bed next to Deborah, in her shoes. Jeremiah sat on the end of the bed taking his off, letting them thump to the faraway floor. The hospital had just that year decided to let the grimy sisters in.

—Hi, hello and welcome, said Jeremiah, standing up in his socks.

Jill and Rose pointed, and Deborah pulled Ruben down to her sweaty, milky, freckly half nakedness for a kiss. Her hospital gown, blue and pink teddy bears, was wrinkled over her shoulder. When Ruben leaned over, Squirrel bumped Deborah.

—Here's the boy!

—Shh.

—What?

—Surely he's not allowed. Nervous Ruben was all but sorry she'd come. The baby was lovely, pink and sweet, but Jeremiah saying Welcome made her shy; people welcomed are outsiders.

—Jill and Rose are allowed. It's a private room. If they ask, I'll say he's my son.

—You have them nine months apart, of course.

—We Catholics are like that. I forgot to mention him, I have so many.

Squirrel cried, but nobody came running. Ruben bounced on her heels and Jill and Rose demanded that she take him out, as if they'd never seen him before. Jill made rude noises into her new sister's face. Let's put him next to our baby and see if he's bigger, she said. Ruben liked that, but she wasn't going to do it. Jeremiah edgily put on one shoe and tied the bow carefully. Ruben found a place in the lounge chair, which was covered with the children's coats and with newspapers and books, and wished she carried enough peace inside her to quiet Squirrel just by circling her hand on his back.

But a nurse came in. That baby's not allowed in here, she said. I'm surprised at you, Mrs. Laidlaw. Introducing your baby to all those germs.

—How about my own kids' germs? They have more germs. They play in the germy mud.

—Sibling visits are permitted. But they'll have to go soon, too.

—Everybody's going, said Deborah.

It hurt Ruben's feelings. I wouldn't harm the baby! she said. She thought she might cry. She could break a rule, but only a silly rule.

—We've got to have some kind of control, said the nurse.

—What do you think I am? Ruben said. She was embarrassed. Not only had her smuggling failed to conceal Squirrel, the nurse hadn't noticed that she was attempting to conceal him. Hey, what do you think I am, the Symbionese Liberation Army?

—What's that? said Deborah.

—You know, Jeremiah said. Patty Hearst.

—Oh, right, Deborah said. Toby thinks Patty Hearst is a phony. I thought she was wonderful.

—She was tricked, said the nurse. She thought she was doing good, but she wasn't.

—That's what Toby thinks, Deborah said, like a queen, a queen with her breasts hanging out and a now sleeping newborn on her arm. Defiantly and wrongly, Deborah could insist that Ruben and the mean nurse make friends, wielding the authority of pink and blue teddy bears.

—No, it's not, said Ruben, who wanted to fight with the nurse. That's not what I think. Patty Hearst doesn't give a damn about people in trouble. She's not a real revolutionary.

—Well, the baby has to go, said the nurse, and Deborah was

apologizing, ordering everyone out: You're absolutely right! I'm so sorry! We should have thought! Deborah wouldn't stop. As if, Deborah said to the nurse, working in this madhouse isn't hard enough, we're making things harder for you!

Which was not true. They had not made things harder for the nurse.

And before anybody could fight with anybody, Deborah went on: I need some rest! All of you chickens and roosters and caterpillars. Get going.

But also saving something Ruben would have spoiled. How delicate. How lovely. Ruben felt loved and held in check for her own sake, a rare feeling she always enjoyed; but she was also angry that she didn't get to have her fight.

She wanted one thump of Deborah's hand on Squirrel or on her head or her shoulder. She wished to outstay the others by a second. But Jeremiah offered a ride home and in a moment she was just a mommy in the departing crowd, helping people on with coats.

Deborah was also dismissing Mary Grace, trusting the nurse with her, which Ruben found unthinkable, and now Mary Grace in her cart was being wheeled out of the room, and Deborah announced that she would have a bowel movement and a nap in that order. The nurse scolded along behind them as they walked to the elevator. Would have thought people would have the sense!

But then Deborah came unsteadily to the door of her room and called Ruben back. Ruben turned, smiling, as the nurse turned, too, stymied, dismayed.

—What is it? said Ruben happily.

—Teach my classes this week?

—Oh, sure, said Ruben, because she and Deborah were casual outlaws together. What Patty Hearst would have been if she hadn't been violent and had thought coherently about just causes! In the elevator she couldn't imagine how she could

teach Deborah's two classes in addition to her own. And was
annoyed with Deborah for not making an arrangement in advance. She went home and stayed up reading instead of preparing so many classes.

————

Jessie stood on our front steps, alone. She stood still for several minutes, while I watched through the window. She thrust
her hands into her coat pockets. The wind on her bare neck
must have felt delightful for a moment and then cruel. It blew
her skirt around her legs and hobbled her. Now I'll start
guessing: she thought about coming back inside, taking Sarah
in her arms. A gesture that could be construed as an apology
would not have come easily to my sister Jessie, but she could
have found a way to joke about it and hang on to her dignity.
It would have helped that our parents were asleep.

Jessie was cold and sorry, but it was late, and maybe then
she remembered the conversation about free love. She didn't
want more questions like that, and didn't want to lie to
Sarah, and couldn't tell the truth—and so she set her shoulders and started down the street.

Or was she waiting for me to come out? Did she know I
was at the window?

Jessie was too upset and awake to go to the room she
rented. She went to a rooming house where a man she knew
lived, knocked on his window, and in the end he sneaked her
in and made love to her. He was called Maurice, and I don't
think he ever hurt her, physically or in any other way. I don't
think they were the least bit in love. They comforted each
other—they were occasional lovers for months or years—
when there was trouble. Who knows what Maurice's particular troubles were? But there were plenty of Troubles at Large
if he lacked personal ones. He drew her skirt up around her
knees with respect and smoothed it before he entered her. She

was grateful for his care. She was also sexually aroused. She cried. Jessie almost never cried, but sex moved her. How do I know all this? I know.

"Shall I steal a carrot for you?" Maurice once asked her. They were passing a pushcart and Jessie was hungry.

She knew he didn't mean it. He wouldn't steal from a poor man. "Would it be all right if the peddler were rich?" she said.

"It would be all right for a responsible group to steal the carrot if the carrot was going to be put to good use."

"Say we were going to feed an irresponsible horse . . ."

I think Maurice was the friend who drew Jessie to the meeting at which their group's role in the strike was devised. He had light brown hair and a salt-and-pepper mustache. Once he recited the Ten Commandments to Jessie, then apologized because anarchists reject government. He admired her short hair, lifting her hat to kiss her scalp. Jessie was at ease in bed with a man by that time. At first it had been strange, despite her strong belief that it was a fine thing for men and women to come together without being held back by laws and scruples. And despite her desire. At first the sight of a man's genitals would scare desire out of her. Not for long.

"Don't be afraid of the mounted policemen," said one of the organizers, at the meeting to which Maurice brought Jessie. "But don't get close to them. Always look around you to see where the crowd is moving. Don't be caught alone."

———

The sitter was rude about extra time. On her way to teach, Ruben broke off twigs from a hedge near the bus stop, thinking about their conversation. She began to walk to the next bus stop, keeping warm, but the bus passed her. Walking, she'd arrive just in time for her own class, and then she'd have to wait an hour to teach Deborah's class. If she'd taken the bus, she'd have had time for coffee in Carlotta's office first. She burst red-cheeked into the dim classroom, and the students all talked about it.

Emma had brought a religious pamphlet, which she tried to read out loud. Ruben kept nodding her head, trying to keep her tongue from supplying the next word too fast. But the pamphlet made tired, flushed (now chilled) Toby Ruben uncomfortable. It was not about God, which would have been fine with Ruben, atheist though she more or less was, but about men and women. The wife, read Emma, should respect her husband's . . .

—Judgment, Ruben said, reading upside down across the table. But think, Emma—is that necessarily true?

—I should hope so, said Emma.

Two of the others sniffed.

—Are you married? Ruben persisted. She thought of Harry and his judgment. For some reason she thought of Harry naked, saying, Your back or my back? Nursing made her breasts hurt and sex was easier if she was on top. But Harry's judgment could be terrible. Harry had wanted to buy a new car so Ruben could drive around town and drive to this class. They couldn't afford it. She was afraid to drive. She'd have an accident; the Squirrel would die. Policemen.

—No, said Emma. I'm separated.

She made herself stop. Well, let's do math.

—When is the test? said Lily.

—I don't know, said Ruben, but I'll ask Carlotta. You're right. It's time to sign you up. You and Cecile.

—Not me? said Emma.

—I don't think you're ready.

—Oh, you don't love me because I'm stupid, Emma said.

—Emma doesn't mean it, said Mary.

Emma was smiling. Cecile's white, that's why you want her to take the test. She was talking in a baby voice, teasing.

When Carlotta came through, shouting encouragement as usual, Ruben asked about the test, but Carlotta wanted to talk about Deborah's baby. Miss Toby, have you seen that new child?

—I have.

—And is she a fine child or not?

—A fine child, said Ruben. A very fine child.

Carlotta left and they looked at the next page in the math book, a chart about taxes. Emma couldn't imagine what a chart might be. They had been through this. But the others grew quicker each week. They answered the questions, fighting and laughing, working it out. Sometimes they could answer more quickly than Ruben. Maybe even Mary could take the test.

When the class was over Emma left in a hurry. The pamphlet from her church, "A Woman Finds God," lay on the table, and Emma ran back and took it. She didn't hug Ruben. When Ruben left it was snowing a sharp gray snow. She couldn't go for a walk after walking to the school in the first place. She didn't want to stay in the basement room.

Amid dingy houses and gas stations she found a coffee shop and had coffee and a doughnut. She left in the stinging snow. Even now it was early. Sometimes an hour will not pass.

When she and Deborah talked, Ruben didn't imagine Deborah teaching at the same table in the same basement. For some reason she imagined a different room, but of course Deborah taught in the same basement room. Deborah had eight students, not just five, and Ruben would have to meet another class in the morning. The feel of the room was different, and for a moment, walking in, Ruben thought it was a different room after all, or a different table. Food was all over the table: Tootsie Rolls and M&M's, which Ruben liked too much, and a box of cookies and a bottle of Coke. Everything glowed yellow; when she looked up she saw a light fixture she'd never noticed. Why hadn't Carlotta showed her?

—Where do you turn on that light? she said, not even stopping to say hello. Hands pointed to a perfectly visible switch on a wall.

—I've been teaching in the dark!

—You're Deborah's friend. Have you seen the baby?

They were friendlier than her own group. There were three white women and five black ones; Ruben was ashamed to have counted. They offered her candy and cookies. They even had small square napkins. She ate. She wondered who had paid for this food. Should she offer to contribute or would that be offensive?

They simply refused to do math. They claimed Deborah said they'd learn more if they did it at home on their own. They sat back confidently, a little ways from the table, not leaning. The table did not jiggle. They kept their hands in their laps or on their broad, no doubt tired knees, each soothing her own long-suffering knees. All their lives they had worked to come to this place, where they could spend an hour in the middle of the day eating candy and talking, but not, please, about math.

It was hard to quiet them. They talked about their nails, and examined their polished nails. It seemed one of the women had polished everybody's nails at the last class.

—In class? Prissy Ruben.

—It was my report.

—We do reports. Today's her report. The woman who would give a report, that day, was wearing a red felt hat with a small curved brim. She was a tiny, mischievous-looking black woman.

—Her report was on nail polish? What's yours on?

—Ghana.

—Oh! All right. Let's hear it.

But it wasn't ready. Ruben opened the big book to grammar exercises. The boy with the big dogs were late.

She explained.

—But the boy was late and the dogs were late. That's more than one. That's plural, said somebody.

Another woman disagreed. It just doesn't sound right. The boy with the big dogs were late.

—We did this one last week, someone else said. Deborah definitely said it's The boy with the big dogs were late.

—You've already done these?

—No, she's just saying that. She likes mixing you up.

—We don't usually do these book questions.

—Well, what do you do?

—Lady, we don't do very much, said one of the women. And that is a fact.

—We're tired, said somebody else. It's late.

The hour-long class took four hours. Ruben ended it ten minutes early and tried to spend a lot of time gathering her belongings, but still it was eight minutes early when she left the room, turning off the light. In the office, where Ruben had to pick up her check, Emma was talking to Carlotta, with a baby on her hip. If Emma could bring a baby to class, maybe she could learn. Maybe her brain was on her hip and the baby would stimulate it.

Ruben walked into the office, stood behind Emma, and ran her hand over the baby's back. Emma didn't turn, but she said, He doesn't need to be poked. He's overtired.

Doesn't it soothe him? She wanted Emma to turn and see it was she, and laugh and apologize for speaking grouchily to her. But Emma looked over her shoulder and turned back, and Ruben thought that she'd been complaining about her, prob- ably complaining that Ruben wouldn't let her take the test. Carlotta looked at Ruben curiously, frowning a little as if she were quite slow, but it was necessary to get something across to her.

—I must put this child to bed, Emma said.

—We'll talk, said Carlotta.

Emma walked past Ruben and out of the office. The little boy whimpered.

—Did you like that crowd of ladies? Carlotta said. That is a big class. I wouldn't give such a big class to anybody but Deborah.

—It's not too big, Ruben said.

—And you are a fine teacher, too, I am sure, said Carlotta. You don't have Deborah's experience, of course.

Ruben thought she was a better teacher than Deborah, and adding up a job here and a job there, she had more experience. Deborah had worked here longer, and Ruben had never taught in a program quite like this before—that much was true. But she was angry. She wanted to be praised because her ladies were ready to take the test.

—I wish Emma could take the test like the others, Ruben said. I know it's hard for her that she isn't ready.

—Oh, I don't think she minds much, Carlotta said. She doesn't need her equivalency diploma for this job. She just wants to please you. But you know, Miss Toby, there is something I must discuss with you. Carlotta sat down in her chair and Ruben leaned on the table opposite her. Carlotta said, Emma's faith is important to her.

—Her faith?

—She said you made light of her faith today, said Carlotta.

—Oh, no, I would never do that, Ruben said.

—She said she had a pamphlet from her church, and you told her it was untrue. Now, she respects you, Miss Toby, and I can see that you are a strong intellect, someone we are proud to have here. But a woman's faith. Well, maybe it's hard, but we try to understand one another's faith.

Ruben, who could make a speech at breakfast about freedom of religion, didn't know what to say. Then she said, The pamphlet was not about religion. It was about something else. About men dominating women.

—It was from her church. I am sure you will remember, next time. Carlotta searched on her desk for the envelope with the check and gave it to Ruben, and Ruben turned to leave.

Then she found herself turning back. Funny about Deborah, she said. Of course you're right. She's a fabulous teacher. Obviously they all love her.

—They do.

—Yet they spend their time eating candy and having their nails polished in class. I wouldn't do that. Somehow she teaches them anyway. Somehow they get ready to take the test.

—Their nails?

—Well, I guess they are giving reports. One of them gave a report on nail polish, and she polished all the others' nails. Ruben was laughing a little, trembling a little. But they take the test anyway! she said in a high voice, shaking her head in wonder. She knew that only one of Deborah's students had taken the test in a year, and Deborah had said that one was different.

—Most of them don't care about the test, said Carlotta. They just want the skills.

—Polishing nails? Look, I'm white, Ruben said. Some of these students are white, some black. She quoted the Carlotta of her imagination, who would be scandalized if Ruben did what Deborah was doing. I think not teaching them anything is condescending. As if black people couldn't learn.

—You think your friend is not teaching them anything?

—Well, maybe it's not that bad, Ruben said. I don't know. It doesn't seem as if she is. And she hurried home, where Squirrel had screamed for an hour and a half and the sitter was in tears. Ruben paid the sitter and sent her home, nursed her frantic baby in bed until she was calmer and Squirrel fell asleep, his head on her numb arm. If she moved him to his crib, he'd wake up. If she eased her arm out and left the room, he'd roll off the bed. In tiny movements minutes apart she extricated her arm. Now he lay on his stomach, slanted across the bedspread, his bottom hunched up. The brown hair on his head swirled around its place of origin. How did it know where to begin? The Squirrel wore a blue shirt and a cloth diaper and rubber pants. Ruben felt the diaper: damp but not sopping. She curved her body around his and reached for the book on the table

next to the bed. As always, her glasses were dirty, and she
licked them, which really didn't help.

––––––––

When the trolley men went out in January 1921, the city of
Boynton, Massachusetts, did not immediately lose its temper.
Women bundled up in the clear, cold air and walked to the
shops, calling "Does you good!" to one another. Men walked
to work or took out the Ford that ordinarily waited in the
garage until Sunday. Since autos had become so popular, they
pointed out, the trolleys didn't matter as much. Of course
that was why the fare was going up to eight cents and wages
were being cut. Riders were disappearing. Still, people told
one another, the trolley men had legitimate needs and con-
cerns, and perhaps the company would find a just way to
solve this problem quickly.

The company immediately hired scabs, who, however,
would come from Boston and would not arrive for several
days. The newspaper called the scabs "strikebreakers," which
made them seem noble. Like the *Denver Post*, the *Boynton
Herald* opposed the strike. I read the editorial aloud at our
dinner table, and dug my nails into my palms. The newspaper said that as soon as the strikebreakers arrived, the trolleys would run again and everything would be fine. The
strikers would learn their lesson.

Surely, the women in the shops told one another, patting
their chests and smiling after their unusual exertion, surely it
would all be settled and the scabs would never come at all.
Meanwhile, with everyone out except two obstinate motormen who could not act as part of a group, the trolleys were
in the barn and the silence on Main Street was startling.
Horses were more in evidence, but in truth, not many in
Boynton still kept a buggy.

A nephew of my father's was one of the striking motormen. "Uncle Saul, we must eat!" Cousin Joe had said at a family dinner on Sunday.

"But I never saw Cousin Joe do anything *except* eat," Sarah whispered to me. Joe was fat and ordinarily silent. "Maybe," said Sarah, "he just means it's time for dinner!" Sarah was worried about the strike, but she was excited, these days, exuberant. "One more week until Warrie's birthday party," she said to me as we walked home that night from our aunt and uncle's house.

I had to think for a minute before I remembered Warrie. Then I was shocked. "But the trolleys may not be running," I said.

"Oh, they'll fix the problem by then," Sarah said.

The first day of the strike was a Wednesday. "They've got to run on Sunday, they've got to," Sarah said, leaving for school. My father and I got up an hour and a half earlier than usual that day and walked to work. If it hadn't been for my nervousness about his uncertain temper and about Jessie, it would have been a carefree adventure. We walked together for a mile, and then he turned and trudged down the hill to the dress factory where he labored all day. He was sturdy, but rather little—built like Jessie. He mingled quickly with the other workers. I saw him wave abruptly to a couple of friends as he marched toward the building.

Walking to the millinery shop, I heard distant shouting and realized it came from the trolley barn in Randolph Square. Long before I reached it, I could see people running. The trolley barn was a dilapidated wooden structure next to a small brick building where the company had its headquarters. Between the buildings a yard laid with tracks ordinarily contained several of the red Boynton trolleys. Now the trolleys themselves were locked in the barn, but picketers carrying signs filled the yard. The crowd in front of the office was shouting. I made out the name "Harris"—the president of the trolley company. A stone was thrown at the strikers; I

was surprised, because most of the crowd that had gathered
seemed sympathetic to them. A cry went up, and some of the
pickets rushed toward the crowd. Again the shout, "Harris!
Harris!"

A window opened in the building, and a man leaned out
and said something.

"Harris, Harris."

The man shouted unintelligibly. I was late, and I was
afraid of seeing my sister. I kept walking, looking down at
the paving stones and picking my way between snowy places.
My shoes were thin, my feet were wet and chilled, but I
reached the store at last. We didn't sell many hats that day,
but I liked being among the quiet, unargumentative heads,
which looked as serene and haughty as ever. Even whiny,
scared Miss Fredericks seemed soothing.

Jessie, I learned later, was not among the picketers that
day. She went to work. She needed rent money. But she had
trouble pleasing the ordinarily affable Mr. Franklin, her boss.
Once, months earlier, he'd said to her, "You have something
between your ears," and Jessie had made a great joke of
studying her head in the mirror to see if it was true. He'd
said "ears," she added, in a funny tone, a tone suggesting
they were somewhat more than ears, somehow. Now he sometimes started conversations with her. She would tell him
nothing about herself, but surely there were rumors at the
mill. Today he was biting back fury. "What do you think of
this strike, Miss Lipkin?" and "Think they can just walk
away from their jobs, let the rest of us go to blazes."

At first Jessie was silent. Then she turned to him, a newly
typed letter held against her chest as if to shield her. "I don't
agree, Mr. Franklin," she said.

"Don't agree."

"No," she said. "I'm on the side of the strikers."

"Well, Miss Lipkin!" but that was all.

Jessie was absent from the picket line that day, but she

later became a familiar presence there. Her principles won out. Mr. Franklin fired her immediately, though she was not in the office to read his tersely worded dismissal. Jessie was at the trolley barn, shouting hoarsely, her black hat pulled down over her aforementioned ears. Some of the men were embarrassed by her and avoided her; others had heard rumors about her life and scorned her, or were afraid of her. But for many of the strikers my sister was inspiring. Her certainty that the strikers simply had to be victorious, the definiteness of the way she moved—she bustled, with her arms bent just a little so her elbows stuck out—must have given them strength, just the way her energy had speeded me up when we were children. She had screaming matches with policemen who wouldn't hurt her because she was a woman but hated her because she took advantage.

One morning she was hit by a rock on the side of her forehead. She came to the millinery shop for me to wash the blood off. Luckily there were no customers—this was the third day of the strike, and walking to Main Street for a new hat no longer seemed like a delightful outing—but even so Miss Fredericks was haughty. I kissed Jessie and soothed her and loved washing the blood and soot from her face in our little back washroom. I should have locked her in the washroom and left her there for a few days.

When it became evident that the scabs would be coming before any settlement could possibly be reached, the trolley men and their sympathizers, including the anarchists, grew tenser and more determined. If scabs were going to run the trolleys, the strikers' position would immediately become much worse. The public had to be prevented from using them. Opinion, I gather, was still divided. Some of the leaders feared a repetition of Denver and insisted that persuasion was the only legitimate method—and that it would work. On the whole, the townspeople were sympathetic, but of course their patience was not unlimited.

Jessie and others thought that force might be necessary to keep people off the trolleys. They didn't say they intended to hurt anyone; they'd just set up human barriers. "And what's to keep a man from picking up a paving stone?" cried one of the strongest defenders of peace and orderliness. "Once you start pushing, people will push back."

"Let them," said my sister. No, I wasn't there. I was home washing dishes, as always. But I can hear Jessie's hoarse voice saying it.

Where did her clear-eyed courage come from? Jessie grew up, somehow, thinking that certain activities might well be all right, though other people were quite sure they were not all right. How did that happen? I grew up in the same house as she did. Sexually, I wasn't far behind her. I had lovers—not then, but not much later. I never thought there was anything wrong with that, and I'm not sure how people who think sex is wrong know that it is, or where they get the idea. Maybe our parents forgot to tell us. And yet my father shrieked with rage over Jessie's sexual looseness. I married, but it didn't last, and I had lovers again.

But this other, this violence. Why did Jessie think it was allowable to throw paving stones at people who wanted to use a trolley being run by an unjust company? Certainly the company was unjust; no doubt about that—although it also had its troubles. Ridership was down and yet wages had to be paid. I don't know whether Mr. Harris or somebody else, troubles notwithstanding, was extracting an unfair profit; certainly that's possible. The trolley company had built the amusement park. Maybe it was not a financial success and the company was trying to make the trolley men absorb the loss. I'm speculating: at the time these issues didn't occur to me. Now I can't find out.

But how does violence come to seem acceptable? Jessie didn't hit me when we were children. She wasn't a brutal person. Maybe she wasn't violent. Maybe she never agreed to throw things; maybe she was simply courageous enough to endure the risk that they would be thrown at her. Maybe nothing of what took place was her fault.

By Sunday the scabs had arrived. The trolley company, in fact, had staged a little show on Saturday afternoon: one trolley, operated by scabs, traveled down Main Street, crossed by means of a curved section of track to the opposite side of the street, and ran back again. The only passenger was an old lady everybody knew was daft, who explained as she boarded the streetcar that she was the mayor's sweetheart and he required her presence.

Saturday night it snowed, and people awoke Sunday morning wondering whether the company would try to run the trolleys at all, just on account of the snow, but it was a sunny day, and crews of men were out shoveling early. Now crowds of strikers and sympathizers formed as quickly as the scabs appeared, and soon snowballs—some with stones in them—were in the air. Rumor had it that one thousand state troopers were on their way. Someone produced the latest antistrike editorial from the *Boynton Herald*, and it was jeered loudly. "It is not for nothing that these sympathizers are referred to as Bolsheviks," it said.

Around noon on Sunday, the first trolley of the day rolled out of the trolley barn. It was a red trolley from the Main Street line. The crowd had been waiting for hours. It surged forward. Men and women carrying hoes and rakes tried to tear down the wires. These were not ruffians; they were decent people who smelled of damp wool and of houses where cabbage was cooked.

No, I still wasn't there. I was home arguing with Sarah about, of all things, whether or not she was going to Warrie Livingston's birthday party. What can I say? Sarah kept her promises, and she'd promised to go. Sarah wasn't political. "I just don't understand why not," she said. "I'm only one girl. The trolley company isn't going to change its mind because one girl goes to a birthday party. The company doesn't care about me. The strikers don't care about me. But Warrie cares." She sat at the breakfast table long after we'd all finished, arguing with anybody who walked past her. My parents, of course, were hysterical. They were afraid of twenty things they could name and twenty more they couldn't even imagine. They were afraid that if Sarah went, she'd be corrupted by Jessie, who, they were sure, was leading the strike. They couldn't calm down enough to understand that if Sarah went, she'd be going *against* Jessie's wishes. My father was a political man, but he wouldn't listen now, or maybe he thought Sarah was so impressionable, she'd switch sides and become a freethinking anarchist like her sister the moment she got to Randolph Square. All he could do was shout. He forbade Sarah to leave the house, but he couldn't say why in a way that might persuade her.

All I can say in defense of Sarah's position is that we didn't have a telephone and I don't remember whether the Livingstons did. Canceling would have been impossible. The strike was being reported in the newspaper but not, as it would be today, on radio or television. If Sarah didn't appear, nobody would know why. Of course, I kept telling her, she could explain later. She could write a letter.

Sarah bruised her fists on the table in a rare show of temper. Her hair was coming loose. I remember one of her tight braids slipping down so she looked lopsided. She'd been crying for so long that her eyes were red and swollen. Everybody was yelling different things at her, but everybody agreed that she had to stay home. At last, when she banged on the table one more time and a plate fell and broke, my mother walked up to Sarah and slapped her face hard—several times. Sarah ran to our bedroom, sobbing. When I looked in later she was asleep. I swept up and washed the dishes.

At the trolley barn, a little band of would-be passengers was cheered as it boarded the first trolley—and jeered much more loudly. A man smiled confidently and waved at the crowd as if he were running for office. The troopers arrived then, marching from the railroad depot, and they in turn were cheered and jeered. Some predicted there would be no further trouble, but then the trolley was overturned, with a dreadful crash, by a crowd that moved forward like one organism, and the confident man was injured and carried off in an ambulance. Now strikers and sympathizers were throwing paving stones, bricks, stones, and lumps of coal. The soldiers filled the square and rushed to right the trolley that had been knocked over. Its windows were smashed and young boys tore off decorative metalwork from below the roof. As soon as it was righted, it was knocked on its side again. Meanwhile, someone opened a fire hydrant and soon buckets of water were being poured on the tracks. The day was not bitterly cold, but it was cold enough. Everyone knew the trolleys couldn't run on ice.

The water was swept away, though, before it could freeze, and when the troops massed and raised their weapons, the crowd sobered. Only a few still threw rocks and lumps of coal. At last one of the red trolleys, looking innocent and ordinary, moved slowly along Main Street. And then came a green trolley: the Lake Avenue Interurban.

Our trolley company ran crisscrossing local lines in town, and three interurban lines: The Lake Avenue line, the Prospect Avenue line, and the Hillside Road line, each of which traveled fifteen to twenty-five miles into the country, eventually arriving in another town, or, in the case of Lake Avenue, at a trolley park. It's not necessary here to repeat the familiar paean to our country's lost interurban trolleys. As has often been said, they were a cheap, slow, charming mode of transportation by which a traveler could eventually traverse huge distances. Periodically someone would discover that you could go by interurban from Boston to Pittsburgh, or some such, changing and changing, but of course most people used

them to commute to work, to get to the amusement parks the
trolley companies built, or to shop or go visiting.

The interurban cars run by the Boynton company were
green, not red. They were longer than the regular cars and
more elaborately decorated, with gold curlicues, if you please.
It always felt like a bit of a treat to ride them. We'd ridden
the Lake Avenue line to the Boynton Lake Amusement Park
more than once, and of course Sarah and I had taken that
line to the Livingstons' house just two weeks earlier. Unlike
the trolleys in town, the interurbans had controls at both
ends and ran on a single set of tracks. The rights of way
were too narrow and the tracks too expensive for two pairs
of tracks to be laid. Every now and then there was a siding,
so a car could leave the main track to allow one coming the
opposite way to pass.

As the interurbans began to run slowly down Main Street
that Sunday, while the crowd watched restlessly and the soldiers looked bored, the day grew colder and clouds spread
across the sky, which was the color of dull iron. Now I'm
speaking of what I remember: I'd gone out to look for Sarah,
who was suddenly missing, not in her room and nowhere else
in our apartment. I had hurried out to search for her, hoping
she was not on her way to the birthday party.

When I reached the square, I learned from bystanders that
a second green trolley, with its gold curlicues, bearing a scab
motorman and conductor plus three passengers, was making
its way into the snow-covered countryside. It must have been
beautiful out there. The passengers must have looked out the
window at the small shabby houses, which were farther and
farther apart, at dogs running in their yards, at children
having snowball fights, and bare, wintry trees.

———

The baby woke up. Ruben's body was stiff and she was hungry.
She would read more that night, or tomorrow. She kissed her

baby's face and carried him into the next room to change his
soaked diaper. By now everything he was wearing was wet,
and she brought him naked into the bathroom and gave him a
bath. Squirrel liked to be bathed. He laughed, patting the water. Ruben couldn't remember why she was ever impatient with
him. The phone rang. She wrapped Squirrel in a towel, hoping
he wouldn't pee on it, and carried him into the other room. It
was Deborah on the phone.

—Carlotta came to see me, she said.

—That was nice of her. I thought they were letting you out
today.

—Tomorrow. She brought me a bib.

—That was sweet of her.

—She told me what you said.

—What did I say? Ruben's insides began to hurt.

—Carlotta said, You got some funny friendship, said Deborah.

—A funny friendship?

—She said you told her I'm no good.

—That's not what I said.

—Toby, if you didn't want to teach my class, you could have
said.

—I was shocked at your class, Ruben said. They aren't doing
anything.

—But I care about them. I talk to them, we talk about all
kinds of things. I try to help them make sense of the world.
They've never thought about numbers. They've never thought
about what's in the news. About deciding who to vote for. It's
not just a matter of that stupid book.

—But what about the test? Why else are we there?

—If they pass the test, where will that get them? They'll still
have minimum-wage jobs changing diapers.

—Deborah, she said, can I call you back? I just took Peter
out of the bathtub and I need to dress him.

—Don't bother to call me back.

—Deborah, she said. I love you.

—You don't know a thing about kindness, Toby. You're dangerous, and I'm scared of you. If Carlotta was any different, I'd be out of a job. You simply went and told her I'm a bad teacher. What kind of a friend does that? Here I am lying here with these stitches killing me, and the baby won't nurse . . .

—It wasn't like that, said Ruben. I'm sorry.

—I can't be friends with you, said Deborah. You think abstract ideas are more important than people. You think the test is what matters. I can't believe that. I can't believe how disappointed in you I am. I wanted to be friends with you forever.

—What did I say? What did she say I said? How do you know she's telling the truth?

—Oh, don't give me that, Toby. The nurse is here. I've got to hang up.

Toby Ruben's hands were shaking. She took Peter into his room and finished drying him, and dressed him in a diaper and rubber pants and his pajamas. She laid him in his crib and then she went back into the bedroom. She was in too much pain to cry. She picked up the book, and her eye fell on a sentence in the paragraph after the one she had just read. What it said was unbearable. She had not realized what was coming. She had not known it was that sort of book, with that sort of pain. She had no interest in such a book. She would read no further. She tore off a corner of a page of a newspaper that was lying on the dresser next to the book. She closed the book, marking her place with the scrap of newspaper. She put the book in a pile of Harry's books on the dresser, three down, so she wouldn't pick it up again soon and upset herself. Then she lay down on the bed, clutched the blanket, and tried to keep her eyes closed.

DEBORAH'S big yellow-haired daughters could recite the rules of games. They made identifiable objects from clay or cloth, while Ruben's boys, Peter and Stevie (such fern fronds, such forest creatures) fooled with sticks and bark; could barely be coaxed to breathe near your ear. Ruben had left her intricate boys alone, though they were only eleven and nine, so she could drink with Deborah, but she wouldn't be gone long, and Harry was coming home soon from the office where, this year, he calculated the cost of fire engines.

She hadn't told Deborah, but later she was going out again. And she'd just come home from teaching. She'd rushed through her house. Peter spoke, as he often did, mysteriously. Steps must not be taken! Stevie, who'd agreed at birth to make explanations, explained: He has a kingdom upstairs.

In the crowd at the bar where they'd come to celebrate, quickly, the forty-fifth birthday of their department chair, Janet Grey, Ruben and Deborah met in the doorway. Now Deborah's freckled shoulders led the way. Janet Grey waved two fingers from a small table. Two years ago, she'd hired Ruben to teach part-time at an odd little college where she timidly ran English. Ruben had told Janet Grey about Deborah. They were adjunct instructors, two courses each, a thousand dollars a course. Ruben and Harry needed more money than that. Now it was September, but hot. They'd begun to teach again. It was the time of year when Ruben believed she'd keep a neat note-book. Deborah wore a bright blue sundress. She didn't mind air-conditioning and wasn't hurrying fall. Ruben liked cold weather.

—Your hair! breathed Deborah to Janet Grey. In the noisy bar, Janet's corner was hushed. That was Janet. Deborah's voice rose and sang. Perfect!

Never mind what Janet Grey had finally done to her hair. Ruben wasn't sure, but she didn't like it. She had a beer.

Deborah fussed about having a beer, as if she didn't know how it would taste. Let's order something disgusting! she said, and ordered something with too much cheese.

Ruben didn't care whether Janet Grey had a birthday all alone, but she didn't mind when Deborah told her what to do—liked being told, and liked doing it—whining, nonetheless, like a little sister. Ruben loved and deplored Deborah's long, solid blond-fringed arm reaching past Ruben's nose for the best cheesy bit. With every gesture, Deborah proclaimed party, but it was no party. Deborah pretended for Janet Grey, but there was something Deborah gave or threw away, to do so, that Ruben wanted her to keep.

Toasts to Janet.

—By the way, my niece . . . whispered Janet.

Deborah with her glorious and irritating kindness probably kept track even of the often-mentioned niece's birthday, the niece's earwax. What if Harry hadn't come home to look after the boys and their kingdoms? What if they had died, falling down the stairs on their heads, while Ruben drank the deli-cious, bitter beer? But she was used to mothering now. She knew that even if she became slightly drunk, it was unlikely that they had died. They were sensible boys, or at least Stevie was, and meteorites rarely fell on houses. It was good, not bad, to drink beer and talk about tall skinny boots, the present subject, with her friends Deborah and Janet. The niece and Rose and Deborah and Janet had all bought boots or thought about buying boots. Ruben had also thought about buying boots, but she didn't say.

—You're the most interesting person I know, said Deborah, appallingly, to Janet Grey. Do you use a computer? I can't imagine—

—My niece does.

Ruben had enrolled in a drawing course, though it cost money. She couldn't draw. She didn't want to tell Deborah; Janet even less. If the conversation stopped, she'd have to tell. It didn't, but the first class began in an hour and a half, and people must be fed first. If Ruben didn't cherish secrets, it would be easy to explain and go.

Jill, Deborah's oldest, smoked. And was not friendly: the hardest of their children, but the second hardest was Peter, who was friendly and often obedient but seemed not to have heard about requirements others had heard of. Once Peter stole a pie, a cheap commercial pie in a box, from the corner store. He walked out with it in his hands and nobody saw him, or nobody stopped him. He was seven. He claimed he hadn't known about money. He served it to the rest of the children. Rose told. Then he baked a pie, naturally without permission, but with astonishing care: pot holders, rolling pin, baked pie shell, blueberry filling from a can that the children bought. They had crossed the street in a body behind Jill, the only one who was allowed. Strips of dough over the top.

Peter was never at ease in one way of being for long. These days a pie wouldn't interest him.

—Firsties are like that, said Janet Grey, but she didn't mean unpredictable Peter or imperious Jill, she meant her silly niece, who had learned how to use a computer. Happy Birthday, Janet Grey. Ruben kissed the back of Deborah's obstinate, darling head, standing up fast because suddenly she did need to hurry. But wouldn't explain—probably seemed bored, disdainful, generally a bad person. Kiss on the hard head beneath the fluffy hair, some money on the table, out the door with a squeeze to Janet's birthday shoulder. How could Deborah say Janet was the most interesting?

Nobody had died; quickly Ruben made supper.

The drawing class was at an art school in an old factory: brick walls, new big lights, safe banisters. All afternoon children made pots and painted pictures there, even Peter and Stevie last spring, though they preferred to pile pebbles and speak secret languages in their own backyard. Deborah's enterprising girls had carried home paintings from the art school to be spread with joy on their parents' walls, big paintings like sails for small boats, which they swung by a dripping edge; green and yellow ellipses and parts of ellipses.

Ruben wanted to draw her students, her fern-frond boys, Harry with his flat hands and the wide, flat briefcase that he laid on the table, still wider and flatter. These days, nobody taught her anything. She was nervous, going into a class when she was used to being a teacher. Her fear interested her. In the drawing class, she thought, she would be quiet at a table, looking at the look of something, holding a pencil, feeling a calm she would carefully transfer to the page as a line. Then a second line.

At the art school, Ruben entered a high-ceilinged room in which three classmates already sat. They half smiled and looked away. She sat down. A big, ugly, echoing room, a few chairs. Then a sleek-haired, pink-cheeked man in a jacket and tie hurried in, his jacket open—and of all things he was Deborah's husband, Jeremiah. For a second, Ruben thought if she looked away and he didn't see her, it would never be necessary to speak, but that made no sense. And she had no quarrel with

Jeremiah. Jeremiah sat noisily down and looked left and right quickly, as if the instructor might be hiding. Ruben waved like Janet Grey, with two fingers, and when she waved she became Janet Grey and felt to her surprise that Janet Grey really liked having a drink on her birthday with Ruben and Deborah, felt happy to visit but not (heavens!) live in their twoness.

—I know you! called Jeremiah.

—I know you, too.

He snapped his head sideways at a noise. The noise was the teacher, a man with long fingers full of objects: a big white iron dustpan you'd sweep up a factory with, a grayish battered muffin tin for dozens of muffins, an ugly green statue of a naked woman with her arms in curves above her head. It wasn't a muffin tin but part of a machine, and now the teacher went to a closet and brought out a small door with hinges, and two doorknobs. And pieces of ugly cloth in wide gray stripes or big prints that he flopped and draped and hung.

—Ten of you? said the teacher. There were eight. He shrugged and pointed. Heavy, tall easels made of gray-green iron were shoved together in a corner. Ruben seized one and pulled, but it was caught behind another, and the top clanged against a third easel. She hurt her hand. At last she wrenched the easel free and dragged it into the center of the room. She set it up next to another woman's easel. It tipped, and the teacher came over and tightened something. Next the students had to bring drawing boards to the easels: big heavy wooden oblongs, which balanced unsteadily on tiny supports. From a closet came huge sheets of paper. The teacher distributed strips of masking tape with which to tape them to the drawing boards.

When the teacher walked by with the tape, Ruben, already tired, called, I don't know your name.

—Gregory, he said, and stopped and raised his eyebrows, but she couldn't think of another question.

Jeremiah competently brought out an easel for himself and

one for a confused young woman. When they had to draw, though they'd been told to bring pencils, he had none. Gregory looked annoyed, borrowed a pencil from another student and handed it silently to Jeremiah. Gregory was a long-armed man with pale hair. He waved his right arm when he talked. The students were to draw the pile of objects, all those pieces of machinery and drapes and vases and the ugly statue and another one. Not what Ruben had expected. Afraid she might suddenly cry with nervousness, Ruben began to draw. She didn't like drawing while standing up. She began with the green statue. The teacher walked behind them.

She heard him talk to Jeremiah. Fill the page, he said. Ruben tried to fill the page. The teacher watched her for a while, then walked on without speaking. She was so bad at this, apparently, that there was simply nothing to say. She was angry at Jeremiah for coming. He would carry her shame back to Deborah, and Ruben would not be able to make this her own funny story when she was ready to tell it. When Gregory spoke to the other students, she could hear him but didn't know what he meant. Ruben filled the page with hurried lines, trying to put everything in. After drawing a vase next to a statue, she noticed that in truth a big ladder stood between them, with ceramic pots on its steps. Ruben drew it in the space above the statue. She was tired of her picture before the teacher told them to stop.

At last he said they should tape their drawings to the wall. He walked the length of the row of pictures, all different. Ruben thought hers was the craziest, with lines all over the place. Several were beautiful. The teacher pointed to a vase on one picture, the draped cloth on another. He said, That's interesting. That's interesting. He thought a chair Ruben had drawn was interesting. Then the teacher asked them to choose the most interesting part of their drawings and to make that part the subject of a whole drawing on a new sheet of paper. Ruben didn't know what he meant by interesting, but she drew the ladder again. In both her drawings, the pots seemed to be sliding off the steps of the ladder.

After the second drawing, the class took a break. Jeremiah walked right over. Toby, let's get coffee, he said. Ruben didn't exactly want coffee, but she followed him. She wasn't sorry he was there, after all, though she didn't know him well, even after all these years. Jeremiah was a lawyer. She thought he worked for a business, an import-export firm. Somewhere, containers were swung by cranes onto ships, their arcs modified by Jeremiah.

He put on his jacket, left it hanging open, and stomped purposefully down the stairs.

—Where are we going?

—Coffee at the greasy spoon around the corner.

—Do we have time?

—Sure.

She caught up. Have you taken classes here before?

—Nah, but I know the routine from waiting for the kids. I've spent hours in that luncheonette.

While he drank his coffee, and Ruben had Sanka, he said, So what brings you here? She was tired and cranky.

—I've thought about taking a drawing class for a long time, she said, sounding phony to herself. What about you?

—So you don't know why you're doing this?

—Well, no. I mean, I don't have some practical purpose.

—You don't know, but I do, he said.

—You know why I'm here?

—No, how should I know why you're here? I know why I'm here. They were sitting at a little table and he put his elbows down on either side of his coffee cup, keeping his hands in the air and his fingers spread.

—Why?

—Funny you should ask. Now, didn't you think *he'd* ask? That teacher? What's his name?

—Gregory. Suddenly they were buddies. Don't you think he should have said his name?

—I don't care what his name is, said Jeremiah. But I think he might have taken the trouble to find out our purpose in coming. Mine is quite specific. Maybe the advice he'd given me would be different if he knew. Fill the page, he said. Well, what I want to draw is quite small.

Suddenly they were not buddies. What is it?

—The markings on model trolleys. You can buy decals, but they're expensive, and they aren't always made accurately. If you study old photographs, you can see that some of the markings are incorrect on the decals you can buy.

—You make model trolleys? She'd never seen them, though she'd often been in his house. Probably he made them in the basement. She thought only a trivial person would make model trolleys, and she tried to recall if Deborah had ever mentioned them. How could Deborah be married to someone who built model trolleys? But it was time to go back to class. He offered to drive her home when it was over, but she had her car. He said, Next week I'll pick you up. It's hard to park here.

—Thank you. Ruben presented herself with the gift of a ride from Jeremiah. These days she drove everywhere, but never fearlessly. She'd heard the fear went away if you kept at it, so ordinarily she didn't let herself accept rides, but this class was hard enough.

Now Gregory asked them to fill another huge sheet, now with the contents of a quarter of the second drawing. A piece of Ruben's ladder grew larger while she thought about her friend's husband, a lawyer who made model trolleys. She imagined herself asking him, in the car next week, Why aren't you bored by the very idea of making model trolleys? Her arm ached from stretching to the top and sides of her drawing.

At home, she complained about the art class, the teacher, and Jeremiah, but Harry liked her drawings. They seemed to turn him on, though they were just jagged objects, all cluttery and falling off the page. But she was too tired for sex. No, not quite. Fingers groping quickly before sleep, as if newly, as if in discovery. Lovely.

—Why didn't you tell me you were studying art? said Deborah. I can't believe you and Jeremiah are studying art together. He's been talking about it all summer.

—It's not *studying art,* said Ruben obnoxiously. It's just drawing. If I'd known he was going to be in it, I think I wouldn't have done it.

—Why not? What's wrong with Jeremiah?

—He's weird, all that stuff about trolleys.

—Oh, that's been going on for years. Didn't you know about that?

—It does sound familiar. I knew, but I forgot. But still. She laughed. Drawing the markings?

—Why not? It was one of Deborah's why not days.

Never mind. They had driven in Ruben's car to a kitchen-ware shop across town where Deborah wanted to buy a wedding present for somebody Ruben didn't know; then Ruben had to pick up Stevie at a friend's house. Like suburban moms, they said. Ruben had never been to the store, and she gazed at everything she couldn't afford: stew pots with curved handles and softly glowing flat bottoms burnished in circles; whisks and ladles and tongs as graceful as the necks of cormorants. She wanted to draw everything, if she couldn't own it. An old man watched them, the only customers, from behind his counter. He called out, France. Ruben had to touch the pots. The store was a museum where she could touch. I love good pots, she said, when Deborah walked past her with a tray.

—Enamel ones in colors, said Deborah. Red, orange . . .

—I like copper and stainless steel better, said Ruben. Before she had children, she had cooked seriously, now and then. Long, happy Sundays with a French cookbook. She said, If

Janet would give me a full-time job, I'd shop here. She ran her
hand under the bottom of expensive cast-iron pots and up their
sides.

—Not likely, said Deborah.

The man said, Would you ladies mind the store while I walk
around the block? They were surprised enough to say yes. He
strode out, already swinging his arms, but cautiously. He was
a small, neat man.

Ruben circled the store as if she planned to stay, and she'd
already noticed a handwritten sign near the cash register: Help
Wanted: Part-time. If I worked here, she said, I'm afraid I'd
break things.

—You'd work here?

—We could use the money. I like it here.

When he returned, she asked him. You'd enjoy it, he said
quietly. He was delicate, scholarly, with dry hands and lines
around his eyes.

—What if I broke things?

—I doubt you would.

When she went back the next day at the time they'd agreed
on, Archie nodded and put her to work in the back, unloading
shipments of flowered mugs. Ruben learned to use the cash
register. The first time, she sold nothing but a few sets of mea-
suring spoons and salt and pepper shakers, but a woman
looked for a long time at a yellow Le Creuset cast-iron frying
pan. She walked away without buying, and Ruben was disconsolate, but the woman returned another time and bought it.
The next time, Ruben had to gift wrap a heavy steel stockpot
for a shy, smiling young woman. The store had rolls of colored
ribbon to wrap around the packages. When the gift wrapping
was done, Archie was dissatisfied. He threw away the ribbons
and paper and did it himself. The young woman seemed mor-
tified, but Ruben didn't mind much; kindly he showed her each
step.

The night of the next drawing class, Jeremiah called to say

he was leaving the house, so she'd be out front. What a bully, she said to Harry, who was trying to calculate while Stevie explained something long. But she was glad not to drive.

—You actually signed up for a drawing course so you could learn to draw the markings on model trolleys? she said as she got into the car.

—I'm weird, he said. Hey, I'm glad I'm getting to know you better. We've been friends for a long time, but we don't really know each other.

—Deborah and I don't go in for husbands much.

—You don't like your husbands? I think Deborah likes me.

Flustered, she said, We just don't like those little foursy friendships—the two couples.

—Oh. I didn't get it. Well, it's too bad. I like women, but I don't meet women except at work, and Deborah's friends. I'm not going to cheat on Deborah, you understand. That goes without saying. So—

—I get it. She laughed at him while he drove around a corner and abruptly parked half a block from the art school.

—You laugh at me. Women do. Even Deborah. Painting curlicues on model trolleys. But I'll tell you about the interurbans. General Motors killed them, did you know that?

She liked being "women." It felt sexual, but safe.

In class they were still carrying heavy easels, filling pages with many ugly objects. Ruben drew a woman who stood drawing opposite her, when there was a blank corner at the bottom of her page and the woman came next.

—Have you any idea about the interurbans? Jeremiah said at the break. He was the worst student in the class. The teacher spent time on Jeremiah, who seemed to resent it, though even Ruben could see what he was doing wrong. He drew tight little pictures like diagrams, nothing like what she saw when she looked and drew. She was pretty sure what she did was better than what Jeremiah did, but the teacher didn't praise her.

Jeremiah was in a hurry for break and seized his jacket as
soon as the teacher began to wave his arm toward the door.
Ruben hurried after him. Interurbans, she learned, at their fast-
est could go a hundred miles an hour. The largest number of
lines was in Ohio. Farmers put milk cans on the trolley.

—General Motors destroyed them?

—Well, there's some dispute. Of course, the automobile destroyed them. But I think GM made it happen faster, yeah.
They bought up trolley lines and shut them down.

—I didn't know.

—All sorts of strikes and trouble, because ridership was
down and the lines were losing money. The truth is, the only
ones that ever made money were the lines tied to real estate
deals. They'd build a suburban development at the end of a
line. You know, there are interurban buffs all over the country,
just like me. There are trolley museums and fairs and compe-
titions, and you can buy kits and people collect them and share
little wheels and so forth. But these are all innocents who do
this, like people who think life in the country is pretty cows.
They don't want to think there was ever any trouble. Maybe
they'll admit that GM was bad for the interurbans, but that's
as far as they go. Nostalgia is all right. But if you read your
history, there was plenty of trouble.

—Accidents? said Ruben, thinking she could tell Peter all
this. Peter liked trouble. Again she had Sanka. She liked picturing a trolley hurtling through the empty countryside. Think
of it, Jeremiah had said, before he got to the subject of trouble:
a pasture with cows and a donkey, and a long beautiful trolley
zipping through it.

—Accidents, he said now. Strikes. Stupidity. Oh, it's like
anything else. Now, this art school. Where did they find this
teacher? What's his name?

—Gregory, said Ruben. I think he might be good, but we're
too stupid for him. She didn't mean stupid.

—Speak for yourself, Toby Ruben. Gregory. Why doesn't he have a last name? said Jeremiah. Gregory sounds like a hairdresser or a pope.

—He doesn't know any of our names, said Ruben, who learned her students' names during the first class. She was even learning names of regular customers in the pottery store. There were people who bought pots and pans every week. Imagine, she said to Jeremiah. She'd already said it to Deborah.

Driving home that night, they passed Gregory on a bicycle. Can't afford a car, said Jeremiah, as if that proved something. Really, Jeremiah was disgraceful. How could Ruben feel chummy with glittery Jeremiah?

—What kind of law do you do, Jeremiah? she said. Do you work for an import-export firm?

—Not anymore, said Jeremiah. I used to. Deborah doesn't keep you up-to-date, I guess. I'm in Woodbury and Dawes now. He gestured downtown, and Ruben remembered seeing the firm's sign.

—You do business law?

—A little. It's a small firm. We do whatever comes in the door. Mostly wills, small claims, a little p.i.

She wanted to disapprove of him, but it sounded innocent enough.

When the teacher had them draw with charcoal, Ruben first hated, then loved it. She was instantly covered with grime; she liked her smudged, childish hands, but then, not thinking, she'd push her glasses up and smudge them, too. She'd fumble in her handbag for eyeglass cleaner, which she never seemed to have brought, and make everything grimy. At home, the children tried charcoal and the house was streaked with charcoal. Peter cried when she took back her charcoal. He was getting old for crying and it startled her. I thought you trusted me, said Peter.

Ruben loved drawing with charcoal, but didn't love keeping track of her supplies and carrying them to class. Gregory had them use huge sheets of paper; when Ruben carried her big pad, it flopped open; pages fell. Her fingers tired: she knew no good way to hold it.

Jeremiah's jacket, smudged with charcoal, swung open as he walked around the classroom. Ruben wondered why he didn't take it off. Nobody else dressed like him. Most of the students were younger people, with a couple of gray-haired women.

If it had mattered at all, thought Ruben, how much this art class would have mattered! When her own class mattered to students—a few each term—they seemed to grip it in their teeth and never let their jaws relax; Ruben sometimes felt a scary power to hurt. Ruben didn't care about this drawing class, not really, but she couldn't help feeling competitive, and she never won. The teacher walked past her without comment, though her charcoal shadows, she thought rebelliously, were as murky and spooky as anybody's. To her surprise, she noted that the class mattered to Jeremiah. She wondered why she was surprised, and laughed at herself for having assumed that people who worked in offices had some protection she lacked.

One night Gregory explained contour drawings. Ruben thought she would like contour drawings and be good at contour drawings. The idea was not to look at the paper, just to look at the object's edge and move one's hand. That resembled the old notion she'd had: looking, letting joy make the mark on the page. But she had never imagined herself drawing while standing up. That made everything hard, no matter what shoes she wore.

In the middle of the explanation Jeremiah said, Could I ask a question?

The teacher looked.

—Do you know an artist named Berry Cooper?

—I know *of* her. A sculptor. What's the connection with contour drawing?

There was no connection. Gregory shrugged. He didn't even look annoyed with Jeremiah.

At the break Jeremiah said, I'm naive, I know. I think all artists know each other.

—Who is that sculptor?

—Oh, she's very interesting. You in particular would be interested in her. She's Jewish. She doesn't let on, but she is.

Ruben was startled that her Jewishness was close to the surface of his mind.

—Do you like her work?

—I don't know it.

—Does she make statues of trolleys? She was teasing. They were on their way back to class in a hurry, Jeremiah sloshing coffee and she gulping her sugared Sanka. She thought sugar would give her energy for the second half of the class, but her arms ached anyway.

—She could have. There's a book about her. You'd be interested. I should lend you the book. I have it somewhere. I picked it up in a used bookstore years ago. I think she lives around here. If she isn't dead by now. God knows how old she is.

—She has something to do with trolleys?

—She went to prison. She was a Jewish anarchist, around 1920. She was accused of causing a trolley wreck. Her sister died in it. The signals were switched. It was during a strike.

—This sounds familiar.

—Maybe you read the book. You English teachers read all sorts of things. Maybe you came across it.

And then Ruben remembered. Oh, Jeremiah, she said, and stopped in the street, put her hand on his arm. Oh, Jeremiah, I read your copy. I started to read it. Deborah lent it to me the day we met.

—She lent it to you?

—I never finished it. It was upsetting. The sister—

—I told you. The history of trolleys is not all peace. Not all cute little clang clang clang went the trolley riding over the hill. San Francisco. Cable cars. Tourists. By no means. Not much

has been written about the wreck, but feminist scholars look
at it, because she was a radical, a political type. Everybody else
wants to be cheerful. We hobbyists are idiots, and historians
are cheerful about the trolleys because they correctly think that
the interurbans were a marvelous thing that has been lost. But
here's this little reality that has always interested me because
I'm different from other people, sort of gloomy, although I
don't let it show.

They were back in the classroom. That night they made collages, which could be accomplished sitting down. Ruben had
forgotten scissors, but she tore paper and glued it to other paper. The teacher liked her collage. He seemed excited, but she
felt as if she'd been wasting her time. It was like tearing a
napkin in a restaurant, just keeping the hands busy. Drawing
never felt like a waste of time.

When Archie was out and no customers came to the pottery
store, Ruben drew the lovely pots, struggling to show their
smoothness and well-proportioned shapes. She couldn't evoke
the solid feel of them, their weight. Sometimes she brought Peter along, while Stevie played with a friend or was babysat by
one of Deborah's girls. Peter drew, too, or did his homework,
or watched her and didn't do his homework. He liked to sit in
the back. I never was in the back of anyplace, he said twice.
He was docile and shy and lowered his head, smiling. On the
way home he was loud and obnoxious. Peter was never the
same for long.

Stevie, watching her make supper one night, finished the
drawings she'd started at the store, put faces on the pots, wrote
captions. A big bowl had a face drawn on it and was saying,
If I only had a brain.

—I was going to take that one to class, said Ruben.

—Take it. But she didn't. When she left, the boys were quar-
reling and Harry was considering pieces of fire engines—hoses,
ladders?—in his study. She felt exhilarated, sneaking out, even

carrying the heavy drawing pad. Jeremiah said to her, first thing, But Toby, you don't still have that book, do you? I've searched the whole house. Deb says you returned it, but who knows? Ruben promised to look. At the break she asked him, But how do you know that artist is the woman in the book? I forget her name.

—In the book her name is Jessie Lipkin. That wasn't exactly her name—it was Gussie Lipkin.

—How do you know?

—I found something else about her. You can look up these things in indexes.

—But maybe it's a different person.

—No, it's the same person. The way I found out that she was Berry Cooper. Well, I read the book. A dotty old woman sold it to me at a used bookstore on Linwood Road—it's gone now; there's a housing development. Anyway, she told me Lipkin lived around here with a different name. I don't know how she knew. I thought about the book for years. Then someone told me about the *New York Times* index. Did you ever use that?

Ruben wasn't certain.

—Oh, very wonderful! You should take a look at it. Any library will have it. It has a volume for each year, and it's an index of all the articles in the newspaper by subject. Heavy books. I just hauled them off the shelves one by one. I looked up Gussie Lipkin in every single year starting in 1921, when the wreck occurred. That year there were three articles about her. This was in Massachusetts, and the *Times* wasn't too interested. The next year, none. The next year, one. Then none. Then, in the thirties, someone gave a lecture on the trial. And then there was a review of a sculpture show and it was listed under "Lipkin, Gussie. Alias Cooper, Berry." I looked it up and it said there was a sculpture show in New York at a gallery— this was in the late thirties, some Communist festival no doubt—by Berry Cooper, whose former name was Gussie Lipkin. I don't think she goes out of her way to let people know who she is, but sometimes it comes out. Anyway, there it was. After that, every few years there's something about Berry Cooper. And locally, too. She does live here, or she did. Naturally I looked them all up and there's never another reference to Gussie Lipkin, but I didn't need another reference. Then I found a historical piece in a Jewish magazine that could have told me everything. It said Gussie Lipkin is Berry Cooper. It said she's dead, but I think that could be wrong, because I have references to sculpture shows after the date of that piece. And they don't say she's dead. Of course, by *now* she could be dead.

—Was she a good sculptor? said Ruben.

—She mostly did abstract stuff. I don't know much about that.

On the way home, they passed Gregory on his bike. Even when it's cold, Jeremiah said. That goes beyond fitness. That's obstinacy.

—Maybe he can't afford a car, Ruben said. That's what you said last time.

—Oh, he can afford one, Jeremiah said, as if he knew.

—I'll look for the book, Ruben said when she got out. She was pretty sure she had never returned it.

But she couldn't find it. They'd moved twice since they'd lived in the apartment where she'd read half the book and stuck it somewhere. Surely she'd have returned it when they moved. She remembered bringing Deborah piles of borrowed possessions, and Deborah had done the same when she and Jeremiah and the vigorous girls moved to a bigger house with more wall space for paintings of yellow and green ellipses. Ruben didn't remember returning the book to Deborah, but memory is faulty. She remembered toys, baking pans, records, a cookbook, and Deborah's notes for teaching freshman composition, which Ruben had disagreed with anyway.

—Help me find a book, she said to Peter and Stevie, but they wouldn't, and she couldn't remember what it looked like, except that it was old. The boys ran up and down the stairs, fighting and getting along. When she scolded them for fighting they were never really fighting, and Stevie explained anything odd Peter might have done recently. The rooms upstairs, today, were a newspaper office. The boys were reporters. Downstairs were earthquakes and robbers. Ruben thought the book was black, or had a black spine. She'd simply look at every book she owned. She made herself go slowly, acknowledging—all but greeting—each book on each shelf, then each book on the next shelf.

Now Stevie took an interest. Peter had gone downstairs to cover a fire and disappeared; she thought he was reading. She could recognize the change in the air when anybody in her family, anywhere in the house, began to read. The air was roomier, because the reader was elsewhere.

—What's it called? said Stevie.

She'd asked Jeremiah. *Trolley Girl.*

—It's about a girl?

—A woman.

—Why's it called girl then?

—People sometimes say girl when they mean woman.

—I don't think I'd like that book. I don't like books about women. But I like books about trolleys.

—I don't think you'd like it, said Ruben.

She couldn't remember the book. She remembered what was upsetting: somebody was killed in a wreck. That was when she could not read any longer. Which was odd. It wasn't the only book she'd ever read in which somebody died! She remembered thrusting the book into a pile of newspapers and other books on the dresser. Maybe, eleven years ago, it had been thrown out with the newspapers. Now that she knew Jeremiah better, it would be unforgivable if she'd thrown away his favorite book about trolleys.

—You spend all your time in libraries, she said to Jeremiah.

—A lot of it.

She told him she was still looking for the book. She didn't say she was afraid it was gone.

The next day, Deborah said, We are finally acquiring a dog, and Ruben said she'd go along to pick him up. Deborah had agreed to adopt a dog her mother had taken in. She likes it, said Deborah, but she doesn't love it, and she doesn't have the energy for it.

It had been ascertained that the dog was a boy dog. And thank heaven for that! said Deborah. I have enough girls, heaven knows! she said, belying her words by scrubbing her fingers all over the heads of the nearest two girls, Rose and Mary Grace, who shrieked and ducked. They were in Deborah's kitchen. Mary Grace sat on Deborah's lap, though she was too big, and gave her mother a wet kiss.

—Moozum, said Jill, walking by.

—What's moozum? said Ruben, though it sounded familiar.

Deborah said, It's our word for menstrual blood, I'm afraid. Jill has her period. Ruben was jealous: she'd never have said such a thing to her mother, and she had no daughters.

—What's a period? Mary Grace said, but Rose hushed her. You *know*.

On Saturday, Deborah, Ruben, Mary Grace, and Stevie rode north in Deborah's car, forty miles to the small city where Deborah's mother lived. They'd been talking about getting dogs, both of them, for years.

—Oh, mothers, said Ruben.

—I forget when yours died.

—Thirteen years ago. Before we met. But Ruben wasn't ready, yet, to talk about it. Good leaves right here, she said. It was October, and besides acquiring a dog they were inspecting leaves.

—Peak! said Deborah. Peak! Maybe a smidgen past peak. They had left the highway and were riding on a road that got more wind and sun, or was up on a ridge, because here the leaves were redder and browner and in some places nearly gone.

—I like them better this way, said Ruben.

—Too sad, said Deborah. Better when they're crazy and yellow.

They stopped for ice cream and the children ran in the leaves. Nobody could be as beautiful. Ruben's shriveled relatives would have tied red ribbons to keep off the evil eye, and she knew why, watching Stevie of the delicate lashes and eyebrows and blond Mary Grace run toward her, their hands full of leaves. Not Ruben's mother; she wouldn't have tied red ribbons. Her grandmother would have.

—I'm sad, anyway, these days, said Deborah. Maybe Ruben could talk about her mother? At last? They were sitting at a picnic table in the sun, behind the stand where they'd bought the ice cream. It was cool, but not too cold for ice cream. They were in sweaters. Their ice cream was nearly gone. Their legs were stretched out and their backs were against the table edge, and Ruben thought she'd never been so happy, sitting next to Deborah watching the sharply, achingly perfect children, her back intersected by the soft warm wood of the picnic table. A little dog awaited them, and maybe Ruben would mention the death of her mother and it would not be unspeakable, just a death.

—Why are you sad? Ruben said. I'm happy.

—Happiness makes me sad, said Deborah.

Ruben laughed. She thought of Jeremiah's book. Do you remember—

—I think about Janet Grey too much, said Deborah.

—Janet Grey?

—The boss lady.

—I know who you mean.

—I teased her too hard, said Deborah. Now she's suspicious of me.

—She's boring.

—Oh, no, said Deborah. She's not boring. She just pretends to be boring because life hurts her so much. Or that's what I think. Do you think I've invented that?

—Could be. Ruben was jealous, again. She ran her hand down Deborah's shoulder and arm. Deborah's live mother had knitted the sweater Deborah wore, tweedy gray with flecks of color, cables on the sleeve. It made her look like a Swedish matron, with her light hair. Ruben played with Deborah's arm.

But she liked hearing about whatever upset Deborah. She liked that kind of talk.

—You don't think I'm dumb to think about her? Deborah said.

—Well, how much do you think about her?

—A lot.

—Is this a sexual thing?

—Oh, said Deborah. Oh. I don't think about going to bed with her, she said, but you know the way she carries her purse? She grasps it by the handles as if it weighs forty pounds, picks it up, and I want to just grab her.

—Is all this because she's the boss? Ruben asked.

—Probably. I know that's silly. I went for a long walk with her the other day.

—When?

—After our classes. We carried our papers and books.

—How far did you go?

—Like one of our walks, in the park.

—I wouldn't want to carry stuff.

—I didn't like that part.

—What did you talk about?

—Her love life.

—Recent?

—No.

Behind the ice cream stand was a little woods, filled with leaves and bits of garbage. Ruben could see the children down there, and then she couldn't see them. They were right down the hill. Stevie would go anywhere Mary Grace led him. Mary Grace came back first. She was the chubbiest and blondest of the girls. Her hair was long and wavy. She wore a bright green jacket. There's a dead dog at the bottom of that hill, she called.

They moved toward the car. Deborah said, So you like going to art school with Jeremiah? He's pretty weird, isn't he?

—Frankly, yes. Do you remember lending me a book? When we first met? Did I ever return it?

—He asked me about that, said Deborah. I thought you returned it. Didn't we both read it? I remember talking about it.

—You never read it, and I didn't finish it.

—Are you sure?

—Pretty sure. I wish I could find it. Poor Jeremiah.

—I know. He's rather special, said Deborah. Like a child with crutches. You don't want to lose his stuff.

The dog—not the dead dog at the bottom of the hill, but the living dog, Mac—was a big yellow Lab. He's blond, like the rest of you, said Ruben, though Jeremiah wasn't blond.

Deborah's mother had put his dish and leash into a plastic bag. She didn't seem sorry to give up the dog. She kept looking past them, over their shoulders, and twice Ruben turned to see if someone was there. Deborah's mother was smaller and quieter than Deborah, and sad. In the car on the way back, the dog licked the children's faces and tried to jump into the front seat. During a lull in dog hilarity, Deborah said, My mother makes me sad.

—She seems sad herself.

—I'm just like her. I've always been sad.

—No, you haven't, said Ruben.

—Yes. You don't really know me.

—Of course I know you! Who knows you? Janet Grey?

—Hush, said Deborah.

—What?

—Nothing. The children.

—What about the children? said Mary Grace.

—Nothing.

Mary Grace said, You're not changing your mind about the dog, are you?

—No, M.G., of course not.

—Don't call me that. That's a car.

—I'm sorry, said her mother, glancing into the rearview mirror. No, Mary Grace. We are keeping this dog!

—Mommy, said Mary Grace. What's wrong with Granny?

—She's always been like that, honey.

—I kept thinking someone was coming.

—She's always done that.

Ruben said, Is she looking for your father?

—I suppose, said Deborah, but I don't think she misses him much. Maybe she's hoping for a boyfriend.

—Maybe she has one, said Ruben.

—Maybe she does.

—What is it like to be old? said Ruben, although Deborah's mother was not terribly old.

—We'll find out if we're lucky, Deborah said.

—Why would it be lucky? said Stevie from the backseat.

—She just means it's better to be old than to die young, said Ruben.

—How do young people die? said Stevie. I knew a boy who died who was six.

—People die at any age, said Ruben. But it hardly ever happens.

—How old are dogs when they die? said Stevie. How did that dog die?

—Murder, said Deborah.

—Really? Really murder? said Stevie. Should we call the cops?

—No cops, Deborah said. Some mysteries are supposed to stay mysteries. Like what you did with Jeremiah's book, Toby.

—What *could* I have done with it? And why?

—Oh, it bothered you. I was surprised, I remember. You tried to make me feel guilty for letting you read it. You're awfully sensitive. I had no idea. Now I'm more used to you.

—I don't think I'm so sensitive. It was something about this book in particular. I like upsetting books, on the whole. It was something about the way it was written. I like upsetting movies.

—No, you don't, said Deborah.

—You say I don't know you, said Ruben, but you don't know me, either.

—Well, maybe not, maybe not.

But that would be terrible, all that not knowing. What was the point, then? Just rides to look at leaves and collect dogs? When Deborah stopped at Ruben's house to let her and Stevie out, Stevie got out and ran to the door. Ruben came around to the driver's side and Deborah rolled down the window. Ruben said, I want to tell you what became of my mother.

—What became of your mother? Deborah glanced into the backseat, but Ruben ignored Mary Grace.

—I killed her.

—No, you didn't.

—That's true. I screamed at her, said Ruben. She was at my house. On her way home she stopped at a gardening supply store and slipped on a wet piece of broken pavement, and broke her hip. They could never get her to walk again, and then she got pneumonia and died.

—Why did you scream at her? said Deborah.

—She was criticizing the way I watered my houseplants.

—Were you nice to her after she broke her hip?

—Reasonably nice. She was hard.

—I know how you feel, said Deborah. Not that it makes sense. It wasn't your fault, though.

Ruben kissed her and went into the house, happy again. She looked for Jeremiah's book until her mind changed the subject. In a bookcase where she thought she hadn't been attentive before, she put her finger on every book. Wasn't it just as Deborah said? Toby Ruben was a coward about books.

Gregory the art teacher gave specific homework assignments, but usually Ruben didn't do them. She kept drawing, though. At the pottery store she drew bowls, pots, and a terra-cotta teapot. She drew the teapot again and again, hoping no one would buy it. At first she had sketched when Archie was on his walks around the block, but after a while she drew when the store was quiet and they were together. Once he looked over her shoulder and pointed out that the handle of a fry pan was longer than she'd made it. Of course it's longer, he said. Look. It would have to be longer, and it is.

She laughed at that. She liked it. It would have to be and it is.

Ruben didn't usually bring her drawings to class. Some students brought homework, which everyone discussed with great respect. Once, they were supposed to make collages at home. Jeremiah brought in a collage of a decorated trolley, green construction paper on a white background, with decorations of gold foil, carefully cut and glued. Jeremiah explained that this trolley was a replica of one that had run in western Pennsylvania from 1912 to 1927. He'd done it precisely and the teacher didn't like precision. The teacher tried to explain to Jeremiah that that wasn't the idea.

—Condescending bastard, said Jeremiah to Ruben at the break.

—I think it's a different point of view, said Ruben. A student in a composition class, years ago, had wanted only to parse sentences. Maybe to Gregory, Jeremiah seemed like that woman, whom Ruben had loathed. The woman's expression had seemed to accuse clever, creative Ruben of being lazy. She'd had a fight with Deborah about it, but she couldn't remember why they argued.

She wanted to sympathize with Gregory, be serious fellow teachers together with Gregory, and forget Jeremiah. In imaginary discussions she mediated between them, but in life Gregory didn't answer when she spoke. He still didn't know her name.

Jeremiah had a rosy face and dark hair, not like Deborah and the girls. His hair waved neatly over his forehead, which made him seem old-fashioned: like a trolley conductor! and that was his way, too—friendly but impersonal. Jeremiah confided in Ruben, but she thought he'd say these things to anyone, and when another student joined them at the greasy spoon, Jeremiah was the same as ever. Almost the same. He told everyone about trolleys and interurbans, but only with Ruben did he talk about the sculptor who once was a Jewish anarchist, and the lost book. The book stayed lost.

One evening Jeremiah brought homework and the teacher liked it: a charcoal drawing of three bowls on a shelf. Gregory said it was interesting! He talked more that night. He said he'd been thinking they could chip in and hire a model for the last meeting. Use the eraser to change the texture, he said to Jeremiah, and then he said the same thing to Ruben. She erased the charcoal and it changed. Not too much, said Gregory. She was elated. He'd spoken to her.

Jeremiah, at the break, said, What did you think of my still life?

—It's great. She was drinking tea. Sanka was unbearable.

—A woman in my office did it.

—You're kidding.

—I can't draw like that, said Jeremiah. Don't you know that? The woman in his office knew about shadow. In class, when they'd drawn cylinders and spheres, the teacher pointed out the way light fell on the forms, but Jeremiah didn't seem to know what he meant. He always said, The light comes down from the ceiling.

—Well, I wondered, said Ruben. But she was upset. She said, I thought you converted. No more trolleys! Just cylinders and spheres.

In Ruben's fantasy, she took unfriendly Gregory aside and told him, teacher to teacher, what Jeremiah had done.

Meanwhile Ruben's life continued. A black-and-blue mark on her thigh, where a falling easel hit it, turned yellow and slowly disappeared. She sent a birthday card to her aunt, whom she didn't like. Harry whistled when he walked from room to room, and Ruben couldn't think whether it was new or if he'd always whistled in doorways. In the ladies' room at the college, she heard, Who do you have for English?

—Ruben.

—Is she hard?

—No. She whistles when she walks around the room.

One morning Peter walked out of the house to go to middle school and ten minutes later the phone rang. She knew from Harry's voice that it was bad. Peter had stepped off the curb into a moving car. Harry made her take off her nightgown and put on clothes before she ran. Ruben ran down the street. It was the day in November—it happens once a year, after a rainstorm—when many leaves fall at once. Suddenly there are more open spaces than leaves, and everything's yellow. Ruben ran crying in the new yellow day, with new sky. Near the school, Peter lay on the ground next to an ambulance, a collar around his neck.

But he was fine. The teacher who called Harry had begun by saying, Peter's all right, but Ruben hadn't believed him.

For a week, she and Deborah, day after day, said, There is no safety. There is no safety. Ruben's uncle died. Harry's uncle died. Two young women in Ruben's class brought her presents on the same day: a piece of spanakopita and an apricot Danish. She ate one before class and one after, feeling cared for. The baby-faced girl with long curls who brought the spanakopita said, You talked about spanakopita once. You said you liked it. Yes you did, yes you did.

And Stevie's teacher's dog had puppies, and the Rubens

adopted a gray puppy. Stevie named her Granny because he had no Granny. He had liked Deborah's sad mother.

Deborah acted like such a puppy expert. Put bitter apple on the furniture, she said. There's no need for this chewing!

—I'm always running there, she said.

—Where? said Ruben.

—To my mother. She's sad, she forgets, her belly hurts.

On the way to class, Jeremiah went through a light that had just turned red. Fuck this, he said.

—Fuck what?

—I don't like this class. *Gesture*, he says. I don't know what that means. I'm not getting better at drawing.

—Lately I like the class. Ruben had made a pen-and-ink drawing of the boys eating cereal from big curved bowls. It pleased her like nothing she'd ever drawn before. She kissed the top of Peter's head with her pen. And Stevie's, too. Everyone seemed rescued lately, much of the time.

—I like bringing in drawings, said Jeremiah. He laughed cynically. I do like that. This week I had a contest in the office. Three people entered, and I picked the best.

—Do you think Gregory believes you do them?

—Why not? He thinks he taught me something.

—But each person has his own style.

—In the office, I tell them, Pots! I distribute charcoal and they go home and draw the pots in their kitchens.

Ruben laughed, but she didn't like it.

—What's wrong? said Jeremiah. This isn't medical school. I'm not going to be taking apart brains under false pretenses, just drawing pitchers, he said. Then, pleased: Drawing pitchers! Drawing pitchers!

She laughed again. She knew he could tell she didn't like it.

—Jeremiah, she said, to change the subject, I still can't find that book.

—Well, that's a shame. I'd like to have it. But maybe it's not at your house. Maybe you did return it, and Deb stuck it somewhere. She does that.

—I don't think so.

—I'd love to find *her*, he said, and for a moment Ruben thought Deborah was missing. A week later, he began to talk about the artist as soon as Ruben got into the car, as if they'd had one unbroken conversation. I found that article about her, from the Jewish magazine. It was in a file at the office. I made you a copy, and then I forgot it.

—What does it say?

—Oh, it's all about the strike. This would interest you.

—Why? Because I'm Jewish?

—In part. But it's terribly interesting.

—Why? said Ruben. Why do you need to find this old lady? Do you want to see her sculptures?

—I just want to talk to her, Jeremiah said. We'd have a lot to say.

—I suppose you tried the phone book?

—Of course.

Ruben said, Listen, does Deborah know you bring in other people's drawings?

—Of course not. All these cars. It's disgusting.

Now *he* was changing the subject, but she didn't much care. She said, You'd prefer trolleys, of course.

—Naturally trolleys. Why not trolleys? The irony is, said Jeremiah, people believe in public transportation. They don't know they believe in it, but they do. You know about Bernhard Goetz?

—The man in New York who shot the kids in the subway.

—Right, said Jeremiah. Black kids. They asked him for money and he shot them. Now, why do you think this is a big story, huge outcry, so forth and so on?

—I read that he was acquitted, said Ruben. Just recently.

—I know he was acquitted. Disgusting. But why? Why the outcry? Why disgusting?

—Because he was a racist, said Ruben.

—No, said Jeremiah. Not because he was a racist. Or only in part because he was a racist.

—Then why?

—Why. Because it was in the subway. People feel safe in the subway. There is to be no shooting in the subway!

—But nobody feels safe in the subway!

—Oh, yes, said Jeremiah. Public transportation is a big womb. We are carried. We do not drive ourselves. The engineer takes care of us. That's why stories and songs about trolleys and trains are cute. But if something goes *wrong* on public transportation, it's much worse than anyplace else. Why is crime on subways so scary? Because trains are our mother. Somebody holds up the train, he's killing our mother. Think about it.

Ruben didn't want to think about it.

At the break he said, Tell me how to talk about pictures.

—Pictures? Oh, the drawings.

—We have a woman who comes into the office once a week, Jeremiah said. Payroll. She does the best drawings.

—Jeremiah . . .

—I need to be able to talk about them, said Jeremiah.

—Okay, okay, say you're interested in the volumes of the shapes. Say volumes. Gregory keeps saying volumes.

And a few days later, just to see if she could, in one evening she taught Harry to draw, hid his best effort, and gave it to Jeremiah.

A young woman said, I drew my dog, and brought out a charcoal drawing of a dog.

—Cool, said Gregory. Anybody else?

—The view from the back window, said Jeremiah, but it was the view from the Rubens' back window, drawn by Harry.

—Interesting how you did the bushes.

—At first they seemed just to be part of the background, said

Jeremiah, but I wanted them to be important. I wanted them to have volume.

—Excellent, said Gregory.

Jeremiah and Ruben winked and shook hands as they set up the easels. Ruben's arm was giddy with this childishness, and she drew rapidly and gorgeously, swirls and flowing circles of ink. That week it was ink.

—Think of Anna Karenina, said Jeremiah at the break.

—Anna Karenina?

—Threw herself under the wheels of a train. Why a train? Much more awful that way. Much more terrible. Public transportation. Didn't you ever read that book? She comes to Moscow or St. Petersburg, one or the other, I forget. She comes on a train and sees her lover for the first time in the station. And everyone's upset because someone's been crushed under the wheels of the train, a guard or a peasant. And then she herself—when that same lover grows cold to her . . .

—*Anna Karenina,* said Ruben to Deborah, a few days later.

—*Anna Karenina?* Deborah had said Jeremiah never read books.

—He was talking to me about *Anna Karenina.*

—Then there must be a trolley in it.

—Well, a train.

—I'm glad you're friends with Mr. Impossible, Deborah said. Toby says, Toby says . . . That's all I hear lately. They were drinking wine in Deborah's kitchen, though it was only three in the afternoon. But it was Deborah's birthday. Ruben had brought her the bottle of wine.

—You're kind of annoyed with him, I detect, said Ruben, wondering whether Deborah had found out about the drawing fraud, which seemed embarrassing at this distance from the school.

—Oh, he's all right. Mr. Folk Songs. Mr. Fuck Songs. Mr. Fuck Brain.

Mac the smiling yellow dog came in looking expectant. You're not Mr. Fuck Brain, Deborah said, pulling him toward her and stroking his side. You're Mr. Noodle Brain. Mr. Doodle Brain.

—Mac has a nice smile, said Ruben. He looks like Mary Grace. They both have those smiles from underneath, as if they're pretending they don't know they're smiling. Mary Grace and Rose were out in the backyard. Mac went out, scratched at the door and came in, scratched and went out again.

Ruben was cold. Deborah's house was full of wooden planks—the floor was made of them, and so was a partition between the kitchen and an old playroom where nobody played—and somehow wind came through all the chinks between them, even the indoor chinks. She sat in Deborah's kitchen wedged between the shellacked wooden table and a big yellow dresser, once a changing table, now cluttered with mail and papers and paintings. She ran her hand across its much-painted side, detecting air bubbles under the paint. The doorbell.

—I thought the kids were in the back, said Deborah, but the person at the door was Janet Grey with a wrapped birthday present. She said, Do you mind my just turning up? Happy Birthday, Deb. Oh, Toby, hi, I should have known I'd find you here. Toby *Laidlaw*. Deb's wife. Janet looked to make sure Ruben didn't mind the joke, then said, Could I possibly borrow a child?

Janet wore a gray coat, like her name, and a silk scarf arranged around her shoulders. Her eyes were gray, too, Ruben noticed, or they looked gray in this early December light. The room was light, but it was cloudy outside. Looking from her corner, between table and dresser, Ruben told herself to like Janet's humorous but limited eyes.

—Just one child? said Deborah. We have a sale right now. A three-for-one sale.

—Just one. Janet explained that she was going Christmas
shopping for her niece. She wanted a consultant.

—May I open this? Ruben was upset that Janet Grey called
her Toby Laidlaw, but also pleased, and impatient that Deborah had asked if she could open the present. Why do people
ask that? What else would they do with a present? It had a
bow. Ruben's present, the bottle of wine, had no wrapping of
any kind, but came with a note and a drawing of Deborah that
Ruben had copied nervously from a photograph. It was better
than what she'd have done a few months ago, but it looked
childish. Janet's present was a wonderful pair of red-and-yellow
socks, and Ruben coveted the socks and the brains to buy the
socks. Deborah took off her shoes and her gray socks and put
them on.

—Thank you! Kiss! said Deborah, which was something
Deborah would not say. She offered one, wide-armed. Janet
mimed a hug and a kiss from across the room, then thought
better of it and stepped forward to Deborah, who stood waiting
in her big cream-colored sweater, and they kissed.

Ruben wouldn't have let her children go shopping with Janet
Grey. Deborah's girls were playing picturesquely in the backyard, scrubbed by the glorious cold air, and why should they
be squashed in cars, sent out on the dangerous, smelly roads,
corrupted by cynical stores offering gaudy rags?

But Deborah said placidly, That would be nice, and called,
Kiddos! opening the back door. Jill came down from upstairs.
She raised her long arm and rested her hand on the doorjamb,
taking up the doorway but coming no closer. What is it?

Apologetic flutters from Janet Grey, who didn't mean Jill.

—I'm too busy, anyway, said Jill.

But Rose and Mary Grace came inside with cold flying off
their cheeks and their hair tumbly, and demanded diet Cokes,
of all things.

—I wonder if one of you ladies might, began Janet Grey.

Both of them wanted to go. Janet Grey said, I think just one, and Deborah chose Rose. Mary Grace cried. Janet apologized. I'm just not used to children!

—It's fine, said Deborah, and then the doorbell rang again as Mary Grace cried harder. Pray for something distracting, Deborah said, hurrying.

—We wondered if our mommy was here, Ruben heard. Peter's precise talk, on days he wasn't wild. In he came, he and Stevie and Granny. Stevie said, There's something wrong with Granny.

Mac wagged and sniffed while Granny wagged and sniffed and peed on the floor. Nothing was wrong with her.

—But she was holding up her foot!

Deborah looked over Granny's feet. She said, Maybe she had a pebble between her toes. The prayer had been answered, and Mary Grace looked over Granny's feet and Mac's feet. Soon everybody was on the floor playing vet. Now Janet and Rose climbed over the dogs and children, and left.

—Oh! said Deborah. I shouldn't have let her go. She has homework.

—Why did you let her?

—I was flattered, laughed Deborah.

—I don't know what you see in Janet Grey, said Ruben, feeling guilty because of the socks. She's so fussy, with her little scarf around her neck and spread out on her shoulder.

—We should wear scarves like that, said Deborah. Let's go shopping and buy silk scarves and wear them spread out on our shoulders.

—I don't like shopping.

—I love shopping, said Deborah.

—But I'll go with you, if you mean it, Ruben said.

Deborah did mean it. Real silk, okay, not polyester? Good colors. Do you want to go now? Wouldn't it be fun to go now? Maybe we'll run into them. Where were they going?

—But I'm so comfortable, lied cold Ruben. And what about all these children?

—Jill is here.

—Jill! Jill won't baby-sit. I'm scared of Jill. I wouldn't even ask. When she came down I thought she was going to preach a sermon at us.

—Just now she's religious, it's true, said Deborah. She's probably mortifying her flesh up there.

—You mean hurting herself? said Jewish Ruben.

—I am kidding, Toby. I am kidding.

But Jill turned friendlier and they did go shopping. Giddy from their half glasses of wine, they drove to the mall and with exaggerated enthusiasm picked out two big silk scarves, expensive, swirls of green (Ruben's) and yellow (Deborah's). Ruben's went with her coat. She looked like an old lady with her glasses and the scarf, which wouldn't, in the mirror, appear artfully arranged. It just looked as if she was cold. But she let herself be persuaded. One alluring midgreen blob was almost blue. She couldn't resist having a present on Deborah's birthday. They paid for each other's scarves. Ruben's cost a dollar more. Ruben carried her scarf home in Deborah's car, feeling it on her lap in its plastic bag, so pleased she couldn't look at it. That bluish green was certainly her favorite color.

—So some things she does are all right, said Deborah.

—Janet Grey? Lots of things she does are fine. She's just a little boring.

—But what makes her boring? said Deborah. Are we boring? Ruben said, Maybe we're boring to her.

—Obviously not. You just said that out of guilt.

—That's right. Deborah abruptly turned right and took a brisk shortcut around a cemetery and an old factory. Ruben said, You're not boring because you go straight where you're going. You don't futz around.

—That's what I always think about you. It's true, she has to stop and hold little observances.

—Does she really like her niece, or is she talking herself into it? said Ruben.

—Oh, I think she does, said Deborah, turning again. Or maybe not. She never says a bad thing about that niece. Nobody's that wonderful. She must not like her.

They drew up to Deborah's house, where every light was lit and children could be seen racing past uncurtained windows. With self-satisfaction they made their way up on the porch, arm in arm.

Ruben said, Oh, we're just the way we're supposed to be! and they laughed at their audacity, but meant it. In the hall, they shouted names of children and dogs and eventually everybody appeared, including Rose, who had been properly returned. Then juice had to be drunk, but at last coats went on. Ruben snapped the leash onto Granny's collar and took her scarf and they finally departed in the cold and dark, she and Stevie and Peter and Granny. Peter held Granny's leash but then Stevie began whirling and staggering, whirling and staggering, and Peter handed the leash to Ruben so he could whirl and stagger and bump into his little brother. They shrieked and laughed down the block in the twilight, but then Deborah and Mary Grace came running after them.

—We were supposed to give you this! Jeremiah said I should give you this! called Deborah, hair flying.

—Elephant platypus! screamed Mary Grace.

Oh. Yes. The article about the anarchist. She hugged Deborah hard and took the folded sheets of paper. Deborah and Mary Grace ran back home—no coats!—and Ruben and the boys walked on.

—Elephant platypus! the boys screamed after Mary Grace. Then, Elephant giraffe! Elephant orangutan. In the dark, they spun in circles again and staggered forward and spun in circles, a taller and a shorter one, outlined like the dark trees.

—Porcupine, they gasped, giraffe, platypus.

—No, no, platypus, elephant platypus.

—Elephant platypus! When they spun past her, she reached to touch their hair. Each boy in turn stopped and then they

took the leash from her and she walked between them and
again touched a hand to each head. Their hair was fine and
silky, with snags and tiny roughnesses, and she felt a few hairs
for nits—two years before, all of Deborah's girls and both
her boys kept giving one another head lice; Deborah said,
You're in our nitwork. But now everybody was clean. Nobody
had any troubles at all. There were no troubles anywhere on
earth.

THE LITTLE ANARCHIST
GUSSIE LIPKIN AND THE BOYNTON TROLLEY WRECK

[The article, unsigned, was from *Jewish Monthly*, November
1972, pp. 24–28. It was accompanied by photographs, one of a
woman and one of a trolley car, but they had been photocopied
and were hard to see.]

"The *Boynton Herald,* Miss Lipkin, reported that 'wrenches,
auto cranks, paving blocks, bottles, coal, and missiles of all description' were thrown at the strikebreakers. Miss Lipkin, did
you throw bottles and paving blocks?"

"No, sir, I did not."

"Did you throw anything, Miss Lipkin?"

"Mud, sir."

"You threw mud?"

"Yes, sir."

"And how did you acquire this mud, Miss Lipkin?"

"I knelt in the yard of the trolley company and scooped it up
in my hands, sir."

"In your hands?"

"Yes, sir."

"Miss Lipkin, this event took place on January ninth, did it
not?"

"I believe so, sir."

"And there had been a snowfall the night before, is that right?"

"Yes, sir."

"And yet you ask us to believe that you scooped up mud in
your hands?"

"The yard was in the sun, sir. The snow where I was standing had melted."

"I see. And did some of this mud fall on your dress, Miss Lipkin?"

"Yes, sir."

"Miss Lipkin, you are nineteen years old, am I correct?"

"Yes, sir."

"And you are Jewish, are you not, Miss Lipkin?"

"Objection, your honor. The defendant's religion . . ."

"Objection sustained."

The above quotations—which I discovered by chance one rainy afternoon in the Boynton, Massachusetts, Public Library while doing research for a graduate dissertation on the history of the New England textile mills—are from the transcript of a long-forgotten but fascinating trial that took place in October 1921 in the grimy Massachusetts mill town of Boynton: the trial of a young Jewish girl, daughter of an illiterate immigrant mother and a father who loved to read, a trial not for mud throwing, it turns out, but for murder. "The Little Anarchist," as Gussie Lipkin was called by that very same *Boynton Herald*, or sometimes "the Emma Goldman of Boynton," has nearly been forgotten by Jewish historians, by feminists, and by historians of the radical left, but she might well be of interest to all of these. Bright though uneducated, this woman at fifteen joined an anarchist cell that had met briefly in her parents' living room. Three years later she was apparently its leader and spokesperson. Short, plump, and not attractive—judging from the single surviving photograph—with a low forehead and rather thin, cropped hair, Gussie Lipkin had been born in Boynton in 1902 to Jewish immigrants from Russia who went on to have two other daughters. They had landed at Ellis Island a year before her birth, and were drawn to the small, desperately poor Jewish community in Boynton by the prospect of work in the mills. By the age of eighteen, Gussie Lipkin had become estranged from her parents and lived briefly as the common law wife of a factory worker and union leader who was rumored to have left a wife and child behind in Europe.

In 1921, Warren G. Harding became president of the United States. Hitler's storm troopers were becoming active. The first radio broadcast of a baseball game was made from the Polo Grounds in New York. And, though the "Red Scare" was dying down, Sacco and Vanzetti were found guilty of murder. Just a year earlier, national hysteria about possible Bolshevism in America had led to extreme measures, including the deportation of a shipload of radical aliens, including Emma Goldman and Alexander Berkman. In January 1920, Attorney General A. Mitchell Palmer ordered raids on leftist organizations. Known radicals, aliens, and unlucky bystanders were illegally rounded up, held under appalling conditions, and in some instances deported.

Also in that year came the death of the inventor of the rubber tire, which was changing the lives of Americans. Twenty years earlier, people had gotten around mostly by trolley: on the still familiar urban trolleys but also on interurbans, which ran for dozens and sometimes hundreds of miles from city to city. Now that system of ubiquitous public transportation was changing. An article in *The New Republic* entitled "Passing of the Interurbans" (August 20, 1919, pp. 92–93) points out that there was a decrease in passengers everywhere. The writer, C. J. Finger, attempts to persuade his readers of the futility of increasing fares, an expedient he calls "foolish."

The trolley was doomed, and yet hundreds of lines existed and thousands of men worked on them. With the decrease in use came increases in fares—from six cents to seven, even eight—and wage cuts. And, inevitably, there were strikes. A savage strike took place in Denver in 1920 and one nearly as brutal in Albany and Troy, New York, in 1921. The trolley men of Boynton, Massachusetts, received news of a 25 percent wage cut, which seems outlandish but was typical, just before

Christmas in 1920. On January 5, 1921, the conductors and motormen struck the line, and scabs were hired.

In the late afternoon of January 9, 1921, as a trolley operated by scabs made its way through the snowy New England countryside, it collided with one coming in the opposite direction. One person was killed. To the horror of the Boynton community, the dead young woman was Sarah Lipkin, the youngest sister of the known radical Gussie Lipkin. No one knows why Sarah Lipkin was journeying on the trolley that afternoon. Her body had barely been removed from the wreckage when rumors spread through Boynton that an arrest had been made. Gussie Lipkin had been found walking along the trolley tracks. Obviously, the frantic townspeople insisted, in conspiracy with the strikers and other sympathizers—and possibly in some mysterious collusion with her sister—Gussie had somehow altered the signals and caused the crash. She was dirty and exhausted, and readily confessed that she had been among the crowd of sympathizers who attempted to keep the trolley lines from operating, by any means at their disposal, that morning. Yet Gussie Lipkin insisted on her innocence of the crime with which she was charged: murder. Murder of her own sister.

"Hang the little Jew" was one of the slogans found painted on factory walls and fences in Boynton in the next few days. We can only speculate, decades later, on how much anti-Semitism existed in the town at that time. The newspaper ran one editorial commenting on the high percentage of Jews in the "radical organizations among us." "Let our Jewish neighbors look after their own," said the editorial. "Law-abiding citizens desire nothing more of them than the same adherence to the rules of right and wrong, the ideals of our country, that we ask of ourselves." Certainly there was no major anti-Semitic rally or demonstration; yet even in the courtroom testimony quoted above there is implied prejudice.

The trial lasted for seven weeks. The motormen of both trolleys, one of whom had been injured in the crash, testified at length. The jury found Gussie Lipkin not guilty. A year later she was arrested again, after a small demonstration by an anarchist group at a strike of women seamstresses. Clearly the authorities were determined to make some charge stick, and Lipkin spent eighteen months in the Boynton city jail after a successful prosecution on a charge of disorderly conduct and inciting to riot.

Gussie Lipkin left Boynton in her midtwenties and lived for a time in New York, then later in Paris. She studied art and became a sculptor. At some point she took the name Berry Cooper—Cooper being the name of her second husband. Her sculpture is not unknown. In midlife she returned to New England. In the last reference to her I can find, she was exhibiting sculpture in a show designed to raise money for the Freedom Riders in the early sixties. I can find no record of an obituary, but an artist of my acquaintance has told me she died of emphysema several years ago, while living in the west.

It's tempting to speculate on why Gussie Lipkin has been so totally ignored. Her trial was somewhat notorious. The *New York Times* sent a correspondent to Boynton, although in the end it ran only two short mentions of Lipkin, buried in the back pages. A Jewish law student from New York University, Jacob Lauterman, wrote an amicus brief on behalf of a Jewish philanthropic organization and sent it to various left-wing organizations, without any results.

Maybe the energy of the left was already absorbed. It was the time of the Sacco and Vanzetti case, of Red-baiting and vigorous protests all over the nation. Even devoted servants of justice must choose their causes. Certainly the Jewish community was divided. There must have been embarrassment, and the fear that possibly Gussie Lipkin was not being framed, but was guilty. At her trial, her lawyer portrayed her as a selfless, idealistic young woman, overcome with grief at the death of her sister. In any case, Gussie Lipkin deserves some belated attention from all of us. Disturbing the dust on the yellowing pages of the *Boynton Herald* is evidence of a fiery spirit, a woman who refused to allow others to think for her, a stubborn, intelligent girl.

———

All week Ruben wondered if the model would wear clothes. Then Jeremiah was so slow picking her up on Thursday night she thought he wasn't coming. She shifted the clumsy drawing pad to her other hand as she waited in the street. Her fingers, reaching around the edge of the pad, were cold, even in gloves. The pages blew open: her lumpy drawings in the dark.

He showed up. You know anything about this shit?

She touched the drawing pad on her lap. What shit? She thought he was upset that they'd had to chip in three dollars apiece to pay for the model. She was tired of Jeremiah's objections to the drawing class.

—This dame Janet Grey hasn't told you?

—Told me what?

—She's dumping Deb.

Janet Grey had phoned an hour ago, while they were eating, and told Deborah that she needed only one adjunct teacher for the spring term because enrollments were down, and that she preferred to hire Toby Ruben.

—But why?

—Enrollments.

—But she's so close to Deborah.

—Apparently she likes you better.

—Is Deborah furious with me?

—It's not your fault.

Ruben thought they should skip the art class and go to Deborah, but she couldn't bring herself to miss drawing the model.

—Deborah and I teach two classes apiece now. Couldn't we each have one? Janet Grey told me yesterday she wants me to teach two sections again in the spring.

—I don't know the details.

They were going into the building. She tried to stop thinking
about Deborah and Janet Grey. She was afraid Deborah would
think she was in cahoots with Janet Grey. Yet how could Deborah imagine that? Deborah was the one who liked her. Ruben
didn't like Janet. She'd had maybe three conversations alone
with Janet. She and Janet taught on Tuesday, when Deborah
wasn't there. Once, they had talked about Deborah, only a
little. Janet asked Ruben, Would you consider Deborah an intellectual? Ruben didn't know what she meant. She didn't
know whether it would be good or bad to be an intellectual.
What had she said?

She had said, Sometimes I'm surprised at things she hasn't
read. Oh, my. She had said that.

Gregory told them how they'd draw from the model, who
would change poses every two minutes. They were to try to
draw the *gesture:* a few swift lines. The students clumped into
the cluttered corner as usual and dragged out easels. Ruben set
up her easel. She took two pieces of charcoal from her smudgy
plastic bag. She was always dropping and breaking charcoal.
There was no place to set it down. She taped four or five big
sheets of paper to the easel with masking tape, and all but the
top one slipped out from behind and fell. She put the charcoal
on the floor and retaped the paper with more tape. She had
never learned to do it right.

Gregory, talking about gesture, waved to someone behind
them. Opposite Ruben, Jeremiah coughed. The whole class had
colds. They had never come to know one another, but they
snuffled in unison, unable to blow their noses because their
hands were so dirty with charcoal. They were all bundled in
thick sweaters because the room was always cold.

Gregory plugged in a space heater near the platform on
which, all term, he'd set jugs and broken statues and ladders
and tables. On the platform was a chair. Then he nodded, and
a rosy-skinned naked young woman, whose crinkly reddish
hair was pulled into a big ponytail, walked from behind Ruben

and stepped onto the platform. She crossed her legs and stretched her arms above her head, fingers just touching.

In a corner of her page, Ruben began to draw a small, tight naked woman whose legs were too short for the rest of her. Before she could finish, the woman thrust one leg out in front, as if she were running, brought her arms down, and bent them, as well, like a runner. Ruben tried again. She wanted to draw the woman's face. She wondered about the men in the class, whether this experience was erotic for them. It was erotic for Ruben; well, it was sort of erotic. It was new, it was brave. The woman was perfectly formed, with shapely, smooth thighs. Her breasts were rounded and firm, not very large. Ruben tried to draw the woman's breasts.

Gregory passed behind her. Just the gesture, he said.

The woman changed poses again. Now she knelt on the platform. Ruben tried to imitate the line of her body with the charcoal.

As usual Gregory spoke to the other students, hardly ever to her. That's fine, that's fine, she heard him say. It was simply one of the loveliest events on earth for this woman to take off her clothes and stand before them, just so Ruben could try to draw her with charcoal. She wished Gregory would talk or listen to her. She had no way of saying it made her happy to draw this woman.

The woman sat on the platform, one leg stretched in front of her. Maybe the other students' happiness would show in their drawings. Ruben thought Gregory might be a good teacher. When he had occasionally left the room, Ruben had told a few people her name. Once she'd complained to an older woman that Gregory didn't know their names, and the woman, who had not said her own name, said, Names don't matter.

The break was delayed. When they finally stopped, Ruben was elated and exhausted. She didn't want to talk to Jeremiah and drink Sanka. At last the model stepped behind a screen, then strode out ahead of them, dressed in a sweater and jeans.

Thank you, Ruben said as the woman passed, not knowing whether you were supposed to pretend you didn't know it was the same person. Jeremiah ran toward Ruben and took her by the elbow. Come on, come on. She went. He said, Wasn't that something? Wasn't that just something? Here all term I've been—

But then he shook his head and didn't say anything more as they hurried to the coffee shop in the cold. When they got there, Jeremiah stopped. Do you want anything?

—Not really.

He steered her around. I don't want to break the mood.

In the empty classroom, they took off their coats and separated to look over their drawings. Gregory and the others came in.

Gregory asked each student to hang a drawing of the model. Ruben had one she rather liked. They all carried their sheets of paper to the usual wall and taped them with leftover bits of tape. When she looked around, Ruben was startled at how different everyone's drawings were. A young man had made the model ugly, with strange angles and shadows. Two drawings looked stormy and elegant, as if made by complicated people, though they were the work of two women who looked like drugstore cashiers and wore big plastic earrings in bright colors.

Gregory walked, talking. The model had enlivened him, too. You don't usually draw this way, he said to one woman, glancing from her drawing to her. Ruben was surprised that he knew whose it was. There's more sense of the edge of the paper here. Do you see?

The woman obviously did not see, but he went on to the others. He praised a line, a tucked-in head, the curve of a neck. Some students had omitted the model's hair. Ruben hadn't thought not to draw her hair, and all her drawings included that grand ponytail.

But you, Gregory said, looking at Jeremiah. But you. Ruben

thought Jeremiah's drawings were the best he'd ever done. She imagined herself saying to Deborah, For once, what he drew didn't look like a trolley. Then she thought how Deborah was upset, how they must hurry to her.

Gregory said Jeremiah's drawing had a sumptuous curve. Ruben wouldn't have called it sumptuous. Now Gregory stopped and turned to face Jeremiah, his back to Jeremiah's drawing, as if he wanted to conceal it. By the way, he said, and Ruben saw her own feelings reflected in the body of one of the women with plastic earrings, who suddenly shifted as if something frightening had entered the room.

—By the way, said Gregory, I know perfectly well what you've been up to all this time, and I think it's truly stupid. Just thought you ought to know.

He moved on to the next drawing, which was Ruben's. He was angry with Ruben, too, or else he was overcome with what he had just said. Nice line here, he mumbled.

—Do you mean the homework? said Jeremiah.

—Yes, that's what I mean.

—I have some thoughts on your methods.

—I'd rather not hear them, Gregory said.

Jeremiah moved away from the group and walked to the window, glanced out, and returned. Of course the window was dark. There was time for one more drawing. Gregory said they could put together their own still life groups, if they wanted, or they could leave, if they preferred to do that. It was the last meeting of the class. All the students packed up and left. The older woman thanked Gregory and said she'd asked her husband to buy her an easel for Christmas. Ruben and Jeremiah walked silently out of the room and the building, to Jeremiah's car. Easing out of the parking space, they were passed by a man on a bike.

—Was that Gregory? said Ruben. She wished—well, she had many wishes. She imagined Gregory telling his artist friends

about two middle-aged idiots in his class. She started to laugh
a little. She was going to say to Jeremiah, We are idiots (since
she couldn't seem to separate herself from Jeremiah), and her
statement was going to make a difference. But Jeremiah
rounded the corner sharply and there was a thump, and the
sound of metal breaking, and then Jeremiah was cursing, pulling over to the curb right at the corner and jumping out.

Afraid to look, she followed him. He had knocked over
Gregory and his bike. She started to scream, pressing her hands
on her mouth, and then took her hands away and screamed
some more. All she could do now was be loud. She couldn't
bear to look closely, but then she did. Gregory was standing
up, leaning over the bicycle.

—Oh, man, said Jeremiah. You're going to think I did that
on purpose. How can I ever—? Are you all right? Shall we call
the cops, or an ambulance?

—I'm all right, said Gregory. I need for you to get the fuck
out of my life, is what I need.

—Of course I'll pay for the bike! said Jeremiah.

Gregory was holding one arm with the other. My own stupid
fault, he said quickly. I knew you couldn't see me when I turned.

—Gregory, said Ruben, finally a grown-up—exaggerating
the mommy tone—I know you're angry. You should be angry.
But you must let us help you. Is your arm hurt?

—I just scraped it on the ground. The back of the bicycle
was hit, but I personally was not hit. He passed his hand over
his face. Look, I just don't need anything more from you two,
okay? I really just want you to get the hell out of here.

—Whatever you say, said Jeremiah. Send me a bill for your
new bike.

—Go to hell, said Gregory. Jeremiah got back into his car.
Ruben stood there a while longer. Finally she said, I learned a
lot from the course. I really did. And drawing the model was
fantastic.

Then she got into the car. Five blocks closer to home, Jeremiah pulled over to the side of the street, shifted into park, rested his arms on the wheel, and hid his face in his hands. His shoulders shook. Then he sat up, shifted, and drove toward Ruben's house.

—No, she said. I have to talk to Deborah.

—It's late.

—Even so.

—No.

—Yes.

Deborah said, What are you doing here? She wore her pink fuzzy bathrobe and slippers, and under it a light blue flannel nightgown. Ruben hugged her and rested her head on Deborah's chest and cried a little. Then she knew why Jeremiah hadn't wanted her to come. Maybe he wasn't going to tell Deborah what had happened. He was afraid Ruben would. Well, she wouldn't do that.

—If you're here to comfort me, I don't need it, said Deborah. I told Jeremiah not to tell you.

—But what did Janet say?

—Let's not stand here in the hall, at least, said Deborah. Ruben phoned Harry while Deborah made Almond Sunset tea. Ruben thought Jeremiah would go upstairs, but he stayed and drank tea.

—You'll be peeing all night, Deborah said.

—I do anyway, after that coffee.

—We didn't have coffee tonight, said Ruben.

—Oh, right.

—Why not? Deborah said.

—We were too overcome, said Ruben. The model.

—What was she like?

—She was naked.

—I'm sure you liked that, Deborah said to Jeremiah. He was warming his hands on his mug. He drank the tea quickly, even though it was scalding. Ruben considered that Jeremiah's

tongue might be calloused from many hot drinks. She found
herself, for a moment, wondering how such a tongue might feel
inside one's mouth or stroking one's clitoris. She stared hard
at Deborah to dispel the late-night thought. She had never been
attracted to Jeremiah. Now, she found herself assuming he had
run into Gregory's bike on purpose. Yet surely he hadn't. She
argued with herself, looking at Deborah.

Deborah was talking, telling the history of the last two days
as it pertained to Janet Grey. Janet had waved from a passing
car, but did not stop. Janet had called and left a message with
Rose for Deborah to call back. Deborah had called and Janet
had said she couldn't talk right then but would call Deborah
later.

—Then she called just when we sat down to eat.

—Jeremiah told me.

—At first I didn't know what she meant. She was talking in
a low voice, and I could scarcely hear her. She said, I have to
make some changes. I thought she meant changes in her life. I
thought she wanted to confide in me. I was pleased! Deborah
lowered her big, dignified blond head into her hands and her
hair fell forward. What did I do? she said.

Jeremiah got up and left the room, and Deborah watched
and waited to speak until he was on the stairs. Then she spoke
quickly. Was I obvious? Does she think I'm after her, you
know?

—I'm sure she's scared of intimacy . . .

—You never liked her, but she likes you. What did you say
to her about me?

—Hardly anything. Why do you think it was me? said
Ruben. Listen, why can't we each teach one course if she has
only two for next term?

—Oh, no, she's just getting rid of me. You'll see—she'll hire
someone else. She says because of your specific expertise, blah
blah blah. Believe me, I asked her. I was quick to suggest taking
away one of your classes!

—Well, of course, said Ruben, quickly wondering whether she could work more hours at the pottery store and whether she would like that. She said, What do I know that you don't?

—You have more experience, actually. Or more on paper.

—I doubt it.

—Oh, you know, said Deborah. Some of that stuff before you moved here sounds good.

Ruben was frantically tired. She had drunk her tea. She was getting cold, as always in Deborah's kitchen. She wanted to put her coat on, but if she did that Deborah would think she was in a hurry to leave. How did Janet *sound*? she said. I can't imagine this. I can't imagine it in the same universe with the red-and-yellow socks. And Rose going shopping with her. She hasn't even handed over that present yet!

—Oh, she started by saying we'll always be friends, she values my friendship . . . She sounded like my friend. She sounded as if she was telling me about getting rid of somebody else. As if I was supposed to sympathize because this was so hard for her.

—Should I talk to her? Ruben said.

—I think her mind's made up. I think something made her decide I'm just not very bright—and you're her star.

Sometimes Ruben stood in the hall and heard Deborah teach. She thought that what Deborah said was a little oversimplified.

—What did she say when she visited your class? she said, not knowing why she was asking the question. She got up and put on her coat.

—Oh, it was all right. I don't remember what she said. But there's not much you can do with freshman English.

—Oh, there's a lot, Ruben said, though she knew she shouldn't. Her coat was on and she picked up her drawing pad and her plastic bag of stuff, and took a step toward the door.

—Whose side are you on? said Deborah. You think I'm no good, don't you? Did you tell Janet Grey you think I'm no good?

—No, said Ruben. No, no, no, no, no.

—I'm not sure I believe you.

Ruben was sorry she'd come. She felt almost sick, cold and headachy. She couldn't bear to leave with Deborah saying these things. She walked over to her. Deborah didn't push her chair out from the table to meet her.

Ruben knelt next to Deborah's chair and put her arms around Deborah's waist. I'll tell Janet Grey it's both of us or nothing, she said.

—No, you won't.

—Why not? But she was wondering if she would. She was waiting for Deborah to release her from the obligation of saying that to Janet Grey. She sat back on the floor, feeling awkward and bundled up in her coat. She knew of nothing good in herself, nothing she could count on.

—Come to bed, Deborah, said Jeremiah, coming into the room. Now he was also in a bathrobe.

—I'm sorry, said Ruben. She stood up. I'm sorry I'm still here.

—I didn't realize you were still here, Jeremiah said.

Ruben hated leaving with everything unresolved.

Jeremiah said, Shall I put on my pants and drive you home? I forgot about you.

—No, I can walk.

—It's not a great idea.

—I do it a lot, said Ruben.

—I guess this is it, then, he said.

For a moment she thought he meant the friendship was over. What do you mean, *it*? she said. Deborah knows it's not my fault.

She realized what he meant as soon as she had spoken. He said, No, I mean the course is over. The drawing course.

—It's over? said Deborah. I didn't realize.

—It's over, said Ruben. Then she could not stand herself to such a degree that she had to change things, even if it was going to make them worse. Jeremiah, she said, that was awful. Tell her. Tell Deborah.

—Tell Deborah what? they both said.

—Oh, Jeremiah, said Ruben.

—The model? said Deborah. What, was she an old girlfriend of yours?

—No, the model was great, Jeremiah said. She was gorgeous. For the first time, I wanted to draw. I could draw her. Toby, did you see my drawings?

—They were great, she said.

—Let me show you, Deb, Jeremiah said, and he picked up his drawing pad. He had put the sheets they'd used that night between the other pages, and now he pulled them out and spread them on the table. Deborah didn't look terribly interested, but she moved toward the table.

—She took a different pose every few minutes, Jeremiah said.

His drawings were almost abstractions—quick, hard strokes that seemed different from anything Jeremiah had done before. Jeremiah, you didn't make her look like a trolley, Ruben said.

Deborah sniffed, and looked without speaking. Then she began to look at the other drawings in the pad. There were many, some stuck together, some folded. She took out a smaller charcoal drawing, a still life of a pitcher and a bowl. When did you do this? she said. Why didn't you show me?

—Oh, that was a homework assignment, Jeremiah said.

—You did it here? But we don't have a pitcher like that.

—Well, said Jeremiah, somebody in the office brought in a pitcher for me to draw.

—Somebody brought in—? Who?

—Carol.

—Why would Carol bring in a pitcher? Deborah stood up and straightened her bathrobe, staring at Jeremiah, who had moved toward the doorway again. They looked across the room at each other in their robes, like Mom and Dad on Christmas morning. Ruben was ashamed to be there.

—Oh, God, Jeremiah said. Oh, Christ.

—What?

—Carol didn't bring in a pitcher. Carol drew the pitcher. The picture! The picture of the pitcher, he said, was drawn by Carol.

Deborah looked at it, put it down, and turned. So what? she said. Are you trying to tell me something terrible about you and Carol?

—No, said Jeremiah. For Christ's sake, you certainly don't trust me, do you? I'm not trying to tell you anything about me and Carol. I'm trying to tell you something about the goddamn art class. The art class was a crock. No, I was a crock. I was lousy at it. I couldn't do it. So I started bringing in homework by other people. Carol did the most, but lots of people did them.

—You lied about it to the instructor? said Deborah. Toby, did you know about this?

—She helped, said Jeremiah. I know, it sounds stupid. It *was* stupid.

—You made drawings and said Jeremiah had done them? Deborah said.

—No, but Harry did one, said Ruben.

—Harry? What is this? What kind of kid stuff is this? Didn't the instructor see through you? I hope he did, Deborah said. I hope he let you have it.

—Well, he let me have it tonight, Jeremiah said. I don't know how long he knew.

—You were cruel to him! Toby, how could you take part in this scheme? How would you feel if your students did that? Or don't you care about other people at all? Is all you care about your fabulous brain, that can figure out such a scheme?

—Don't be so self-righteous, Ruben said. They were still all standing up, now leaning on things. They were so tired.

—Self-righteous? said Deborah.

—Look, said Jeremiah. You don't even know the worst of it. I might as well tell you.

—There's something worse?

—I ran him down with the car.

—You ran him down? said Deborah. The instructor? You mean you killed him?

She looked wildly toward the door. Ruben and Jeremiah laughed and tried to stop laughing. No, he's all right, said Jeremiah. But his bike is smashed.

—You ran into his bike? said Deborah.

—I didn't mean to.

—Well, I should hope not!

Deborah pulled out the chair she'd been sitting on before. She sat down. I don't know when I've ever felt so bad, she said in a low voice. She sounded frightened.

Ruben couldn't understand how she had become stuck there, stuck in this scene, how she had somehow participated in depriving Deborah of her job, and how she had become a conspirator with Jeremiah.

She said, We're not Hitler.

—Well, of course not, said Deborah. You didn't kill him. She sounded as if she meant it, but then her voice became sarcastic. You didn't kill him! How kind of you! How kind of you not to kill the instructor! My best friend and my husband. Two disgusting people.

—You think I turned Janet Grey against you, said Ruben.

—I don't know what I think, Deborah said, with cold anger. I think you're both people with no feelings. You want to strip the world naked and draw it. You want to make fun of it. You want—I don't know what you want from me, the instructor, or anybody. Here, she said, standing up again. She moved away from the table and undid the belt of her bathrobe. You want to draw naked women? That's what you want? She pulled off the robe and threw it on the floor.

—Stop it! screamed Ruben.

Jeremiah came toward Deborah, reaching for the bathrobe.

Deborah struck him in the face and he stepped backwards,

and in that moment she pulled her nightgown up over her head. There she was, what Ruben—she understood suddenly—had wanted to see for years: naked, beautiful Deborah, fatter than the model, with creases in her belly and pocked thighs, but lovely swinging breasts and those big smooth shoulders in one unbroken line that led to her breasts and her long summer arms.

Ruben cried with longing and misery and guilt, and fled from the house, clutching her drawing pad.

—Deb, she heard Jeremiah say as she ran, it's so cold, so cold in here.

Ruben ran with her pad in the night, then had to slow down. She would never think about the drawing class again, she decided. She would never think of Gregory or his bicycle, nor of Jeremiah, his missing sculptor, his deceitful drawings, his lost book.

WHEN Ruben walked out of her house, her old dog, Granny—who had been Granny even when she was young—rushed barking down the wet street, her gray ears flung back. Ruben caught up and attached the leash, and Granny strained at the leash. Ruben could see Deborah coming toward her a block away, under the stripped, wet trees, in a bright green raincoat, although it had stopped raining and intermittent sun made the yellow leaves translucent. It was a Friday afternoon in November. Deborah's dog, Mac, had never used a leash. He came running ahead of Deborah, and Ruben tensely watched his yellowness, afraid as usual that he'd rush into the street. But when he did the light had changed, and Mac crossed before any cars turned.

Ruben hugged the sticky green raincoat and Deborah hugged back. A plastic bottle of Poland Spring water stuck out of Deborah's pocket. Lately they were always thirsty. They walked toward the park.

—We've never gone up the North Peak, Ruben said. Stevie

had shown it to her when he was home from college. A short climb: they couldn't reach the main peak before dark today.

In the woods, Ruben's sunglasses made everything rosy. She took them off and the woods became brown, with blurry edges. She'd forgotten her clear glasses. She put the sunglasses on again. It was almost winter. The woods were still wet and soon wet leaves dampened her feet.

Deborah said, Did you see that woman, in the paper? Lying on her stomach.

—What woman?

—In Rwanda.

They had talked and talked about Rwanda. What if you had to watch your child be shot? Deborah had said, again and again.

—Not Rwanda, today, exactly, said Deborah. Zaire. The woman was in Zaire. One of the refugees. She fled from someplace, but there was no safety, and she had to go back into danger.

—Oh, yes, more fighting there.

—Those refugees are caught in the middle. They're being starved to death while people fight around them.

They crossed the street into the park. But aren't they the bad guys? said Ruben. I can't keep them straight. The Hutu and the Tutsi.

Deborah said, Did you know those tribes used to be called the Bantu and the Watusi?

Ruben said, No, I didn't know.

—When I read those words—months ago—said Deborah, it made it different, because I recognized the words: Watusi, Bantu.

—Just the words, said Ruben.

—Just the words. Not even something like Trafalgar Square. I've *been* to Trafalgar Square.

—I know. Just the words.

They were on the wide, tended path and then they crossed

the river on a footbridge, came to the trailhead, and started down the trail. The dogs stayed shoulder to shoulder on the bridge and then separated, came together again, and ran in loops. The trail was a little muddy, a little slippery.

—I think these refugees are in the worst situation possible, said Deborah. Don't you sometimes spend hours figuring that out, just thinking what the worst possible situation might be?

—I don't want to live like that, said Ruben. Shut up.

—But the rebels are pulling them out of the camp and shooting them. Children.

—I think these are the bad guys, said Ruben. Aren't they the bad guys?

Deborah stopped and her green raincoat glowed. Her hair was still blond, but faded. What do you mean, bad guys? These are children. There was a picture in the paper, a man carrying a child onto a boat. They're just refugees.

—But I think they're the ones who massacred the Tutsis. I think they're the Hutu, these refugees.

—Children didn't massacre anybody.

—Sometimes they did. And they were silent. A man with a dog came toward them, and Deborah called, Friendly! The man didn't answer.

—Good day for a walk! Deborah called.

—Don't, said Ruben.

—Don't what?

—Nothing. She didn't like Deborah's calling to strangers. She was too tired to be friends with everyone on earth, even people in foreign countries who massacred their distant cousins. Ruben had not read the story about the war in Zaire and the refugees. It was so complicated. You still think about dying babies, all the time, Ruben said.

—I do. I worry about our babies, still.

Ruben said, When they were little and we stayed home with them, I'd clean up their shit and walk in the park, thinking,

What if they die? But now I have other things to think about,
like pots and book orders.

—Oh, God, said Deborah. Book orders. I just got an e-mail
from my chair about book orders. Deborah taught full-time at
a college ten miles away. Ruben usually taught two courses at
two different nearby colleges, but just now she had only one.
Ruben worked many hours in the pottery store. Archie came
in only a few hours a week. Friday was her day off at the store,
but she taught on Saturday mornings. She was annoyed that
Deborah usually wanted to walk on Fridays when Ruben was
getting ready to teach.

Ruben was fatter than Deborah though, so she didn't turn
down the suggestion of a walk. Deborah was bony, these days,
and she was always walking, with or without Ruben. Ruben
looked for clothes that made her look thinner. She liked clothes
with buttons, flaps, and zippers, as if they sectioned her off
into acceptable parts. She was wearing a khaki shirt with flaps
buttoned down over her breasts, and a heavy sweater under it.

She got fatter when she worried, and she'd worried that fall
about Peter, who had dropped out of college and come home.
For a long time he just slept. Stevie would call from college and
demand to talk to him, and Ruben would awaken him. If she
tried to wake up Peter without being told to by Stevie, Peter
was angry, which might mean silence and might mean rage.
Now he had a job—a new job—but it didn't take many hours
of his week.

—Peter has a job, she said.

—Oh, that's great, said Deborah. I knew he'd be all right.

—I'm not sure it's great, and I'm not sure he's all right, said
Ruben. But it's a job. He's working for an artist, an old
woman.

—Doesn't he do art? Deborah said.

Since he was small, Peter had made things in the backyard
out of twigs and dirt and grass. No art student, nothing like

that, but he fiddled with things. This fall, all he'd done was iron autumn leaves between sheets of waxed paper, like a kindergartner. It had cheered him, but depressed Ruben. He'd come to the park to gather the leaves, and when he was done ironing them, he'd tape the waxed paper creations to the refrigerator. Ruben didn't know how much irony he intended, if any.

—Who's the artist? said Deborah.

—A sculptor, said Ruben. I think her name is Cooper.

—What does he do for her?

—Mostly he drives her to Stop and Shop, but I believe the idea is that he can help chisel the marble, or whatever sculptors do nowadays. She has an old car that she doesn't drive anymore, and she lets him drive it around.

—I don't think they chisel marble, said Deborah. Can you imagine how expensive that would be? Maybe she gets grants. Is she famous? The name sounds familiar.

—Not to me, said Ruben. Wasn't it always expensive? They didn't know. They were quiet for a while, not knowing, together, about the history of sculpture. As they walked, Ruben looked out for deer, but although there were deer in this park, she was sure they wouldn't see any. Of course the deer hid from the dogs. The dogs were friends and Granny followed Mac.

—I should have figured this out by now, Deborah said. I should have done book orders. They're making me teach two sections of freshman comp.

—I like freshman comp.

—You always did. I don't.

—I have this one lady, Ruben said. Then she said, I'm tired of my husband.

—What about the lady? said Deborah.

—I know, I'll get to the lady, but I hate Harry—doesn't that come first?

The trails were marked by color: the Blue Trail, the Yellow Trail. She was trying to remember which trail led to the North

Peak. Maybe they'd be lost—but they wouldn't be lost. They were too close to where they lived to be lost. They were perfectly safe. They were half a mile from the playground where they had met when the babies were little.

—It was a hard week, said Deborah.

—Husband, children, or work?

—Oh, all that. And the news. Toby, I still think about that woman all the time.

—What woman?

—My imaginary woman. Every time there's news about Rwanda, I think of her. I picture her sitting in some kind of building, and people come and yank her daughter out and shoot her. I always picture Mary Grace, but black.

—But she's imaginary, said Ruben. Maybe it didn't happen.

—What do you mean, Toby? There are thousands dead.

—I know, said Ruben, but maybe none of them happened to see their children shot. Maybe they got shot first. Maybe the kid was shot behind a tree.

—So she heard the gunshot! So what?

—It's sloppy to spend the whole week thinking of something that vague.

—Vague, said Deborah. I don't know what you call vague. You have a kindness defect, Toby.

Ruben felt bad for the woman whose child was shot, but she wanted to talk about Harry. Deborah wouldn't agree, but she, too, might be angry with her own husband, and Ruben liked to hear about Jeremiah, who still glittered, although less, and who had cried twice in Ruben's presence: when he'd knocked the art teacher off his bicycle, and then, five years later, when Jill turned up pregnant and had to have an abortion, Catholic or not.

—I'm sorry I have a kindness defect, she said, but let me tell you about Harry. Yesterday I went out for milk and fruit, and Harry saw me walking as he was driving home. So he parked the car and got out and walked with me.

—He didn't just give you a ride? Was that what made you angry?

—No, he felt like a walk. I did, too. It was just getting dark. I'd been at work at the store all day. I like the way things look at twilight at this time of year.

—I know, said Deborah. I love it every year. The trees are black and the sky is fluffy.

—We walked to Gagliardi's, she said. On the way back we passed a group of young black men hanging out, leaning on a car. It was that block on Porter where there's parking on only one side of the street, because it's so narrow, and cars were going by fast. One of the men was holding a baby. I saw him hold it up—a three-month, dangly sort of baby.

—I know what you mean, said Deborah.

But the story was not going to be interesting. She had thought, all day, that it was interesting. She went on, though. The baby was overwhelmed by its clothes.

—Right.

—He sat the baby on the roof of the car. As we passed, he lowered his head and kissed the baby's face. It was in a floppy hood. He had to burrow in to kiss it. I saw the baby's curled hand, and it was white. I was so happy, watching them, Deborah. I said, That baby's hand is white. And Harry said, So what? And I said, So nothing. It was just interesting. And Harry said, You think he kidnapped a white baby? You think it's not safe to put him there, with the cars whizzing by?

—Was that what you thought? said Deborah.

—Of course not.

—It doesn't sound safe. What *did* you think?

—I don't know what I thought, said Ruben. I thought nothing. I thought looks. The way it looked—like a painting. Maybe the baby wasn't white. Maybe it was a trick of the light. Maybe he looked white under a streetlight, or in a passing headlight.

—African-American people have light-colored palms, said
Deborah.

—No, it was the baby's fist, Ruben said. But it wasn't important. I mean, it wasn't *racial*.

—Maybe his wife is white.

—No, that's just my point. I mean, maybe she is. I don't know. But it wasn't racial.

—But why did you talk about the baby's color then? said Deborah.

—Because I could see it. I was talking about what I saw. Like a painter. Like Peter. But Harry. He just jumps to the nearest category. I say black person, white hand, he thinks the history of race in America. If I said fur coat he'd think baby seals getting clubbed. I might just mean fur coat.

—I don't think you can mean just fur coat anymore.

—Bad example. I thought, I have to divorce this man. He is keeping me from thinking.

—I know, I know, said Deborah, and now Ruben knew she would talk about Jeremiah. All of a sudden you hate them, said Deborah. All of a sudden, after all these years, you cannot stand them. What I cannot stand about Jeremiah is he pees like a waterfall. I hear it all over the house.

—Does he leave the door open?

—Sometimes, but even if he doesn't.

—Day after day, you don't mind it . . .

Deborah said, I remember minding it even before we got married. But it gets to me more lately. I thought I was a better person than that. Is that menopause, when you can't stand the sound of your husband peeing?

—You think he pees less often so more comes out? said Ruben.

—I don't know. He pees pretty often.

—Maybe it's the way he aims it that makes it so loud.

—Is your period heavier these days? Deborah said. Mine is heavier. I think it's menopause.

—I don't have periods very often.

—Imagine, said Deborah. No periods. No more moozum.

—No more what?

—Menstrual blood, said Deborah.

Ruben wondered if she'd mind loud peeing.

Deborah said, So did you fight with Harry about the baby with the white hand?

—Oh, I did. Of course he didn't know what I was talking about. I didn't, either. I didn't even want to know. I didn't want to understand it. That would mean *I* was thinking in categories.

Deborah didn't answer and they walked on the trail. They scuffed the damp leaves with their feet. It was darker under the trees. Ruben liked the feel of the leaves. She wanted to step through leaves. The dogs circled back to them and Granny came over and stretched her round, gray head up to be stroked. She liked to make sure everyone was there. They came to a fork and Ruben remembered which path to take. The trail began to climb. Around them in the woods, the leaves still on the trees were dark red and dark orange. Ruben took off her sunglasses and put them away, even though she didn't have her clear glasses. But she wanted to see the true color of the leaves, even if she couldn't see their exact shapes.

Deborah said, One of my students said something I never expected. We were talking about Halloween. Of course we weren't talking about Halloween, that makes it sound like first grade. We were talking about Toni Morrison and somebody talked about ghosts, because you know she writes about ghosts a lot.

—I get bored with her ghosts, said Ruben.

—Somebody said Halloween ghosts are different, Deborah said. And one of the students said, When the ghost of my aunt comes to see me, we play checkers.

—Did she mean it?

—I don't know. She has a nose ring.

—Did anybody laugh?

—Nobody laughed.

—Does she really see the ghost of her aunt? said Ruben.

—I told you about it, said Deborah, because it was unexpected. You wanted Harry to say something unexpected.

—Yes, that's right! said Ruben. That's *exactly* right.

—The point of the man kissing the baby, said Deborah, could be men and babies. It doesn't have to be race.

—Why does it need a point? said Ruben.

—Good point, said Deborah, and laughed.

Ruben said, This student hates me.

—My student?

—My student.

—So what? said Deborah. That was the matter with Deborah as a teacher. She didn't mind being hated. But maybe it was good to be hated, and Ruben taught in a foolish blob of good fellowship, despite her kindness defect. Could a person with a kindness defect teach in a foolish blob of good fellowship? Yes, unfortunately, thought Ruben in an instant. The good fellowship wasn't real. She was competitive. She was nice to the students so they'd think she was the best imaginable teacher. She said, Well, I don't want to be hated. She doesn't hate me. She disapproves of me. She's the youngest in the class. I have all these prejudices. I think the youngest should be the most lighthearted.

—I forget what you're teaching this term.

—Freshman comp to grown-ups, same as before. Saturday morning. Deborah, why can't you *remember*?

—But today's Friday. Why aren't you home getting ready?

—Good question.

—I mean it, said Deborah.

—You're the one who insisted on Friday, Ruben said.

—I didn't know.

—I've been teaching on Saturday mornings for five years.

—I thought it changed. I thought it was Tuesday evening.

—Last spring. In addition to Saturdays. Never mind.

—Why are you angry? said Deborah.

—I'm not angry.

—You are. Of course you are.

—I'm not. Anyway, I guess she's twenty-eight. Most of them are in their forties. She works for the phone company. First she's angry because I don't start on time. Her name is Maddy and she's always mad at me. But I wait, because I feel sorry for the people who drive a distance. They come in with coffee and two doughnuts apiece.

—You let them eat in class? I'd never do that, said Deborah.

—But I learned from you! You let those women eat in class, back in the GED program.

—Oh, no. I wouldn't do that. Do you eat?

—No, said Ruben, but I get coffee at the break. There's a coffee machine. It's magic. It's supposed to dispense coffee, milk, and a cup, and it almost always does. *But not in the same order each time.*

—You mean sometimes the milk comes before the coffee and sometimes after?

—No. Deborah's sense of humor was faulty. She had a humor defect. No, Deborah. Sometimes the *cup* comes before the coffee and sometimes after.

—But then you can't drink it.

—Right. You watch it go by. Anyway, this young woman, Maddy, disapproves of my coffee. When I complain about the cup coming last, she says it doesn't happen to her.

But they were reaching the peak. The White Trail crossed the Blue Trail, and Ruben picked it up, though at this point it didn't matter. The peak was right before them. They could see it, an outcropping of stones. They climbed silently. The dogs raced off through the woods below them. Maybe they'd heard an animal, or smelled one. Ruben could see both dogs a long way off through the bare trees. Then she watched them come back.

The North Peak was just a little peak with a few rocks on
top. They each stood on a rock. They could see the woods
below them, and a piece of the city beyond the woods. The sun
was just setting, bright red. The wind had come up. Ruben
stepped off her rock and put an arm on Deborah's shoulder.
This raincoat is sticky, she said.

—It's not warm enough, Deborah said.

Deborah mussed Ruben's hair and she mussed Deborah's.
Do you want to go? Deborah said.

—I want to see the sun set, said Ruben.

The sun was a red disk opposite them. It would disappear
behind a hill, but not for a while. Deborah was impatient. Mac
whined. Ruben took her sunglasses from her pocket. She also
had a small bottle of eyeglass cleaner, and she cleaned them
and wiped them with a tissue. Deborah took a drink of Poland
Spring and gave Ruben a drink.

—Are you cold? Ruben said.

—I'm worried that it will get dark. We won't be able to find
our way back.

—Oh, the woods are so small, the trails are just for fun,
really. We just walk downhill.

—I don't know, said Deborah. You could wander around
here for a while.

—You think they'll find our skeletons?

—No, I don't think they'll find our *skeletons*.

At last a chunk of sun went behind the hill, and then it
seemed to move faster. When the sun set, the air became less
red. It was grayer and colder right away. Ruben watched a little
while longer, then she turned, belatedly worried about Deborah
in her thin raincoat, and led the way down.

The spot just below them was flatter and freer of underbrush
than most of the woods, and the dogs ran ahead. Then they
ran back and forth, side to side, in the flat place. Then Ruben
heard someone coming. She thought she saw the whole woods

spread out ahead of her, but someone she didn't see was coming. Maybe there was a trail around the peak.

Ruben and Deborah walked side by side for a few yards, and then Deborah stepped ahead. They were awkward, shuffling down the short steep stretch just below the peak. What a middle-aged lady Deborah was, in her raincoat, her hands grabbing air on both sides of her for balance. Again Ruben heard someone rustling, and then someone stepped out of the woods just to the left of where they were coming down, a man wearing something white. He stopped, and at first Ruben thought he had seen them and was waiting for them, but then she thought he was peeing—like noisy Jeremiah—and she wasn't sure, but she thought she might hear the sound of his urine hitting the leaves. He was just far enough away that she didn't know whether Deborah had seen him or not. When they came closer he was zipping his fly. The dogs circled back and approached him, and Granny barked.

—Cool it, the man said to Granny, who did not stop barking. The man crouched and Ruben was afraid he might be feeling for a stone.

—Granny, she called.

The man eyed Granny and stood up. Those people took everything I had, he said.

—What people? said Deborah.

The man took a worn leather wallet out of his pocket. The people at the crossing.

—I don't know what you mean, Deborah said.

—I never bothered them, he said. He had on a dark sweater over a white shirt. He was a youngish man, maybe in his thirties.

—Did they ask you for money? Ruben said.

—I gave them all my money.

—Was it a man with a dog? said Deborah. He's the only person we've seen.

—Are you in a hurry? said the man.

—Yes, said Deborah. She started walking.

Ruben didn't know whether to be afraid of the man or concerned for him. Where are you going? she said.

—It's getting dark, Deborah said.

—Take care, said Ruben.

Deborah was already ahead of her, the raincoat looking brighter in the dusk. It looked very manmade. Ruben followed the raincoat. The dogs were ahead with Deborah, then Granny came back to her. For a while she wondered whether the man would follow or even hurt them. She didn't like keeping him behind her when she couldn't see him. They came to the intersection of two trails, and Deborah looked back at her for directions. Ruben stepped into the right-hand trail, which she was almost sure was correct, but in truth she wasn't certain.

—Did you ever go to Barcelona? Deborah said.

—No.

—When I was in Barcelona, said Deborah, one night I was alone in a bar. A man spoke to me, and I went for a walk with him. He was Swedish. He spoke English with a beautiful accent. He kept telling me how much he hated Barcelona, and after a while I noticed it was because of everything everyone else liked about it, the liveliness and the history. He was afraid of himself. He told me he was afraid he might hurt me or kill me. I didn't want to run away, because it would let him do what he was picturing. It would be like joining him in his mind.

—What did you do? I can't believe you never told me this story.

—I slept with him.

—I can't believe that, said Ruben.

—Well, I did. Then when he was still naked in his hotel room, I picked up my clothes and went out into the corridor before he could stop me. I'd been careful to leave them in a pile, despite my passion. I really was terribly attracted to him. I knew he wouldn't follow me without clothes on. I was praying. I was praying to Jeremiah as well as God—it was just after we'd met, but he was home in the States. I thought somebody might see me come out naked, but it would be better than dying. Nobody did, though.

—A nice Catholic girl! Ruben said. Then she said, Did you see? That man was peeing.

—He was masturbating.

—No, he was peeing. My god.

—He was masturbating, said Deborah.

—Why did you talk to him?

—You talked to him more than I did. You have to prove there's no such thing as crime by talking to a criminal.

—He was a harmless nut, said Ruben. What would a criminal be doing in the woods?

—The woods are a good place for crime.

—But nobody comes here, said Ruben.

—We come here.

—You think he waited all day for us? said Ruben. If I were a criminal, I'd have more important things to do.

—I think you'd like being a criminal, Deborah said.

—I would, I would, said Ruben. Wouldn't you?

—No, said Deborah. I don't want to hurt anybody.

—And you think I do? said Ruben.

—I think sometimes you do.

Now they walked in twilight. They crossed a paved road that was closed to traffic, and Ruben knew they were in the right place. They stepped back into the woods on the other side, and Ruben was aware of the greater darkness, though she could see the trail. The dogs had no trouble. She wished she had her other glasses. She was still wearing her sunglasses. Things were too blurry-edged without glasses.

What was it Deborah had just said? Something twisted inside Ruben, as if something in her body—below her neck, above her stomach—tightened or rose against her.

—Everybody likes to hurt people at times, she said.

—Well, you think that, said Deborah. You forgive yourself a lot.

—You think I forgive myself for something I shouldn't?

—Oh, you let yourself fight with Harry. You let yourself say things to me. There's a lot of letting going on. Especially about Peter.

—Well, I don't hide things. That's true, said Ruben.

—I just think you should watch yourself.

—I've spent my life watching myself. Then she said, What about Peter? Do you think Peter's in worse shape than I know?

Deborah said, Oh, I guess Peter's all right. But sometimes it takes my breath away, the things you say to him. You have no tact, Toby. You forget he's only a kid. You loom over him.

—He's twenty-one!

—But to him, you're still a grown-up, and he's a kid. I'm sure you do things to him—well, like the way you talked to me. When I talked about my student, and the ghost of her aunt. I could just feel you thinking, What stupidity is going on in that classroom!

—But I wasn't thinking that.

—You don't think I'm a good teacher, said Deborah.

—I think you're a great teacher!

—No, you don't. You think I'm just going through a set routine and the students don't get their lives changed. You're always talking about how your students change. Even this one who hates you. Is this a full-year course?

—Yes.

—Well, I guarantee you by April you'll have some great thing going with this student. You'll love each other. I'll be certain that nobody understands love but you.

—I don't think this is fair, said Ruben.

—Well, probably it isn't, Deborah said.

They came to the trailhead in silence. Now they walked on the park path. Ruben had to hurry home or the chicken wouldn't be cooked in time for supper. But she said, Sometimes I suddenly see myself through your eyes, and it scares me.

—Well, you scare other people.

—Do I scare you?

—I never know what you're going to say, said Deborah.

—You want to know what I'm going to say?

—No.

—That would be boring, if you knew what I was going to say. We just agreed that, didn't we?

—Well, of course. But you're critical.

—I don't think I'm more critical than you, Ruben said.

—How could you say that? You want to divorce Harry just because he thinks you mean race when you don't?

—I didn't really want to divorce him.

—Oh, I know that. I'm not that dumb. But I wonder what you'll want to do to me the next time I misunderstand you.

Ruben held Deborah's arm. Deborah, I love you.

—I know you love me. But all the same, sometimes I'm at the lower limit of what you can stand.

—No.

She followed Deborah home. She couldn't separate at the corner. You have to tell me you don't think these things! she said.

But Deborah wouldn't. How about Janet? she said. How about what happened with Janet Grey?

—Oh, Janet Grey, Janet Grey. That was ten years ago.

—I should forget it, I know . . .

—You will never forget Janet Grey!

—Why did you do it?

Ruben had done it. She had told Janet Grey she wasn't sure Deborah was a good teacher, and Janet Grey had fired Deborah. Two years later, Janet had made friends again with Deborah, and that was what she said.

Deborah said, Maybe a little dull. That's what she said you said.

—I know. I know that's what she told you. I just don't remember it.

They stood in the light of the streetlight. It was cold, and
Ruben had to go home and make supper. She looked up at
Deborah. I'm sorry, she said.

—I know you're sorry, Deborah said. I have to go home. I'm
going to see my mother after dinner.

—Your mother? Tonight?

—It's only an hour away. I'll stay over.

—But you never mentioned your mother. I don't know
what's happening with her.

—Oh, the same. She fell. She didn't break anything, but she's
bruised. And I haven't seen her for two weeks. Tomorrow I'll
help with her shopping.

—I'm sorry we didn't talk about your mother.

—It's all right. Deborah hugged her lightly and walked away,
and Mac followed her.

—Wait, said Ruben. She ran after Deborah, and when Deborah turned she took Deborah's head in her hands and kissed
her on the mouth.

Deborah said, Hey, it's all right. She touched the tip of
Ruben's nose and turned away.

Ruben walked home. Her house looked dark. Ruben stepped
into her square front foyer. She stood still. The living room and
dining room and Harry's study were dark, and in front of her
the wooden staircase looked smooth and elegant in the dark,
though she knew it needed to be scraped and stained. Beyond
the stairs, there was a light in the kitchen. She was cold. Once
the sun had gone down, she'd wanted a hat and coat. Granny
went into the kitchen, and she heard Harry greet the dog. She
didn't call out, but went upstairs and took off most of her
clothes. She put on sweatpants, slippers, a turtleneck, and her
longest, loosest, oldest sweater. She was still protesting to Deborah, scared and apologetic, and also angry, because she knew

Deborah was nutty at such times; and also not angry, because Deborah was right.

Now she went downstairs and into the kitchen. Granny's water dish was empty. I thought you were Peter, Harry said.

They heard Peter come in. I'm microwaving that spaghetti sauce, said Harry.

—There's a chicken, said Ruben.

Harry said, Did you find my watch?

—Is it missing?

—I told you it was missing. I guess you didn't find it.

—When did you tell me?

—This morning.

Peter said, I didn't take it. Honest, I didn't take it. He cringed and squeaked.

—I know, I know, said Harry.

—How's your sculptor? said Ruben.

—Oh, she's good, Peter said. She's always good. Good and rich.

—Rich in money, or rich in something else? Harry said.

—Not rich in money. Rich in marriages, said Peter. She was married three times.

—And they're all gone? said Harry.

—All the husbands gone. Maybe I'll be the fourth. She's started a book. She can't see well enough to type. Or so she says. I think she just likes the shock effect—dictating and watching me react.

—What's her book about? Ruben said.

—Her life, mostly in the fifties so far, when she lived in Malta. She had a husband who cut off her hair while she slept. He sold it.

—Like in O. Henry but backwards, said Ruben.

—That's right, Peter said. You know that story, The Gift of the Magi? Well, this is The Madge of the Gifti.

Harry said, Which story is that? and Ruben said it was about

a woman who sells her hair to buy the man a watch fob while
the man sells his watch to buy her combs.

Harry said, I've never known what a watch fob is.

—I don't know, either, said Peter.

Ruben got the chicken ready. She would cook it in a pot on
top of the stove because she was so cold. There would be good
hot broth. Deborah made me feel bad, she said.

—Oh, you're always upsetting each other. Toby, I'm
cooking.

—What are you cooking?

—Spaghetti. I told you. I'm heating that sauce.

—There isn't enough. We'll have chicken, too. She filled
Granny's water dish and fed her. Granny lay under the table,
already asleep, but she got up and walked over stiffly when
Ruben put her dish down.

Ruben put the chicken into the pot with water and an onion.
There was still parsley in the garden. She went out in the dark,
getting cold again, to find it.

Harry said, What did the sculptor's husband do with the
money when he sold her hair?

—It must have been nice hair, Peter said. He got a lot of
money.

—What did he buy?

—He bought loot, I guess. She's always talking about loot.

—She was stubborn, he continued, after a pause to open a
beer. They were poor and she wouldn't do anything to help.

—Why didn't he sell something of his own? said Ruben.

—His watch, said Harry. That's what you did with my
watch, Toby, you sold it.

Peter laughed and laughed. Then he said, I made most of
that up. I made most of that up about her hair.

—You mean he didn't sell her hair?

—She said he gave her a haircut while she was sleeping.
That's all she said.

—What about the Madge of the Gifti?

—I made that up, said Peter.

It worried her; she wanted to just find it amusing, that he turned and turned like that, but she couldn't. She wondered if the sculptor minded. Maybe she liked it. The water for the spaghetti boiled. She wondered if this sculptor called Cooper might like to know her.

—She stayed married to him a long time, Peter said.

—Is *this* true? She tried not to sound harsh. What would Deborah say about the way she sounded?

—Oh, yes, this is true.

—Did they have kids?

—I don't think so.

They carried plates of spaghetti into the dining room. Ruben took only a little, leaving room for chicken, but Peter and Harry ate and wandered away. When the chicken and broth were ready, Ruben ate some. She drank wine all by herself.

Peter came back into the kitchen while Ruben was still eating. He took a beer from the refrigerator, opened it, and came to sit with her. I'm attracted to Cooper, he said.

—Really?

—Sort of. She has short white hair that sticks out from her head and I want to press it to her head. He spread his long hands.

—Well, I'm glad, said Ruben. That's the sort of surprising feeling I wanted you to know about, when I was trying to grow you.

—I'm glad you're glad. When you were trying to grow both of us?

—Of course. Then Ruben said, I want to meet Cooper.

—Oh, I think that could be arranged.

—Are you working this weekend?

—A little, said Peter. She wants me to drive her someplace. Ruben finished her chicken. She scraped her plate into the garbage and went for her teaching folder. She still had five papers to mark and then she'd plan her class. She was tired and achy, as if she might catch cold. Peter drank his beer and Ruben settled down to work at the dining room table.

This time she'd asked the students to write two letters, each making the same argument, one to a friend and one to a stranger. The first paper she looked at that evening was about the broken computers at the public library. The student pretended to write one to her cousin and the other to the mayor. The students wrote lively letters to their friends and boring letters to the mayor; they thought it was inappropriate to be interesting when writing to the mayor.

The next paper was Maddy's. She'd taken the opposite position in the two letters. Maddy wrote a letter to her boss, thanking him for her job evaluation. She said, I sincerely appreciate your many constructive suggestions. In the letter to her friend, she said the boss was crazy and that she disagreed with everything he'd said.

Ruben wrote, You didn't follow instructions.

Peter left the room.

The next two papers were short. While she was reading the next to the last one, the phone rang. It was a little late for a call. She hoped it wasn't for her. She stood up. She'd been sitting on her foot and it was asleep. She shook it as she picked up the phone, wondering where in the house Harry and Peter were.

—Toby, said the voice. It's Jeremiah. Deborah was in an accident. She's in the hospital.

She couldn't speak. She kept nodding, knowing while she was nodding that Jeremiah couldn't see her. Deborah had had an accident on the way to her mother's house. A driver had lost control of his car and crossed the median divider and rammed into her car. The hospital had called Jeremiah, and he'd had to call her mother. He didn't know how bad it was. Now he was leaving for the hospital.

—But what's wrong with her? Ruben said, even though he'd said he didn't know.

—I don't know. I'll call you. Would you let the dog out in the morning?

—Of course.

—I have to go.

—Wait!

—What?

—Nothing, she said. I love you both.

—I'd better go. He hung up.

She held on to the phone, then she heard the dial tone and hung up. She was sitting. At some point while listening to Jeremiah, she'd sat down and pulled her chair up to the table. Now she had to stand up and walk around the table to hang up the phone. Her arm hurt from holding the receiver. She hung up and sat down in the nearest chair and rubbed her arm.

She pictured flames, and Deborah in the raincoat. Maybe there were no flames. Probably Deborah had been wearing a jacket, not the raincoat. If nothing much was wrong, the hospital would have told Jeremiah what was wrong. She couldn't stop imagining flames, though he had said nothing about fire. A car was in flames and Ruben ran to the car, but the door was locked. She made herself imagine opening the door and pulling Deborah out, wrapping her in a blanket. She pictured a white blanket with a blue border she kept folded on a chair in her bedroom in case of an unusually cold night. In her mind she held it with her arms stretched wide and then stepped toward Deborah, who was clothed in flame, and wrapped first one arm and then the other around her friend in a saving, smothering hug. But in Ruben's mind the flames continued out each end, at Deborah's head and feet, and soon the body she was hugging was diminished, though the flames were gone, and she was afraid to open the blanket.

Peter came into the room. Deborah's in the hospital, Ruben said.

—What happened?

—She was in a car accident.

—Weren't you just with her?

—She went to her mother's after supper.

—How bad is it?

—I don't know.

She had trouble talking loudly enough for Peter to hear her. He walked out of the room and now Ruben began to cry. It was as if Peter had known more than she did and walked out of the room so as not to tell her. She cried only a little. She didn't have the breath to cry. She saw the papers she'd been marking on the table. They looked sweet. Three of them happened to be in the arrangement of a fan, spread out, and others were upside down near them, but they were all spread wide, as if a trusting, innocent person had been reading them and pushing them energetically and happily around. She had not been happy. She'd been tense about Deborah.

Harry came running. What happened?

—Deborah's in the hospital.

—Which hospital?

—I don't know. Where her mother lives.

—Where does her mother live? Maybe we can call and find out.

Ruben couldn't remember the name of the town where Deborah's mother lived. Ten or twelve years ago she had gone there with Deborah and the children to adopt Mac. They'd driven for about an hour, she thought. Harry began naming towns, but they weren't right. Ruben said, No, you're going in the wrong direction.

Harry named towns an hour in the other direction. About some of them, Peter, who had come in behind him, said, That's less than an hour.

—Depending on traffic, said Harry.

—But even if we know the name of the town, said Peter, we won't know the name of the hospital.

—We'll call her mother, said Harry. It's intolerable not to know more.

Ruben was afraid to know more. And surely Deborah's mother had gone to the hospital. She'd have called a neighbor to take her. Still, they could try. Deborah's mother's last name was Walker, a common name.

Harry called directory assistance, asking for Walkers in town after town. Ruben couldn't remember Mrs. Walker's first name. She thought it might be Elizabeth. There were dozens of people named Walker, and many named E. Walker.

—I didn't plan my class, she said. She was so tired.

—Cancel, said Peter.

—I can't, Ruben said. They come from so far. They'd come for nothing and find a note on the door. She sat down and straightened the unruly papers. She lowered her head and cried.

—She may have minor injuries, said Harry.

—Jeremiah sounded scared.

So they went, back and forth.

Wearing her nightgown, she was still dialing directory assistance. It was too late to call Deborah's mother, and she had no way of knowing which of these many people—she kept writing down numbers—was Deborah's mother. If any. She called none of them. Late at night, the phone rang. Ruben, awake in bed, seized it, but it was Stevie.

—I wanted to talk about Thanksgiving, he said.

—Stevie.

—What is it, Mom? Is something wrong with Squirrel?

She told him. How bad? said Stevie.

—I don't know. When the phone rang, I thought maybe it was Jeremiah.

—Probably it's not bad. There's no reason for it to be bad. Mom, I don't know what I feel.

—About Deborah?

—No, about Jessica. I called to talk about Jessica. I want her to come home with me for Thanksgiving. But I don't know.

—I forgot about Thanksgiving.

—She doesn't have much money, but that's not it. She has enough for a ticket. Or I can help with the ticket. She loves me, no doubt about it.

—That's good.

—But if I let her come . . . We have fights about it.

—Baby, love. I need to hang up.

—Don't worry. Deborah will be all right. I'm sorry. I've just been thinking all night about Jessica, and I called her, but she was angry.

—Why was she angry?

—Oh, she was writing a paper. She didn't want to talk.

—And now your mother isn't letting you talk, either.

—It's not the same, Stevie said. I won't cry over it.

—No, don't cry over it. Ruben felt as if she had been awakened. It was dark in the room. Maybe she'd been asleep. Harry had turned over and fallen asleep again.

—Don't you cry about Deborah, Stevie said.

—I don't know whether I should or not.

—Jeremiah will call in the morning.

She slept again. At least Stevie wasn't in the hospital. She woke and got out of bed and went to a window. I'm sorry, she told Deborah. I'm sorry I told Janet Grey you are a dull teacher. Oh, you are, you are. Students say it about you. I have seen you teach. But I love everything about you, dull or not. I want to touch your neck and your back.

She didn't know what was hurt. Deborah might look different. She might be paralyzed, and Ruben could heroically push her in a wheelchair for the rest of their lives.

In the morning she thought, But I don't have a key. How could she let Mac out without a key? She was not frightened about Deborah now, but worried about Mac, who would need to go out. Of course Deborah was all right. It was probably just a fracture. Of course the hospital had called Jeremiah, because when you end up in the hospital, they call your husband.

She took a shower. Harry was still asleep. Peter had gone out late and she hadn't heard him come home, but things had been moved in the night. His sweatshirt was on the hamper in the bathroom. On the table in the hall was a small cardboard box that looked as if it had held paper clips a long time ago. The writing was rubbed off. She didn't look inside. She ate breakfast.

Ruben always walked to the college, for the exercise and because driving still made her tense, and she had to drive to the pottery store day after day. Today she'd need extra time, so she could figure out how to let Mac out. She stuffed her papers into her briefcase. She was trying to teach her students that there are words, she thought wearily. Her students used words, sometimes well, but they had never noticed themselves using words. Every week she gave them a poem to read. They complained that poems were hard, and she laughed at them. By now the giving and receiving of a poem was an act of love, though the women (this year, all the students were women) still made a point of pretending to be outraged. Not another one, they'd say. What's *this* one about? *What* are these oranges?

—I give you poems because I love you, she'd said last week. Some of them looked ready to cry, their plump middle-aged made-up faces distorted with affection. She'd glanced at Maddy, who looked disgusted.

Today was colder than the day before, bright and sunny. She walked alone, hearing her own footsteps. Then a runner passed in sweatshirt and shorts, a tall, gray-bearded man she'd seen before who ran with great leaps like a deer, making a scalloped path in air, and like a deer he seemed slow when he was air-borne. She wanted to be that man, or to run with him. She imagined he was a psychoanalyst: at peace with trouble in the soul. I hurt my friend and she is hurt, she would say to him.

At Deborah's house she tried the doors, but of course they were locked. She looked under an overturned flowerpot. She walked slowly around the building. She had allowed extra time,

but not much. She was worried about Mac. It was as though
Deborah were trapped in the house. Mac watched from inside.
Mac, she said tearfully, open the door.

She stood crying and examining doors and windows for a
long time. At last she tried the basement windows, which were
old. She knew Deborah and Jeremiah didn't have an alarm. She
crouched in the alley next to the house and pushed as hard as
she could on one of the low, wide basement windows. But it
opened out. It had a hinge at the top and a metal toggle that
swiveled up and down into a well on the sill. Ruben laid down
her briefcase. She searched in the backyard for a rock. I
mustn't, I mustn't, she told herself, but she found a broken
brick with an edge and saying Life before property, plunged it
into the glass.

The glass tinkled and Ruben sat back and looked around,
frightened. No one came. Her hand was cut, and a shard clung
to it. She pulled it out. Deliberately she broke off enough glass
to put her hand in, and she reached inside and opened the hasp.
The window stuck. She banged the brick on the frame. At last
it budged, and opened. The opening was small and dirty.
Ruben in her teaching clothes considered whether to go in
faceup or -down. Down. She held the window open with one
arm and put her legs into the opening. Then she twisted until
she was facedown. The window fell on her shoulders, and she
cried again, but she was able to reach up, from inside now,
and hold it. She was just small enough to squeeze in. She had
to twist her shoulders. She turned her face to the side. Her legs
found something, but it gave way. She scraped her arms getting
in, but then she was inside—elated. She had saved Deborah.

She swatted at cobwebs on her arms and face. She had
knocked over a small table. She righted it, reached up to lock—
pointlessly—the broken window, went upstairs, and opened
the door into Deborah's kitchen. She stepped into the yellow
room, startled, though she had known where she was going.
On the table and in the sink were dirty dishes. Deborah must

have left right after supper, and Jeremiah was getting around to cleaning up when the call came. The plates on the table held scraps of lettuce and something dark. Mac came to meet her. He barked once, then wagged his tail and licked her hand. There was blood on it, and now she saw a spot of blood on the floor. She bent to kiss Mac's yellow head and let him out the back door.

There was something Ruben ought to do here, but she couldn't think what it was. She went into the bathroom, washed her hands and face, found a Band-Aid, and tried to brush off her coat. Then she thought of the phone. Maybe Deborah's mother's number would be written on the wall next to it. But no numbers were posted. She picked up the phone and looked at it. It was the kind with a memory, but she couldn't tell whose numbers were in it. Would Deborah's mother be number one? Ruben pushed the button and heard the extended tune of a long distance number. The phone rang three times and then a sleepy young voice said hello.

—Mary Grace? Sweetie?

—This is Jill.

—I'm sorry, said Ruben. It's Toby. I'm at your house. Did your father call you last night?

—It's pretty bad, said Jill, who sounded rational, as always, but scared.

—Your mother.

—They don't know if she's going to make it. I'm coming home today. Jill was in law school in California.

—Jill. I didn't know—

—Then why did you call me? Jill said in a clear, puzzled, but not unfriendly voice, as if she welcomed the distraction of a small social mystery.

—I knew . . . I knew something. What happened?

—Someone slammed into her.

—You mean she might die?

—I couldn't get a flight last night. I'm glad you woke me up.
I'd better go.

—Jill.

—What? You're sorry about my mom. I know. 'Bye, Toby.

Ruben hung up the phone and walked through Deborah's exuberant yellow kitchen, neater now that the girls had moved out (Rose was a teacher in Boston and Mary Grace was doing badly in her sophomore year at the University of Massachusetts at Amherst), but full of light and funny pottery. Ruben didn't have time to clean the kitchen. Her body felt insubstantial, bruised from breaking in, but light, as if it didn't touch things. She opened the door and Mac came in. She locked it again. She would be late to class. She didn't know if Deborah was conscious. She moved through the sunny, dust-flecked air in Deborah's house. Everything—even the dirty dishes—seemed expectant. What if she didn't go to class? But she let herself out the front door, pulled it shut, and tested it. For a moment she panicked about the briefcase, but then she remembered it in the alley. Now she walked so fast her stomach began to hurt. Then slowly. She often waited for her students. Today they could wait for her.

She had not planned the class. She had not planned it, and now Deborah might die. Maybe Jill had misunderstood, but of course she wouldn't. Once, when Jill was about six, she had run back and forth between Ruben and Deborah, kissing their legs; later she'd turned serious and withheld. She'd spent a year traveling through Asia when she was halfway through college, and her parents hadn't heard from her for weeks. The day she was six and kissed their legs, she had run faster and faster. Ruben remembered the little kisses on her bare knees. They all wore shorts; it must have been summer. One for *you*, Jill had called, and *you*. And *you*. And *you*. At last she had slapped them each lightly instead of kissing them, and run away.

How could Ruben live if Deborah died? Of course it was

partly Ruben's fault. She hadn't driven the car that slammed into Deborah's, but she'd delayed Deborah with anger, the sunset, and kisses. Worse, Ruben had been pummeling Deborah's life for years and years. Everything in it had been at least slightly changed by obnoxious, ever present Ruben. Deborah was her only work of genius, whom she had never appreciated and whom she had made incorrectly anyway. She'd made Deborah wrong, after all, and now Deborah had been hurt, probably for want of right making, and Ruben didn't know what to do.

Her students, many of them mothers, understood sorrow. It was the kind of group that could be told, but telling would probably be a bad idea.

The class was three hours long. That was always scary, but ordinarily Ruben planned it in sections, so it seemed shorter. First, while the students were sleepy and silent, she taught them about apostrophes or run-on sentences. Next she teased and scolded about the papers she was returning. Then came the assignment; then, invariably, an argument about the poem of the week . . .

It was a long walk. She should have gone home from Deborah's and taken the car, but it hadn't occurred to her and now she was too far along. She walked past silent houses, wondering whether people in them were sobbing with grief for someone sick or hurt.

—God, she said, in the quiet street, and screamed a little. God didn't care. She stopped and pressed her face into the hard, rough bark of a tree, but only for a moment.

When she reached the college, a little place, she saw no one. The dorms were elsewhere, the residential students asleep. Some years, hers was the only Saturday morning class. She was ten minutes late. In the ladies' room she washed her face again. Her shoulders hurt. She didn't know why, then remembered the window falling on her. She hoped nobody would break into the house through the broken window. Deborah would be

proud of her, not angry, for breaking it. They'd joke about
Mac's trials of conscience and bladder control. Or maybe Deborah would tease. They'd walk in the woods again, years from
now. You were hysterical, Deborah would say, still making fun
of her years later. All I needed was a collar for whiplash. And
you're breaking windows!

The classroom was plain, with harsh lights and metal chairs,
but it had become dear. Ruben liked it, as she had come to
love the rolls of colored ribbon and the cranky cash register at
the pottery store. The green chalkboard had an aluminum sill
shaped in channels so the chalk would not roll. Years of chalk
dust had softened the look of the metal so it looked like pewter.
She liked resting her fingers in the channels when she stood at
the chalkboard. She wrote happily on the green chalkboard and
each year was teased for bad handwriting. The students' writing was always better.

Another comfort was a lectern made of oak, which sat on
the teacher's desk. Ruben, when she sat, used a student's desk.
When she talked, she stood and walked. She couldn't stand still
long enough to lean on the lectern. Each Saturday she moved
it from the desk to the floor beside it so she could dump out
her briefcase on the desk. The lectern was the room's only
wooden object, and she appreciated its weight and grain. Today it had already been moved. The students were waiting,
their chairs in a semicircle. Maddy looked annoyed.

—I'm sorry, said Ruben. She counted them. Who's missing?
Rosemary and Chris were missing. One day Maddy had said,
If you had a list . . .

But Ruben liked names. She liked learning and saying their
names, and knowing them so well she knew who was missing.
Somewhere was a stack of cards. She said, I want to talk about
its.

—I always get it wrong. Did I get it wrong? said small gray-
haired Lillian, from the last chair.

—You all get it wrong constantly, said Ruben. The jokey

tone felt phony at first, and her voice was unsteady, as if the joke might turn to a sob, but then she was all right.

—So maybe we're right and you're wrong, said June. Majority rules.

—A likely idea, Lynne said. She was younger, fat, and cynical.

Ruben babbled about "its," half remembering. She said, The poet Milton used the word *its* twice in *Paradise Lost*. Before that, people wrote "his." June's thoughts, she wrote. She said, They used to write June his thoughts. Was that true? How was it relevant?

—Why not June her thoughts?

—I don't have any thoughts.

—This is a little elementary, said Louise, a friend of Maddy's.

—But Toby says we get it wrong, said Lillian, calling across the room to Louise.

Most of them called her Toby. A few said Ms. Ruben and one or two said Mrs. Ruben. Norma, the oldest, who left her coat on, called her Mrs. Ruben and she said it now. Mrs. Ruben, can you explain something else I never understand?

—Of course, said Ruben. Or maybe I can't. Maybe I don't understand either.

—I'm sure you do. You know, your glasses are unusually smudged today. I can see that from here.

—Thank you, said Ruben. She reached into her pocket, but she had no eyeglass cleaner. She said, I'll wash them at the break.

—We can wait, if you want to clean them.

—Her pants look dusty, too, said someone.

Someone else produced eyeglass cleaner.

—What I don't understand, said Norma, is advertising. I mean the writing in advertising. Why writing like that is allowed.

—You mean mistaken uses of *its*, with or without an apostrophe? said Ruben.

—I just mean the writing. I'm diabetic. I could die from
sugar. But some of those ads! Each of the students' statements
seized Ruben's attention for one second, so she forgot Deborah,
and then she'd fall through the floor of the remark and be in
a howling place where Deborah might die.

—Mouthwatering, someone said. Luscious chocolate . . .

—Or cigarettes. Or beer.

—Sex! someone said.

—Sex? said another voice.

—What about willpower? said Maddy. The ad isn't making
you.

But someone else was almost screaming—and it was Lynne,
her tiny features cramped in her big face. Legal! You listen to
lawyers? They shouldn't be allowed to use words that hurt.

—Wait, said Ruben. The First Amendment?

Lynne's young, skeptical voice was ugly. When people talked
that way, Ruben wanted Granny, who didn't talk. But the
thought of Granny was connected to Mac and Mac was connected to Deborah. Are words so dangerous? Ruben said. What
if Deborah could hear her? What would she say about hurting
with words?

Ruben wrote on the blackboard, You have taught me language and my reward is I have learned to curse. She said, But
I think I've got it wrong. It's from *The Tempest*. Caliban says
it. She told them about Caliban, the monster captured by Prospero. Prospero is a magician, she said, but he uses words. She
wondered what she was getting at.

Frieda—almost as old as Norma, tall and proud—spoke, bel-
lowing: *You taught me language, and my profit on't is, I know
how to curse. The red plague rid you for learning me your
language.*

Everyone laughed with fright and then quieted.

—Nigger, said Lynne, in the silence.

—I hate that word, said Deirdre, who was black.

—Grounds for arrest, said Norma.

They fought until the break and past the time they usually took a break.

Maddy shouted, Can you stop and think for a minute? screaming at them all, including Ruben. Ruben was writing on the chalkboard, nothing sensible or legible. Maddy said, If this class had a few rules! The words I want to hear are Ms. Ruben explaining what's wrong with our papers.

—I think maybe this discussion matters, Ruben said wearily.

—It's not appropriate, said Maddy. She had medium-length light brown hair and a thin face. Ruben thought she looked something like a donkey, with brown ears hanging down on each side of her face. All my life, Maddy said, I have never used commas correctly.

—What about pornography? said Louise, Maddy's friend, who wanted to keep fighting. But commas, she added. Commas also matter.

Ruben looked at her watch. I'll give you your papers, she said. We'll take a break and you can look them over. She was exhausted. Suddenly Deborah, once again, was dying. Ruben took the papers and began walking around the room, inefficiently handing Lynne's to Lynne, Norma's to Norma, too tired to call anybody's name. She had not read Lillian's. She would explain to Lillian at the break. Lillian, dumb but kind, would tell Ruben not to worry about her paper. Maddy stood and snatched half the papers away, and for a second Ruben thought she was the victim of an assault.

—June, called Maddy, and June, who had a craggy, good-humored face, patted Ruben's shoulder as she reached past her to Maddy for her paper. Frieda.

Ruben fled to the faculty lounge, out of breath, sobbed, gave that up. She could call Harry. Maybe he'd had news. She didn't. She looked at her mail. Everything claimed importance. She threw away the papers and went for coffee, though she'd meet the students near the coffee machine. She put her coins in and, just as she had described it to Deborah, the coffee came out before the cup. She watched the coffee go by. Ruben so badly wanted the moment when she had told Deborah about the coffee, she reached out her arms for it.

Maddy watched her. Could I ask you a question?

—Sure.

—Would you read a poem I wrote?

—I'd like to. So Deborah was right. Maddy would be hers by April.

Together they walked back to class. Maddy said, Some Saturdays, it's hard to come. I think it will just be a waste of time.

—It's not a waste of time, said Ruben. She walked into the classroom and thumped her briefcase on the teacher's desk like an exclamation point.

The poem she'd given them was "To His Coy Mistress."

—I didn't get it, said Deirdre.

—I think I got it, said June, who was good-natured with poems, as always, but brisk, as if she and the poems were opponents in a casual softball game.

—A masterpiece, said Frieda.

Ruben read aloud, "Had we but world enough, and time,/ This coyness, Lady, were no crime . . ."

—Love poem, somebody said.

—Yes. But Ruben was reciting for Deborah.

—Trying to seduce somebody.

—Words to get a woman into bed.

—Sneaky.

Ruben said, "But at my back I always hear / Time's wingèd chariot hurrying near / And yonder all before us lie / Deserts of vast eternity . . ." and suddenly instead of emphasizing the wonderful *ah*s and *ar*s, she was sitting at the teacher's desk after all, in a chair she didn't remember, her head down on her arms, sobbing loudly, her tears splashing the paper on which the poem had been photocopied.

Arms held Ruben. Well, it was the most embarrassing moment ever. Someone knelt and held her. She looked up: little old Lillian. She said, I forgot to tell you. I didn't have a chance to read your paper . . .

—It doesn't matter, said Lillian, who had graying curls all over her head. Someone offered Ruben a tissue.

—A friend is in the hospital, Ruben said. Someone I love.

The group was quiet. Lynne said, I am bisexual. Whereupon everybody laughed.

—I just mean, said Lynne, it's a love poem.

—Yes, said Ruben. Yes, it's about a woman. Yes, my friend, who is hurt, is a woman. I don't know how badly hurt. It just happened. Ruben stopped. But my dears, she continued, when she could next speak. I think everything is sexual, everyone is sexual. We are all—

—You're not going to tell us that we're all bisexual? said Norma.

—Multisexual, Ruben said, with new wisdom. We can love trees. We can love anything. Fire hydrants.

June said, At least they're phallic.

—I don't have a poem for next time, Ruben said.

—We'll forgive you, June said. But what about an assignment? No assignment? June's craggy, wide-awake face with its long nose smiled at her with astonishing sweetness.

—Shhh, said several women. Couldn't you let her forget?

—I like the assignments, said June.

—All right, said Ruben. For next week, write whatever you want. Write something you've always wanted to write.

—What makes you think—?

—There must be something. Something you've always wanted to say but never said.

She thrust her papers into her briefcase, and the students crowded around her to hand in the papers they'd written.

—I'm sorry you have to read these when you're worried about your friend, said Norma.

And Ruben left the room. Embarrassment caught up to her at the door but dissipated by the staircase. She went down the stairs. But she let the metal door smack her in the forehead when she left the stairwell.

She started for home. Students waved from the parking lot: offering rides. She started up the hill and along the street alone.

Someone was walking quickly toward her, and in a moment she saw from the way he sliced the air that it was Harry. He had never come to meet her before. He came quickly and looked upset. Well, she couldn't tell how he looked. He was wearing a baseball cap. He'd been a Giants fan since childhood.

He waved as if she might miss him, although she was coming straight toward him. She waved back. She was tired. Maybe he'd take her briefcase.

—Jeremiah called, Harry said from a distance.

—What is it?

He came up to her. He gestured: both arms up, down, pushing air. Well, it's rather bad.

She thrust her hand to her face, keening. She's dead?

—No, no, she's not dead.

—Then why did you say it's bad? Never do that. Never say there's bad news if it isn't the worst possible news.

—In fact she's in some danger. I hadn't thought she might be. A crazy accident. They don't know why it happened. A man in his forties, not drunk. Suddenly he lost control.

—But I already know she's in danger, said Ruben. How could it be that—now—she was having an argument with Harry?

—How do you know?

He didn't know about her conversation with Jill. She said, I broke into their house to let Mac out. I called Jill.

—You broke in?

—Yes.

—Yes, all the girls are on their way.

—Can I go to the hospital? she said.

—Jeremiah says no.

There they stood in the street. He put his hand comfortingly on her arm, and she shook it off. He says no? It's an hour away and he says no?

—Well, it's *because* it's only an hour away. You could be summoned in a hurry, but the girls couldn't be.

—But I have to see her. Is she conscious? What's wrong?

—Internal bleeding. Liver damage . . . a lot of internal damage. She's conscious. But I really don't think you can see her. I think just family, very briefly.

—But I'm family! she shouted. They began to walk. She said, Why didn't you bring the car? You might have missed me.

—I thought if I brought the car I'd miss you. And I wanted a walk.

—That was selfish, she said. She didn't mean it, exactly. She meant something hard to explain. If she were really family, Harry would have brought the car whether he wanted a walk or not, because the shape of their day would be totally changed by Deborah's accident. And if he'd brought the car though he wanted a walk, that would mean she was family after all. She couldn't say all that, and it made no sense. She cried. They walked together. He didn't comment on her tears or offer to take the briefcase. She could scream at him about the briefcase, and she was afraid she might. She had a kindness defect. She brushed against him and he came to life. He touched her arm, and she cried into his arms and asked him to carry the briefcase.

They walked home, stopping at the market for a sandwich to share for lunch, and agreed on chicken cutlet. At home, they unwrapped it and Harry cut it. They sat on stools at the kitchen counter and ate it. Ruben was hungry.

—It's her liver? she said.

—Her liver, and other things.

—Did you find out the name of the hospital?

He had written it down.

—Can I call her?

—Jeremiah said to wait.

The sandwich, which they ate off the deli wrapping paper, had shreds of lettuce in it, and the lettuce was all over the table between them. Ruben played with bits of it. I cried in class, she said.

—You told them about Deborah?

—Sort of.

—Well, they're used to you.

—Not that used to me.

She heard a key in the door. Peter came in, and someone was with him.

—Racing into the sea, said an old woman's loud voice.

Peter and an old woman came into the kitchen. Granny got up from under the table and barked. Ruben, tears on her face, pushed back her chair and gestured to straighten the shreds of lettuce by magic, to line them up like iron filings under a magnet.

Peter and the old woman, who was Cooper, stood side by side the way he had stood with high school and college friends, waiting for the grown-ups to speak. Cooper was short, but she stood straight, so she looked less old. She moved a little stiffly. She had broad shoulders. Berry Cooper, she said. The name startled Ruben momentarily. It sounded like a name she had heard, but that was probably because it sounded like Gary Cooper.

—My parents, Peter said. Then he said, I left Cooper's box here.

—I saw it this morning, said Ruben.

—Why don't you sit down? Harry said. I'm making coffee. Do you drink coffee, Mrs. Cooper? Berry?

—Black, said Berry. With sugar. Her short white hair stuck out. She wore a heavy dark green smock, a costume for Robin Hood.

—What's in the box? said Ruben boldly. She remembered something from childhood: talking normally with undried tears still on her face.

—You didn't look? said Berry. Fingernail parings.

—Oh, Cooper, that's not true, said Peter, not affectionately.

—I am a liar, Berry Cooper said.

Harry made coffee.

But Ruben had believed the old woman, for a moment, and she'd thought that if she were that kind of person—by which she seemed to mean a person who dealt in tangibles—she'd have saved fingernail parings, and now she'd have some of Deborah's.

—How's Deborah? said Peter, suddenly murmuring, coming closer to her, putting his hands on her arms: like an adult full of compassion.

Harry said, Not good.

—Was it a drunk?

—No, Harry said.

—Was the other driver hurt? Ruben thought to say to Harry.

—Only slightly.

—My friend's in the hospital, said Ruben to Berry. She was in a car accident last night.

—I must have put it in the hall, Peter said. He went to look for the box.

—Canine interference, said Berry. Granny had put her front paws on Berry's lap and was sniffing her face. Berry tipped her face downward. You like paint, doggie? she said.

—I thought you were a sculptor, said Ruben.

—I am. Berry sat down on Harry's stool and spread her knees wide and rested her arm on the counter, pushing the paper from the deli off it.

—Right now you're painting? Ruben said, not knowing why she was persisting in this tea-partyish manner.

—This morning Peter and I painted a protest banner, Berry said. It was his idea.

—And what were you protesting? said Ruben.

—Old age.

—You don't like being old.

—I feel the way I did when I was young, Berry said. Where is Peter?

—He went to look for your box.

—I'm decrepit, said Berry, but not that decrepit. The other day I painted a big picture. A large gray shape. If I showed it to a critic he'd say it represented my death.

—And what did it represent to you? said Ruben.

—Not my death, I can tell you that much.

—I'm afraid my friend will die, said Ruben.

—So she'll die, Berry said. Why does that make you afraid?

Peter returned with the box and they had coffee. Berry put the box in her pocket.

—I had a husband who lost things, Berry said to Peter. You better not be somebody like that. She had round eyes that stood out from her face a little. When she talked, she had the impatient sound of a child. She didn't fit herself into the conversation the way adults did.

—Which husband? said Peter.

—One of them.

—I'm not, said Peter with authority.

—Petey, said Berry. Carry me upstairs. I want to see the rest of the house.

—Carry you? Ruben said.

—I don't climb steps, Berry said. May I have more sugar? She'd drunk half the coffee.

They gave her more sugar and then she walked slowly to the foot of the stairs. Peter made a chair of his arms and easily carried her up. She looked bulky. Ruben, surprised, followed: the hostess, yet with that dragging sensation inside her. It was hideous to do things unconnected to Deborah, but she didn't seem to have the authority to clear everything else out. On the second floor, Berry walked from room to room. May I sit here a little? she said, in the bedroom, and Ruben considered that probably Berry hardly ever went visiting these days. She felt sorry for Berry.

Berry said, Go, Petey. When I'm ready, Mom will help. Or I'll call you.

Peter nodded and withdrew, and Ruben listened to his footsteps, oddly pleased, as if Berry had schemed to be alone with her. Berry sat down on the side of the bed. Ruben's nightgown was bunched next to her, and the underwear she'd worn the day before was on the floor. The bed was not made. Ruben sat down on the floor and crossed her legs. She was in her dusty teaching clothes: pants and a jacket with a blouse underneath.

—I don't pay Petey much, Berry said.

—But the job is good for him, said Ruben.

—Maybe more in a few months, said Berry sadly. I might get some money.

—He's all right. He can't afford to move out, but I don't think he minds.

—Of course he minds! said Berry, slapping the mattress. I remember how I felt, living in my father's house.

—Well, maybe he minds. But it's all right. If Ruben had to talk, she needed to talk about Deborah.

—My second husband, said Berry, almost died twice. Now Berry spoke directly and in an almost friendly way to Ruben. Ruben felt as if after all they were the same age. But Berry was extremely old. Her skin had wrinkles upon older wrinkles, as if she'd lived many lives. Berry went on: The first time, I was afraid. He had a burst appendix and in those days people usually died from that. But he didn't. I was miffed that I'd spent all that time being afraid. The second time he almost died, I kept working. I had a WPA job painting a mural in a post office in Arkansas, and he was in New York. I didn't go to him.

—What did he have?

—Pneumonia.

—Why didn't you go?

—Oh, if he was going to die, it was his death, not mine. It wasn't that I didn't love him. I did love him, then. I never stopped, really. He left me, later, for a man. I loved him, but

I had some respect for his death if it was going to be a death.
It was none of my business. It didn't belong to me.

—Didn't you want to take care of him?

—Other people took care of him.

—Was he angry that you didn't come?

—I don't remember.

—I guess money was part of it. In those days.

—Oh, I don't know. We always got money, one way or another.

—Weren't you afraid *for* him? I'm afraid for my friend. I think how afraid I'd be.

—Well, stay out of her way then. She doesn't need two people being afraid.

—And I'm afraid of losing her.

—Stay out of her way, stay out of her way, said the wicked old woman. If you're going to lose her, you'd better find a new friend. Berry got up and looked around the room, at the bookcases and then at a couple of reproductions of paintings, at Toby's and Harry's dressers and a chair heaped with clothes. Then she walked to the stairs and walked down slowly on her own. Ruben walked behind her. She wanted to push her. She wanted the old woman to have a heart attack.

When they reached the bottom, there was no sign of Peter. She was angry with him for leaving her alone with Berry, as if Peter were Berry's baby-sitter or guard. She left Berry standing in the living room and walked into the bathroom and locked the door and cried. Then she peed, but then she stayed there. She heard Peter come along. Where's Mom? he said.

—Wouldn't know.

—She just left you here?

—Looks that way.

—Well, I'll take you home now.

—I'd like to make wee-wee first, if you don't object.

—Of course not, said Peter, and Ruben heard him lead the way to the bathroom. Before he and Berry could reach the door, Ruben opened it, smiled slightly, and walked past them like a stranger. She got her coat and sat in the dining room until, after an interminable time, Berry had used the bathroom and Peter had ushered her out of the house. Then Ruben went looking for Harry. She met him on the stairs. She said, I'm going to the hospital.

—But Jeremiah said no.

—Well, I'm going anyway. Do you want to come?

—I'll go partway, said Harry, and she remembered why she approved of him. They decided he'd come along and wait for her someplace near the hospital.

—You are kind to me, said Ruben.

Harry drove. They didn't talk. At a traffic light Harry put a tape into the tape player, and anger flashed through Ruben once more. It was an endless, stupid book about economics, read in a woman's voice with self-conscious diction. Why are we listening to this?

—I have to give a talk on it.

—It's stupid.

—Parts.

The highway was busy. She thought he changed lanes too much. She didn't think it was safe to listen to a tape while changing lanes on the highway. They would have a fiery crash and end up in the hospital in the room next to Deborah. Leave me alone, Deborah would say. What are you doing, stealing my death?

She asked Harry, Do you think Deborah is going to die?

—I don't know.

The tape went on. Certain fluctuations of this nature . . .

She said, I want you to say, No, of course not.

—I wish I could say that. He sounded like an old rabbi facing tragedy. Ruben tortured herself by deciding how she'd have spent the afternoon if Deborah had not been hurt. She'd have done the grocery shopping and maybe bought herself a sweater.

She wanted another long, loose sweater, with winter coming.
Maybe she'd have taken everything home and put the groceries
away and cooked something, maybe a dessert. She hardly ever
did that.

The hospital, an hour away, was in a town where they'd
never been. Where should I wait? said Harry.

—I don't know.

—Is there a library?

—How should I know? They got off the highway and found
the hospital, a big brick building with curving paths and tame
landscaping. He drove past it.

—Where are you going?

—I'll find a place to wait and give you the car.

It made sense, though it seemed silly. They drove through a
peeling downtown. There was a library. Harry kept going. I
really want a coffee shop, he said, the way he said he'd wanted
the walk. Harry always knew what he wanted. He drove into
what was obviously the wrong kind of neighborhood—all
houses. Then he turned around, but when he found a place, it
had shut down. Ruben felt like a passenger trapped on the
wrong bus—no, someone in a nightmare. At last they found a
little old-fashioned luncheonette.

—That old place will have rice pudding, said Harry. I'm going to have rice pudding.

—Enjoy it, said Ruben bitterly. He waved, as if Deborah
weren't hurt, and got out, and she slid into the driver's seat
and drove off. At first she got lost, looking for the hospital
again, but at last she remembered.

She parked in the visitors' lot. Getting out of the car, she was
afraid. She could take a nap in the car, or she could go back
and get Harry. But she bravely got out and walked toward the
hospital, conscious that anyone looking out the windows in
front could see her. Jeremiah? As if the risk were Jeremiah's
anger. As if that were the danger.

At the information desk in the lobby, she gave Deborah's name to a young woman with braids who looked like an illustration from a children's book about farmers.

—I'm afraid both passes are out, said the young woman.

—Both passes.

—Deborah's allowed only two visitors, said the woman, as if Deborah was a friend of hers. There are two people upstairs now. She's in intensive care, so it's only family, just a few minutes every hour. Are you family?

—I have to see her, said Ruben. She was going to shout, but the woman would not be shouted at.

—I know how you feel, said the young woman. Once my best friend was sick, and they wouldn't let me in. I went home and cried and cried. I was maybe thirteen. I thought she'd die, but of course she didn't.

Ruben began to cry. I'm afraid my friend will die, she said. That's what I'm afraid of. I'm afraid I'll never see her again.

—Her condition is guarded, said the young woman. A line had formed behind Ruben, but this girl was in no hurry. Guarded isn't good, but it could be worse. I wish I could tell you more.

—They told me not to come, said Ruben. They'll be angry.

—They won't be. Go sit down. When one of them comes down, you go up. If anybody asks, say you're her sister.

—I *am* her sister.

—Well, there you are. Don't tell anybody I said this. I'm just a volunteer.

Ruben sat on a slippery couch at the side of the lobby, watching people come in and go upstairs. Everyone but Ruben was immediately allowed up, even two toddlers. But the young woman with braids wasn't kind to anyone else. She just handed them passes. Then she left, and was replaced by an older woman. Ruben went to find a ladies' room. When she came back, she saw Mary Grace in a big puffy coat coming into the lobby with a green duffel bag, her long blond hair tangled with the strap of the bag. Ruben stepped forward and Mary Grace was suddenly sobbing in her arms and clutching her, and they were both sobbing while the duffel bag fell against Ruben's leg and settled there.

—Oh, Toby, Toby, did you wait for me? Did you know I was coming? The two of them rocked and cried, and people walked around them. Ruben couldn't talk, feeling the joy of Mary Grace's tangled light hair on her cheek, dragging into her tears.

Ruben said, They won't let me go up. I don't know if they'll even let *you* go up.

—Of course they will. In a moment Mary Grace had a pass. She turned back, hugged Ruben once more, her pudgy, red face looking disheveled and wild, openly terrified but loving, about to abandon Ruben easily. She hurried to the elevator, swinging the duffel bag onto her shoulder. Ruben started after her to say, Tell Jeremiah I'm here! but a guard was in the way, and after all she didn't want to fight with a guard.

She returned to the slippery couch and tried, unsuccessfully, to read *Glamour*. She was angry with herself for all she observed coursing in her soul, not just love and pity for Deborah but feelings she didn't want to have: fear of Jeremiah's anger, fear of the girls' anger, jealousy of them all. They would tell Deborah she was demanding and selfish, and Deborah would die angry with her. Sitting in this ugly light green lobby with a bad painting opposite her, she had become ugly.

Suddenly Jeremiah was beside her and she threw her arms around him—she felt his surprise—and sobbed, while he sobbed with her. At last she was behaving the way people should behave here, sobbing with Mary Grace and Jeremiah. She stood up and so did he.

—You didn't get the message? said Jeremiah.

—What message?

—I told Harry we wanted you to come but they wouldn't let you in.

—He just told me not to come.

—Well, it's not so good that you came.

—What's going on, Jeremiah?

He shook his head and looked as if he was trying to speak, and then she saw that in his hand was the pass. Jeremiah had aged faster than the rest of them. He was plump and jowly and gray. And slow. I'm her sister, she said, and while he looked puzzled, she snatched it from between his fingers. It was a large laminated card. Just wait, she said. I'm sorry. Then she flew past the guard, waving it, and opened a staircase door and ran up, afraid to wait for the elevator. She stopped on the landing and looked at the pass. It said 718. She couldn't run up seven flights. She left the staircase and pushed the button for the elevator, terrified of being stopped. At the seventh floor, she walked into the Intensive Care Unit. A nurse looked up and she gestured with the pass. I'm sorry, the woman was saying, but Ruben saw that the room before her said 716 and the one to its left said 714, so she walked fast into the room to its right and there was Deborah, in a twisted hospital gown that left her almost naked. She looked asleep, and had tubes and bottles all around her. I'm very sorry, came the angry voice of the nurse behind her. But Ruben had pushed through the curtain near the bed, and she dropped the pass and put her arms under Deborah's arms. Deborah opened her eyes and looked right at her and reached to hold her tightly and pull her close.

THE trouble was that Deborah died, and there didn't seem to be a way to figure out that it hadn't happened. Often Ruben let herself imagine that it wasn't true. She imagined herself in the dining room eating supper and marking papers. She ran her mental tongue over the events and licked the spot of time in which she read the next to the last paper. Then the phone did not ring. Ruben listened in her mind to its exquisite silence, and in her mind she picked up Lillian's paper.

Or, it did ring. The phone did ring. The phone rang and it was Jeremiah, but he said, Deborah just called. Her mother died.

Apparently someone had to die.

—Deborah wants me there, said Jeremiah. Would you let Mac out in the morning?

—I don't have a key, said Ruben. Whenever she played this hard game, she said sensibly, I don't have the key. Sometimes, if she was alone, she actually screamed the words aloud: I don't have the key! I don't have the key! Sometimes that was the end of the game. She stopped where she was—carrying laundry down the stairs, in the bathtub, in the street—and emitted small screams.

When it wasn't the end of the game, she talked. In an offhand voice, acting the part of Jeremiah, she said, Oh, I'll drop an extra key off at your house. Or, Oh, I'll put my key under a flowerpot on the back steps. When she got that far she was in a tumult of smiles and sobs. Nobody stopped and questioned her when she cried in the street. Once she sat down on the icy sidewalk to hold herself. Across the street, somebody walked by but ignored her.

She didn't have her hair cut and when the frame of her glasses broke in the middle she taped it together. She canceled one class but held class after that. The students asked about her friend. Some had seen the story in the paper. Deirdre offered to lead the class in prayer, and Ruben accepted, though she didn't usually pray and now she hated God. I think prayer is inappropriate in this setting, said Louise after the prayer.

Ruben had last heard prayer at Deborah's funeral. She was a pallbearer. The coffin was heavy. Arriving early at the church in the car with Harry, she saw men removing a coffin from a van, and she knew Deborah was inside. The men carried it into the church as if it were any box. Ruben made Harry keep driving. He drove as if he couldn't see, straight ahead down the street where the church was, and block after block on that same long street. It seemed as if he'd drive out of the city. At last Ruben said, Go back now, and he made a U-turn.

At the church, people were walking in, and Ruben and Harry joined them. Peter and Stevie came in Berry's car and sat with them. Jeremiah and the girls walked in, holding on to one another. All through the service, Deborah's mother, in the front, looked around, over her shoulder, searching the church. Ruben sat between Harry and Peter. Peter's hand, on his knee, shook. At last she took it, but soon he took it back to blow his nose.

At the store, Ruben was sure she'd break things, but she
didn't. Deborah's better hands had become hers. Archie teased
her when she broke no crockery for a month. He nodded
gruffly at her whenever she wiped her eyes, but didn't seem to
want to talk about Deborah. Three months after Deborah died,
Ruben was working one day at the back of the store, unpacking
a shipment of big blue goblets. She liked them. She was careful.
Archie called to her that he was going out, and she knew he
was taking one of his walks around the block, even though it
was a bitterly cold, icy day. He used a walking stick with a
point that he jabbed into ice. In a moment she heard the chimes
as he left, and a while later chimes again. She finished taking
a goblet out of its paper wrapping, holding it by the stem, and
set it on a shelf. The glass of the blue goblets seemed to draw
in light and make it blue.

Ruben walked to the front of the store. The customer was
Deborah. Deborah was dressed in a coat Ruben remembered,
though she hadn't seen it for a long time: a blue coat, not warm
enough for this cold day in a cold winter. A *dressy* winter coat.
Around her neck Deborah wore a yellow silk scarf. Her hair
was caught in a red-and-yellow crocheted hat with earflaps.
Some of her hair fell forward over her face. Deborah had put
her gloves on the counter, and Ruben, sucking in her breath,
touched them. The counter was between Ruben and Deborah.
The gloves were made of yellow wool. Between the thumb and
forefinger of one glove, the knit was worn and stretched, and
a broken piece of yarn extended, loose. Deborah's eyes followed Ruben's finger and acknowledged the torn place as if it
was something to be slightly ashamed of. Deborah looked
steadily at her: pity, love, a warning. She said, I'm wondering
if you carry long spoons.

—Long spoons, said Ruben. She could not speak properly.
She was happy for the first time in a long time. She suddenly
understood that it didn't matter that Deborah had died. People
can come back to life. She said, Do you mean for a barbecue?

—Someone I know is pregnant, Deborah said. If I bought her a long spoon, she could stir the soup.

—Who is it?

—Nobody you know.

Ruben said she'd see if they had long spoons. In the winter they did not usually carry barbecue tools. She went to the back room and looked, though she knew she wouldn't find any, and when she returned, Deborah was gone. She was glad it was over, and astonished to be glad. For a few minutes she remembered why it was all right for Deborah to have died, and then she couldn't remember, and it was no longer all right.

Ruben had been afraid to drive that morning because of ice, and Harry had dropped her off. Now, when Archie came back, she could take the bus home. It was Friday. Her hours had changed; she now worked Fridays. She would have to get ready for her class. It was the annual class on structure. Ruben had discovered that people don't think about structure. She wanted her students to know about balance and symmetry and shape; it would make them better writers. It was too bad she couldn't bring one of the goblets to show them. The stem was just the right length. She enjoyed the stem. Seeing Deborah had lightened her, even though Deborah had had to return to being dead. Archie would let her take the goblet home if she asked, but she would slip on the ice and drop it. She heard Archie come in, and she put on her coat.

—I think about increasing your hours, Archie said.

—I'm really a teacher, said Ruben. She still loved the shiny underside of pots, their curved surfaces, the competency of good knives, and the delicacy of small mugs covered with flowers. Best of all she liked heavy metal pots, but there was much to be said—and Deborah had said it—for enamel pots in red, orange, and yellow. Ruben had sold plenty of those, talking to customers as if she were Deborah. This cunning blue frying pan . . .

Ruben said good-bye to Archie and walked to a little store

for milk. Ice connected tree to tree. Sections of old sidewalk
were planes of ice tilting against different sections like geolog-
ical strata preparing for an earthquake. In the store window
gleamed Ruben's mother: Ruben was closer to old than young.
These days she liked remembering her mother. She knew she
hadn't killed her mother.

She didn't take the bus but kept walking, carrying the milk,
and came to the edge of the park where she and Deborah had
walked, the last day. Though it was so cold she walked into
the park with the milk, not cold (she should have been cold)
except when the wind increased. Ice formed on her glasses, but
she walked on the bridge spanning the river, where ice lay in
chunks, to the trail where three months before she and Deborah
had walked. She walked on brittle, springy iced leaves. In her
imagination Deborah was coming nearer, not in the dressy coat
but in that silly green raincoat that would be far too light for
this weather.

Like any of the dead, Deborah had become naive. Hadn't
she even known winter would come? Walking beside Deborah
in the green raincoat was her own self, who knew nothing:
idiotic, bulky, and grumpy. These two crossed Ruben's path:
Deborah picking her way and Ruben arguing too loudly. As
they passed, she pinched her own three-months-younger stupid
arm: foolish Ruben was leading her friend up to the peak. If
she would turn back, Deborah would leave for her mother's
house earlier and would not meet the wild man who killed her.
Ruben could not get dumb Toby Ruben, who was her own
imagining and should be obedient, to notice her.

—Notice me! she shouted in a low but intense voice. It was
grisly fun. This time somebody heard: a man with a black Lab
stepped out of the woods and looked over his shoulder, then
looked away and kept walking. Ruben hurried forward, past
him and his dog, with the foolish idea of climbing the North
Peak, but she slipped on ice and crushed her glasses against the
bark of a tree. The lenses came out and the frame separated at

the center, where she'd taped it. The grocery bag fell and the cardboard milk container burst. She took off her gloves to try to put the glasses together, but she couldn't. Nobody heard the noise she was making. The man had disappeared. Milk was all over the icy ground. She put on her gloves, left the milk container where it was, and walked out of the park. She walked, milk on her gloves, to the optician's, which was nowhere near the pottery store, where she'd begun, or near her house, but quite in a different direction.

Without glasses, Ruben could see cars and buildings, but signs on poles were unclear. Objects on the ground might be dead animals or flaws in the sidewalk or leaves. In her pocket lay her disgraced glasses.

The eyeglass store was warm, full of burnished wood surfaces and perfectly shaped clean lenses. The walls were hung with posters of wide-eyed, amazed people in glasses that apparently contained no glass. But the place was closing. The people there spoke impersonally and Ruben yelled and sobbed so they thought she was crazy, but they drew her into the store to fit her with a new pair of glasses.

—The shape of your face, they said, and similar lies. Ruben's face had no shape. Covered with frozen tears, her cheeks slid away from her nose and her chin was gone. In the mirror she saw only frames, no face. A man had now remembered her, knew her for a respectable lady with credit card, tears or no. He brought another pair. These are slightly different. They were metal.

His hands slid the frames into place over her ears, and it was as if the man—a thin man with long grooves down the side of his nose and mouth—had spoken softly in her ears. She wanted to put her arms around him. She and the man would roll slowly on the carpet, stroking and soothing.

—Are you parked far from here? Your cheeks are red. He pointed as if he might touch them. The man had written down numbers and measured what he seemed to believe was the dis-

tance between her eyes, which were two miles apart just now.
He looked up her prescription. He would make glasses for her,
possibly spending the night himself in a basement room forging
metal to circle her lenses. She hadn't worn metal frames for
decades and now she'd have them again. In the playground,
meeting Deborah for the first time, she'd worn gold granny
glasses.

—I walked.

—But it's so cold. Maybe someone can give you a ride. I'd
take you myself, but I have to pick up my daughter from her
cello lesson.

At last she let herself be cajoled, and called Harry at his office
to come and get her. The man lifted the phone over a partition
so she could use it. The receiver touched her ear as if it loved
her. Harry said he'd come.

In the car she said, Deborah came into the store today.

—Good, he said.

It made her furious. Good? He should have said either, No,
she didn't! or, A miracle! So she said, You drive as if you hate
sex.

—And how would one do that?

She hated *And*. She hated *one*.

—Nothing gets to you, does it? she said. What kind of a
place do you live in?

—I live here.

—Fools live here.

—What do you mean, what kind of a place?

—Why don't you take off your gloves and hold the wheel
tightly? she said.

—It's too cold.

She'd had to wait outside the store, because it closed before
he could get there. I'm colder than you, she said.

—Look, you didn't have to walk there. If you'd gone home
from the park and called me, I'd have left the office and driven
you.

—Now I have to teach without glasses.

—Oh, baby. Don't you have your old ones?

Suddenly he sounded as if he loved her.

—It doesn't matter, she said. Maybe I do.

—We'll find them.

—You think no problems are real, she said. I suppose you think Deborah will come back to life.

—It sounds as if you're the one who thinks that, Tobe.

—I told you what happened, that's all I did, said Toby Ruben. I just told you what happened. Oh, I wish I hadn't! Now I don't have it anymore. She cried, yet again, on this terrible day. Then she said, We need milk.

He stopped at the convenience store. Shall I get something for supper? he said. Do you want to wait here?

—I don't know. I think there are leftovers.

He folded his arms on the steering wheel, not yet getting out. Peter called me, he said.

—What's wrong? said Ruben in a hurry.

—I'm sorry. Nothing's wrong. He's going to Massachusetts.

—To Massachusetts? In what?

—I assume he went in Berry's car.

—But it's too icy. That car is so old. The tires must be bare. Why did he go to Massachusetts?

—To visit Mary Grace Laidlaw.

—Why?

—That's all he said, Tobe. I'm going to visit Mary Grace. I'll see you, Dad. Now Harry got out and slammed the door and went into the store. Probably he only slammed it because the street was sloped, or maybe he slipped a little. When he came back, she said, Is he coming home tonight? Does Berry know about this?

—He didn't say anything else.

Ruben had written two letters to Mary Grace, but they hadn't been answered. As children Peter and Mary Grace played together, but more often she'd played with Stevie. These

days Peter said he might not like girls. I might like old ladies.
I might be in love with Berry.

—But she's a hundred, Ruben said.

—A hundred and five. But sexy.

She hadn't seen any of the Laidlaws since the funeral. Once,
she saw Jeremiah across the street, and he waved mournfully.

They went home and ate leftovers, and then good Harry read
aloud to Ruben the papers she hadn't yet read, because she
couldn't find her old glasses. In big letters, Ruben wrote com-
ments on each paper. It took a long time. She had already prepared the reading assignment: an essay and a poem, "Travel:
After a Death" by Jane Kenyon, but mostly she'd talk about
structure. Peter did not come home. As they were falling asleep,
Harry said, I'm not a good person.

In the morning, she looked out the window for Berry's car.
She looked for Peter's coat. No Peter. Harry was asleep. As she
was leaving for class, the phone rang. Could you ask Petey to
telephone when he awakens? said someone: Berry. I presume
he is sleeping.

—He's not here.

—Out this early?

—He didn't come home.

—Sex, sex, sex, said Berry. Good-bye, Mrs. Ruben.

Did that mean Berry didn't know where he'd gone with her
car? Probably. It made her stomach hurt that Peter had gone
without permission, not that Berry's permission would have
made it safer. Ruben had to walk to the college. She couldn't
drive without glasses, even if she weren't afraid of the ice.

—What's different about *you*? said June. June's voice had a
jokey roughness: as if Ruben were being predictably naive and
childish. But maybe she was.

—She does look different, Deirdre said. Deirdre was taking
off a brown coat and a big brown sweater under it. Underneath
it all she was a skinny long-waisted black lady in a black silky
blouse. Maybe she'd pray again, for Ruben's poor glasses.

Ruben envied Deirdre for being comfortable in the cold classroom in just a blouse. Ruben kept her sweater on and looked round and clumsy. She yanked down the ribbing at her waist.

—A haircut? said nice Lillian. No, I guess not.

—You really don't know? Norma, the oldest, said. She always sat under the window, with light behind her. The authority. She's not wearing glasses.

—Oh, that's right, said Lynne, from across the room. Did you get contacts? No, they really broke, didn't they? I could have told you that would happen, Mrs. Ruben.

Ruben had worn tape between her eyes for weeks. She'd been teased for it. Sometimes all her students were her mothers, making up for the one she'd lost. When she taught structure she always began with a limerick. She began inventing one on the blackboard:

A discerning old teacher named Toby

Loved books: *Pride and Prejudice, Moby-*

Dick. She taught writing,

Which she found exciting,

And some of her students found it exciting, too.

—Uh . . . no, said Norma.

—Why not?

Ruben discussed the shape of the room, the shape of their hair; they looked embarrassed, probably because her own was messy. How could she get a haircut when Deborah was dead? Some things were possible, others were not. She had brought in a reproduction of a painting by van Gogh, and the students pointed out that the bed looked as if it was sliding down the floor, and that the floor was tilted.

Maddy said, Moby and Dick have to be on the same line. Maddy had changed.

—Not that I see the point of all this, said Maddy, after all.

—Oh, you never see the point of anything, someone said.

—She's a rebel, said a voice from the corner.

—No, she's not a rebel, said Norma. Toby's the rebel, and we're going along with her. Maddy's a loyalist.

—Loyal to *what*? someone said.

But they didn't keep to the topic. There really was a topic. Why was teaching them so hard?

—Lightbulb in the sky! Ruben shouted then. I just understood what's wrong with you guys! You have no sense of structure!

—Lightbulb? A voice from the right.

—You know, dummy, like in a cartoon. A voice from the left. She's finally figured us out.

But Ruben couldn't keep them on that topic, either.

Ruben remembered that she had thought it would be useful to read Louise's essay out loud. She didn't remember why. She couldn't read her notes. Nor could she read the essay without glasses, but she asked Louise to read it. Louise was not a good reader. But Ruben hoped the essay would clarify the point she was struggling toward. She wanted this shapeless crowd to think about shape: the bad limerick. The limerick had been lost in the discussion.

—Things have shape, and can be made more shapely, she said. She ought to have known: June made jokes about breast size, and they were off again. There were those with big breasts, those who favored (and had) small breasts, those who believed exercise might enlarge one's breasts, those who believed that talking about breasts proved that men ruled their lives, a woman who confessed that she had had silicone implants (and there is nothing wrong with them, she said), another who knew someone who'd had her large breasts cut down (general astonishment) and the treasurer of a chapter of La Leche League. At any time, an untaught, nonspecific feminist roar might come out of this group. Only Maddy believed in what they called the Way Things Used to Be.

—Life with My Nine-Year-Old, read Louise. The essay concerned heartwarming and difficult moments with her daughter. Much of it was boring. Then Louise read, One problem I had with Stacy was when she decided to write a story. My mother was in the hospital having a hysterectomy. Stacy wrote a story called The Death of Grandma. Only she didn't tell me, and she read it aloud to my mother when we went to visit her in the hospital. In the story the little girl wasn't named Stacy. She was named Lacy. At the end the grandmother died. Well, I almost collapsed when Stacy read this aloud to my mother. Some people would just laugh, but you don't know my mom. On the way home I told Stacy she had to change the story, and go back the next day and read a new story in which the grandmother didn't die. She said no. She is so stubborn. Finally I promised to get her a new outfit for her Barbie if she'd do it.

—Well, I see why you liked that paper, said Norma. Norma, who was big, had a way of sitting under the window in the small college chair that made the chair seem silly. Only a chair in which Norma looked good would be a good chair. Norma said, It would be nice if we could change life so people don't die, the way we can change stories.

Ruben, astonished, had had no idea that was why she liked the paper. In fact she didn't think she'd liked it much. It was just an example. She thought Louise should have written the whole paper about the incident with the story and the grandmother. The rest of it was pointless and obvious. The point she wanted to make was that in a revision Louise could select and shape her material.

Deirdre's favorite part was about how cute Stacy looked at Halloween, dressed up as a witch, but Ruben wanted Louise to cut that part.

Ruben said, Don't you see? The paper just naturally wants to be about Stacy and the story of the grandmother.

They did not see. Wait a minute, said June. What right do you have to tell your daughter what to put in her story?

Louise said, You'd know if you knew my mother.

Lorna said, Toby seems to think she has the right to tell us
what to put in *our* writing.

—I know just what Louise means, Deirdre said. I have a mother like that.

—Is that the point? said Ruben.

—Wait, said Lorna. I think Stacy has a right to make the story come out the way she wants it.

—Did she change it? someone asked.

—I bought the Barbie outfit, and she changed it, said Louise. Then she changed it back. She wouldn't read it to my mother with the change.

—She's a conniver, said Maddy.

—No, Lorna said. It's not her fault. She didn't realize how important it was to her to keep it as it was, until she tried changing it.

—Does she want her grandmother to die?

Lynne said, I agree with Louise. You don't let your kid go to the hospital and read her grandmother a story called The Death of Grandma. You just don't!

—But if Stacy needs to write this story, said June.

—If it just had to be that way, Lillian said.

—There's no such thing, said Lynne. Nothing just *has* to be any which way.

—Art, said Ruben. You're talking about art, and the next thing she knew, she'd promised to invite Berry Cooper, the first artist who came to mind, to visit the class and discuss this problem. She didn't like Berry much, and at present she felt the students deserved a crabby guest speaker. But Berry was undoubtedly an artist, and presumably an expert on the question of whether art must follow rules or be free. Never mind that the art under discussion was by a child. Never mind that the topic was structure. Maybe Berry could be persuaded to talk about structure as well. Just before the class ended, Ruben heard running footsteps in the quiet corridor and suddenly Harry flung himself into the room, waving her old glasses, the ones she'd worn years ago. She was furious, especially because he ran. The students cheered and cooed, and she had to put on the glasses. She hated the old frames. And the prescription had been right four or five years ago, when Deborah was too busy to be dead.

Harry drove her home, but they had to go to his office first. He'd left in a hurry the night before, and wanted some numbers. Harry no longer priced fire engines. He was the budget director of the parks department, and he directed others to price the dredging of polluted streams and the leveling of tennis courts. Meanwhile they ate lunch at Bosey's, an old restaurant that still had booths. Ruben, docile without glasses, was too tired from teaching to be angry with Harry for making what she called the Spectacles Spectacle; he laughed when she made the joke and they were reconciled. She put on the old glasses and sat with her hands braced on either side of her on the scarred vinyl, crying without blowing her nose when she remembered being there with Deborah, years ago, accompanied by several babies. They'd stopped during a walk for cold drinks, and Deborah had worn a straw hat.

—I'll have whatever you have, she said, and Harry ordered chicken souvlaki and tea. His office was around the corner, and they walked on the ice, grabbing each other's arms. It was less cold. The patches of ice had gray edges.

Harry had a dark green office in a corner of the third floor of City Hall, with a window that opened and let in light. He had a view of a bank. That month he was preoccupied with a pocket park to be constructed in a slum. He was considering indestructible basketball hoops. It took him a while to put onto a disk all the numbers he wanted. Ruben sat at his desk chair, which he never used, preferring a smaller chair near the computer table. She nosily looked over Harry's papers, sure there would be no secrets. Next to the phone was a white pad and on it was written, Peter. Mary Grace. Laundry.

—Laundry? said Ruben.

—Oh, God, Harry said.

—What's wrong?

—I forgot twice. Peter said he'd promised to do Berry's laundry. But he didn't do it. He wanted to know if I'd go to her house and get it, and wash it at our house.

—I didn't know he did that for her.

—I guess he does. But I forgot. I suddenly remembered while I was falling asleep.

—You said something.

He said, When I thought of it, as I was falling asleep, I got terribly scared. It felt as if Berry's dirty laundry could make Peter have an accident on the ice and die. But in the morning I forgot again.

—I didn't know you worried about accidents, too, said Ruben. It was necessary that Harry believe her worries were foolish, though of course they were not. She and Deborah had talked about death for years, and sure enough. But they had worried about the children.

She needed to go home in a hurry to make sure there was no bad news about Peter. I'm not really worried, said Harry, when she jumped up. I don't ordinarily worry. It's just Deborah.

But at home, putting the key into the lock, she heard talking. Look, Harry was saying behind her. Berry's car was parked on the sidewalk near their house. He'd left the driveway for them. Nice boy. Peter and Mary Grace were sitting on the fake oriental rug, pulled up to the coffee table.

Mary Grace had on snow boots that stuck straight out in front of her, visible under the table. The children had a red and white teapot between them. They had mugs of tea, but they looked not settled but restless. Disheveled—or, the house around them was disheveled and they had not needed to straighten anything, but had added their gear to the disarray. A green puffy jacket was about to slip from the sofa; one sleeve hung down. Newspapers were slipping off the sofa on which

Peter leaned backwards, the afternoon sun coming in behind him. Ruben had not cleaned in weeks. She saw dust in the air and dust on the dark staircase and knobby dark wooden banisters. Dog hair on the rug. Granny rose, stretched, and came lurching to meet them, and Mary Grace slowly lifted her big tangled blond head and, midword—she'd been speaking as they came in—looked up without smiling and started to rise. She stood on the wrong side of the coffee table, hands at her sides. Ruben couldn't reach over the big wooden table. She dropped her briefcase, walked around the table, and took Mary Grace into her arms. They stood, as in the hospital, rocking, crying, hugging each other. Ruben felt as if she'd been waiting to put her arms around Mary Grace all these months, and hadn't known. And hadn't thought to wonder whether there was anything these girls needed from her. She should have visited Mary Grace and brought her home, as Peter, who knew about people, had.

She didn't know whether Peter had brought Mary Grace so that she and Toby Ruben could be together, or brought her for himself. Once they stopped hugging, the visit became a little awkward. Ruben was still in her coat. She hoped Peter had washed the teapot, which usually stood on a shelf unused. Teabag labels stuck out from under its lid.

—Hi, everybody said belatedly. Peter was pretending ease— she knew the look. Ruben said, Berry called this morning.

—I could have guessed, he said.

—Are you supposed to be with her today?

—According to who?

—Cooper's needy, said Mary Grace, as if she'd been in touch all along. Maybe she had.

Harry had gone into his study, across the hall on the other side of the staircase. He was already on the phone saying numbers. He didn't seem to need time between events. Or maybe he wanted an excuse to be out of the room. Ruben took off her coat and tried to decide what to do next. She could go upstairs and take a nap. Instead she went into the kitchen, fixed herself a cup of coffee, and carried it into the dining room, where she sat at her usual chair, but was really with Peter and Mary Grace, because the dining room and the living room were the ends of the same room. Sitting there, though, she didn't have to talk to them unless she wanted to, or unless she was invited to.

Mary Grace said, You're funny.

—How am I funny? Ruben said, glad to be included.

—Not you. Peter.

—How is Peter funny?

—Oh, he already knows. And Peter did seem to know, but he wasn't amused, he was angry. Anger appeared in the room from someplace. Ruben drank her coffee. A narrow window in the dining room wall had small colored circles in it, and elaborate dark woodwork. That window always pleased her.

She was perfectly visible there, drinking her coffee and looking at the little red circles on the window, which made her think of cherries she and Deborah might have eaten. Her side was toward Peter and Mary Grace, but when they began to speak, it was as if she weren't there.

—Why does that make you mad, what I said? said Mary Grace.

—It doesn't.

—He said furiously, said Mary Grace.

—Don't you think she'll find out? Mary Grace said.

—I don't think she'll look.

Ruben couldn't help it. She said, Am I she?

—No, Mama, said Peter. Cooper is she.

—What will she find out? That you used her car?

—We had a little trouble with her car.

Ruben got up and carried her coffee cup into the living room and sat down. What happened?

—We had a fender bender. Are those different glasses?

Ruben drew in her breath sharply.

—No, said Mary Grace. This was a necessary and all right fender bender. It's an old car. Nobody was hurt. This is the fender bender to prove that not all accidents kill somebody. Somebody had to have one. So Squirrel has very kindly done it.

—How nice of him, said Ruben. They're my old glasses. I hate them. What happened, really?

They'd slipped in a parking lot and plowed into the back of someone's car.

—Did you leave a note?

They had not left a note.

—You have to leave a note, Ruben said. Hadn't she taught him that?

—But I don't have any money.

—Peter, did Berry say you could take the car to Massachusetts?

Now Peter really got angry. Look, can we talk about something else, please? This is entirely my business. I will deal with it. I wrote down the license number of the car we damaged, and I will find out from the authorities whose car it is, and make proper payment. So you can stop wondering about my ethics. And no, if you want to know, Cooper didn't know. But she wants me to use her car. Cars need to be driven.

—Not on ice, said Ruben. Who knows what she'll do when she finds out? She's crazy. Or evil.

—Would you kindly stop it? Peter said. You know nothing about her.

Ruben stood and left the room. Peter called, Am I scaring you away?

—I should have stayed over there drinking my coffee. I shouldn't have come over to your part of the room.

But Peter had shifted moods again. He couldn't seem to bear himself sometimes; he had to make himself change. But I wouldn't have said that in your hearing if I didn't want you to hear it, he said charmingly. I need you to remind me of my responsibilities.

Ruben stood in the doorway with her cup. The coffee was cold by now, but she liked carrying it around. Well, I guess I knew I was visible, she said. We all knew I was there.

—You were visible, said Peter. And audible. You farted once.

—Squirrel! said Mary Grace.

—Peter, said Ruben, I'm your mother.

—Well, so you are. Maybe I need to have my mother know what I'm like.

—Did you really write down the license plate number? said Ruben.

—No, said Peter.

She sat down again. She said, I miss your mom so much.

Mary Grace bent her wide, pretty head and held it down for a long time. She said, Once my mom told me something about you I think I wasn't supposed to know.

—What?

—That she'd broken something here, something you cared about—a cup, I think. And she lied to you. She couldn't bear for you to know that she'd broken it.

—Didn't I see her break it?

—I guess you were in the bathroom, or answering the phone, and she broke it. She just wrapped it in a newspaper and threw it out, hoping you wouldn't miss it for a long time, and then you'd think somebody else did it. It makes me cry to think of my mom that way. I can't believe she did that.

—It doesn't seem like her. Ruben couldn't remember such a cup. She wondered if it was true that she'd cared about it. She wished she could remember. So many years. It could have happened in any of three kitchens.

—Squirrel, I'm so bad, Mary Grace said, now turning from Ruben. It suddenly reminded her of Harry talking about Berry's laundry, and she wanted to ask Peter if he'd been bringing it home and washing it, a woman's underwear, handled tactfully by this young man who made so many mistakes. Mary Grace was not bad. She had run away from school. She was supposed to be in her dorm room writing a paper.

—Hey, Peter said. I ran away and never even went back. You'll go back.

—But I won't write that paper.

—So you'll flunk a course or two, Peter said. It turns out it doesn't mean your life is over if you fail a class in college. A closely kept secret. Peter looked older than he was. He had a beard. He always seemed to wear blue. He was tall and he liked clothes that had straight up and down lines, corduroys or twills or narrow pants. He looked angry and potentially destructive, sitting there, lounging against the sofa, sometimes tipping his head back as if to show off his straight black beard.

I need sweetness, said Mary Grace. Peter stood up and Ruben thought he was going to lean over and kiss Mary Grace, but instead he walked out of the room and into the kitchen, just beyond it. She turned and watched him coming back, and he was carrying the canister in which Ruben kept sugar. She started to rise with anger. She thought he was mocking the girl's sadness.

But Peter set the canister in front of Mary Grace, and she opened it, reached her hand in, brought it out with some sugar in her palm, and began to eat. Ruben folded her arms and put her head down on the coffee table and cried. The young people ignored her, and Harry, from whom work noises had been coming for a while from the room beyond the staircase, also ignored her. When she finished crying she heard Mary Grace say matter-of-factly, This is how we live at Dad's house, too, and Ruben was startled by *Dad's house* and also wondered whether Mary Grace meant they sat around crying, or they ate sugar, or both.

When Ruben looked up, Mary Grace was still scooping sugar out of the canister and licking it off her palm.

—You've gotten saliva into my sugar, said Ruben affectionately.

—I'm sorry.

Ruben moved closer to Mary Grace and put her arm around
Deborah's baby. And your teeth, lovey, what about your
teeth?

Peter left to do Berry's laundry, and Ruben took a nap on the
couch. Mary Grace watched television and then she took a
nap, too. They waited and waited for Peter and finally had
supper. Ruben liked being with Mary Grace and none of the
other children. Then Peter came home and took Mary Grace
to Jeremiah's. Ruben went back into the living room. When
she'd napped, someone—Harry or Mary Grace—had put a
blanket over her, and it seemed like a good idea to get under
it again. Lying there, she heard Peter come in. He went into
the kitchen and she could hear him opening a can. Soup probably. After a while Ruben got herself up, wrapped the blanket
around her, and went into the kitchen, where Peter was perched
on a stool eating soup and crackers. She's pretty fucked up, he
said.

—Berry?

—No, Mary Grace. My new love.

—Is she your love?

—She is my love. I think I want to marry her.

—But you just got the idea. Aren't you just being kind to
her because of Deborah?

—No. And I didn't just get the idea. You think I'm stupid
because I left college.

—That's not true.

—Or because I'm kinky.

—Are you kinky? she said.

—Sure, he said. I like old ladies. I want to fuck Cooper, even
though I also want to be faithful to Mary Grace. And I like
women's underwear. I do Cooper's laundry so I can look at it,

handle it. Does that truly horrify you? Maybe you were a bad mother to raise me to be this way. He laughed in a childlike way that made her feel better. She went to bed.

Mary Grace did not go back to college in the next few days. On a night when Peter was out, Toby Ruben and Harry ate spaghetti and broccoli with garlic and hot pepper flakes at their old oak dining room table, which was older than the children and full of dents and gouges.

Harry said, When you said Deborah came into the store, did you mean her ghost?

—Is that possible? said Toby.

—I would assume not, Harry said. I thought you meant you imagined her.

—I wouldn't have been surprised then, Toby Ruben said.

—That's true.

They fed Granny the leftover broccoli. Ruben said, Does Granny like broccoli more than anything?

—Not more than running in the woods, said Harry, and Ruben remembered the two dogs running in the November woods, and how she'd thought they might be chasing a deer. Maybe they were pretending.

—What do you like best? Ruben said.

—Best of everything? Best in the world? Harry said. I have to think. I like fucking a lot.

—I like pretending Deborah's alive, but then I cry.

—I don't think you can ask yourself yet what you like best, Harry said.

—I like weather, Ruben said. It was true that being out in rough weather was still good, but now Deborah couldn't be with her. She said, I hate it so much that Deborah died.

—I know.

—Do I say that every hour?

—Just about.

She said, Why should I be able to walk in the cold when she

can't? There we were together, and then one of us was gone.
Why should it be Deborah and not me?

—I know, he said.

She said, But I love it when Peter laughs. I love it when Stevie feels he has to explain something. Do you know that Stevie thinks nobody understands life except him, and it's his responsibility to explain it?

—No, said Harry. He had pushed back his chair and was folding his napkin. I never noticed that.

—I can't think of a good example. Yes, I can. When he comes home, the first night, he looks around at us and tells us what we're up to. He says, I see you're buying lots of red things, if I've bought red pot holders. That's not a good example after all . . .

—Maybe what I like most, said Harry, is reading, at a certain point in the book, when you can't stop and yet there's more.

—Fucking followed by ice cream, Ruben said then, deciding that that was something she really did like a great deal, and it was feasible, so they left the dishes on the table and took each other a bit shyly in each other's arms. They weren't used to approaching it from precisely that direction. They went to bed and in the fervor of experiment tried this and that. For the first time since Deborah died, Ruben didn't weep when the first good, loose feelings went through her. After they'd made love and lain in the bed for a while, Harry said, Now the ice cream.

There was mocha almond ice cream in the freezer and they were eating it in the living room, naked under their bathrobes, when they heard feet and voices on the porch. Granny, who'd been eyeing the ice cream bowls, ran to the door and barked as a key turned in the lock. Harry pulled his robe over his knees. In came Peter, Berry, and Mary Grace. Toby Ruben stood up and checked her robe and offered ice cream all around. Sure, said Berry.

—One of my parents' best traits, said Peter. Ice cream in the house all the time.

—We never had that, said Mary Grace. She was wearing an old black wool coat that Ruben was pretty sure was Peter's.

—When we're married, said Peter, there will always be Ben & Jerry's, no matter how poor we are.

—To your health and that of your bride, Berry said hoarsely, with a huge yellow-toothed mocking smile.

—Mary Grace, said Ruben, are you on vacation? She was being parental and difficult on purpose. She knew Mary Grace was not on vacation.

—She's taking an unscheduled break, Peter said.

—I'm playing hooky, Mary Grace said, with an unconvincing smile. Anxiety filled the living room, squeezing out sexual sweetness. Berry and Peter and Mary Grace sat in a row on the sofa.

Mary Grace said, I should call Daddy. He's crying tonight. But she didn't stand up.

Berry said, Why is he crying?

—Because my mother died.

—Oh, yes, said Berry. I forgot. Berry's dark eyes bulged slightly and her white hair stuck out all over her head. It was as short as a man's. She had big features. She wore the same dark green smock she'd worn the only other time Ruben had seen her, when she came to their house the day after Deborah had been hurt. Ruben hadn't seen her since then, and she felt angry at Berry before she remembered why: because Berry had said if her friend was dying, she'd have to find new friends. Berry sat with her elbows on her knees. She'd put her dish on the floor for Granny to lick without asking whether that was all right. She looked around mischievously at all of them. She was an old woman, but she sat like Peter, like a kid.

Berry had to have known it was unsettling to toast Peter and Mary Grace as a bride and groom. She was unsettling.

Then she said, Nothing fancy in this house. I can come in my work boots.

Berry did wear leather work boots that looked dusty. Mary
Grace wore her snow boots.

—Berry, said Ruben, slightly mollified, do you still make
sculptures?

—We all make sculptures, Berry said. You are making one
right now.

Ruben had her ice cream bowl on her knee. Her leg was bent
at the knee and the bowl was on top. Berry sketched in air a
shape that consisted of a straight line and a broken line and a
round object.

—Will you visit my class? Ruben said. I promised my students I'd invite you.

—What time is this class? When Berry heard that the class
met in the morning, she said she'd visit it if Ruben would buy
her breakfast beforehand. I like The Paragon, on Winthrop
Street, she said.

—Sure, said Ruben. It'll be fun.

—Since I take it you are not offering me an honorarium.

—No, said Ruben. Of course I should, but the college won't
give me any money for it. She wondered if she should pay Berry
herself.

—Cooper's rich, said Peter. He had said it before. She can
do it as a good deed. Famous people should give a little.

—Are you famous, Cooper? Mary Grace asked her seriously.

—I am, said Berry. And they all laughed. She said, Five or
ten years ago, I didn't know whether or not I was famous. I
thought I'd go and take a look at my outdoor pieces. There
were seven, but two were destroyed, one accidentally. The five
were widely separated. It took weeks. They were in parks, and
the parks were alike. I'd leave my car and walk until I found
the park, courthouse square, what have you. I liked catching
sight of what I'd made. Once, it was a windy day. This was in
upstate New York. I walked—finally I saw a patch of green,
and there it was. It's called *Magnet*. It's a big curved stone and

riveted to it is a shape like a bird. It has been described as cynical and witty, but I wasn't amused when I made it, which was during the war. Of course it was covered with pigeon droppings—Berry grinned around at them all. She continued, Not much was going on in that neighborhood. I sat down on the ground and waited for something to happen. Now if this was television, a wise old black man and a smart little kid would come along, and say my piece had consoled them through heartbreak. But nothing happened except the thing sat there and I sat there.

Berry stopped talking and Harry said, But what made you know you are famous?

—You don't think I am, do you?

—I have no evidence one way or another, said Harry. But I thought this story was going to be how you realized—

Berry said, People nowadays have predictable minds, which is worse than evil. People who think evil but unpredictable things are not as bad as people with predictable minds.

—Do you mean I have a predictable mind? said Harry. I happen to be extremely interested in this story, because I am the budget director of the parks department for this city. We've installed some sculpture ourselves, and considered doing more, and I'm always looking for insights.

—I don't agree, said Mary Grace, to Ruben's surprise. Look at Hitler. If he hadn't been creative maybe he wouldn't have figured out the gas chambers.

—Boredom is the worst, said Berry, giving her a big smile. You can't help all this delicate moral deliberation, Hitler and the like, because your mother died. Get over it and go back to thinking clearly.

—I never thought clearly, said Mary Grace.

—Poor motherless child, Berry said. Then she smiled at Ruben. Are you naked beneath that soiled wrap? Ruben pulled it more tightly, said, Of course not, stood up.

But Harry said, She is, she is, and so am I!

—Carnal adventures! said Berry. I'm afraid we interrupted you.

—We were going to lick the ice cream off each other, Harry said.

Ruben was upset that Mary Grace was hearing these things, and hearing them about her, who should have done nothing all day but mourn Mary Grace's mother. She left the room and climbed the stairs, her hand seeking comfort from the dark carvings on the banister, which often seemed like something she hadn't earned and wouldn't have expected to have. The dark curved woodwork belonged in a fancier, cleaner house. Mary Grace was laughing and blushing and looking in all directions when Ruben looked over the banister at her. Berry was giving Harry her big grin, full of yellow teeth.

Peter had one leg bent at the knee, the ankle crossed over the other knee, and he rocked forward and back, just a little, like a boy pretending he was old. Ruben could see that he, too, was a sculpture, and wondered whether Berry meant that these days she just looked at the shapes of things, the shapes things happened to make. Climbing the stairs, Ruben worried for a minute about Peter, but sometimes the worry was terrifying and just now it was not. In the bedroom she took off her robe, put on a flannel nightgown, and went to sleep, her living room full of people, her arms around dead Deborah under the blanket.

For days and days, not much of Peter. He'd spent nights at Berry's before, and when he passed through, sometimes he said he was staying there. Some days he stayed with Mary Grace.

—Jeremiah doesn't mind?

—He doesn't notice.

Sometimes Peter appeared in the kitchen, sitting on the step stool at the counter, eating cold cereal any time of day. Once, she heard the television in the night, but he was gone by morning. Harry said one morning, He dropped out of college and now he's dragging her out of college, and Ruben felt Deborah's dismay from where she was helplessly dead.

—He learns as much from Berry as he did in school.

—And is she learning from Berry?

—They're always together. A threesome.

—I'm not so sure. I think he tantalizes each of them with the other, Harry said. I think Berry's a witch. She's teaching Mary Grace to worship the devil.

—Witches are like Druids, Ruben said. Not wicked.

—I don't mean Berry's a Druid, Harry said. I mean she's a bad old woman.

Ruben was surprised, because she thought Harry liked Berry, and she had liked her more after the ice cream night, though she didn't know why. One day she waylaid Peter in the kitchen. I want to see Berry's sculpture, she said. She thought she might describe it to the students in advance of Berry's visit, which was set for the last class of the term.

—I'll take you, Peter said, but she had to ask twice more. Ruben realized that she expected the sculpture, somehow, to be comforting, despite Berry's peculiar notions. Berry seemed to understand that feeling bad is sometimes necessary. Some of Ruben's friends tried to help her feel better, but that was not allowed, was not possible, was not desirable. Whenever Ruben stopped and looked inside herself, she saw a woman flinging her arms wide and screaming, a sculpture of grief.

Berry lived in a small two-story house with aluminum siding, in a dilapidated neighborhood. Peter drove Berry's big old green Ford into the driveway. She's home? Ruben said. She doesn't mind?

—She's always home. And I don't know what she minds.

A yellow dog came to the door when Peter turned the key. He looked like Mac, but he was a somewhat bigger, younger dog, with a slightly different expression. He licked Ruben's hand solemnly. He had made his way around something and he blocked the door. Ruben pushed him to enter. A shape as tall as she stood just behind the door, so it couldn't open all the way. It was a stone carving, almost abstract, of a man's head. Ruben said, I didn't think they'd be so big.

—This one was outside for a long time. In a garden of a private school in Pittsburgh. When the school closed, they told Cooper she could have the sculpture if she'd come and get it. She drove down there and got people to help, and put it on her truck.

—She has a truck?

—She used to.

The head was so big that its bigness—in the ordinary room with its two windows side by side and broken Venetian blinds—was more noticeable than whether it was good. Ruben had a feeling it was good, because it stirred her. She wanted to touch it. She wanted the huge stone tongue, which protruded slightly, to lick her.

Now she heard sounds. Berry was coming down the stairs. She came in saying, Is this the day? She was in the familiar green smock and sweatpants, and her hair stood straight up.

—The day? said Ruben.

—No, Peter said. It's two weeks off. She means visiting your class.

Berry looked doubtful, and Peter said, Come off it, Coop. Stop pretending you're senile. It won't work with me.

Ruben said, I came to see your sculptures.

—Big enough for you? she grinned. She slapped the head affectionately. Berry looked powerful, but she was short, smaller than what she'd made. Your mother has new glasses, she said to Peter. They were Ruben's new metal-frame glasses.

—Is it all right to touch them? Ruben asked.

—Sure. Kids climbed on this one. Berry slapped it again and looked at it critically. I don't like the left nostril, she said.

Ruben looked. The nostrils were cone-shaped indentations in the stone of the nose. They were at different angles from each other. She said, Your left or the head's left?

Frank. I call him Frank. Frank's left. But maybe it's all right. Maybe it is effectively disturbing. Ha! She gave a half laugh, half snort.

Ruben looked at the two other sculptures in the room. There was no furniture. Berry said, I used to rent this place. The landlord was afraid my stuff would break through the floors. So I said, Shut up—I'll buy it.

—The floors look all right, Ruben said.

—Of course they are.

—Of course they are *not*, said Peter. You know you were warned about that. He spoke as if he'd been with her for years, as if he'd always partly been Berry's. It was a relief.

The other two sculptures weren't quite as large as the head. One was painted in wide orange and green stripes. It looked like a big orange and green rock. The other was blue, a big uncontrolled shapeless thing. Ruben loved it, for some reason. The surface was pitted like something you might see in a planetarium, and Ruben wondered if all the holes and marks had been made by Berry's chisel. The dark blue paint must have been poured over it, because in some places it didn't quite cover and in other places it had pooled. It was hard not to try and stick one's fingers into the paint-filled holes. I love this, Ruben gasped, and giggled a little. She felt love for the sculpture in her abdomen, in that sore place that was always worn out from crying, and she hoped she was not going to cry again. It was April by now. She was tired of constantly feeling terrible.

She looked again at the less dangerous orange and green rock. It had been painted with a careless wide brush; she could see the ridges the brush had left. Some of the stripes overlapped and made strips of brown. Ruben looked around, not knowing what to say about the orange and green rock and the sad little brown strips. She could see into the next room—more sculptures; several more heads. She went to look. They looked like Easter Island sculptures and made her uncomfortable in just the way those always did: she was afraid of being screamed at

by the maker. In the case of the Easter Island heads, it seemed
that the sculptors, hidden for millennia, would emerge and protest all this crappy staring and photographing. She thought
Berry might object to her looking, too, as if the heads were
secrets.

She and Peter and the dog toured all the sculptures in the
room while Berry stayed in the front room, poking and mut-
tering. Peter said, There are more upstairs, and they went upstairs, too. The rooms seemed dustier and more disorganized,
as if the sculptures there had been left half done and Berry still
meant to get back to them.

—Are these newer?

—Mostly.

—I don't like these as much, Ruben said.

—Most people don't, said Peter, but these got her a lot of
notoriety. He ran his hand along a heavy metal tube. There
were many of them, laid in piles or fastened together with riv-
ets, in heaps like huge piles of pick-up sticks.

—They look like gun barrels.

—Yes.

But before Ruben had finished looking, Peter became restless.
I have to go, he said. I have to meet Mary Grace. She thought
he didn't want her to see the back rooms of the second floor,
where Berry lived. She followed Peter down the stairs and out
of the house. Shouldn't I go and thank her? she said, as if Peter
was any authority on etiquette.

—No.

—Doesn't she need to be carried up the stairs?

—No. She just does that for show.

They got back into Berry's big car. As he backed it up, Berry
Cooper appeared on the porch, hands in the pockets of her
green smock, and called clearly, I'll need a slide projector.

—Fine, fine! Ruben shouted eagerly back. Thank you! But
they were already in the street.

Peter drove fast. About Mary Grace, Ruben said tentatively

as they drove. All this with Mary Grace...I *love* Mary Grace....

—You don't know what it is to love Mary Grace, Peter said. He glanced toward his mother, just a long enough look to make her worry about his driving. She looked away and scanned the quiet street, which had no traffic at all. It was Sunday morning. Peter looked sensible and serious, older than he was, with his beard and narrow face and gray shirt collar under a blue corduroy jacket. She always forgot he was less than a year older than Mary Grace because he had been alive all that winter while Mary Grace had been Deborah's pregnancy.

—Mom, I'm going to marry her. She's my wife.

—You haven't already married her?

—No.

—Sweetie, she's twenty-one. You're twenty-two. She's a mess. Can't you watch out for her, a little?

—Will you shut up? said Peter. They'd reached their house and he swung the car to the wrong side of the street, so she'd be nearer the curb, reached across her, and opened the door.

—Shouldn't—but he was getting ready to drive away. She got out, angry with herself because she wasn't angry enough with him. She didn't see him for days after that. Then came brief sightings. Cold cereal. She hoped he was eating something, someplace, in addition to cold cereal. A lot of his clothes were gone. He'd moved out, apparently to the Laidlaws'. She didn't see Mary Grace or Berry. Sometimes she came home and found Peter in the kitchen reading the paper, standing next to the counter with it spread out in front of him. Sometimes she thought he came home simply to read the paper, although surely Jeremiah got it.

On the morning of the last class, with mixed feelings about sharing this odd group the last time she'd see them, she drove to Berry's, not knowing if the old woman would have remembered or taken her seriously, but there she was on the porch with a big old tote bag. They went out to breakfast, as prom-

ised, and Berry had a big omelet. Ruben wanted to talk about
Peter, but they didn't talk much. Ruben tried to tell Berry about
the course and the students.

—Grown women, Berry said. I approve. In the car on the
way to the college, Ruben said she hadn't seen much of Peter
lately, and that reminded Berry, who sat forward in the passenger seat, playing with the clasp of her shoulder harness, of
the time she'd told off a gallery owner because the gallery was
never open, and what he'd said to her. One of my pieces could
be seen through the window, Berry said. Just a corner of it.
And that was all.

—Do you mean all I can see is a corner of Peter? Ruben said,
laughing, but Berry didn't answer.

Finally, as she ushered Berry out of the parking lot and into
the classroom building, Ruben said, Now, Peter's doing his job,
isn't he?

Berry stopped and faced her, her huge toothy smile indulgent. It will work out, she said. I'm not so bad off, you know.
I don't need pity.

—Of course not! said Ruben. Of course not.

As they walked through the corridor, Berry stuck her hands
in her smock pockets and wedged the canvas tote bag under
one arm. It slipped out, and folders of slides fell on the floor.
She stood and grinned at Ruben, hands still in her pockets,
while Ruben knelt and gathered ancient envelopes and folded
papers and plastic slide covers as well as naked slides in cardboard frames. Some seemed to be from sets that Berry had
bought—or stolen, Ruben found herself thinking—while some
looked as if she'd made the photographs herself. Berry continued to smile, as if everyone knew her hands were fastened into
her pockets. Maybe she couldn't bend. Ruben feared she'd
brought a mad, incoherent speaker.

The students were subdued, for them. Some found the setting
up of the slide projector, which had to be tilted over a book
so it would aim properly at the screen, hilarious. A boy set it

up. Ruben had forgotten this college included young boys, but during the week, presumably, there were crowds of them.

—I almost stopped twice, Berry announced, by way of an opening, marching to the front of the room. The students organized themselves, and one or two scooted back where they belonged, having been visiting their friends across the semicircle of chairs. The chairs had attached desktops, and some of the students could barely fit into them. They were a fat group, and they stuck out their big behinds to make jokes. Now two of them, Rosemary and Lorna, scooted backwards, behinds thrust out, to their chairs: a kind of apology.

Berry waited. Then she said, When I was young, my husband died. I had to have money. I could have stolen it, but that would have been a crime, so I worked in a restaurant. Carving stone is costly.

The students looked baffled. They were probably surprised that Ruben hadn't greeted them and introduced this old woman, and Ruben was surprised, too.

—But the second time, Berry said, was different. I was already old. I wasn't too weak to make things, although, you know, you have to be strong. She raised her fist to show off her muscles. But I had a son in trouble.

She stopped.

—Excuse me, I don't see the connection, Maddy said, but Berry ignored Maddy.

—I decided to do something else. I didn't know what. Maybe I'd work in a restaurant, except I was too old to be hired. They want you young and cute. She grinned at them. Her grin made Ruben, who was leaning on the cold radiator at the side of the room, think of a skull, of Deborah.

—I would go away, Berry said. I could put my belongings in one of those storage places.

The students nodded. They knew about storage places.

—I would go to Wisconsin, where I'd never lived. If I stayed

around here, I'd have to work. I would answer the phone and
it would be the gallery owner. Berry paused. This is how much
I loved my son.

Norma was nodding vigorously. Ruben thought Norma
might stand up and kiss Berry.

—Did you do it? said Norma.

—No, I didn't, she said.

—And what happened to your son? someone asked.

—He died, said Berry. He stole a car and died driving it. He
had robbed a gas station and the police shot him as he was
trying to drive away.

The class stared at her, and Lorna hid her face in her hands.

—Slides, Berry said. Deirdre stood and pulled down the window shades. Everyone looked at Deirdre, and beyond her,
through the three windows, at the Science Building opposite.
There was just a small square of grass far below, between the
buildings. They met in the Humanities Building because they
were human, one of them had said. The Science Building was
just like theirs: five stories high, with big windows. They were
on the fifth floor, and just exactly opposite, quite close, a scaf-
fold hung from the roof of the Science Building, and on it a
window washer, arm working up and down, was vigorously
and in a somehow lonely way washing the big mindlessly shiny
windows of the Science Building. He was hidden when Deirdre
closed the first shade.

—Now that was a work of art, someone said.

—He had a nice butt, said June.

The third window had no shade. The room was less bright
than before, but not dark. Ruben felt bad about the missing
shade, whose absence she'd never noticed. With annoying slow-
ness, Berry prepared her slide show. The student who had set
up the projector offered to run it.

The slides went by. Sculpture is three-dimensional, Ruben
now remembered, and the slides were two-dimensional and

faint, worse in the incomplete dimness. She undertook to ask questions. The students, for once, had turned shy. When was that made? she said. Who made it?

—Hepworth, said Berry. 1928.

Ruben exaggerated what she felt for the students' sake. I don't know how to look at it. Why do you like it?

—Because it makes me feel sexually aroused, said Berry.

—It's porn? came June's saucy voice.

It was a rounded thing, really a big rounded rock.

—All art is pornography, Berry said impatiently, while lowering her arm to signal she wanted the next slide, which resembled the previous slide. Ruben noticed that Berry's arm had come down on Louise's shoulder and Louise was rubbing her shoulder.

—No, said Maddy. Art is uplifting. At least, that's what Mrs. Ruben taught us this year.

—Well, maybe she taught you wrong. Three more slides rapidly went by as Berry's arm worked up and down like a hatchet.

—I have had three husbands and innumerable lovers, said Berry. And then she said, *So far,* with perfect comic timing— and Ruben felt the students swoop over to old Berry's side, at least for the moment. Berry went on, But the best orgasm I ever had was while looking at a show of paintings.

—Who painted them? said Rosemary.

—Willem de Kooning, Berry said.

The ways in which nobody in the room could respond to that were many, and nobody responded.

This is a piece called *Three Forms,* Berry said now. No, that is wrong. It is called *Three Uprights with Circles, Mykonos.* I am fond of it. The slide showed three vertical slabs of what looked like white marble. They had holes in them, and were visible through one another. Even the imperfect photograph made Ruben want to walk around and see how they'd look from another direction.

—Is that porn? said Rosemary.

—No, said Berry slowly. She stared hard at it. Not porn. No
arousal.

—Then why do you like it?

—It's good, said Berry. Can't you see that? Maybe you can't, just seeing the slide. Didn't you go to the Hepworth show at Yale? She stared at them. They looked uneasy. Ruben had not gone, either.

—New Haven is less than forty miles from here. I walked there to see it, Berry said.

—Surely you didn't, said Ruben.

—I did. But I suppose none of them is terribly bright. I don't think this college has a lot of terribly bright students, she said conversationally to Ruben.

At that Frieda stuck her legs out, leaned back in her chair, and laughed hard, and soon everybody else had decided to be amused rather than offended.

—Giacometti, called Berry cheerfully, as the slides went by again. Moore. I like abstract sculpture, don't you? she said chummily to the class, and now they nodded happily. Maybe they did. You know, said Berry, it's not supposed to *be* anything? Suddenly, after she'd insulted them, she was the students' great friend, and they were full of questions, sharp and naive both.

At last came a slide that was easy to see; it happened to be a dark piece, and it showed up on the screen.

—Is that Barbara Hepworth again? Ruben said.

—No, that's mine, said Berry. It won a prize.

The sculpture was a tall perforated disk. A tree stood near it, so they could see how tall.

Berry slapped her stomach. Let it in and see if it wants anything, she said. See if it makes you feel good. And the students began slapping their stomachs and joking.

—That one tastes good, said Lorna.

—Tastes! Louise said.

—For me, everything is food, Lorna said in the half dark.

Did you see in the paper? An old man with three or four kinds of cancer wanted to die, so he asked his doctor for medicine to die. The doctor said no, he'd go to jail. Then the doctor said to the old man, Some people starve themselves, and the old man says, But eating is my greatest pleasure.

Berry ignored her, but three or four of the women commented on the morality of physician-assisted suicide and the pleasure of eating.

—I mean, said Lorna, he didn't want to die at all!

Ruben wasn't sure. She didn't know. Would Deborah have— Oh, enough about Deborah.

The students began asking Berry questions. She was sitting now, on one of the desks, a dim slide forgotten behind her. They wanted to know how she worked, and Berry talked about carving stone and casting bronze. These days she sometimes fooled around with cardboard and string. You can make garbage sculpture, she said.

—I think sculpture must be fun, Deirdre said.

Berry looked happy for the first time. Oh, it is fun. It is fun, she said, almost kindly. She said, Resistance. Resistance is fun. Garbage, wool—that's all right when you're old. But when I was young! Well, you see, I had no money when I was young. I worked—I was even a prostitute, she said. A whore.

Ruben wondered if it could be true, but she had learned that sometimes things are true after all.

—Could I ask a question? said Louise. Why did you tell us about your son? I've been thinking about it all this time.

There was silence for a while, and Ruben noticed that the boy showing the slides had sat down, put his arms down on the desk, and lowered his head in the dimness.

—Why did I tell you about my son? Berry said. She looked confused. Maybe she couldn't remember talking about her son. But surely she remembered. Ruben thought everything Berry did was for effect and she was in charge of everything. It's wicked to be in charge of everything, she decided. Good people leave holes. And she thought of the holes in Berry's sculptures.

—You can't be good if you want to be an artist, Berry said. If I had been good, I'd have stopped doing art and he wouldn't have died, but I am not good.

—That makes no sense, said Norma firmly. No sense. Berry was not in charge. Norma was. Suddenly Ruben remembered it was the last class, and soon she'd lose these students. She felt great love, just then.

She had taught them nothing.

Maddy said, You had no reason to think it would help your son if you gave up art.

—Art doesn't go by reason, Berry said.

—I don't think you're like that at all, Norma said. You want us to think you have no morals, but I bet you do, like anybody.

Berry was grinning and looking out the unshaded third window. Look! she said. Look! And everyone who could not see what she saw jumped up, Ruben included. Suddenly they were not a class but a little crowd, standing behind Berry, who was looking out the window. The window washer, obscured by the lowered shades, had made his way along the opposite building with its huge blank windows until Berry could see him, now directly opposite the unshaded window, moving his squeegee up and down.

Everyone watched. Nobody objected that he wasn't worth looking at. I do like his butt, said June.

—If you notice, Berry said, he works high up on scaffolding without a belt. I used to do that. I installed some pretty tall things. I never used a belt.

—But the platform is pretty big, Ruben said.

—Not that big, Berry said. I will show you that artists have no morals. I'll startle him, and he'll fall.

At that she moved forward, clapping her hands. The window washer didn't turn or hear her. She opened the window, leaned out, and bellowed joyfully, You have a nice butt!

Maddy yelled, I'm calling the police! and rushed from the room.

Now Berry was continuing to yell, I command you to fall! I command you to fall! The window washer turned his head and everyone screamed, and he waved his arm amiably and went back to work. Ruben moved forward and closed the window. She began to talk about the assignments she was returning. Her hands shook and her throat felt strange. Maddy came in with a security guard, and Ruben told him nothing was wrong. It was a misunderstanding. She apologized.

—No problem, he said. Anytime you think you might need me, it's always better to call. He left.

There was a long, exhausted silence. Everyone including Berry and Ruben sat down and looked thoughtful. Ruben wondered if the class might be over.

Then Norma said, Could I ask a question?

—Certainly, said Berry.

—Do you have a religion? I mean, it's hard for me to understand how somebody with a religion could do what you just did.

The class murmured.

—I am Jewish, said Berry, and Ruben said, You *are*? out loud.

—Not all Jews are named Rabinowitz, said Berry.

—But I wonder about Norma's question, said Ruben. I'm not sure I accept the assumption behind Norma's question.

—You don't think that was terrible? Norma said. Trying to kill the window washer?

—I'm not sure, said Ruben. And I'm not sure what it had to do with religion.

—No religion in the civilized world would sanction that, said Norma. I'm not Jewish, but I assure you no rabbi would say it was all right to do that. He could have been killed.

—It's not easy to commit murder, Berry said. I ought to know about murder. I was once accused of it.

—Did you go to prison? asked Louise.

—I was acquitted. It's ironic that you ask about my religion. At that time, because I was Jewish, it was thought I was more likely to have done it.

Something stirred in Ruben. There was something she was supposed to remember.

Berry said, They called me the Little Jewish Anarchist. Do you know what an anarchist is?

The class did not know.

—The screaming headlines said it was someone who believes there should be no government, Berry said, which is not what I believed. Believe. I am an anarchist because I don't believe it's possible—Ruben was listening closely; there was something she needed to find out—I don't believe it is possible to enact fair laws and follow them, in the personal soul or in the state. It isn't possible to decide in advance. That's why I became a sculptor and made these pieces. People think some of them are in favor of revolution. But they're all just what they're made of.

—What was your name, before it was Berry Cooper? said Ruben. She was standing up. Why did she think Deborah would return from the grave when Berry answered?

—It was Gussie Lipkin, said Berry, turning in her seat and grinning. A good Jewish name. I'm a famous person. You've heard of me.

—How do you know? said Ruben.

—My sister wrote a book about me, Berry said. She called me Jessie in the book. I saw it in your house. It's on the bookcase in your bedroom. On the right. On the lowest shelf.

Ruben listened. She didn't reply, but she heard herself make an odd noise. Then she hugged all her students and said goodbye. She remembered the article about Gussie Lipkin that Jeremiah had given her, years ago, when they took the drawing class. Once in a while, Ruben took out a drawing pad and drew something, still. She remembered searching for that book, helped by Stevie, who was about eight. She'd never found it. She'd given up. Now she bundled Berry home and didn't want to talk, but before Berry got out of the car, she said to Ruben, who was thanking her for coming, trying to make it sound as if ordinary things had happened, You know, I've never had children.

—But your son! said Ruben. Your son the robber, who died.

—Yes, I was tempted to save him by giving up art, said Berry. But that wasn't my son. That was your son.

She got out of the car. Stunned and full of rage, Ruben still did not drive away, but conscientiously watched the short, sturdy old woman in her green smock until the door had firmly closed behind her. Then Ruben drove home.

Mary Grace was sitting on Ruben's porch steps. Ruben sat down beside her, too exhausted to invite her in, inquire whether Harry was around, or even take out her key. Mary Grace leaned her big yellow head against Ruben's chest.

—What?

—I'm sorry.

—About what? as Mary Grace snuggled into her chest like a baby. Sweet darling, about what? Ruben stroked and fondled her favorite of Deborah's daughters, the one she'd always wanted.

—Didn't Cooper tell you?

—What? She told me plenty.

—I've been thinking all morning she'd yell at you because Peter is leaving her.

—Peter is leaving her?

—Peter and I are going back to Massachusetts. We're going to get jobs and in the fall I'll go back to school.

—When are you going?

—Today. I sneaked over here. He didn't want to say anything to you. He's probably furious with me. I had to tell you.

—But why?

—I have to get away from here. I should go back to school.
But we can't be apart, she said.

—But where will you live?

—Oh, we'll stay with friends until we find something. Mary
Grace sat up and patted her hair and clothes back into shape,
all set for new seriousness.

—What about Berry?

—He told her this morning. He went to her house at seven
o'clock this morning and quit. She'll be all right. But he took
her car. We're just borrowing it. He kept the key, and we went
just now, when we knew she'd be at your class, and took it.
She doesn't need it. She's less helpless than she lets on. She's
the kind who lands on her feet.

—He told her this morning? said Ruben.

—I should go, said Mary Grace. I'll have to lie when I get
back. He wouldn't like it that I told you.

—He just wants us to worry?

—He knew you'd think it was wrong. But it's not that simple, she said, in Deborah's voice, and Ruben got up, hugged
the child hard, and entered her house. The key seemed to be in
her hand after all. She closed the door with Deborah's child
outside it, rather than go on with this conversation for even
one more minute. She went up to her bedroom, not stopping
to leave her briefcase downstairs. She knelt near the bookcase
and drew out *Trolley Girl*, which looked familiar though she
hadn't seen it in twenty-two years—a battered black book that
smelled of a used bookstore—and sat down on the floor with
the book closed in her lap. Deborah was never around anymore
when she was needed.

Ruʙᴇɴ told herself she'd return *Trolley Girl* (at last, twenty-two years late), as soon as she had a chance to look it over, but she didn't look it over. It would bring to mind too efficiently the year she'd been lent it. She neither opened it nor returned it to glittery Jeremiah, proprietor of holes in the air, of scooped-out places where Deborah once lived. She didn't want to tell Jeremiah who Berry was, though he'd want to know. Jeremiah was hard. Berry was hard.

Peter and Mary Grace were gone. Teaching had ended for the summer. Even the pottery store would close for two weeks in August, and in July business was slow and Ruben worked fewer hours. She would have liked money for housecleaners and house painters, but she liked time, too, time to paint the first-floor hall and clean; yet she did little. She carried a portable phone around. Stevie came home from school, listened to her speculate on where Peter might be, then returned to college for a summer job leading tours of prospective students. He said,

I like telling people things they don't know. I like walking backwards.

When the four of them had toured colleges, Peter's senior year in high school—a time that felt tiny and distant, as if seen through a long tube—Peter had convinced his little brother, Stevie, that students auditioned to be guides by walking backwards; he'd enacted elaborate tryouts in motel rooms at night. Now Stevie said, Once, a guide made up crazy statistics and facts.

—You wouldn't do that!

—Of course not. This guy said the biology department kept live leopards for research, and an animal-rights person complained. That's how they caught him.

Stevie was still like a curled fern frond deep in the forest, full of surprises that didn't bring pain. All summer, she didn't hear from Mary Grace or Peter and neither did Stevie. Sometimes she tried directory assistance in Massachusetts towns, but nothing.

After Stevie left, Harry walked around the house naked, though someone could come up on the porch and look through the window. She liked the innocence of his genitals, which moved slightly as he walked from his study to the kitchen for ice water or orange juice.

—I don't seem to know anything, Harry said. Deborah. Peter. He said, I feel naked. I might as well be naked.

Once he lay on the living room rug on his back, and raised his hairy legs in the air. Come here, he called to Ruben as she passed. She was hot, rushed, on her way to make a phone call. It was Sunday, and she meant to wash the kitchen floor. She stood over him.

—What?

—Take off your clothes and lie with me.

—I don't think I feel like it.

—I don't mean fucking.

Feeling like a girl, though her red hair was gray and her waist was thick, Ruben took off her clothes, and stepped out of her sandals. She lay down and felt the rug on her bottom, and began laughing. Coached by Harry, she scooted closer to him, and they raised their legs between them and pressed their buttocks and then the soles of their feet together. And laughed.

—What gave you the idea? she said.

—An ad for women's tights, he said. The bottom half of two women.

Reading, Ruben would interrupt herself to think of Deborah, but once when they went to a film she forgot Deborah while it was on the screen and remembered her only in the lobby. Deborah was excluded forever from seeing this or any other movie. Ruben herself would die at some point and see no more movies, while other people would go on making and seeing movies, but that knowledge didn't change the desolation of Deborah's exclusion.

One day in August, Rose was in town and came to see Ruben. They drank iced tea and talked stiffly about Deborah. How's your dad? Ruben said, and Rose shook her head back and forth. He blames you, she said. Rose looked older than she was. She had little blondish curls with a ribbon in them that made her look like a middle-aged woman pretending to be a girl.

—Because Deborah died?

—Of course not. Because Mary Grace dropped out of school.

—Isn't she going back to school?

—I don't think so, said Rose.

Sitting cross-legged on her dining room chair with her bare legs under her, Ruben felt young, foolish, and desperate, wanting to defend love, to defend Peter and Mary Grace. Rose wore a cream-colored long-sleeved shirt, despite the weather, and now she unbuttoned the cuffs and rolled them up slowly, looking and smoothing while Ruben admired and disdained this process, and both of them stopped speaking as if it required concentration.

—M.G. was talking about nursing school, according to Dad, Rose said eventually. But he doesn't think she meant it.

—She told me she was going back to college.

—Maybe she thought you wanted to hear that. Dad thinks she conned you into lots of stuff. Ruben was stung.

—He said she didn't talk to him the entire time she was home. He doesn't know how she spent her time.

—She helped Peter.

—Caring for that senile old lady?

—She's not senile. She's an artist.

Jeremiah would recognize the name Berry Cooper, or possibly just Berry or Cooper, even after so many years. Given time, she and Deborah might have remembered together. Apparently Mary Grace had never said the name to Jeremiah.

Berry wasn't senile, or even, in truth, terribly awful. The window washer had not died, and it wasn't Berry's fault, exactly, that she had been the subject of a book lent to Ruben by her dead friend Deborah, though it was hard not to blame Berry, even to blame her for Deborah's death, as if she'd sculpted Deborah and thrown the piece out the window, where it would fall as the window washer might have fallen.

Thinking about falling, Ruben wondered if the huge head with the conical nostrils had broken through the floor yet. It was not Deborah's head, Ruben knew that perfectly. The next day in the store, as she stood waiting, one foot out of her sandal, while a fussy man examined teapots, Ruben made up her mind (stroking the floor with her bare toes, though she'd picked up splinters that way before) to close early, drive past Berry's place, and see what had become of the old woman and her laundry. It was the laundry nagging at her, as it had nagged at Harry last winter.

And she did. Nobody answered the doorbell, but the door was unlocked. The head had not fallen through the floor. As before, the door opened only partway, because of the head. The head frightened her; the protruding tongue, this time, seemed not sexy but lewd. The house smelled stale and dry. Beyond the head was the blue rock, smaller than in memory. An intruder, Ruben was quite afraid, but the head still had the power to distract and please her. The air was less emptied of Deborah with these stone objects in it. Berry's windows were closed, and in the old summer air all the heavy pieces looked dirty. On the floor was a twisted green blanket, and Ruben wondered where the dog was.

—Berry! she called. She listened hard. The house didn't feel empty; but what did she mean by that thought?

She was afraid to leave the room where she stood, where the head and the rocks stared back at her. She didn't want to turn her back on the big things in this room. At last she sat down on the floor. She wondered whether she'd eventually just get back in her hot car and drive home, but after twenty minutes or so, she thought she heard sounds, maybe a toilet flushing, which pleased her so much that she understood she had feared finding a corpse. More time passed, and then—slowly, slowly— Berry came down the stairs.

Ruben made noise. She went to stand below as Berry's legs and torso appeared. It's Toby, she shouted into the dimness.

The white-haired old woman who descended was not wearing her green smock. Instead she had on a flowered cotton housedress in pink and red, which made her look more like a regular old lady. Her hair had grown out a little. For the first time, she looked Jewish—maybe because now Toby Ruben knew she was Jewish. She looked like Ruben's aunt or her grandmother—or even Ruben's mother.

—My little dog died, said Berry. She spoke in her usual firm voice.

—It was a big dog, Ruben couldn't keep from saying. Then she said, I'm sorry. When did he die?

—Last night.

—But where is he?

—Upstairs.

—I came because I was worried about you, Berry, said Ruben. Are you all right?

—Your son stole my car, said Berry.

—I know. I'm sorry.

—I'm going to prosecute, Berry said.

—But what about the dog?

They climbed the stairs together. Berry smelled not quite clean. The dog was not in the front room, with the warlike sculptures made of metal tubes. The second room, where Ruben had never been, was full of dilapidated wooden bookcases filled with books, and more books on the floor, not new paperbacks but old books with black and brown covers. Berry's bedroom, where a single mattress lay on the floor instead of a bed, was otherwise filled with about ten piles of clothes. Ruben was afraid of rotting food and maggots, but she saw nothing like that. The dog lay next to the bed. He looked asleep. Maybe he really had died only the night before. Small piles of dog feces lay about the room.

—I am reduced, Berry said. I am reduced. For the first time, Ruben could tell Berry had shame and self-consciousness like other people, not just theatrical defiance.

She turned and touched Berry's hand. Was he sick? The dog had looked young.

—He must have been, said Berry solemnly.

—We'll take his body to the vet, where it can be cremated, Ruben said.

—Shall we? I think he'd like fire. Better than earth.

The dog was bony. Ruben wondered if Berry had fed him. She brought the green blanket from downstairs, and was trying to make herself lift the dog and put him on the blanket when Berry lowered herself to the floor, and, in a sitting position, leaned over and did it. Ruben wrapped the blanket around him and then she was able to lift him and carry him downstairs. She could hear Berry coming down behind her, but instead of waiting, she reached under the dog to turn the doorknob and open the front door. The sunshine outside seemed harsh and startling. Ruben wished she'd opened the trunk of her car in advance. She had to lay the dog on the sidewalk, then go back inside and squeeze past Berry, who was coming down with one hand flat against the wall, the other clutching the banister, then clutching it lower down. Ruben put her hand on Berry again to make sure she didn't jostle the old woman. She had left her purse in the room upstairs. She couldn't make herself wait, but maneuvered past Berry again on the way down. She had opened the trunk and closed it with the dog inside before Berry came out.

—I forget his name, Ruben said, as they drove away, once Berry had her seat belt fastened around her, which required leaning over her; Berry's body seemed softer and fleshier than Ruben expected; in her mind Berry was all bone, but Ruben felt breasts.

—Sasha.

—Yes. Had she ever known? She said, He wasn't old, was he?

—Dogs have a different system, said Berry.

The people at the vet's office assumed that Berry was Ruben's batty old mother, and patted the old woman's arm but talked sensibly only to Ruben, who paid the cremation fee. Berry said as they left, Appreciation is heartfelt, and the vet's assistant stared. Then Berry walked confidently although slowly, with a slight lurch, to the wrong car in the parking lot, and stood there looking at it until Ruben came up behind her and put her arm on the flowered pink shoulder. Berry took Ruben's hand. When she didn't speak, she seemed much older. Ruben got her into the car and walked slowly around to the driver's side. When we get back, I'll help you clean up that dog shit, she said, turning the key. She was not such a nice person as this. She had a kindness defect.

The shit was dry and not disgusting, but hard to scrape off the floor, though Ruben had found some rags and a knife. She looked over the piles of clothes, far too many for her washing machine. Berry had not followed her upstairs. There was a phone on the floor near the mattress and Ruben phoned Harry, who was home from work by now. He said, This I need in my otherwise perfect life?

—I need help carrying all the dirty clothes down the stairs.

When Ruben came downstairs with the first load, she left it on the floor near the staircase and ventured into the kitchen, where Berry was eating a bowl of cold cereal. At different places in the kitchen were three unmade sandwiches: two slices of bread, side by side. Next to one was an open jar of grape jelly. Harry arrived. They put the laundry in his car.

—Shall I bring you a hamburger, Berry? said Ruben.

—With ketchup.

—We're going to do your laundry.

—I miss Sasha, Berry said.

Harry said, Was Sasha the dog?

—Sasha the dog. A pile of ashes, like many of my friends.

Toby and Harry Ruben commandeered seven washing machines in a Laundromat. Toby Ruben said, I'm just getting off on being Lady Bountiful. They had supper at a Thai restaurant—hadn't they earned dinner out?—then stopped at McDonald's.

Berry seemed surprised when they returned, and surprised by the hamburger.

—You didn't remember I said I'd bring one? Ruben said.

—I thought it was a hamburger in theory only.

—No.

—Your son stole my car. I suppose you owe me a hamburger.

Ruben felt rage outline the veins in her arms, then recede. They drove home in separate cars. Ruben listened to the radio. The news from Zaire was now the news from Congo. Deborah had been right. The rebels who'd liberated the country had also massacred refugees. Now the U.N. was investigating.

—You were right to worry, she said to Deborah, who couldn't hear her, a fact she never doubted. People had said to her, Now Deborah will always be with you: meaning, apparently, that Ruben could pretend to talk to Deborah and pretend to hear her answers. But when she did that, she had at her disposal only her memory of what Deborah had said in the past. If Deborah were alive, she would not say exactly what Ruben imagined she might say. She never had. Ruben found she was imagining telling Berry all this. She'd missed the rest of the news, with all this thinking.

In the morning Harry said, We have to make an arrangement. A social worker . . .

—She's not senile.

—She can't care for herself.

—The dog's death upset her.

—Or she couldn't remember where the dog food was, and he starved to death.

—I don't think it's that bad, said Ruben. There was a bowl of dog food in the kitchen.

—It might sometimes be that bad.

For three days Ruben led her life and then she went over to Berry's. She offered to take Berry shopping and was pleased when Berry said no.

—I have food, she said, but no dog and no work.

Again, Berry was wearing the pink housedress. What do you do all day? Ruben asked. The house had no television, and the books didn't look as if anybody read them.

—I remember my life, Berry said, but her voice didn't have its usual boldness. Today I remembered the Second World War,

which changed everything. I would enjoy reading, but I've lost
my reading glasses. And my teeth. I've lost my teeth.

Her jaw looked sunken. Ruben helped search for Berry's teeth in dresser drawers and desk drawers and cabinet shelves. The clean clothes were where Ruben had last seen them, and she helped put them away.

Harry said, that night, I bet she doesn't even have a will.

—She's poor.

—How do you know? She could be rich. And she has the statues. There don't seem to be any relatives. What will happen to the art?

The next time, Ruben asked Berry questions. The gallery in New York no longer existed. Berry had no kin. Ruben had requested a glass of water, and they sat in Berry's kitchen like two ladies. The white-haired woman opposite her leaned forward, but her back was straight. Her hair was wild. Ruben could believe she'd been a political activist, despite the pink housedress.

—Don't you have another sister?

—Dead.

—The one who wrote the book?

—The one who wrote the book.

The next time Ruben visited, a week later, Berry was wearing the green smock, and that made Ruben feel better. It had been among the dirty clothes. Everything made sense. She didn't wear it when it was dirty, but did when it was clean. In the smock, Berry looked like a crazy artist, which was much better. Are you eating? said Ruben pleasantly.

—No, I'm talking to you.

—I mean in general. Have you eaten today?

—Pears. By now it was early fall. Stevie had come home and was gone again. Mary Grace and Peter were still silent and gone. Pears were a good choice in the fall. Now Ruben could smell them. She said, Did someone bring you pears?

—I bought them. I bought a big bag of pears.

The kitchen was bare but clean. Not much cooking went on there, but a plastic bag of yellow Bartlett pears was on the table. Some had brown spots. Ruben washed the pears, cut out the brown spots, and found a bowl. She put them into the refrigerator.

—What else do you eat?

Berry didn't answer and Ruben snooped in the cupboards. Berry ate breakfast cereal.

Ruben went home and called a state agency. A social worker called her back. Suddenly Ruben was a primary caregiver. The social worker was surprised that Berry lived alone. Possibly she should be living in Ruben's house? Wait a minute, said Ruben.

There followed telephone numbers and kindness. Even the social worker, once she got the point, was kind. People were surprised that Ruben was making these calls about someone who wasn't her relative. She's my friend, Ruben said. Don't friends count? She'd get off the phone and cry about Deborah. Friends count. She thought of the hospital where friends didn't count.

—Friends count, she said to Berry.

—Of course. Once, a friend died for me. I have a corn on my toe, but the drugstore has shut down.

Ruben bought corn plasters and washed Berry's feet and applied the thing in the package, with Berry's stubby foot on her lap. Drying Berry's foot, she felt happy.

It turned out there was money. Berry had a bankbook, and the bank had not closed its doors.

Harry said, We need a lawyer. She has to make a will, and she ought to give somebody power of attorney. Probably us.

Later he said, She's our hobby.

Washing a few dishes, one day, in Berry's kitchen, Ruben felt the entire pain of not knowing where her child was. Mostly, she decided, she felt it half strength. Bad enough.

Harry said, We have to call Jeremiah. Jeremiah is a lawyer.
He's that *kind* of lawyer.

She said, Jeremiah has been trying to find Berry for years and
years.

—What do you mean?

They were in bed, interrupting themselves during the prelim-
inaries. Ruben sat up. In her youth, Ruben said, needing to
keep laughter from her voice because the story made her nervous, Berry was a revolutionary. I think I told you.

—I don't think so.

—I heard the story years ago, but I didn't make the connection. Then she told my class. Ruben interrupted herself. Oh—
that's why I didn't tell you. It was the day the kids left. Anyway, she blew up a trolley, I think. There's a book about it,
which, Toby Ruben said archly, I have been borrowing from
Jeremiah for more than twenty years. She'd imagined the first
words she'd read if she ever opened the book: Deborah didn't
love you, and Peter and Mary Grace are dead.

—What do you mean, a book? Where is this book?

—It's there.

—Where?

—On the bottom shelf, on the right. The last book. That
black book next to the green one.

—That book? Harry started to get up.

—Hold my breasts, said Ruben. Lie here. She spread her legs,
and when Harry moved onto her, she clamped her legs over
his back. Harry was buying the city a playground that fall. He
was happy and excited, and she liked a happy husband.

She still didn't read the book. Days passed. She didn't call
Jeremiah. The children didn't phone. These days, when she
looked inside herself, someone was still screaming, but Ruben
cried mostly in the bathtub and when she was alone in the
house, or even in the store, in the back room, knowing Archie
was hard of hearing. Soon he'd retire; sometimes Ruben
thought she might take out a loan and buy the store. How

unfeeling to consider changing her life without Deborah's knowledge.

—Did you call Jeremiah? Harry sometimes asked.

At the store, now, she usually selected the stock. One afternoon Ruben was arranging a display of new bowls, terra-cotta with blue enamel inside. She placed them near a shelf of dishes by a local potter whose work she liked; thick glazes, secret color rising to the surface. She wondered if the potter made pitchers, and the words drawing pitchers, drawing pitchers played tauntingly in her mind. It took her two days to place them: Jeremiah and the art class. She remembered that Jeremiah was in pain and was funny; he was not merely difficult.

So at last, that evening, she called him. Dialing, she rehearsed: she'd explain who Berry was, ask about a will, apologize for keeping Berry to herself. The voice saying hello sounded like Deborah. Who's this? Ruben said.

—Mary Grace Laidlaw. Toby?

—How long have you been there? She was amazed, hurt.

—A week.

—Why didn't you call me?

—Oh, Toby. Because I don't know where Peter is.

—But I haven't known where Peter is for months.

—But I did know.

The girl was crying. Mary Grace, Ruben said. Mary Grace. She was angry, then merely needy. Mary Grace, come to my house. Now.

Okay. The phone was clicked down and a minute later it rang. I don't have a car. Come get me?

—I'll meet you in front of the house in five minutes.

Young people have no strength. She and Deborah used to walk the six blocks over and over, back and forth. Ruben waited in her car at the curb, and then Mary Grace came out of Deborah's old house and ran down the porch steps and got in. She turned to face Ruben, who was held back by her shoulder harness. Ruben released the harness and took Mary Grace in her arms. Mary Grace's hair was short. Ruben ran her hand over it. You cut off your hair?

—One sad day.

—Where have you been living?

—My father doesn't open the curtains, said Mary Grace quickly. Now and then he calls a cleaning service and they push everything aside and vacuum the middle of the rooms. Things are piled on things.

Ruben drove home. It was early in the evening on a Thursday in October, and Harry wouldn't be home for a while. It was dark. Ruben brought Mary Grace into her kitchen. Sit, she said. Talk to me. Mary Grace sat on one of the kitchen stools, and Ruben took off her coat and began cooking: eggplant, zucchini, yellow squash, mushrooms. On the counter were three tomatoes so red their skins were beginning to stretch and wrinkle, and a lot of basil and parsley she'd bought because she'd been too sad in the spring to grow any.

—Mostly we were in Boston, Mary Grace said now. We sublet a place in J.P. I don't think he loves me anymore.

—You broke up?

—I didn't know he was leaving. He was just gone, one day. I had to tell the lady he worked for. He left while I was out.

—He has Berry's car?

—If it's still working. It wasn't doing so great.

—I thought you went back to school.

—No.

Ruben cut up the vegetables. She couldn't just cook vegetables, though Mary Grace was sometimes a vegetarian. Maybe rice with them . . . She said, Why didn't you call us?

Mary Grace was silent for a long time. Then she said, Peter said you'd be mad about the car, about a lot of things. I think he didn't want to have the conversations you'd have . . .

—But he could have said . . . All I wanted was to know you were alive!

—You thought we were dead?

She considered. Well, no, technically I didn't think you were dead.

—My mom was like that, Mary Grace said. Anytime anybody was ten minutes late, she started planning the music for the funeral. After a while it feels like a person's trying to kill you off. People just don't die that easily.

Ruben clamped her jaw to keep from saying, Your mother did. She knew Mary Grace was thinking it. She said, You're right. We overdo it. Mostly when people are late, they aren't dead.

—Did you ever think what it's like to receive all that worry? I think Peter feels as if there's just too much worry over him in this family. Oh, I don't know what Peter feels. The last week, he hardly talked to me.

—What kind of job did he have?

—Baby-sitting. He took care of two little kids while their mother worked, then he got an older one from kindergarten. Little black kids. Peter likes taking care of people.

—He walked out on them, too? Ruben sat down in the dining room to take in all this information, and Mary Grace began fussing in the kitchen—making herbal tea, Ruben saw. All right. Ruben watched—her vegetables sitting on the counter in pieces. When Mary Grace handed her a mug, she drank. It was a blue mug from the store, and Mary Grace had taken the one that matched it for herself. A middle-sized, chunky girl, she sat on the stool, hunched forward, her short blond hair on her cheeks, blowing on the tea and drinking while watching Ruben across in the dining room, as if to make sure her mother's old friend drank her tea. Ruben drank half of it. Want to walk to the store with me? she said then, standing up and thumping her mug on the counter. We'll get some bread. Cheese. That would be enough supper: vegetables and rice and bread and cheese. They put on their coats and Ruben stuck her wallet in her pocket. Now they walked side by side in the dark. It was cold and Mary Grace walked fast; she did have strength. She

was taller than Ruben, with long swinging arms and a good
smell, probably shampoo. She had on her green parka, getting
old and saggy now, heavy for October.

Halfway down the block, Ruben said, Before you were born,
Deborah and I took walks in the dark. Mary Grace didn't answer. The store was a little Italian market, brightly lit, filled
with people on their way home from work. Toby Ruben and
Mary Grace chose a round loaf with a thick crust and some
cheese, and waited together on the long line to pay, not speaking except when Mary Grace asked if they could also have
olives, and Ruben, delighted to be asked for something, agreed.
When they emerged, Mary Grace took the bag from Ruben as
if Ruben were old and bread were heavy. Her arms freed,
Ruben touched Mary Grace's arm, and at that, still standing
in the light in front of the store, the girl thrust the groceries
back at Ruben after all, and put both her cold hands on
Ruben's head, as if it were an apple she might pick. But she
held Ruben's head tightly, held her hair, then slowly moved her
hands greedily over Ruben's scalp and then her face, while
Ruben held the brown paper bag and felt something resembling
happiness begin in her throat. For a long time Mary Grace
touched the skin and bones of Ruben's face, and touched her
ears, while uncurious shoppers hurried out of the store and
down the street or to their cars. In the background, car engines
caught and cars drove away from the corner. Soon the store
would close. At last Mary Grace leaned over and kissed Ruben
on the mouth. Her face was wet. Ruben kissed back, then put
her free arm around the girl and turned her toward home, and
they walked together.

—You wouldn't mind if I cried every day, Mary Grace said.

—Hell, no, I cry every day, said Ruben. You'd better live
with us.

—Peter got tired of it. My dad hates it.

—Doesn't he cry?

—Yes, but I think he thinks I'm faking, after all this time. My sisters can't believe how much I cry.

—You were her baby. You're too young to be on your own.

—I'm pretty grown up. I'm older than Stevie.

—Stay with us, sweetie, Ruben pleaded. You must stay at our house starting this minute.

—I have to take care of my father.

—No, you don't. And anyway, you aren't.

—It's true, I just sleep.

—What did you do in Boston?

—I worked as a temp. I was the one who made money. I kept working after Peter left, but then the people whose apartment I had came back, so I had to leave.

—You really don't know where he is? Ruben said.

They crossed the street, Ruben looking for cars, Mary Grace not. I don't. The note he left was about stuff between us—bad stuff. But then he said, I feel as if I killed your mother.

—How could he feel that?

—Didn't we all feel that?

—But Peter?

—Well, said Mary Grace, my mother said you once let him fall out of the carriage when he was a baby. Maybe he got bonked on the head.

The food was more than acceptable, and Harry was surprised and pleased to see Mary Grace. He seemed to feel sure that if Mary Grace had come, Peter couldn't be far behind. He asked questions about the car's problems, speculating on how far Peter might have gotten with it. Not California, he said, with satisfaction. Doesn't sound as if he'd make it *that* far.

—I don't think he wanted to go to California, said Mary Grace.

—Where do you think he wanted to go? Ruben said.

—I don't know.

After supper Ruben went with Mary Grace to Deborah's house. It was the first time since Deborah died that she'd gone

inside. The yellow kitchen was still yellow. The house was dirty
and disconsolate. Jeremiah was getting fat and gray. He had a
funny way of nodding his head up and back like a pigeon.

—Dad, said Mary Grace, I'm going to stay at Toby's for a
few days.

Jeremiah said, I read about Harry in the paper. He's crazy.

—What about?

—Tennis courts in Brandon Park. No way. Vandals will finish them off in ten minutes.

—He thinks they're special tennis courts. And mostly it's going to be basketball courts.

—Ten minutes.

—Jeremiah, she said. I have to ask you something. Do you
do wills? Power of attorney?

—Sure. It's my bread and butter.

—There's an old woman Peter used to work for . . . Jeremiah. I think you used to be interested in this woman. I don't
know if you remember. I forgot for a long time, but then she
talked about her life. It's Berry Cooper.

Ruben and Mary Grace had gone in by the back door and
were facing Jeremiah in the kitchen. Now Jeremiah stepped
forward and reached for something on the counter beside
him—a long spoon, though he didn't seem to be cooking or
eating anything—and poked it in the air in her direction,
not threateningly but questioningly, like a microphone. Berry
Cooper?

—Yes, do you remember—when we took that class, all those
years ago?

—Peter knows Berry Cooper? She's alive?

—Well, I know her myself. I go to her house.

—Why didn't you tell me?

They arranged for him to visit Berry. He would take care of
her will and power of attorney. Of course. Ruben and Mary
Grace went home, exhausted with feeling. Ruben told Mary
Grace she should sleep in Peter's room, put sheets and pillow-

cases in her arms, and left her watching *Seinfeld* with Harry. Ruben went upstairs, brushed her hair, and put on her night-gown, though it wasn't bedtime yet.

Ruben walked to the bookshelf. She knelt and drew out the thin, old black book, which still smelled of a used bookstore. She opened it at random, still afraid of what it might say to her. She read the words "What do you think of" and closed the book. Then she walked to the bed and sat down on the edge of it. In middle age it is not necessary to read books while walking in the street pushing a baby carriage. Or, it is not possible. Ruben started reading *Trolley Girl* at the beginning, and read, uninterrupted, into the night, until she reached her old bookmark: a yellowed corner of a piece of newspaper with the number 17 on it. Then she brushed her teeth and got into bed with the book. Harry came up the stairs, took off his clothes, and got into bed. He touched her leg and ran his hand up and down it under the blanket. Ruben said, Do you mind if I keep the light on?

—Just tip it. It was what he always said. She tipped the shade so the light fell on her. She sat up in bed and arranged the blanket so it covered Harry, who was lying down, and Toby, who was sitting. She put the old scrap of newspaper on the table beside her and continued reading what came next.

––––––––

I persist, more than forty years later, in imagining Sarah, who was one of the passengers on the second green trolley, look-ing out the window to the side. I don't want her to look out the front and see what's coming, but she probably did. When *I* sit in the first seat of a public conveyance—which is where, we eventually learned, Sarah was sitting—I look out the larger front window, not the side one.

The first interurban trolley had traveled to the end of the line, arriving empty: its two passengers had disembarked two thirds of the way along, at Ridgefield. It was returning empty. These trolleys didn't have a place to turn around; they had two fronts, and so the scab motorman carried his key from one end of the trolley to the other, accompanied by the conductor with the few cents he'd taken in. Then they set out again. Their task probably seemed simple. They just had to traverse the track they'd already traveled, back to the trolley barn.

Either they didn't understand the signals, or the signals had been tampered with—by my sister Jessie or by others—for the purpose of bringing the cars to a halt, or for the purpose of destroying them. Or the motorman and conductor of the second trolley didn't understand. Or nobody understood. Sitting on the front seat of the second Lake Avenue Interurban with a homemade present for the Livingstons' little boy on her lap, Sarah saw the first car speeding toward her. With a crash that sickened and terrified people in the shabby little houses on either side of the right-of-way, the two long green elegant trolleys collided head-on. Both motormen and one conductor were badly injured, and my sister Sarah was crushed to death in a moment.

I was at the trolley barn, searching the crowd. Of course we knew nothing. I was hoping the trolley that had left was not the Lake Avenue Interurban but one of the others. I resisted asking; the one person I stopped wasn't sure. I also hoped Sarah had been dissuaded by somebody she happened to meet, or by the general sense of confusion and disorder, or by fear of the angry crowd.

After a while I saw a man I knew, and he told me with certainty that the Lake Avenue trolley had indeed departed; he'd seen a young girl who might have been my sister Sarah getting on. I kept looking, though. Then all at once something changed; I've tried to think, over and over, all these years, what changed. I think what may have changed was the kind of noise. People had been making angry, excited, uncertain noise; suddenly there was fearful noise.

When the trolleys collided, there were witnesses. People in neighboring houses hurried to the wreckage. The second trolley was lying on its side. The front was smashed into the rest like a partly closed accordion. A Mr. Brewster somehow climbed over the still vibrating wheels, while people screamed that he'd be electrocuted. Of course the wire was overhead and everyone knew that, but I suppose it had been torn. Mr. Brewster managed to break a window and reach the two surviving passengers and the injured scab workers.

Meanwhile the electricity up and down the line stopped. I don't know if there was a way the trolley company could detect that, but I believe that Mr. Brewster's daughter walked to a house not far away where she knew there was a telephone, and phoned the trolley company, or the police. We at the trolley company suddenly saw men in suits, quite different from the working people in the trolley yard, hurtling from the company's offices. A car drove up and several men got in. It sped away. Somehow the crowd knew these people weren't just avoiding unpleasantness. A few people ran forward to block the car, but others blocked them. Soon rumors were everywhere and it was no longer possible to remember how one had received the news.

I knew a girl was dead. The rumors, at least, were that a girl was dead.

I found the crowd intolerable, and now people were clutching one another and screeching. In a terrible way, people enjoy that kind of trouble. I made my way to the edge of the crowd and found myself walking back and forth in a vacant lot that was scrabbly with weeds in summer but now covered with snow. My feet were already damp but soon they were soaked, and I had the dim knowledge that my shoes would be ruined and that neither my family nor I could afford to buy new ones. It was a double knowledge: my shoes, my feet— and, simultaneously, my sister Sarah. I held the knowledge of what had happened to Sarah away from myself. Maybe some other girl had taken the trolley. Rumors can be false; perhaps no one had died. As darkness came on, the crowd dispersed. No trolleys were running.

The man I'd talked to before, who was the proprietor of the fruit and vegetable market where my mother shopped, came to the edge of the lot. He didn't call to me; he just waited. When I turned, I saw him and walked toward him. I remember how he looked. He was dressed in brown, and was holding his brown cap fast to his thigh as if he'd caught a mouse in it. Because he had already taken off his cap on such a cold day, I knew he had to tell me bad news. I thought he was going to say that an identification had been made and Sarah was dead, but instead he said, "I am sorry to tell you, miss. They are saying your sister was arrested by the police."

He meant Jessie, of course. I experienced a moment of wild joy. Sarah was not dead, she was merely, somehow, a criminal! Then I understood. Jessie had been arrested. She'd been arrested for murdering Sarah. Gradually we all learned that the police thought Jessie had walked miles along the right-of-way next to the Lake Avenue line, in the cold, and deliberately turned off the signal lights that the conductors had lit, in order to cause a trolley wreck. She had been discovered walking near the right-of-way, far out in the country, alone.

I heard over and over again that Sarah was dead and Jessie was being blamed. Oh, others were arrested, too, other known radicals, but Jessie was the only suspect found anywhere near the tracks; Jessie was everyone's culprit. People were kind to me. Jessie had been regarded as our family's bad luck for years. Now we'd been truly cursed. Kind women, or those who throve on melodrama, enclosed me, sobbing, in their arms and coats. Someone led me to the store, where, even though it was Sunday, Miss Fredericks had materialized. She washed my face in warm water. I remember that her touch felt frightened, as if she thought my face might burn her hand. Then I was escorted home. I felt rage more than sorrow. I blamed myself, my parents, the trolley company, the scabs, the stupid Livingstons, and Sarah. I'm not even sure I blamed Jessie at first. Jessie was the only one who at least thought she knew what she was doing.

By the time I got home, my parents knew. For hours, we weren't alone, and it was just as well. Rabbis and prayerful old men appeared, though we didn't belong to a synagogue. Neighbors, relatives, busybodies. Food was carried in. Tea was forced on us. My mother and father sobbed, but I was silent; maybe the neighbors thought I was a co-conspirator. Later, when we were alone, my parents screamed. "She should die in the electric chair!" my father shrieked. I went into the bedroom I shared with Sarah and felt absolute terror that she was gone. And it was unthinkable. All through her life, Sarah had barely left our block except to go to school. The room seemed enormous. Never in my life had I spent a night alone in a room, without the sound of breathing nearby, the breathing of one sister or the other or both. I didn't go to bed but spent that night wringing out wet cloths and patting my mother's face with them, as Miss Fredericks had frantically patted mine. My father left the house and was gone for hours.

I thought my mother would never speak intelligibly again. The few words I made out were in Yiddish. When I remember that night, I understand why, through the years that followed, I never let myself get close enough to a man to consider bearing his child. My mother was not a particularly intelligent or strong woman. If she'd had an easy life—if there is such a thing—maybe she'd have carried it off well. But nothing much happens to anybody that's worse than what happened to my mother that night.

I don't know how much my mother understood of the American justice system, and I don't know when she made up her mind between anger at Jessie and fear for Jessie. By morning she knew which she felt, and it was anger. And for

the rest of my mother's life, after that night when I bathed
and kissed her over and over again, the serious quarrel between us was about pity and love for Jessie or anger at Jessie.
I explained, that night and on many other nights, that it
wasn't certain Jessie had done anything wrong—that she had
been arrested, not convicted. To my mother, though, Jessie
had done wrong when she first had left our house and taken
lovers, and those actions were the cause of Sarah's death.
Not that my mother hoped for Jessie's conviction. She
wanted to scream at Jessie and hit her, not to have the law
take an interest in her.

I don't remember much of Sarah's funeral, which took
place the day after her death. I remember a small room, narrow corridors made smaller by black drapery, crowds jostling
in the narrowed halls, crying and lamenting. I remember
Sarah's schoolmates and their parents presenting me with
their distorted faces. Crying makes people ugly, and nobody
was decorously sorrowful.

A day or so later, when my mother was being tended to by
relatives—she was like a sick person, mostly in bed, bargain-
ing and stalling for hours before she'd accept morsels of food
from patient cousins and sisters-in-law—I slipped out of the
house, concealing my coat by crushing it against my body
until I got outside. Then I put it on and walked to the city
jail.

I thought I'd have to wheedle and plead, but a frightened
policeman, a young, skinny Irish cop, who'd obviously never
expected to have to deal with a serious crime, listened to me
respectfully, nodding vigorously and too many times, as if he
himself were the accused person. "You can see her in the parlor," he said incongruously, and even in my distraught state I
marveled that a jail would have a parlor.

Of course it didn't; he meant what we'd call a waiting
room. He showed me into a plain, narrow room with
benches along the walls and a big dusty oak desk in one cor-

ner, with nothing on it at all. He pointed to a bench and I sat down. Then he left, and in a while I heard the sound of a door, and he brought Jessie into the room.

She stood still. She looked angry. Her bobbed hair was matted and stuck out, seeming to make sharp points around her face. She was wearing her own clothes: her gray dress. She looked buxom and square, stubborn. The policeman stood beside her for an instant, then turned and moved toward the empty desk as if he meant to sit there, supervising our conversation. The desk had no chair. Narrow and dark in his uniform, he stood and looked at the desk a moment, and then he left the room, almost on tiptoe, walking in back of Jessie, as if she were the authority figure.

Jessie and I stayed where we were. I didn't stand and take her in my arms; she didn't step forward or cry. Her arms and legs, under the demure dress, seemed rigid, and they were spread a little, clumsily: limbs hacked off by torturers and carelessly refastened. Her face held only horror and rage. She didn't seem to see me.

I leaned to the side and began to make a sound, a shriek that I muffled with my hands because we were in a place where I could not let go. I hadn't shrieked before. I had cried, but mostly I had kept silent, bringing wet cloths. Now I was afraid I'd vomit on the floor and the jailers would be angry. At long last Jessie sat down on the bench, not close to me—as far away as someone could and still be in a conversation. "Miriam," she finally said urgently. "Miriam." She sounded stern. At length I stopped making sounds, passed my hands over my wet face, and sat up. I turned in her direction.

"How's Mama?"

"In bed."

"And Papa?"

"Oh, very bad."

"I never thought she would go," Jessie said. "She never did anything like that."

"I didn't think she would. I had no idea," I said. But I was
thinking that if Jessie didn't expect Sarah to take the trolley,
it meant she knew there would be trouble. I was overcome
with fear. It was physical. I was so afraid Jessie would die in
the electric chair that I couldn't stand up, as if my bench
were perched up in the sky and if I stood I'd plunge to my
death. At last I moved closer to her, and put my arms around
her. "Jessie, if you did it, never tell me," I said. "Promise me
you'll never tell me. Tell me you didn't do it."

"I didn't do it," she said.

We held each other. I wasn't close enough to feel her soft
breasts. We were both pretending, as though the jailer was
watching us after all. I felt that the wrong sister had died,
and it was my fault because I'd always preferred Jessie's intelligence and wit to Sarah's stupid goodness. Jessie's political beliefs, her ideological beliefs, seemed, just then, like dry
pedantry. She'd killed Sarah over fussy little notions. I
stopped being afraid Jessie would die in the electric chair. I
wanted her to die in that hideous manner, in humiliation
and terror, being walked consciously to her death. Now I'd
scared myself so badly, wanting such a thing, that I couldn't
speak, but on the other hand, I was no longer afraid to
move. I stood up and hurried away. The jailer, whom I
found in the anteroom reading the newspaper, was surprised
and embarrassed. He'd have let me stay a little longer. He
pushed the paper away and later I realized he must have
been reading a story about us.

Soon enough, my parents and I were left alone in what felt
like a vast space. I no longer wrung out wet cloths. My
mother said she wanted nothing, and hardly spoke. Neither
she nor my father talked of Jessie or Sarah. Their permanent
lifetime moods were selected that week. From then on, they
were people of bitterness and suppressed rage. I was alone.
Suddenly it seemed that I had no friends. I had thought I had
friends. Edith Livingston, who'd taken so to Sarah, did not

come to her funeral or make contact with me again. From the vantage point of years, I don't blame her. The newspaper didn't report where Sarah was going on that trolley—I suppose nobody knew but our family, and nobody asked us—but everyone knew the crash had been on the Lake Avenue line. Of course the Livingstons knew all about it; but what would have been gained if they'd blamed themselves, or sullied that little boy's life with a notion of responsibility, however indirect, for a death? And of course they had meant no harm with their impulsive, sentimental invitation. I pride myself on being unlike my parents, but I've never done anything impulsive or sentimental since. I've never suddenly begged a friend to come and see me; I've barely invited anybody to come and see me at all, even with advance planning. I have always blamed myself for Sarah's death, and not just for taking her to the Livingstons' in the first place, but I am not responsible for any other deaths.

One night an old friend of my father's, a member of the anarchist group he'd dropped in recent years, came to see us and talked to him solemnly in the kitchen for a long time. He was an old man, not one of the young people Jessie knew best; he'd been in prison in Russia, and was rumored to have written books. When I finally walked into the room, poured them both some schnapps, and then poured some for myself and sat down with them—knowing I was unsettling them—the old man hesitated and then seemed to decide that maybe, after all, I was a more reasonable person to speak to than my father. He told me that anti-Semitic marchers had held walks past the jail several times. They were shabby, nutty, uninformed, and secretive, apparently members of an organization nobody knew about. Then the slogan "Kill the Little Jew" had appeared painted on a large boulder visible from the Lake Avenue trolley. Oh, yes, the trolley strike was over. It was just like Denver. The men gave up when somebody died. Even that made me angry. Were they surprised? Either you

make up your mind to persist in spite of death, or you don't
do what could cause a death in the first place. The old man
who spoke to my father wanted us to make contact with a
Jewish organization that might provide us with a lawyer. The
anarchists, poor wretches, had no money, and several of their
members had been accused, although only Jessie was in jail
and only she was accused of murder. They would make a secret contribution to her defense, he explained, but he thought
she'd be better off if her connection to them could be made
to seem trivial. He thought the anti-Semitism was a good
thing, because it might make one of the large Jewish groups
take an interest.

My father, grief-stricken and now terrified of anti-Jewish
feeling, was incapable of strategic thinking, and only shook
his head, again and again, but I was glad to talk with the old
man. And soon enough a lawyer appeared; I don't remember
just who made the connection. A Jewish organization had
taken us on. The lawyer was a plump, smooth-haired young
man who held his hat on his lap, waving off my offer to take
it, and repeatedly stabbed it with his finger. My mother and
father faced him, watching suspiciously from their armchairs,
and didn't speak. I think his name was Mr. Arthur, or Arthur somebody. He seemed to guess that they didn't know
English well, because after a few minutes he switched to Yiddish, and spoke sweetly. I was surprised. He said he was
sorry, he was sorry, he was sorry for their trouble. He went
back to speaking English when he began discussing the strat-
egy of the case once more; his Yiddish was only good enough
for ceremonial phraseology, I suppose.

He asked me questions that made me impatient; he didn't
understand Jessie. In those days I had abrupt changes of
viewpoint. Sometimes I wanted her to fry and sometimes I
wanted to mount a defense that would get her acquitted at
any cost. The lawyer's notion was to establish an alibi for
her. He wanted to prove that she'd been with us the morning

of the wreck, but she'd been arrested outside of town. We hadn't seen her all day and there was no way to prove that we had.

"Think," he kept saying to me. "Sometimes it helps to remember trivial things. What did you eat? Did she drop in and help cook it?" As if Jessie had ever cooked anything in her life. But he wouldn't let that topic go. I think he had the notion of proving that she cooked for the anarchists, too, that she served chicken soup with matzoh balls to hungry radicals without listening to them.

He had talked to Jessie already. "She says she was out in the country drawing pictures of barns," he said, as if nobody would believe such a thing. "In January. That's what she was doing. Drawing barns. She said she was tired of the strike. She was angry with everybody."

"That sounds like Jessie," I said, and he looked up quickly, then shook his head. "I don't think your sister has confidence in me."

"I'm sure she's grateful—" I began insincerely, but he cut me off. "She said, 'They will execute me because I'm young, female, and Jewish, or they will not execute me because I'm young, female, and Jewish.'"

"I don't understand," I said, but he just shook his head.

My parents and I attended the trial every day, even the selection of the jury, an impassive group of businessmen in stiff collars who all looked alike to me. My mother and father sat in the back of the courtroom, not speaking. For the trial itself the room was filled. I sat in the first row, behind Jessie, and people invariably made room for me. She crossed the room stolidly each morning, like someone on her way to clean a toilet. She wore a black dress that looked tight across her breasts. I suppose it was a uniform of some kind for prisoners. Maybe they'd had to send to Boston for it. Jessie's bulging eyes looked steadily and all but casually around the room as she walked to her place.

The District Attorney was a tall, wide man who flung his arms out and paced rapidly when he spoke. He had thick, straight white hair that fell over his big forehead and that he shook back by bending his head, as if in prayer, then flinging his chin up and out. His hair floated and slowly settled while he himself continued moving quickly. His hair was like a calm, stupefied wife moving at her own pace beside her wide-awake husband—or like a silent, sinister assistant: a hidden resource, another insidious possible form of destruction for us. By now, of course, I longed for Jessie's acquittal with all my soul. In my dreams, when Jessie was acquitted, Sarah suddenly appeared alive in the courtroom, smiling, irritatingly unmindful of all the trouble she'd caused.

The District Attorney spent hours establishing that trolleys are operated by electricity and run on tracks, but he always seemed dangerous, even then. And gradually, slowly, he seemed to trap my sister, almost to photograph her as she walked out into the country and switched the trolley signals. Hours of testimony by employees of the trolley company detailed the way they worked. It turned out that our system was unusual, similar to one in western Pennsylvania. Trolleys ordinarily used a signal system operated by the weight of the passing car, but we had simple hand signals. The track was divided into segments. At the end of each was a siding, where a motorman could pull his car off the main track and wait for an oncoming trolley. When a car entered a new section, the motorman or the conductor had to reach out and flip two switches, one that turned off a string of lights alongside the track on his right, in back of him, and another that caused a new long line of electric lightbulbs to go on. They were on poles stuck in the ground every few yards for the whole segment. If an approaching motorman saw lights on his left, he'd know that a car was in that section of track, coming toward him, and he'd go into the siding and wait. Lights on the right would mean only that another car going in his own direction was ahead of him, and he'd just have to slow down. On the day Sarah died, one long green interurban car entered Section 6—we kept hearing about Section 6—while the other car was coming toward it in the same section. The signal lights had been turned off, or the first motorman had neglected to turn them on, or else they were on but ignored by the second motorman.

Both motormen had been injured in the wreck, but both had lived to testify. The motorman of the first car was a young man with a strong foreign accent. He seemed like a pirate, an adventurer. He could give no good reason for coming to Boynton to work as a scab on the trolleys; he'd had a job collecting trash in Boston, but a buddy had told him of this opportunity for a bit more money and he'd taken it. I thought he had woman trouble and was looking for a reason to leave town. He seemed completely capable of ignoring an explanation of the signals, but he swore that the lights on his left were off, and that his conductor turned on those on his right.

The motorman of Sarah's car seemed more reliable. He was a middle-aged, balding man, well spoken. He'd taken the job because his wife was pregnant with their fourth child. He said he regretted being a scab. He seemed to understand what he was doing. He also swore that when he entered the section, he turned the lights on, and that the lights on the left were off.

Jessie had been arrested walking toward Boynton along the track, closer to town than the wreck. The District Attorney undertook to show that she'd walked to the beginning of Section 6, waited until the lights went on, then switched them off. Painstakingly, he established that the motorman who had turned the lights on might not have noticed that they went off. Regular trolley company employees testified that some of the lights often were unlit. Bulbs burned out or became loose in their sockets, wires were damaged. It would not have been unusual for a stretch of lights within a section to be unlit when the section as a whole was lit. A motorman passing through such a section wouldn't worry; he'd feel sure that the oncoming motorman would see at least one lit bulb on his left, and would retreat to the siding.

The most painful part of the prosecution's case was the examination of witnesses called to testify against Jessie. There was testimony that she was Jewish, that she was an anarchist, that she had lovers. Her lover's wife testified. A man who seemed all but deranged testified that the anarchists had had many more destructive plans. Sometimes Mr. Arthur objected to the more far-fetched or irrelevant parts of all this damaging testimony, but the judge rarely sustained him. Mr. Arthur cross-examined witnesses, but too politely. He couldn't get either motorman or either conductor to say that the lights might not have been turned on, and he spent a great deal of time trying to establish that Jessie's lover might have had as his mistress some other dark-haired short woman, which was nonsense.

When it was time for Mr. Arthur to put on the case for the defense, I was not confident. He called Jessie to the stand, an event the newspaper stories had anticipated for weeks.

"I went for a walk in the country," Jessie said, with a slight stubbornness in her voice, as if nobody had a right to know. "I wanted to think. I wanted to think what we ought to do next."

"It was quite cold, Miss Lipkin."

"I don't mind cold."

"Why did you walk near the trolley tracks?"

"Less snow," she said. "And I wanted to see if the trolleys would actually run. And I was sketching."

"Sketching."

"I sketch. I have piles of sketchpads in my house." The sketchpads were produced. She sketched on newspaper sometimes, in messy black ink, over the printing.

"What were you sketching, Miss Lipkin?"

"The hills covered with snow."

"But your comrades were back at the trolley barn, Miss Lipkin. Why weren't you with them?"

"I was tired of them," said Jessie. "I was tired of the strike." Jessie's claim, made in a loud, slightly hoarse voice, oddly uninflected, was that she had indeed participated in the demonstrations at the trolley company that morning. She had not known of any plan to disrupt the signals. She wanted some time to herself, and she walked out of town with a pencil and pad. What she said chilled me. When had any woman in our town ever wanted some time to herself? I knew the feeling well, though I had never acted on it, but I also knew that my own mother would not be able to imagine what Jessie might be talking about, nor would anybody else I knew. Jessie had drawn hills with a barn in front of them. Her lawyer produced the drawing.

Jessie did take walks. She often walked five miles or more just for exercise. She was the sort of person who must be active or else be consumed by nervous tension.

The District Attorney, cross-examining her later, held up to restrained mockery the notion that Jessie had grown tired of the strike. "If you were tired of the strike, Miss Lipkin, why did you participate? You shouted yourself hoarse. You are hoarse now."

"I have always been hoarse."

He had witnesses to dispute the location of the barn in Jessie's drawing. He suggested that she had not made that drawing in January at all. Even I didn't believe Jessie had walked out into the country the day of the crash to draw a picture of a barn.

Mr. Arthur also produced several anarchists who said that there had been no conspiracy to alter the signals. They were atheists who affirmed rather than swore, and I thought the jury would assume they were liars.

"What are they saying? What?" my mother would ask me
at night. She understood almost nothing, and couldn't seem
to grasp the idea of an adversarial system, a prosecution and
a defense. I tried to explain, but while the prosecution put on
its case, I'm sure she didn't understand that we'd get our
turn, or even that Mr. Arthur was on our side. At least, during the trial, she wasn't against Jessie. My father was grim.
He did understand. I think that, like me, he had come to regret his early rage. Now he might lose a second daughter to
death.

I was furious with Mr. Arthur. He missed opportunities to
object. He was unclear. I could hardly sit still in my seat, hardly keep from jumping up to explain things to the jury, who
gradually took on personality. There was a brown-eyed, serious man with a curious look whom I liked, and another,
with a nervous smile that appeared occasionally on his face
for no reason, of whom I was afraid.

Toward the end of Mr. Arthur's case it began to seem that
he did have a theory that might cast doubt on Jessie's guilt. It
had to do with the spot in Section 6 where the accident had
taken place. Mr. Arthur called a retired motorman who was
familiar with the Lake Avenue line. He was a grandfatherly
man with whiskers. I thought the grandfathers in the jury
box might trust him, if they didn't look down on him as a
mere workingman; they seemed like men of more conse-
quence. The accident had taken place past the halfway point
in Section 6—closer to Section 7, that is, than to Section 5.
All through the trial, that fact had been taken to mean that
Sarah's trolley had been in the section longer than the first,
returning car.

The retired motorman, Mr. O'Brien, testified that trolleys
did not always go at the same speed. He had driven these
very cars along the Lake Avenue line for years; he spoke as
sadly about the wrecked cars as if they'd been his horses.
Parts of the line, Mr. O'Brien explained, were straight and

level, and cars in those parts could reach speeds up to ninety miles an hour, which they actually did, making up for time lost on the more difficult sections of the track. The Lake Avenue line had some difficult sections: hills and curves.

One of those sections, he explained under the somnolent questioning of Mr. Arthur, was at the far end of Section 6, just before it joined Section 7. There was a curve on a hill. If a trolley traveling toward town didn't go around the curve extremely slowly, he said, the overhead rod almost invariably detached from the wire, and the conductor would have to go out and hook it up again. A great deal of time would be lost.

The young fellow from Boston who'd been operating the returning trolley would surely not have gone slowly enough to avoid this time-consuming separation of rod and wire. He'd have had to stop. He and his conductor, a clumsy man who also knew little English, would have had a hard time fixing the trolley out there on its roof in the cold. The overwhelming likelihood, it seemed, was that they had been on the Section 6 track much longer, after all, than the swiftly moving second trolley. The lights could have been turned on or off at either end of the section, but everyone in the courtroom could see that the operators of the first trolley were far less likely to have used the signaling system correctly than the motorman and conductor of the second trolley.

The motorman of the first trolley, back on the stand, testified that indeed he'd had a detachment of the rod. The second motorman, the one who'd been traveling away from town, then testified to no such delay. Suddenly Mr. Arthur's voice took on eagerness and feeling. "Isn't the *likeliest* explanation of the crash," he asked this witness, "that the motorman of the inbound car failed to signal when he entered the section?"

The second motorman hesitated. "Yes, sir," he said then.

The District Attorney cross-examined the second motorman. Wearily, sadly, the D.A. got him to admit that even if he'd entered the section when the other trolley was already in it, he'd have had his own opportunity to turn on the signal lights and avoid a wreck. In order for the wreck to have occurred, both operators had to have failed to use the signaling system—or somebody had to have tampered with it. The motorman had testified that he'd turned on the signals. "Isn't that right?"

"Yes, sir. But maybe," the motorman said quietly, "maybe my mate there didn't look."

The D.A. ignored him and continued asking rapid questions. Couldn't Miss Lipkin have waited at the siding, after turning off the signal lights lit by the earlier trolley? Couldn't she have turned them off a second time? The man said faintly that he didn't know. The District Attorney turned and slogged back to his chair, his shoulders bent. Long after he had seated himself, his hair was still settling.

Mr. Arthur had one more chance. He called to the stand the policeman who'd arrested Jessie. Jessie had been picked up, this man testified, quite close to town, several miles from the wreck.

"If she tampered with the first motorman's signals," Mr. Arthur said, summing up, "the second motorman should have relit them and avoided a wreck, and the first man should have noticed. If she turned off lights the second man lit, she wouldn't have had time to walk so far." It wasn't the kind of dramatic revelation I'd hoped for, but it made sense. I wondered if the jury was paying attention.

While the jury was out, my parents and I sat on a bench in the lobby of the courthouse. I was cold. For the first time I could remember, I wanted my mama, physically, and we sat pressed against each other. My father sat at a little distance, or stood and paced. I'd have liked to have been in my mother's arms, though when she spoke I was generally irked with her because it was her nature to speak, invariably, of the trivial. Nobody bothered us, and the clerk brought us glasses of water and, once, an orange. There's little in life that resembles a criminal trial, and it was more like an elaborate, sinister game than anything else I've experienced—a game in which the loser might be killed. As when I'd visited Jessie, sometimes I'd be so afraid that it was difficult to move, as if any slight gesture on my part might blow us all up.

The feeling wasn't entirely unrealistic. Anti-Semitism was not a big issue in the trial, but we had had a death threat—a letter to my father that arrived at the house in an ordinary envelope; he was afraid to show it to the police. And there were scrawls on walls. Most of the public outcry had to do with radicalism or anarchism, but people assumed that radicals were often Jews, or at least Eastern Europeans. Editorials in the newspaper called for Jessie's death, and a parade was held, with American flags and old soldiers. Of course I didn't see it. The fact that the victim was Jessie's sister seemed to convince people, using a twisted logic, that she was responsible. Killing an innocent girl was so atrocious that the person who did it had to be the sort of person who'd kill her own sister. Something like that. Of course there was no evidence that anybody had specifically tried to kill anyone. Opinion among the left-wing groups was that the anarchists had indeed flipped the switches, but that all they wanted to do was stop the trolleys. The cause of Sarah's death was the trolley company's obstinacy and the scabs' recklessness. Leaflets making this argument appeared in town.

We sat for two days on a cold marble bench staring at a marble wall, memorizing the pattern of streaks in the marble. Sometimes I thought that they had meaning, like handwriting, and if I could only decipher them, the verdict would go our way. Yet when the gentle clerk came to tell us that we had to return to the courtroom because the jury had reached a decision, I wanted to sit there for the rest of my life.

Jessie came in, walking stalwartly with her legs slightly spread, like an older woman, and sat at the table with her lawyer. She lowered her head and raised it. Then she turned and looked right at me. I stared at her and we were alone. I felt that if I could look steadily enough at her I could give her what she needed: safety, forgiveness, justice, whatever it was.

The foreman of the jury announced a finding. Jessie was not guilty. The courtroom was astonished—and looking back, I, too, am astonished. Anarchists were never acquitted. Maybe it happened because of Jessie's youth, or the spell of her power, which was oddly charming. More likely, I suppose, those sober businessmen really did listen to Mr. Arthur. The courtroom filled with murmurs of disappointment but louder ones of jubilation. I had assumed nobody was on our side, but maybe that wasn't true. Jessie was allowed to go free. She walked through the crowd, which separated quickly for her. She walked up to my mother, took her in her arms, and held her stiffly. My father had been walking toward Jessie. He suddenly sat down on the floor and began to sob. I sat down with him. I don't know how long we stayed there. When we got up, the courtroom was empty.

Jessie came home with us, and for a brief time, once more, I could hear someone else's breathing as I was falling asleep. Her landlady had rented her room to someone else; when I accompanied Jessie to pick up her belongings, the landlady expected us to be surprised and grateful that she hadn't thrown them into the street, but had bundled them into her cellar. We walked home together with bags of clothes and books and piles of drawings—Jessie did draw. Before Sarah's death, we'd have been merry about it—the stupid landlady, the clumsy parcels. Now we didn't speak. At times, though, Jessie did talk to me. I didn't ask her whether she knew what caused the wreck, or if she'd caused it herself, and she didn't bring up the subject. She'd lost her job, and seemed afraid to look for another one, and that was probably sensible. I lost mine, too, but not for a while; Miss Fredericks must have made up her mind to get rid of me the day she had to wash my face, but she didn't let me go until spring, maybe out of compassion and maybe because her mother was sick and I was needed in the store.

Jessie stayed home, reading. She didn't go to meetings, and I thought she'd become disenchanted with radical politics. She had little to say to me or our parents, and acted annoyed with us most of the time, while we in turn acted annoyed or downright angry with her and one another, but after a while her old friend and lover Maurice began to stop at the house. He'd come before dinner and stand in the middle of the living room, speaking slowly and evenly, while Jessie sat before him, and I'd tell my mother we had no choice but to set another place for him and make the food stretch. He was a comfort, someone with humor, someone who cared for Jessie and also respected us. He patted his mustache daintily at the table and I thought he was civilization incarnate, introduced into a roomful of brutes who might as well have eaten on the floor, tearing their meat with their teeth.

He talked about the Boston Red Sox, who had sold Babe Ruth to the Yankees but were still his favorite team, and about radio. Baseball games were going to be broadcast on the radio! My father stared at him. After dinner Maurice and Jessie would go out for a walk, even in the snow. For months it was the only time she went out. My mother wanted to know if Maurice was going to marry Jessie, and whether he was Jewish, and I didn't try to explain that anarchists often didn't believe in marriage but lived together without benefit of state-sanctioned ceremony. Then I lost my job. I wanted to move to Boston or New York and forget my family. My mother was hysterical at the mere suggestion, but at last, after a few weeks of unemployment during which I became even more difficult than usual, she shouted one evening, "Go, go!" I knew she didn't mean it, but I went.

I remained loyal. I found a job as a secretary in Boston, eventually moved to New York, took courses at night, and at length received my degree in classics, but I was always hurrying home, spending every holiday with my parents. By the time I had my B.A. the Depression had begun; eventually I secured a WPA teaching job, and spent most of my working life as a Latin teacher at a high school in The Bronx. I had lovers, I married, I divorced. When my father died I brought my mother to live with me, and I put up with her unwillingly, living a private life elsewhere, from that time until a few months ago, when she finally died.

When I visited my parents in the weeks just after I moved out of Boynton, my mother waved her hands in the air and incoherently expressed terror. Jessie was spending more and more time away from home, sometimes overnight. Often I didn't see her; when I did, she passed through the room and out again. She was vigorous and active but seemed as alien as a lodger about whom we knew nothing but the cut of her coat. When I seized her and questioned her, she said, "I'm working." I think she was earning some money copying or transcribing for one of the old anarchist writers, one of the few who had a little money. Then she was arrested. She'd participated in a demonstration in support of a strike of garment workers at a Boynton factory, and for no reason other than a refusal to leave the premises, she was arrested for disorderly conduct and inciting to riot. This time she was found guilty, and spent a year and a half in jail. For my parents, in some ways this event was worse than what had happened before. They understood it and felt ordinary emotions like shame. They were angry with Jessie for causing them more grief, although the charge was so flimsy and the case so obviously rigged that it seems clear the police were simply waiting for her to show her face. I suppose the District Attorney was furious that he couldn't convict her before. This time, when Jessie was released she had little to do with my parents. She left town and we weren't in touch with her for a while. Next we heard that she was married and living in New York. She'd married an artist who'd been her customer when she was working in a cheap lunchroom. Soon she was sharing his studio, taking lessons from his friends, and eventually she went to art school. They lived in Europe; the next we heard, they were divorced. At times I'd see Jessie's name in the newspaper. She was the chairwoman of a committee of artists raising money for the Lincoln Brigade at the time of the Spanish Civil War. Maybe by then she had her new name— her second husband's name, which she kept even when she divorced him and married a third.

I wasn't upset or ashamed, or not very, when Jessie was in jail, and I wasn't curious about her husbands. With Sarah dead and Jessie acquitted, I haven't cared much about any-thing else for the rest of my life. Jessie did care. She never stopped caring. I suppose, even now, she thinks about Sarah more than I do. I feel nothing but bitterness about Sarah, too—most of the time: my strongest emotion when I think of Sarah is still irritation that she couldn't see that it made sense to stay home that Sunday. She wasn't sensible.

We never exactly lost touch with Jessie. I wrote to her when Papa died, and now and then in between, and again when Mama died. I would have addresses but usually not phone numbers. Both times, though, Jessie called me. "Mir-iam, when is the funeral?"

"We had it already. Why didn't you call sooner?" Identical conversations, twenty years apart.

"I was away. Are you still being good, Miriam?"

"I was never good."

"Yes, you were."

"Let's get together," I said both times.

"I'll be in touch."

Nobody as angry as I am is good. Once I visited Jessie in
New York, in a small place in the Village where she was living with a lover. She might have been married to someone
else at the time. I remember thinking that I could have been
shocked, but wasn't, so something shocking must have been
going on. Jessie tidied things quickly when I came in. Maybe
her lover's underwear was on the bed. The place, just a
room, smelled of sex. We talked platitudes, and then she
said, "Aren't you ever going to ask me if I did it?"

"Did what?"

"Changed the signals. Killed Sarah."

"No, I'm not."

"What do you want to say to me, Miriam?" she asked me.
She was beginning to look middle-aged, like a woman who
had had children, though she never did.

It turned out that I knew what I wanted to say. "Jessie, do
you think, do you really think it's all right to break things,
destroy things, maybe hurt people, to bring about a good
cause?"

"I'm not a pacifist, Miriam."

"What has that got to do with it?"

"In a war, do you think everyone who dies is bad and
guilty?"

"Of course not."

"So there's your answer."

Because I am so full of destruction I can barely control, I
cannot endure to think of deliberate destruction. I haven't
seen my sister in decades. Maybe I never will again. Yet I
know I'm writing this account with only one reader in mind.
I've almost forgotten Sarah, but I never spend a day without
thinking of Jessie and wishing her well or ill, mostly ill. I've
gone to her shows—she became a successful sculptor—and I
read her reviews. It's painful for me, whether the critics like
her work or not. I like her work, which moves and scares

me. Huge, greenish stony shapes like big stalagmites, in the last show I saw. I went to the ladies' room and pressed my face against the wall of a booth and wept while the toilet flushed. And to my surprise, I felt joyful. Somehow I know that my sister cares constantly about everything, even though she has behaved like someone who cares about nothing but ideas, or people in the aggregate.

I write these words in a smoke-filled New York apartment, nicer than I could afford without rent control, untidy in a good way. I'm still full of relief that my mother is dead and I can be alone. If and when this book is published, maybe I'll send Jessie a copy. Maybe she'll call me. Maybe this time we'll go for a walk through New York streets together. For some reason I picture us walking downtown, near Wall Street, on one of those narrow streets that haven't changed much since the time decades ago when we did walk together elsewhere. It's a summer evening, hot. Twilight comes slowly. My living sister and I, in rumpled skirts and blouses, walk, smoking, down to Battery Park and watch the Staten Island ferry come in and depart again. The water is beautiful, dirty, and garbagy, like a Turner harbor. I put my arm on my sister's arm and we walk miles, all the way back to Little Italy, where we eat spaghetti and meatballs in a hot little place where the red wine is cheap and bitter.

Call me, Jessie. I think you killed Sarah. I forgive you at last. Call me.

————

Rain fell in the night, and Toby Ruben dreamed that she couldn't find Mary Grace, then discovered her asleep in a wide blue-covered bed behind an oak door, in a room with rain-mottled windows, a room in her own house she hadn't known about. She woke in the dark full of hurry, then heard her guest walk to the bathroom, then walk back to Peter's room.

—Deborah, I read that book.

—What book?

The book she had been afraid to read as a young woman now lay on her bedside table with its antique bookmark, the scrap of old newspaper, next to it. A book one has read is different from a book one has not read.

—Here's a book of yours.

—What book? I don't remember lending you a book.

—Please take it back. I'm done with it.

—I can't. I'm dead. You'll have to give it to Jeremiah.

In the morning Ruben was alone. Harry had hurried away early to a meeting about money, arguing out loud as he dressed; she woke to his voice. She listened, but he finished the argument—won it, surely—downstairs. Few leaves remained on the maple outside her window, and rain pressed detached yellow leaves against the screen. Sorrow can be encompassed, somehow; Miriam Lipkin had written her book, Toby Ruben had read it. At the store, that day, yellow ceramic pepper pots and salt shakers gleamed from shelves while customers scrambled among the wares finding wonders and making reasonably funny jokes about them. When Ruben left the house, Mary Grace had been asleep; in the afternoon she phoned the store, her voice crabby, to ask where Granny's leash was, and if it was all right to take him out. Isn't it raining? Ruben said.

—It stopped, she said, though wet customers shook umbrellas for another hour.

When Ruben left the store in the dark, at last, at six o'clock—no rain at all; it was clear and cold and starry—Mary Grace was leaning against her car while Granny sniffed yellow leaves at the edge of the parking lot behind the store.

—You walked all this way?

—We're a good team.

—What if I'd left early?

—We'd have walked back.

—Granny's old.

—She did fine.

Driving home, Ruben was sorry she hadn't been more en-
thusiastic. She had been looking forward to seeing Mary Grace,
but not just yet. She said, You're not a vegetarian, are you?

—Sometimes I am.

—Are you tonight?

—I'm not too hungry. I ate the leftovers from last night.

—Look, is chicken all right?

—Chicken is fine. Don't worry about me. I can always have
cereal.

—Everybody I know lives on cereal.

—Peter and me?

—Berry, too.

—Oh, said Mary Grace, I miss that old Cooper! Let's take
Dad to see her tonight. He called. He wants to do it. I forgot
to say.

—I'm bringing a lawyer to see you, Ruben said on the phone
to Berry, while Mary Grace set the table.

—You are suing me?

—No. I think you need a will.

—I am interested in prosecuting your son, Berry said
hoarsely.

—You can tell the lawyer about it.

After dinner Mary Grace put the dishes on the floor for
Granny to lick.

—We'll step on them and break them, Ruben said.

—No, we won't! Mom always does this. Did this. Don't
you?

—I scrape the stuff into her bowl.

—No, this way you don't have to scrape them. You can put
them right into the dishwasher.

Harry said, This one looks perfectly clean. Maybe we should
just put it into the cupboard. The wrinkles around his eyes were
more widely separated. He watched Mary Grace expectantly,
as if she were a performer. He had an evening meeting to go
to, but he lingered, then hurried. Now Ruben would have liked

being alone longer with Mary Grace, cleaning the kitchen properly, then talking long about Deborah, about Peter, until maybe they'd figure out where Peter might be. They'd simply get into the car and go look for him. But you have to go in a direction. Mary Grace moved around her kitchen, undeniably there. It was a start.

The doorbell rang. On the step, bulky with sorrow, stood Jeremiah, with a briefcase. You coming, too? he said to his daughter.

—Berry Cooper's a friend of mine.

—You knew her, too? I search for twenty-five years and when everybody finds her nobody bothers to tell me?

—I didn't know you cared about her, Pop, said Mary Grace. And Toby forgot.

—I'm sorry, Jeremiah, Toby Ruben said. He drove and she directed him. She said, It was a long time ago, when we used to talk about her.

At Berry's house, Jeremiah said twice, It's like anybody's house. He squeezed into a small parking space, jumped out, and then dropped back, letting Ruben lead the way. Mary Grace, though, hurried ahead of them both and rang the doorbell. When Jeremiah caught up to her he made a whoosh, like a heavy man, though he wasn't, really. As usual, Berry didn't answer the bell and they went inside, where Jeremiah studied the dusty sculptures like someone in a museum.

—I'll look for her, Ruben said, but then came a tread on the stairs. They waited awkwardly, silently, standing in the hallway and looking up as her feet and then the rest of Berry slowly appeared. Her feet and legs were bare. She was not otherwise bare; she wore the pink housedress, though the day was cold, and the three of them looking up at her were in coats. Berry had more of a humpback than Ruben had noticed before. Her face, with its bulging eyes, was stubborn and passionate. The face was deeply lined, covered with creases and tiny wrinkles. The hair stuck out, as always. More white hairs grew from the moles on Berry's face. The housedress had a food stain on the front.

—I'm busy, said Berry. She stood on the bottommost step with her hand on the newel post.

—Remember me, Berry? said Mary Grace. I'm Peter's girl-friend.

—Did you bring back my car?

—No, the car's not working so well.

—Who is this man, a veterinarian? said Berry.

Ruben introduced Jeremiah. He said, It's an honor to meet you, Mrs. Cooper. I've been wanting to meet you for many years.

—My dog died, Berry said.

—I'm sorry to hear that, said Jeremiah.

It was stuffy in the hallway. Ruben looked around for a window. Her feet hurt. Can we come in? she said. I want you to talk to Jeremiah. He's a lawyer, not a vet.

—Oh, yes, so you said. Well, if this young woman will bring back the car, I don't need to sue anybody.

—You need a will, said Jeremiah.

—A will? I'm an anarchist. Anarchists don't have wills.

—I would imagine, Jeremiah said, leaning back on his heels, which put the back of his head, Ruben saw, against the dusty wall, I would imagine that anarchists have more wills than other people. If you don't have a will, your possessions could end up going to the state. Do you want to support our nefarious government? Help Toby's husband put tennis courts in the park for vandals to destroy? Jeremiah was having a good time.

Berry said, I suppose you want me to leave you my money, Toby Ruben.

—Of course not!

—That would be a conflict of interest. I would be unable to represent you in that situation, Jeremiah said. Do you know to whom you want to leave your money? And could I ask you another question, maybe more important? Do you have a living will?

—A paper that gives you the right to put me to death if I'm troublesome. The big square grin.

—Not at all. A paper that protects you from idiot doctors who want to torture you with futile medicine to drive up your hospital bill, said Jeremiah promptly.

—Oh, I do see what you mean. Berry loved that. She said, Let's talk about my death, shall we? Can you get me a good death? Do you know there was talk of putting me to death in the electric chair at one time?

Jeremiah stepped sideways and bumped into Ruben. I do know that. I do know. I've read the book. The book your sister wrote.

—She has a copy.

—Who does?

—Jeremiah, I do, Ruben said. I have your copy.

—Didn't we figure out years ago that you didn't? Jeremiah said.

—But I do. Berry, could we please sit down someplace?

Berry ignored her. She seemed to like receiving them from the first step, one hand on the newel post. I may have a copy myself, she said. My sister sent me a signed copy when it was published.

—Berry, said Ruben, did you ever call her?

—It was her place to call me.

—But Berry, said Ruben. Berry.

—She called me Jessie. My name was Gussie. She got many things wrong.

—But she was remembering, forty years later. Books like that are always wrong.

—Then why pay attention to them? said Berry.

They couldn't get out of the corridor. They didn't run out of topics, though it took Jeremiah a long time to bring out a legal pad and start leaning on the wall and taking notes for Berry's living will, her last will and testament, and her power of attorney. Mary Grace, in the end, received Berry's power of attorney. Berry insisted.

Jeremiah got tired of leaning on the wall. Now he lifted one foot to the step where Berry stood and leaned on his knee to write. He looked like a fat suitor paying court to her.

—I leave my money and my furniture and my house and my works of art, Berry suddenly dictated, slowly and loudly, to Peter.

—To Peter? Are you sure? said Jeremiah. You mean Peter Ruben? Toby's son?

—To Peter. But not my car. He owes me for the car.

Jeremiah wrote it all down. I'll call an associate in on this, he said. He asked many questions. Ruben was impressed. Berry said Peter appreciated her work. He had cleaned it, arranged it, and talked to her about it. He would come back. Berry said, Peter is my final boyfriend. You think he is your boyfriend, she said to Mary Grace, but he's mine. I'm too used to being selfish, at my age, to be nice to you about it. She laughed her horrible braying, raucous laugh at them all.

Ruben could smell something terrible. Berry obviously didn't bathe. She remembered the dog, but it couldn't be the dog. It was a scorched smell. Then came a bad, sudden noise. They were released. They ran up the stairs past Berry, who was making her way hand over hand. She had been boiling an egg and it had finally exploded. It was smeared on the wall. The saucepan was scorched. Now, released from the corridor at last, they bumped into one another, opening windows, carrying the pot outdoors. Berry was still coming upstairs, protesting and being important. She said, You owe me a pot and an egg.

—Definitely, said Jeremiah.

By now it was late. The single lightbulb in the kitchen made it seem later than it had seemed in that corridor. Ruben didn't

want to look at her watch. She said, Was that your supper?
Was that egg going to be your whole supper?

—Looks that way, doesn't it? Berry said.

At last they got her into a sweater and shoes, then out of the house, and they all drove to the International House of Pancakes, where they bought her an omelet and everybody had something. They sat in the warmth like four happy friends. Berry said, Toby, will you help me wash my hair?

—I will, said Toby gladly, and it seemed like the end of a story, but wasn't, for Jeremiah, who was drinking cup after cup of coffee from the Never Empty pot, said in a voice that irked Ruben, Deborah and I used to come here with the kids all the time. It was a lot cheaper then. And they ate so little! They ate so little!

—Well, we were babies, said Mary Grace.

—That's right.

—I remember wanting my own dinner and always having to share with Rose, she said.

—Oh, no, said Jeremiah. You hardly ate anything. We'd give you one pancake and you'd sit there delicately eating around the edges.

—But later. Later I wanted my own. Maybe even earlier I wanted my own, to feel big. You could have bought me my own!

And Jeremiah gave way instantly. Oh, I should have, I should have. Everything would be different now.

—It's okay, Pop. Now Mary Grace sounded embarrassed.

—No, I should have. If I'd known what would happen.

—If you'd known Mama would die, you'd have bought me my own dinner? That doesn't make sense.

Berry seemed to be ignoring them, vigorously eating a big cheese omelet with potatoes and toast, while Mary Grace, who hadn't eaten much dinner, had pancakes with strawberries and fake whipped cream, and Ruben drank tea.

Jeremiah poured himself more coffee, and Ruben wanted to stop him, as if he were drunk. He went to the men's room, and shuffled back. Why do we make so many mistakes? he said in a quavering voice and Ruben found that she hated him, though she and Jeremiah had certainly both made plenty of mistakes.

But she argued herself into politeness. She said, Oh, I know. I wake up thinking of Deborah. Every day I revise time I spent with her. Every day.

—Boy, I don't do that, Mary Grace said. I try to remember everything exactly the way it was.

—I'm always changing things, said Ruben.

—Changing the past, Berry said with her mouth full. Now that's a human failing!

Feeling criticized, Ruben got angry. Do you want something else to eat, Berry? she said—to make Berry feel like a child being taken by parents for a treat.

—I'm buying all of you dinner tonight, Berry said. I have a credit card. You can pay for this, and I'll pay next time.

As if they'd be together, this bad group of four, forever. As if this were breakfast, instead of a late-night snack, or Berry's dinner. Was it after midnight? Ruben wouldn't look.

—Now, your sort of work, Jeremiah said to Berry. It must have kept you up late very often. Am I right? Don't artists work in the night? Poking holes in pieces of stone in the middle of the night? Eh?

—When a sculpture of mine fell through the floor, said Berry, it killed a man and his lover making love in his bed. It wasn't that late, not later than twelve or one. They hadn't stayed up all night, you see. Neither had I. I was on top of the sculpture. I suppose it was my weight plus its weight that broke through the floor. Beautiful Italian marble. Didn't often get that, I'd won something, to get it. We were able to salvage it. It was cracked, but I worked that in. I sprained my ankle.

—They died? They really died? said Jeremiah, though Ruben was certain she'd made it up.

—Death is a fact of life, Berry said.

—Tell me about it, Jeremiah said bitterly, pouring himself more coffee from the new pot the waitress had brought. He spilled it over his hand. Then he sat back in his chair, wiping his hand on a napkin and shaking his head back and forth.

—Daddy, said Mary Grace, as if to stop something. She was sitting next to her father. Berry was across from her, next to Ruben.

—Well, Mrs. Cooper, said Jeremiah wearily. I suppose you've seen many people die in your lifetime. But for me, my wife Deborah . . .

—I haven't killed many, she said, but I've seen many die.

—You were married several times, I think? I should have asked you this before. He patted his pockets for paper and pen. Are all your husbands dead?

—Now they are, she said. I divorced two of them. The last one died. He was the one I wanted to keep.

—I'm sorry.

Ruben was terribly tired. Her head ached. She would never reach her own bed. If allowed, she'd have lain down and fallen asleep in the aisle of the International House of Pancakes.

—I've known about you for such a long time, Jeremiah was saying. It's strange to know that you're really you.

—I'm me, Berry said.

—I don't even remember that book very well, he went on, but I remember some things. About the trolleys. I'm extremely interested in trolleys.

—Oh, the trolleys, said Berry. The streetcars. Quaint things.

—But the strike—Jeremiah said.

—The strike. We supported the strikers. The company wanted them to work for nothing.

—Surely not for *nothing*, he said. But what did you do to support the strike?

—Well, I was a fine speechwriter, she said, to Ruben's surprise. The main thing I did was write speeches for some of the men in our group. They were better at delivering them, but I was better at writing them. She grinned her wild, untrustworthy grin.

—That's not what it says in Miriam's book, Ruben murmured. Not exactly.

—Oh, she didn't know much.

—But what about the wreck? said Jeremiah. What about the wreck where your sister died?

—Miriam made that up to sell copies. There was no wreck.

—Of course there was, Jeremiah said. It was in the newspapers. There are scholarly articles. You're rather famous, Berry Cooper. You were a famous Jewish anarchist. You went to trial. Have you forgotten?

—I remember everything, Berry said. I remember all of my life. Many lovers. But I don't think I remember a trial.

—Oh, come now, said Jeremiah, and Ruben reached to put her hand on his arm. Oh, come now, he went on. Mrs. Cooper. You were acquitted of murder.

—Of murder? My goodness, Berry said, and she looked sly and wide awake, quite unlike Ruben, who wanted all these people to stop talking and take her home to bed. Berry was still, slowly, eating her toast and her omelet.

—But you did it, Berry, didn't you? said Jeremiah. Didn't you flip the switch and cause the wreck? Didn't you do it? You can tell me. I won't call the cops or anything. But I've always known you did it. The excuse was that sketchbook, but you never sketched scenes in the country like that. I took a drawing course once, just to find out about sketching. I thought about it for years. Berry Cooper, he said madly, I know you did it.

—What was it I did? The grin again.

—You tampered with the signals. You caused the wreck that killed your sister. I think you'd be a nicer person, even now, if you admitted it, Berry.

—And Mr. Laidlaw, Berry said, wiping the last of her egg with a piece of toast and eating it. Mr. Laidlaw. Where was your wife going at the time of her death? Where was she driving?

—What has that got to do with anything? said Jeremiah. She was going to visit her mother.

—But she died on Route 6, Mr. Laidlaw. Her mother didn't live on Route 6.

—She'd taken a wrong turn, said Jeremiah, and Ruben realized she had never known exactly where Deborah's accident had taken place.

—She was going to see her lover, Mr. Laidlaw, Berry said firmly, balling up her napkin and looking around, as if she was the one who'd pay the check.

—Oh, don't be silly, said Jeremiah.

—She told your daughter, who's sitting right beside you, though she never told this supposed friend of hers. She was going to see her lover. She had a lover. Didn't you know? She was going to see her lover, and she told your daughter, and your daughter told Petey, and Petey told me one night, as a bedtime story, to quiet me down. Sometimes I'm hard to quiet down.

—Where's the check here? Jeremiah said. Suddenly he, too, was in a hurry. What kind of nonsense? Of course you're making that up. Mary Grace, tell her to stop it.

—Stop it! said Mary Grace. Of course it's not true! She got up and pushed past him and ran to the women's room, while Jeremiah was suddenly standing and shouting angrily for the check. You killed her! he screamed back at the table, at Berry presumably, but now the waitress was bringing the check and smiling tightly as he took it and threw some bills on the table. You killed my wife! he shouted at the little old lady he'd taken out to dinner. You killed my wife! I mean your sister, he said. I mean your sister.

Mary Grace joined them and said nothing as they drove home. Ruben wanted only silence from Jeremiah and Berry. If she talked all the way home, it might be possible to keep them silent, but she could think of nothing to say. And if she spoke, Berry might reply. What would Berry say to her, if provoked? Oh. She'd say Peter was gone for good. She'd say he was dead.

They drove down the empty street and Berry said, I didn't kill your wife and I didn't kill my sister. It's always love. I was walking out there on the tracks to meet my lover, to try to persuade him to take me back. He'd gone back to his wife. He's the one who flipped the switch. They never even thought of him.

Nobody answered her. Now Ruben knew that nobody wanted anyone to speak. Even Berry, she thought, didn't want anyone to speak. It was always hard to guess what Berry was thinking or what Berry wanted, but Ruben thought that now even she had had enough. Maybe even Berry just wanted to go to bed.

Jeremiah stopped first at Berry's house, and waited while Berry let herself out. Ruben didn't follow her to make sure she'd be all right, but Jeremiah waited until Berry had walked slowly up the walk and onto the porch steps. There was an interminable wait while the lonely old woman stood in front of her own door, and Ruben was afraid she'd have to go and help, but then the door opened, a light even went on inside, and the door closed. Jeremiah drove away. In silence, they continued to drive. Ruben considered saying, I'm sure there was nobody. Could there have been someone in Deborah's life whom Ruben didn't know existed? For her own sake, never mind Jeremiah's, she couldn't endure it.

They reached Ruben's house. She wondered what Mary Grace would do, but the girl got out of the backseat while Ruben got out of the front. As she was about to open the door, Ruben touched her old friend's arm. Good night, Jeremiah, she said. She didn't expect to say anything more, but then she mumbled, Don't worry too much, dear.

As she closed the car door she heard him say, What? What?

She and Mary Grace went into the house together. Inside the

door, with the door closed behind them, Mary Grace kissed
Ruben's cheek and went silently ahead of her up the stairs and
into Peter's room. And that door closed.

Ruben used the bathroom on the first floor, not to awaken
Harry. She climbed the stairs. In her bedroom, Harry was
asleep, his arms and legs flung out all over the bed. Next to
him was a note. Message on machine, it said. Wake me up. I'll
go. Ruben went down the stairs. The answering machine was
in the kitchen. She turned it on. There were two messages. The
first was from Stevie. Mom. Dad. I've got him. He turned up.
He's on his way home. I've got him right here. I'm putting him
on a bus. It gets in at one-thirty. Go and get him.

Ruben started to cry. Then she looked at the clock. It was
two a.m. Harry had meant to awaken, but hadn't. He'd been
sure she'd get in before one-thirty, but she hadn't. The second
message was Peter's voice. Hey, Mom. Dad. I'm here. I'm at
the bus station. I think they'll let me sleep here all night. Maybe
you're out of town.

Ruben hurried back upstairs. Harry was fast asleep. She
picked up the pencil lying near the note, and wrote, *I went.*
Then she reached past the phone and took the copy of *Trolley
Girl* lying there. She went downstairs and ate a cookie, for
alertness while driving. Her car was in the driveway. As she
walked toward it, she saw in the broken light from a streetlamp
that Deborah, her blond hair tumbling out of the red-and-
yellow woolen hat, was waiting in the front passenger seat,
with her frayed gloves in her hands.

It was easy to back the car into the dark, silent street.

—You could write him a note, said Deborah.

—Was it true?

—I love you, Toby, Deborah said.

—Is there a God? Ruben asked, her eyes on the empty street
ahead of her.

—Yes.

—What should I do with Peter and Mary Grace?

—I can't imagine.

—I'm making you up. I do know that.

—Just be kind.

Ruben drew up to the curb in front of Deborah's house and parked. Jeremiah, she wrote on a scrap of paper she found in her bag. Thanks for lending me the book. Berry lies constantly. She has been a wonderful woman, but she isn't perfect and she isn't truthful. Love, Toby. She got out of the car and ran up on the porch. She placed the copy of *Trolley Girl* between the screen door and the real door and got back into the car, which was empty. Then she drove to the bus station.

ACKNOWLEDGMENTS

Friends, colleagues, students, and family members—most noticeably my husband, my three sons, and my honorary daughter —have put up with me and cared about me as I wrote, and I am grateful. For particular help with this book, I'd like to thank Jessica Baumgardner, Susan Bingham, Ruth Buchman, Rebecca Godwin, Donald Hall, Susan Holahan, Edward Mattison, Andrew Mattison, Zoe Pagnamenta, Joyce Peseroff, Sandi Kahn Shelton, and the tireless Claire Wachtel. Additional thanks go to the Corporation of Yaddo, the New Haven Free Public Library, and the Community Soup Kitchen.

The following books have been especially useful:

Avrich, Paul. *Anarchist Voices: An Oral History of Anarchism in America.* Abridged edition. Princeton: Princeton University Press, 1996.

Cavin, Ruth. *Trolleys: Riding and Remembering the Electric Interurban Railways.* New York: Hawthorn Books, 1976.

Fischler, Stanley I. *Moving Millions: An Inside Look at Mass Transit.* New York: Harper and Row, 1979.